THE
JEEVES OMNIBUS 5

Books by P. G. Wodehouse

Fiction
Aunts Aren't Gentlemen
The Adventures of Sally
Bachelors Anonymous
Barmy in Wonderland
Big Money
Bill the Conqueror
Blandings Castle and Elsewhere
Carry On, Jeeves
The Clicking of Cuthbert
Cocktail Time
The Code of the Woosters
The Coming of Bill
Company for Henry
A Damsel in Distress
Do Butlers Burgle Banks
Doctor Sally
Eggs, Beans and Crumpets
A Few Quick Ones
French Leave
Frozen Assets
Full Moon
Galahad at Blandings
A Gentleman of Leisure
The Girl in Blue
The Girl on the Boat
The Gold Bat
The Head of Kay's
The Heart of a Goof
Heavy Weather
Ice in the Bedroom
If I Were You
Indiscretions of Archie
The Inimitable Jeeves
Jeeves and the Feudal Spirit
Jeeves in the Offing
Jill the Reckless
Joy in the Morning
Laughing Gas
Leave it to Psmith
The Little Nugget
Lord Emsworth and Others
Louder and Funnier
Love Among the Chickens
The Luck of the Bodkins
The Man Upstairs
The Man with Two Left Feet
The Mating Season
Meet Mr Mulliner
Mike and Psmith
Mike at Wrykyn
Money for Nothing
Money in the Bank
Mr Mulliner Speaking
Much Obliged, Jeeves
Mulliner Nights
Not George Washington
Nothing Serious
The Old Reliable
Pearls, Girls and Monty Bodkin
A Pelican at Blandings
Piccadilly Jim
Pigs Have Wings
Plum Pie

The Pothunters
A Prefect's Uncle
The Prince and Betty
Psmith, Journalist
Psmith in the City
Quick Service
Right Ho, Jeeves
Ring for Jeeves
Sam the Sudden
Service with a Smile
The Small Bachelor
Something Fishy
Something Fresh
Spring Fever
Stiff Upper Lip, Jeeves
Summer Lightning
Summer Moonshine
Sunset at Blandings
The Swoop
Tales of St Austin's
Thank You, Jeeves
Ukridge
Uncle Dynamite
Uncle Fred in the Springtime
Uneasy Money
Very Good, Jeeves
The White Feather
William Tell Told Again
Young Men in Spats

Omnibuses
The World of Blandings
The World of Jeeves
The World of Mr Mulliner
The World of Psmith
The World of Ukridge
The World of Uncle Fred
Wodehouse Nuggets
  (edited by Richard Usborne)
The World of Wodehouse Clergy
Weekend Wodehouse

Paperback Omnibuses
The Golf Omnibus
The Aunts Omnibus
The Drones Omnibus
The Clergy Omnibus
The Hollywood Omnibus
The Jeeves Omnibus 1
The Jeeves Omnibus 2
The Jeeves Omnibus 3
The Jeeves Omnibus 4

Poems
The Parrot and Other Poems

Autobiographical
Wodehouse on Wodehouse
  (comprising Bring on the Girls,
  Over Seventy, Performing Flea)

Letters
Yours, Plum

THE
JEEVES OMNIBUS 5

P. G. Wodehouse

Hutchinson

London

First published in this collection 1993
© in this collection the Trustees of the P.G. Wodehouse Estate 1993
Much Obliged, Jeeves © P.G. Wodehouse 1971
Aunts Aren't Gentlemen © P.G. Wodehouse 1974
'Extricating Young Gussie' from *The Man With Two Left Feet* © P.G. Wodehouse 1917
'Jeeves Makes An Omelette' from *A Few Quick Ones* © P.G. Wodehouse 1959
'Jeeves and the Greasy Bird' from *Plum Pie* © P.G. Wodehouse 1966

9 10

The Random House Group Limited
20 Vauxhall Bridge Road, London SW1V 2SA

Random House Australia (Pty) Limited
20 Alfred Street, Milsons Point, Sydney,
New South Wales 2061, Australia

Random House New Zealand Limited
18 Poland Road, Glenfield
Auckland 10, New Zealand

Random House South Africa (Pty) Limited
Endulini, 5a Jubilee Road, Parktown 2193, South Africa

The Random House Group Limited Reg. No. 954009

www.randomhouse.co.uk

A CIP catalogue record for this book is available
from the British Library

Papers used by Random House are natural, recyclable products made
from wood grown in sustainable forests. The manufacturing processes
conform to the environmental regulations of the country of origin

ISBN 0 09 177354 7

Typeset by Pure Tech Corporation, Pondicherry, India
Printed and bound in Great Britain by
Mackays of Chatham plc, Chatham, Kent

Contents

MUCH OBLIGED, JEEVES

1

As I slid into my chair at the breakfast table and started to deal with the toothsome eggs and bacon which Jeeves had given of his plenty, I was conscious of a strange exhilaration, if I've got the word right. Pretty good the set-up looked to me. Here I was, back in the old familiar headquarters, and the thought that I had seen the last of Totleigh Towers, of Sir Watkyn Bassett, of his daughter Madeline and above all of the unspeakable Spode, or Lord Sidcup as he now calls himself, was like the medium dose for adults of one of those patent medicines which tone the system and impart a gentle glow.

'These eggs, Jeeves,' I said. 'Very good. Very tasty.'

'Yes, sir?'

'Laid, no doubt, by contented hens. And the coffee, perfect. Nor must I omit to give a word of praise to the bacon. I wonder if you notice anything about me this morning.'

'You seem in good spirits, sir.'

'Yes, Jeeves, I am happy today.'

'I am very glad to hear it, sir.'

'You might say I'm sitting on top of the world with a rainbow round my shoulder.'

'A most satisfactory state of affairs, sir.'

'What's the word I've heard you use from time to time – begins with eu?'

'Euphoria, sir?'

'That's the one. I've seldom had a sharper attack of euphoria. I feel full to the brim of Vitamin B. Mind you, I don't know how long it will last. Too often it is when one feels fizziest that the storm clouds begin doing their stuff.'

'Very true, sir. Full many a glorious morning have I seen flatter the mountain tops with sovereign eye, kissing with golden face the meadows green, gilding pale streams with heavenly alchemy, Anon permit the basest clouds to ride with ugly rack on his celestial face and from the forlorn world his visage hide, stealing unseen to west with this disgrace.'

'Exactly,' I said. I couldn't have put it better myself. 'One always has to budget for a change in the weather. Still, the thing to do is to keep on being happy while you can.'

'Precisely, sir. *Carpe diem*, the Roman poet Horace advised. The English poet Herrick expressed the same sentiment when he suggested that we should gather rosebuds while we may. Your elbow is in the butter, sir.'

'Oh, thank you, Jeeves.'

Well, all right so far. Off to a nice start. But now we come to something which gives me pause. In recording the latest instalment of the Bertram Wooster Story, a task at which I am about to have a pop, I don't see how I can avoid delving into the past a good deal, touching on events which took place in previous instalments, and explaining who's who and what happened when and where and why, and this will make it heavy going for those who have been with me from the start. 'Old hat' they will cry or, if French, '*Déjà vu*.'

On the other hand, I must consider thc new customers. I can't just leave the poor perishers to try to puzzle things out for themselves. If I did, the exchanges in the present case would run somewhat as follows.

Self: The relief I felt at having escaped from Totleigh Towers was stupendous.

New C: What's Totleigh Towers?

Self: For one thing it had looked odds on that I should have to marry Madeline.

New C: Who's Madeline?

Self: Gussie Fink-Nottle, you see, had eloped with the cook.

New C: Who's Gussie Fink-Nottle?

Self: But most fortunately Spode was in the offing and scooped her up, saving me from the scaffold.

New C: Who's Spode?

You see. Hopeless. Confusion would be rife, as one might put it. The only way out that I can think of is to ask the old gang to let their attention wander for a bit – there are heaps of things they can be doing; washing the car, solving the crossword puzzle, taking the dog for a run – while I place the facts before the newcomers.

Briefly, then, owing to circumstances I needn't go into,

Madeline Bassett daughter of Sir Watkyn Bassett of Totleigh Towers, Glos. had long been under the impression that I was hopelessly in love with her and had given to understand that if ever she had occasion to return her betrothed, Gussie Fink-Nottle, to store, she would marry me. Which wouldn't have fitted in with my plans at all, she though physically in the pin-up class, being as mushy a character as ever broke biscuit, convinced that the stars are God's daisy chain and that every time a fairy blows its wee nose a baby is born. The last thing, as you can well imagine, one would want about the home.

So when Gussie unexpectedly eloped with the cook, it looked as though Bertram was for it. If a girl thinks you're in love with her and says she will marry you, you can't very well voice a preference for being dead in a ditch. Not, I mean, if you want to regard yourself as a *preux chevalier*, as the expression is, which is always my aim.

But just as I was about to put in my order for sackcloth and ashes, up, as I say, popped Spode, now going about under the alias of Lord Sidcup. He had loved her since she was so high but had never got around to mentioning it, and when he did so now, they clicked immediately. And the thought that she was safely out of circulation and no longer a menace was possibly the prime ingredient in my current euphoria.

I think that makes everything clear to the meanest intelligence, does it not? Right ho, so we can go ahead. Where were we? Ah yes, I had just told Jeeves that I was sitting on top of the world with a rainbow round my shoulder, but expressing a doubt as to whether this state of things would last, and how well-founded that doubt proved to be; for scarcely a forkful of eggs and b later it was borne in upon me that life was not the grand sweet song I had supposed it to be, but, as you might say, stern and earnest and full of bumps.

'Was I mistaken, Jeeves,' I said, making idle conversation as I sipped my coffee, 'or as the mists of sleep shredded away this morning did I hear your typewriter going?'

'Yes, sir. I was engaged in composition.'

'A dutiful letter to Charlie Silversmith?' I said, alluding to his uncle who held the post of butler at Deverill Hall, where we had once been pleasant visitors. 'Or possibly a lyric in the manner of the bloke who advocates gathering rosebuds?'

'Neither, sir. I was recording the recent happenings at Totleigh Towers for the club book.'

And here, dash it, I must once more ask what I may call the old sweats to let their attention wander while I put the new arrivals abreast.

Jeeves, you must know (I am addressing the new arrivals), belongs to a club for butlers and gentlemen's gentlemen round Curzon Street way, and one of the rules there is that every member must contribute to the club book the latest information concerning the fellow he's working for, the idea being to inform those seeking employment of the sort of thing they will be taking on. If a member is contemplating signing up with someone, he looks him up in the club book, and if he finds that he puts out crumbs for the birdies every morning and repeatedly saves golden-haired children from being run over by automobiles, he knows he is on a good thing and has no hesitation in accepting office. Whereas if the book informs him that the fellow habitually kicks starving dogs and generally begins the day by throwing the breakfast porridge at his personal attendant, he is warned in time to steer clear of him.

Which is all very well and one follows the train of thought, but in my opinion such a book is pure dynamite and ought not to be permitted. There are, Jeeves has informed me, eleven pages in it about me; and what will the harvest be, I ask him, if it falls into the hands of my Aunt Agatha, with whom my standing is already low. She spoke her mind freely enough some years ago when – against my personal wishes – I was found with twenty-three cats in my bedroom and again when I was accused – unjustly, I need hardly say – of having marooned A. B. Filmer, the Cabinet minister, on an island in her lake. To what heights of eloquence would she not soar, if informed of my vicissitudes at Totleigh Towers? The imagination boggles, Jeeves, I tell him.

To which he replies that it won't fall into the hands of my Aunt Agatha, she not being likely to drop in at the Junior Ganymede, which is what his club is called, and there the matter rests. His reasoning is specious and he has more or less succeeded in soothing my tremors, but I still can't help feeling uneasy, and my manner, as I addressed him now, had quite a bit of agitation in it.

'Good Lord!' I ejaculated, if ejaculated is the word I want. 'Are you really writing up that Totleigh business?'

'Yes, sir.'

'All the stuff about my being supposed to have pinched old Bassett's amber statuette?'

'Yes, sir.'

'And the night I spent in a prison cell? Is this necessary? Why not let the dead past bury its dead? Why not forget all about it?'

'Impossible, sir.'

'Why impossible? Don't tell me you can't forget things. You aren't an elephant.'

I thought I had him there, but no.

'It is my membership in the Junior Ganymede which restrains me from obliging you, sir. The rules with reference to the club book are very strict and the penalty for omitting to contribute to it severe. Actual expulsion has sometimes resulted.'

'I see,' I said. I could appreciate that this put him in quite a spot, the feudal spirit making him wish to do the square thing by the young master, while a natural disinclination to get bunged out of a well-loved club urged him to let the young master boil his head. The situation seemed to me to call for what is known as a compromise.

'Well, couldn't you water the thing down a bit? Omit one or two of the juiciest episodes?'

'I fear not, sir. The full facts are required. The committee insists on this.'

I suppose I ought not at this point to have expressed a hope that his blasted committee would trip over banana skins and break their ruddy necks, for I seemed to detect on his face a momentary look of pain. But he was broadminded and condoned it.

'Your chagrin does not surprise me, sir. One can, however, understand their point of view. The Junior Ganymede club book is a historic document. It has been in existence more than eighty years.'

'It must be the size of a house.'

'No, sir, the records are in several volumes. The present one dates back some twelve years. And one must remember that it is not every employer who demands a great deal of space.'

'Demands!'

'I should have said "requires". As a rule, a few lines suffice. Your eighteen pages are quite exceptional.'

'Eighteen? I thought it was eleven.'

'You are omitting to take into your calculations the report of your misadventures at Totleigh Towers, which I have nearly completed. I anticipate that this will run to approximately seven. If you will permit me, sir, I will pat your back.'

He made this kindly offer because I had choked on a swallow of coffee. A few pats and I was myself again and more than a little incensed, as always happens when we are discussing his literary work. Eighteen pages, I mean to say, and every page full of stuff calculated, if thrown open to the public, to give my prestige the blackest of eyes. Conscious of a strong desire to kick the responsible parties in the seat of the pants, I spoke with a generous warmth.

'Well, I call it monstrous. There's no other word for it. Do you know what that blasted committee of yours are inviting? Blackmail, that's what they're inviting. Let some man of ill will get his hooks on that book, and what'll be the upshot? Ruin, Jeeves, that's what'll be the upshot.'

I don't know if he drew himself to his full height, because I was lighting a cigarette at the moment and wasn't looking, but I think he must have done, for his voice, when he spoke, was the chilly voice of one who has drawn himself to his full height.

'There are no men of ill will in the Junior Ganymede, sir.'

I contested this statement hotly.

'That's what *you* think. How about Brinkley?' I said, my allusion being to a fellow the agency had sent me some years previously when Jeeves and I had parted company temporarily because he didn't like me playing the banjolele. 'He's a member, isn't he?'

'A county member, sir. He rarely comes to the club. In passing, sir, his name is not Brinkley, it is Bingley.'

I waved an impatient cigarette holder. I was in no mood to split straws. Or is it hairs?

'His name is not of the essence, Jeeves. What *is* of the e is that he went off on his afternoon out, came back in an advanced state of intoxication, set the house on fire and tried to dismember me with a carving knife.'

'A most unpleasant experience, sir.'

'Having heard noises down below, I emerged from my room and found him wrestling with the grandfather clock, with which he appeared to have had a difference. He then knocked over a lamp and leaped up the stairs at me, complete with cutlass. By a miracle I avoided becoming the late Bertram Wooster, but only by a miracle. And you say there are no men of ill will in the Junior Ganymede club. Tchah!' I said. It is an expression I don't often use, but the situation seemed to call for it.

Things had become difficult. Angry passions were rising and dudgeon bubbling up a bit. It was fortunate that at this juncture the telephone should have tootled, causing a diversion.

'Mrs Travers, sir,' said Jeeves, having gone to the instrument.

I had already divined who was at the other end of the wire, my good and deserving Aunt Dahlia having a habit of talking on the telephone with the breezy vehemence of a hog-caller in the western states of America calling his hogs to come and get it. She got this way through hunting a lot in her youth with the Quorn and the Pytchley. What with people riding over hounds and hounds taking time off to chase rabbits, a girl who hunts soon learns to make herself audible. I believe that she, when in good voice, could be heard in several adjoining counties.

I stepped to the telephone, well pleased. There are few males or females whose society I enjoy more than that of this genial sister of my late father, and it was quite a time since we had foregathered. She lives near the town of Market Snodsbury in Worcestershire and sticks pretty closely to the rural seat, while I, as Jeeves had just recorded in the club book, had had my time rather full elsewhere of late. I was smiling sunnily as I took up the receiver. Not much good, of course, as she couldn't see me, but it's the spirit that counts.

'Hullo, aged relative.'

'Hullo to you, you young blot. Are you sober?'

I felt a natural resentment at being considered capable of falling under the influence of the sauce at ten in the morning, but I reminded myself that aunts will be aunts. Show me an aunt, I've often said, and I will show you someone who doesn't give a hoot how much her *obiter dicta* may wound a nephew's sensibilities. With a touch of hauteur I reassured her on the point she had raised and asked her in what way I could serve her.

'How about lunch?'

'I'm not in London. I'm at home. And you can serve me, as you call it, by coming here. Today, if possible.'

'Your words are music to my ears, old ancestor. Nothing could tickle me pinker,' I said, for I am always glad to accept her hospitality and to renew my acquaintance with the unbeatable eatables dished up by her superb French chef Anatole, God's gift to the gastric juices. I have often regretted that I have but one stomach to put at his disposal. 'Staying how long?'

'As long as you like, my beamish boy. I'll let you know when the time comes to throw you out. The great thing is to get you here.'

I was touched, as who would not have been, by the eagerness she showed for my company. Too many of my circle are apt when inviting me to their homes to stress the fact that they are only expecting me for the week-end and to dwell with too much enthusiasm on the excellence of the earlier trains back to the metropolis on Monday morning. The sunny smile widened an inch or two.

'Awfully good of you to have me, old blood relation.'

'It is, rather.'

'I look forward to seeing you.'

'Who wouldn't?'

'Each minute will seem like an hour till we meet. How's Anatole?'

'Greedy young pig, always thinking of Anatole.'

'Difficult to help it. The taste lingers. How is his art these days?'

'At its peak.'

'That's good.'

'Ginger says his output has been a revelation to him.'

I asked her to repeat this. It had sounded to me just as if she had said 'Ginger says his output has been a revelation to him', and I knew this couldn't be the case. It turned out, however, that it was.

'Ginger?' I said, not abreast.

'Harold Winship. He told me to call him Ginger. He's staying here. He says he's a friend of yours, which he would scarcely admit unless he knew it could be proved against him. You do know him, don't you? He speaks of having been at Oxford with you.'

I uttered a joyful cry, and she said if I did it again, she would sue me, it having nearly cracked her eardrum. A notable instance of the pot calling the kettle black, as the old saying has it, she having been cracking mine since the start of the proceedings.

'Know him?' I said. 'You bet I know him. We were like . . . Jeeves!'

'Sir?'

'Who were those two fellows?'

'Sir?'

'Greek, if I remember correctly. Always mentioned when the subject of bosom pals comes up.'

'Would you be referring to Damon and Pythias, sir?'

'That's right. We were like Damon and Pythias, old ancestor. But what's he doing *chez* you? I wasn't aware that you and he had ever met.'

'We hadn't. But his mother was an old school friend of mine.'

'I see.'

'And when I heard he was standing for Parliament in the by-election at Market Snodsbury, I wrote to him and told him to make my house his base. Much more comfortable than dossing at a pub.'

'Oh, you've got a by-election at Market Snodsbury, have you?'

'Under full steam.'

'And Ginger's one of the candidates?'

'The Conservative one. You seem surprised.'

'I am. You might say stunned. I wouldn't have thought it was his dish at all. How's he doing?'

'Difficult to say so far. Anyway, he needs all the help he can get, so I want you to come and canvass for him.'

This made me chew the lower lip for a moment. One has to exercise caution at a time like this, or where is one?

'What does it involve?' I asked guardedly. 'I shan't have to kiss babies, shall I?'

'Of course you won't, you abysmal chump.'

'I've always heard that kissing babies entered largely into these things.'

'Yes, but it's the candidate who does it, poor blighter. All you have to do is go from house to house urging the inmates to vote for Ginger.'

'Then rely on me. Such an assignment should be well within my scope. Old Ginger!' I said, feeling emotional. 'It will warm the what-d'you-call-its of my heart to see him again.'

'Well, you'll have the opportunity of hotting them up this very afternoon. He's gone to London for the day and wants you to lunch with him.'

'Does he, egad! That's fine. What time?'

'One-thirty.'

'At what spot?'

'Barribault's grillroom.'

'I'll be there. Jeeves,' I said, hanging up, 'You remember Ginger Winship, who used to play Damon to my Pythias?'

'Yes, indeed, sir.'

'They've got an election on at Market Snodsbury, and he's standing in the Conservative interest.'

'So I understood Madam to say, sir.'

'Oh, you caught her remarks?'

'With little or no difficulty, sir. Madam has a penetrating voice.'

'It does penetrate, doesn't it,' I said, massaging the ear I had been holding to the receiver. 'Good lung power.'

'Extremely, sir.'

'I wonder whether she ever sang lullabies to me in my cradle. If so, it must have scared me cross-eyed, giving me the illusion that the boiler had exploded. However, that is not germane to the issue, which is that we leave for her abode this afternoon. I shall be lunching with Ginger. In my absence, pack a few socks and toothbrushes, will you.'

'Very good, sir,' he replied, and we did not return to the subject of the club book.

It was with no little gusto and animation that some hours later I set out for the tryst. This Ginger was one of my oldest buddies, not quite so old as Kipper Herring or Catsmeat Potter-Pirbright, with whom I had plucked the gowans fine at prep school, public school and University, but definitely ancient. Our rooms at Oxford had been adjacent, and it would not be too much to say that from the moment he looked in to borrow a syphon of soda water we became more like brothers than anything, and this state of things had continued after we had both left the seat of learning.

For quite a while he had been a prominent member of the Drones Club, widely known for his effervescence and vivacity, but all of a sudden he had tendered his resignation and gone to live in the country, oddly enough at Steeple Bumpleigh in Essex, where my Aunt Agatha has her lair. This, somebody told me, was due to the circumstance that he had got engaged to a girl of strong character who disapproved of the Drones Club. You get girls like that every now and then, and in my opinion they are best avoided.

Well, naturally this had parted us. He never came to London, and I of course never went to Steeple Bumpleigh. You don't catch me going anywhere near Aunt Agatha unless I have to. No sense in sticking one's neck out. But I had missed him sorely. Oh for the touch of a vanished hand, is how you might put it.

Arriving at Barribault's, I found him in the lobby where you have the pre-luncheon gargle before proceeding to the grillroom, and after the initial What-ho-ing and What-a-time-since-we-met-ing inevitable when two vanished hands who haven't seen each other for ages re-establish contact, he asked me if I would like one for the tonsils.

'I won't join you,' he said. 'I'm not actually on the waggon, I have a little light wine at dinner now and then, but my fiancée wants me to stay off cocktails. She says they harden the arteries.'

If you are about to ask me if this didn't make me purse the lips a bit, I can assure you that it did. It seemed to point to his having gone and got hitched up with a popsy totally lacking in the proper spirit, and it bore out what I had been told about her being a girl of strong character. No one who wasn't could have dashed the cup from his lips in this manner. She had apparently made him like it, too, for he had spoken of her not with the sullen bitterness of one crushed beneath the iron heel but with devotion in every syllable. Plainly he had got it up his nose and didn't object to being bossed.

How different from me, I reflected, that time when I was engaged to my Uncle Percy's bossy daughter Florence Craye. It didn't last long, because she gave me the heave-ho and got betrothed to a fellow called Gorringe who wrote *vers libre*, but while it lasted I felt like one of those Ethiopian slaves Cleopatra used to push around, and I chafed more than somewhat. Whereas Ginger obviously hadn't even started to chafe. It isn't difficult to spot when a fellow's chafing, and I could detect none of the symptoms. He seemed to think that putting the presidential veto on cocktails showed what an angel of mercy the girl was, always working with his good at heart.

The Woosters do not like drinking alone, particularly with a critical eye watching them to see if their arteries are hardening, so I declined the proffered snort – reluctantly, for I was athirst – and came straight to the main item on the agenda paper. On my way to Barribault's I had, as you may suppose, pondered deeply on this business of him standing for Parliament, and I wanted to know the motives behind the move. It looked cock-eyed to me.

'Aunt Dahlia tells me you are staying with her in order to be handy to Market Snodsbury while giving the electors there the old oil,' I said.

'Yes, she very decently invited me. She was at school with my mother.'

'So she told me. I wonder if her face was as red in those days. How do you like it there?'

'It's a wonderful place.'

'Grade A. Gravel soil, main drainage, spreading grounds and Company's own water. And, of course, Anatole's cooking.'

'Ah!' he said, and I think he would have bared his head, only he hadn't a hat on. 'Very gifted, that man.'

'A wizard,' I agreed. 'His dinners must fortify you for the tasks you have to face. How's the election coming along?'

'All right.'

'Kissed any babies lately?'

'Ah!' he said again, this time with a shudder. I could see that I had touched an exposed nerve. 'What blighters babies are, Bertie, dribbling, as they do, at the side of the mouth. Still, it has to be done. My agent tells me to leave no stone unturned if I want to win the election.'

'But why do you want to win the election? I'd have thought you wouldn't have touched Parliament with a ten-foot pole,' I said, for I knew the society there was very mixed. 'What made you commit this rash act?'

'My fiancée wanted me to,' he said, and as his lips framed the word 'fiancée' his voice took on a sort of tremolo like that of a male turtle dove cooing to a female turtle dove. 'She thought I ought to be carving out a career for myself.'

'Do you want a career?'

'Not much, but she insisted.'

The uneasiness I had felt when he told me the beazel had made him knock off cocktails deepened. His every utterance rendered it more apparent to an experienced man like myself that he had run up against something too hot to handle, and for a moment I thought of advising him to send her a telegram saying it was all off and, this done, to pack a suitcase and catch the next boat to Australia. But feeling that this might give offence I merely asked him what the procedure was when you stood for Parliament – or ran for it, as they would say in America. Not that I particularly wanted to know, but it was something to talk about other than his frightful fiancée.

A cloud passed over his face, which I ought to have mentioned earlier was well worth looking at, the eyes clear, the cheeks tanned, the chin firm, the hair ginger and the nose shapely. It topped off, moreover, a body which also repaid inspection, being muscular and well knit. His general aspect, as a matter of fact, was rather like that presented by Esmond Haddock, the squire of Deverill Hall, where Jeeves's Uncle Charlie Silversmith drew his monthly envelope. He had the same poetic look, as if at any moment about to rhyme June with moon, yet gave the impression, as Esmond did, of being able, if he cared to, to fell an ox with a single blow. I don't know if he had ever actually done this, for one so seldom meets an ox, but in his undergraduate days he had felled people right and left, having represented the University in the ring as a heavyweight a matter of three years. He may have included oxen among his victims.

'You go through hell,' he said, the map still clouded as he recalled the past. 'I had to sit in a room where you could hardly breathe because it was as crowded as the Black Hole of Calcutta and listen to addresses of welcome till midnight. After that I went about making speeches.'

'Well, why aren't you down there, making speeches, now? Have they given you a day off?'

'I came up to get a secretary.'

'Surely you didn't go there without one?'

'No, I had one all right, but my fiancée fired her. They had some sort of disagreement.'

I had pursed the lips a goodish bit when he had told me about his fiancée and the cocktails, and I pursed them to an even greater extent now. The more I heard of this girl he had got engaged to, the less I liked the sound of her. I was thinking how well she would get on with Florence Craye if they happened to meet. Twin souls, I mean to say, each what a housemaid I used to know would have called an overbearing dishpot.

I didn't say so, of course. There is a time to call someone an overbearing dishpot, and a time not to. Criticism of the girl he loved might be taken in ill part, as the expression is, and you don't want an ex-Oxford boxing Blue taking things in ill part with you.

'Have you anyone in mind?' I asked. 'Or are you just going to a secretary bin, accepting what they have in stock?'

'I'm hoping to get hold of an American girl I saw something of before I left London. I was sharing a flat with Boko Fittleworth when he was writing a novel, and she came every day and worked with him. Boko dictates his stuff, and he said she was tops as a shorthand typist. I have her address, but I don't know if she's still there. I'm going round there after lunch. Her name's Magnolia Glendennon.'

'It can't be.'

'Why not?'

'Nobody could have a name like Magnolia.'

'They could if they came from South Carolina, as she did. In the southern states of America you can't throw a brick without hitting a Magnolia. But I was telling you about this business of standing for Parliament. First, of course, you have to get the nomination.'

'How did you manage that?'

'My fiancée fixed it. She knows one of the Cabinet ministers, and he pulled strings. A man named Filmer.'

'Not A. B. Filmer?'

'That's right. Is he a friend of yours?'

'I wouldn't say exactly a friend. I came to know him slightly owing to being chased with him on to the roof of a sort of summerhouse by an angry swan. This drew us rather close together for the moment, but we never became really chummy.'

'Where was this?'

'On an island on the lake at my Aunt Agatha's place at Steeple Bumpleigh. Living at Steeple Bumpleigh, you've probably been there.'

He looked at me with a wild surmise, much as those soldiers Jeeves has told me about looked on each other when on a peak in Darien, wherever that is.

'Is Lady Worpledon your aunt?'

'And how.'

'She's never mentioned it.'

'She wouldn't. Her impulse would be to hush it up.'

'Then, good Lord, she must be your cousin.'

'No, my aunt. You can't be both.'

'I mean Florence. Florence Craye, my fiancée.'

It was a shock, I don't mind telling you, and if I hadn't been seated I would probably have reeled. Though I ought not to have been so surprised. Florence was one of those girls who are always getting engaged to someone, first teaming up with Stilton Cheesewright, then me, and finally Percy Gorringe, who was dramatizing her novel *Spindrift*. The play, by the way, had recently been presented to the public at the Duke of York's theatre and had laid an instantaneous egg, coming off on the following Saturday. One of the critics said he had perhaps seen it at a disadvantage because when he saw it the curtain was up. I had wondered a good deal what effect this had had on Florence's haughty spirit.

'You're engaged to Florence?' I yipped, looking at him with a wild surmise.

'Yes. Didn't you know?'

'Nobody tells me anything. Engaged to Florence, eh? Well, well.'

A less tactful man than Bertram Wooster might have gone on to add 'Oh, tough luck!' or something along those lines, for there was no question but that the unhappy man was properly up against it, but if there's one thing the Woosters have in heaping measure, it is tact. I merely gripped his hand, gave it a shake and wished him happiness. He thanked me for this.

'You're lucky,' I said, wearing the mask.

'Don't I know it!'

'She's a charming girl,' I said, still wearing as above.

'That just describes her.'

'Intellectual, too.'

'Distinctly. Writes novels.'

'Always at it.'

'Did you read *Spindrift*?'

'Couldn't put it down,' I said, cunningly not revealing that I hadn't been able to take it up. 'Did you see the play?'

'Twice. Too bad it didn't run. Gorringe's adaptation was the work of an ass.'

'I spotted him as an ass the first time I saw him.'

'It's a pity Florence didn't.'

'Yes. By the way, what became of Gorringe? When last heard of, she was engaged to him.'

'She broke it off.'

'Very wise of her. He had long side-whiskers.'

'She considered him responsible for the failure of the play and told him so.'

'She would.'

'What do you mean she would?'

'Her nature is so frank, honest and forthright.'

'It is, isn't it.'

'She speaks her mind.'

'Invariably.'

'It's an admirable trait.'

'Oh, most.'

'You can't get away with much with a girl like Florence.'

'No.'

We fell into a silence. He was twiddling his fingers and a sort of what-d'you-call-it had come into his manner, as if he wanted to say something but was having trouble in getting it out. I remembered encountering a similar diffidence in the Rev. Stinker Pinker when he was trying to nerve himself to ask me to come to Totleigh Towers, and you find the same thing in dogs when they put a paw on your knee and look up into your face but don't utter, though making it clear that there is a subject on which they are anxious to touch.

'Bertie,' he said at length.

'Hullo?'

'Bertie.'

'Yes?'

'Bertie.'

'Still here. Excuse me asking, but have you any cracked gramophone record blood in you? Perhaps your mother was frightened by one?'

And then it all came out in a rush as if a cork had been pulled.

'Bertie, there's something I must tell you about Florence, though you probably know it already, being a cousin of hers. She's a wonderful girl and practically perfect in every respect, but she has one characteristic which makes it awkward for those who love her and are engaged to her. Don't think I'm criticizing her.'

'No, no.'

'I'm just mentioning it.'

'Exactly.'

'Well, she has no use for a loser. To keep her esteem you have to be a winner. She's like one of those princesses in the fairy tales who set fellows some task to perform, as it might be scaling a mountain of glass or bringing her a hair from the beard of the Great Cham of Tartary, and gave them the brush-off when they couldn't make the grade.'

I recalled the princesses of whom he spoke, and I had always thought them rather fatheads. I mean to say, what sort of foundation for a happy marriage is the bridegroom's ability to scale mountains of glass? A fellow probably wouldn't be called on to do it more than about once every ten years, if that.

'Gorringe,' said Ginger, continuing, 'was a loser, and that dished him. And long ago, someone told me, she was engaged to a gentleman jockey and she chucked him because he took a spill at the canal turn in the Grand National. She's a perfectionist. I admire her for it, of course.'

'Of course.'

'A girl like her is entitled to have high standards.'

'Quite.'

'But, as I say, it makes it awkward for me. She has set her

heart on my winning this Market Snodsbury election, heaven knows why, for I never thought she had any interest in politics, and if I lose it, I shall lose her, too. So . . .'

'Now is the time for all good men to come to the aid of the party?'

'Exactly. You are going to canvass for me. Well, canvass like a ton of bricks, and see that Jeeves does the same. I've simply got to win.'

'You can rely on us.'

'Thank you, Bertie, I knew I could. And now let's go in and have a bite of lunch.'

Having restored the tissues with the excellent nourishment which Barribault's hotel always provides and arranged that Ginger was to pick me up in his car later in the afternoon, my own sports model being at the vet's with some nervous ailment, we parted, he to go in search of Magnolia Glendennon, I to walk back to the Wooster G.H.Q.

It was, as you may suppose, in thoughtful mood that I made my way through London's thoroughfares. I was reading a novel of suspense the other day in which the heroine, having experienced a sock in the eye or two, was said to be lost in a maze of mumbling thoughts, and that description would have fitted me like the paper on the wall.

My heart was heavy. When a man is an old friend and pretty bosom at that, it depresses you to hear that he's engaged to Florence Craye. I recalled my own emotions when I had found myself in that unpleasant position. I had felt like someone trapped in the underground den of the Secret Nine.

Though, mark you, there's nothing to beef about in her outer crust. At the time when she was engaged to Stilton Cheesewright I remember recording in the archives that she was tall and willowy with a terrific profile and luxuriant platinum-blonde hair; the sort of girl who might, as far as looks were concerned, have been the star unit of the harem of one of the better-class Sultans; and though I hadn't seen her for quite a while, I presumed that these conditions still prevailed. The fact that Ginger, when speaking of her, had gone so readily into his turtle dove impersonation seemed to indicate as much.

Looks, however, aren't everything. Against this pin-up-ness of hers you had to put the bossiness which would lead her to expect the bloke she married to behave like a Hollywood Yes-man. From childhood up she had been . . . I can't think of the word . . . begins with an i . . . No, it's gone . . . but I can give you the idea. When at my private school I once won a prize for Scripture Knowledge, which naturally involved a lot of researching into Holy Writ, and in the course of my researches I came upon the story of the military chap who used to say 'Come' and they cometh and 'Go' and they goeth. I have always thought that that was Florence in a nutshell. She would have given short shrift, as the expression is, to anyone who had gone when she said 'Come' or the other way round. Imperious, that's the word I was groping for. She was as imperious as a traffic cop. Little wonder that the heart was heavy. I felt that Ginger, mistaking it for a peach, had plucked a lemon in the garden of love.

And then my meditations took a less sombre turn. This often happens after a good lunch, even if you haven't had a cocktail. I reminded myself that many married men positively enjoy being kept on their toes by the little woman, and possibly Ginger might be one of them. He might take the view that when the little w made him sit up and beg and snap lumps of sugar off his nose, it was a compliment really, because it showed that she was taking an interest.

Feeling a bit more cheerful, I reached for my cigarette case and was just going to open it, when like an ass I dropped it and it fell into the road. And as I stepped from the pavement to retrieve it there was a sudden tooting in my rear, and whirling on my axis I perceived that in about another two ticks I was going to be rammed amidships by a taxi.

The trouble about whirling on your axis, in case you didn't know, is that you're liable, if not an adagio dancer, to trip over your feet, and this was what I proceeded to do. My left shoe got all mixed up with my right ankle, I tottered, swayed, and after a brief pause came down like some noble tree beneath the woodman's axe, and I was sitting there lost in a maze of numbing thoughts, when an unseen hand attached itself to my arm and jerked me back to safety. The taxi went on and turned the corner.

Well, of course the first thing the man of sensibility does on these occasions is to thank his brave preserver. I turned to do this, and blow me tight if the b.p. wasn't Jeeves. Came as a complete surprise. I couldn't think what he was doing there, and for an instant the idea occurred to me that this might be his astral body.

'Jeeves!' I ejaculated. I'm pretty sure that's the word. Anyway, I'll risk it.

'Good afternoon, sir. I trust you are not too discommoded. That was a somewhat narrow squeak.'

'It was indeed. I don't say my whole life passed before me, but a considerable chunk of it did. But for you—'

'Not at all, sir.'

'Yes, you and you only saved me from appearing in tomorrow's obituary column.'

'A pleasure, sir.'

'It's amazing how you always turn up at the crucial moment, like the United States Marines. I remember how you did when A. B. Filmer and I were having our altercation with that swan, and there were other occasions too numerous to mention. Well, you will certainly get a rave notice in my prayers next time I make them. But how do you happen to be in these parts? Where are we, by the way?'

'This is Curzon Street, sir.'

'Of course. I'd have known that if I hadn't been musing.'

'You were musing, sir?'

'Deeply. I'll tell you about it later. This is where your club is, isn't it?'

'Yes, sir, just round the corner. In your absence and having completed the packing, I decided to lunch there.'

'Thank heaven you did. If you hadn't, I'd have been . . . what's that gag of yours? Something about wheels.'

'Less than the dust beneath thy chariot wheels, sir.

'Or, rather, the cabby's chariot wheels. Why are you looking at me with such a searching eye, Jeeves?'

'I was thinking that your misadventure had left you somewhat dishevelled, sir. If I might suggest it, I think we should repair to the Junior Ganymede now.'

'I see what you mean. You would give me a wash and brush-up?'

'Just so, sir.'

'And perhaps a whisky and soda?'

'Certainly, sir.'

'I need one sorely. Ginger's practically on the waggon, so there were no cocktails before lunch. And do you know why he's practically on the waggon? Because the girl he's engaged to has made him take that foolish step. And do you know who the girl he's engaged to is? My cousin Florence Craye.'

'Indeed, sir?'

Well, I hadn't expected him to roll his eyes and leap about, because he never does no matter how sensational the news item, but I could see by the way one of his eyebrows twitched and rose perhaps an eighth of an inch that I had interested him. And there was what is called a wealth of meaning in that 'Indeed, sir?' He was conveying his opinion that this was a bit of luck for Bertram, because a girl you have once been engaged to is always a lurking menace till she gets engaged to someone else and so cannot decide at any moment to play a return date. I got the message and thoroughly agreed with him, though naturally I didn't say so.

Jeeves, you see, is always getting me out of entanglements with the opposite sex, and he knows all about the various females who from time to time have come within an ace of hauling me to the altar rails, but of course we don't discuss them. To do so, we feel, would come under the head of bandying a woman's name, and the Woosters do not bandy women's names. Nor do the Jeeveses. I can't speak for his Uncle Charlie Silversmith, but I should imagine that he, too, has his code of ethics in this respect. These things generally run in families.

So I merely filled him in about her making Ginger stand for Parliament and the canvassing we were going to undertake, urging him to do his utmost to make the electors think along the right lines, and he said 'Yes, sir' and 'Very good, sir' and 'I quite understand, sir', and we proceeded to the Junior Ganymede.

An extremely cosy club it proved to be. I didn't wonder that he liked to spend so much of his leisure there. It lacked the sprightliness of the Drones. I shouldn't think there was much bread and sugar thrown about at lunch time, and you would hardly expect that there would be when you reflected that the membership consisted of elderly butlers and gentlemen's gentlemen of fairly ripe years, but as regards comfort it couldn't be faulted. The purler I had taken had left me rather tender in the fleshy parts, and it was a relief after I had been washed and brushed up and was on the spruce side once more to sink into a well-stuffed chair in the smoking-room.

Sipping my whisky and s, I brought the conversation round again to Ginger and his election, which was naturally the front page stuff of the day.

'Do you think he has a chance, Jeeves?'

He weighed the question for a moment, as if dubious as to where he would place his money.

'It is difficult to say, sir. Market Snodsbury, like so many

English country towns, might be described as straitlaced. It sets a high value on respectability.'

'Well, Ginger's respectable enough.'

'True, sir, but, as you are aware, he has had a Past.'

'Not much of one.'

'Sufficient, however, to prejudice the voters, should they learn of it.'

'Which they can't possibly do. I suppose he's in the club book—'

'Eleven pages, sir.'

'—But you assure me that the contents of the club book will never be revealed.'

'Never, sir. Mr Winship has nothing to fear from that quarter.'

His words made me breathe more freely.

'Jeeves,' I said, 'your words make me breathe more freely. As you know, I am always a bit uneasy about the club book. Kept under lock and key, is it?'

'Not actually under lock and key, sir, but it is safely bestowed in the secretary's office.'

'Then there's nothing to worry about.'

'I would not say that, sir. Mr Winship must have had companions in his escapades, and they might inadvertently make some reference to them which would get into gossip columns in the Press and thence into the Market Snodsbury journals. I believe there are two of these, one rigidly opposed to the Conservative interest which Mr Winship is representing. It is always a possibility, and the results would be disastrous. I have no means at the moment of knowing the identity of Mr Winship's opponent, but he is sure to be a model of respectability whose past can bear the strictest investigation.'

'You're pretty gloomy, Jeeves. Why aren't you gathering rosebuds? The poet Herrick would shake his head.'

'I am sorry, sir. I did not know that you were taking Mr Winship's fortunes so much to heart, or I would have been more guarded in my speech. Is victory in the election of such importance to him?'

'It's vital. Florence will hand him his hat if he doesn't win.'

'Surely not, sir?'

'That's what he says, and I think he's right. His observations on the subject were most convincing. He says she's a perfectionist and has no use for a loser. It is well established that she handed Percy Gorringe the pink slip because the play he made of her novel only ran three nights.'

'Indeed, sir?'

'Well documented fact.'

'Then let us hope that what I fear will not happen, sir.'

We were sitting there hoping that what he feared would not happen, when a shadow fell on my whisky and s and I saw that we had been joined by another member of the Junior Ganymede, a smallish, plumpish, Gawd-help-us-ish member wearing clothes more suitable for the country than the town and a tie that suggested that he belonged to the Brigade of Guards, though I doubted if this was the case. As to his manner, I couldn't get a better word for it at the moment than 'familiar', but I looked it up later in Jeeves's *Dictionary of Synonyms* and found that it had been unduly intimate, too free, forward, lacking in proper reserve, deficient in due respect, impudent, bold and intrusive. Well, when I tell you that the first thing he did was to prod Jeeves in the lower ribs with an uncouth forefinger, you will get the idea.

'Hullo, Reggie,' he said, and I froze in my chair, stunned by the revelation that Jeeves's first name was Reginald. It had never occurred to me before that he had a first name. I couldn't help thinking what embarrassment would have been caused if it had been Bertie.

'Good afternoon,' said Jeeves, and I could see that the chap was not one of his inner circle of friends. His voice was cold, and anyone less lacking in proper reserve and deficient in due respect would have spotted this and recoiled.

The Gawd-help-us fellow appeared to notice nothing amiss. His manner continued to be that of one who has met a pal of long standing.

'How's yourself, Reggie?'

'I am in tolerably good health, thank you.'

'Lost weight, haven't you? You ought to live in the country like me and get good country butter.' He turned to me. 'And you ought to be more careful, cocky, dancing about in the middle of the street like that. I was in that cab and I thought you were a goner. You're Wooster, aren't you?'

'Yes,' I said, amazed. I hadn't known I was such a public figure.

'Thought so. I don't often forget a face. Well, I can't stay chatting with you. I've got to see the secretary about something. Nice to have seen you, Reggie.'

'Goodbye.'

'Nice to have seen you, Wooster, old man.'

I thanked him, and he withdrew. I turned to Jeeves, that wild surmise I was speaking about earlier functioning on all twelve cylinders.

'Who was that?'

He did not reply immediately, plainly too ruffled for speech. He had to take a sip of his liqueur brandy before he was master of himself. His manner, when he did speak, was that of one who would have preferred to let the whole thing drop.

'The person you mentioned at the breakfast table, sir. Bingley,' he said, pronouncing the name as if it soiled his lips.

I was astounded. You could have knocked me down with a toothpick.

'Bingley? I'd never have recognized him. He's changed completely. He was quite thin when I knew him, and very gloomy, you might say sinister. Always seemed to be brooding silently on the coming revolution, when he would be at liberty to chase me down Park Lane with a dripping knife.'

The brandy seemed to have restored Jeeves. He spoke now with his customary calm.

'I believe his political views were very far to the left at the time when he was in your employment. They changed when he became a man of property.'

'A man of property, is he?'

'An uncle of his in the grocery business died and left him a house and a comfortable sum of money.'

'I suppose it often happens that the views of fellows like Bingley change when they come into money.'

'Very frequently. They regard the coming revolution from a different standpoint.'

'I see what you mean. They don't want to be chased down Park Lane with dripping knives themselves. Is he still a gentleman's gentleman?'

'He has retired. He lives a life of leisure in Market Snodsbury.'

'Market Snodsbury? That's funny.'

'Sir?'

'Odd, I mean, that he should live in Market Snodsbury.'

'Many people do, sir.'

'But when that's just where we're going. Sort of a coincidence. His uncle's house is there, I suppose.'

'One presumes so.'

'We may be seeing something of him.'

'I hope not, sir. I disapprove of Bingley. He is dishonest. Not a man to be trusted.'

'What makes you think so?'

'It is merely a feeling.'

Well, it was no skin off my nose. A busy man like myself hasn't time to go about trusting Bingley. All I demanded of Bingley was that if our paths should cross he would remain sober and keep away from carving knives. Live and let live is the Wooster motto. I finished my whisky and soda and rose.

'Well,' I said, 'there's one thing. Holding the strong Conservative views he does, it ought to be a snip to get him to vote for Ginger. And now we'd better be getting along. Ginger is driving us down in his car, and I don't know when he'll be coming to fetch us. Thanks for your princely hospitality, Jeeves. You have brought new life to the exhausted frame.'

'Not at all, sir.'

Ginger turned up in due course, and on going out to the car I saw that he had managed to get hold of Magnolia all right, for there was a girl sitting in the back and when he introduced us his 'Mr Wooster, Miss Glendennon' told the story.

Nice girl she seemed to me and quite nice-looking. I wouldn't say hers was the face that launched a thousand ships, to quote one of Jeeves's gags, and this was probably all to the good, for Florence, I imagine, would have had a word to say if Ginger had returned from his travels with something in tow calculated to bring a whistle to the lips of all beholders. A man in his position has to exercise considerable care in his choice of secretaries, ruling out anything that might have done well in the latest Miss America contest. But you could certainly describe her appearance as pleasant. She gave me the impression of being one of those quiet, sympathetic girls whom you could tell your troubles to in the certain confidence of having your hand held and your head patted. The sort of girl you could go to and say 'I say, I've just committed a murder and it's worrying me rather,' and she would reply, 'There, there, try not to think about it, it's the sort of thing that might happen to anybody.' The little mother, in short, with the added attraction of being tops at shorthand and typing. I could have wished Ginger's affairs in no better hands.

Jeeves brought out the suitcases and stowed them away, and Ginger asked me to do the driving, as he had a lot of business to go into with his new secretary, giving her the low-down on her duties, I suppose. We set out, accordingly, with me and Jeeves in front, and about the journey down there is nothing of interest to report. I was in merry mood throughout, as always when about to get another whack at Anatole's cooking. Jeeves presumably felt the same, for he, like me, is one of that master skillet-wielder's warmest admirers, but whereas I sang a good deal as we buzzed along, he maintained, as is his custom, the silent reserve of a stuffed frog, never joining in the chorus, though cordially invited to.

Arriving at journey's end, we all separated. Jeeves attended to the luggage, Ginger took Magnolia Glendennon off to his office, and I made my way to the drawing-room, which I found empty. There seemed to be nobody about, as so often happens when you fetch up at a country house lateish in the afternoon. No sign of Aunt Dahlia, nor of Uncle Tom, her mate. I toyed with the idea of going to see if the latter was in the room where he keeps his collection of old silver, but thought better not. Uncle Tom is one of those enthusiastic collectors who, if in a position to grab you, detain you for hours, talking about sconces, foliation, ribbon wreaths in high relief and gadroon borders, and one wants as little of that sort of thing as can be managed.

I might have gone to pay my respects to Anatole, but there again I thought better not. He, too, is inclined to the long monologue when he gets you in his power, his pet subject the state of his interior. He suffers from bouts of what he calls *mal au foie*, and his conversation would be of greater interest to a medical man than to a layman like myself. I don't know why it is, but when somebody starts talking to me about his liver I never can listen with real enjoyment.

On the whole, the thing to do seemed to be to go for a saunter in the extensive grounds and messuages.

It was one of those heavy, sultry afternoons when Nature seems to be saying to itself 'Now shall I or shall I not scare the pants off these people with a hell of a thunderstorm?', but I decided to risk it. There's a small wooded bit not far from the house which I've always been fond of, and thither I pushed along. This wooded bit contains one or two rustic benches for the convenience of those who wish to sit and meditate, and as I hove alongside the first of these I saw that there was an expensive-looking camera on it.

It surprised me somewhat, for I had no idea that Aunt Dahlia had taken to photography, but of course you never know what aunts will be up to next. The thought that occurred to me almost immediately was that if there was going to be a thunderstorm, it would be accompanied by rain, and rain falling on a camera doesn't do it any good. I picked the thing up, accordingly, and started off with it to take it back to the house, feeling that the old relative would thank me for my thoughtfulness, possibly with tears in her eyes, when there was a sudden bellow and an individual emerged from behind a clump of bushes. Startled me considerably, I don't mind telling you.

He was an extremely stout individual with a large pink face and a Panama hat with a pink ribbon. A perfect stranger to me, and I wondered what he was doing here. He didn't look the sort of crony Aunt Dahlia would have invited to stay, and still less Uncle Tom, who is so allergic to guests that when warned of their approach he generally makes a bolt for it and disappears, leaving not a wrack behind as I have heard Jeeves put it. However, as I was saying, you never know what aunts will be up to next and no doubt the ancestor had had some good reason for asking the chap to come and mix, so I beamed civilly and opened the conversation with a genial 'Hullo there'.

'Nice day,' I said, continuing to beam civilly. 'Or, rather, not so frightfully nice. Looks as if we were in for a thunderstorm.'

Something seemed to have annoyed him. The pink of his face had deepened to about the colour of his Panama hat ribbon, and both his chins trembled slightly.

'Damn thunderstorms!' he responded – curtly, I suppose, would be the word – and I said I didn't like them myself. It was the lightning, I added, that I chiefly objected to.

'They say it never strikes twice in the same place, but then it hasn't got to.'

'Damn the lightning! What are you doing with my camera?'

This naturally opened up a new line of thought.

'Oh, is this your camera?'

'Yes, it is.'

'I was taking it to the house.'

'You were, were you?'

'I didn't want it to get wet.'

'Oh? And who are you?'

I was glad he had asked me that. His whole manner had made it plain to a keen mind like mine that he was under the impression that he had caught me in the act of absconding with his property, and I was glad to have the opportunity of presenting my credentials. I could see that if we were ever to have a good laugh together over this amusing misunderstanding, there would have to be a certain amount of preliminary spadework.

'Wooster is the name,' I said. 'I'm my aunt's nephew. I mean,' I went on, for those last words seemed to me not to have rung quite right, 'Mrs Travers is my aunt.'

'You are staying in the house?'

'Yes. Just arrived.'

'Oh?' he said again, but this time in what you might call a less hostile tone.

'Yes,' I said, rubbing it in.

There followed a silence, presumably occupied by him in turning things over in his mind in the light of my statement and examining them in depth, and then he said 'Oh?' once more and stumped off.

I made no move to accompany him. What little I had had of his society had been ample. As we were staying in the same house, we would no doubt meet occasionally, but not, I resolved, if I saw him first. The whole episode reminded me of my first encounter with Sir Watkyn Bassett and the misunderstanding about his umbrella. That had left me shaken, and so had this. I was glad to have a rustic bench handy, so that I could sit and try to bring my nervous system back into shape. The sky had become more and more inky I suppose is the word I want and the odds on a thunderstorm shorter than ever, but I still lingered. It was only when there came from above a noise like fifty-seven trucks going over a wooden bridge that I felt that an immediate move would be judicious. I rose and soon gathered speed, and I had reached the French window of the drawing-room and was on the point of popping through, when from within there came the sound of a human voice. On second thoughts delete the word 'human', for it was the voice of my recent acquaintance with whom I had chatted about cameras.

I halted. There was a song I used to sing in my bath at one time, the refrain or burthen of which began with the words 'I stopped and I looked and I listened', and this was what I did now, except for the looking. It wasn't raining, nor was there any repetition of the trucks-going-over-a-wooden-bridge noise. It was as though Nature had said to itself 'Oh to hell with it' and decided that it was too much trouble to have a thunderstorm after all. So I wasn't getting struck by lightning or even wet, which enabled me to remain in status quo.

The camera bloke was speaking to some unseen companion, and what he said was;

'Wooster, his name is. Says he's Mrs Travers's nephew.'

It was plain that I had arrived in the middle of a conversation. The words must have been preceded by a query, possibly 'Oh, by the way, do you happen to know who a tall, slender, good-looking – I might almost say fascinating – young man I was talking to outside there would be?', though of course possibly not. That, at any rate, must have been the gist, and I suppose the party of the second part had replied 'No, sorry, I can't place him', or words to that effect. Whereupon the camera chap had spoken as above. And as he spoke as above a snort rang through the quiet room; a voice, speaking with every evidence of horror and disgust, exclaimed 'Wooster!'; and I quivered from hair-do to shoe sole. I may even have gasped, but fortunately not loud enough to be audible beyond the French window.

For it was the voice of Lord Sidcup – or, as I shall always think of him, no matter how many titles he may have inherited, Spode. Spode, mark you, whom I had thought and hoped I had seen the last of after dusting the dust of Totleigh Towers from the Wooster feet; Spode, who went about seeking whom he might devour and from early boyhood had been a hissing and a by-word to all right-thinking men. Little wonder that for a moment everything seemed to go black and I had to clutch at a passing rose bush to keep from falling.

This Spode, I must explain for the benefit of the newcomers who have not read the earlier chapters of my memoirs, was a character whose path had crossed mine many a time and oft, as the expression is, and always with the most disturbing results. I have spoken of the improbability of a beautiful friendship ever getting under way between me and the camera chap, but the likelihood of any such fusion of souls, as I have heard Jeeves call it, between me and Spode was even more remote. Our views on each other were definite. His was that what England needed if it was to become a land fit for heroes to live in was fewer and better Woosters, while I had always felt that there was nothing wrong with England that a ton of bricks falling from a height on Spode's head wouldn't cure.

'You know him?' said the camera chap.

'I'm sorry to say I do,' said Spode, speaking like Sherlock Holmes asked if he knew Professor Moriarty. 'How did you happen to meet him?'

'I found him making off with my camera.'

'Ha!'

'Naturally I thought he was stealing it. But if he's really Mrs Travers's nephew, I suppose I was mistaken.'

Spode would have none of this reasoning, though it seemed pretty sound to me. He snorted again with even more follow-through than the first time.

'Being Mrs Travers's nephew means nothing. If he was the nephew of an archbishop he would behave in a precisely similar manner. Wooster would steal anything that was not nailed down, provided he could do it unobserved. He couldn't have known you were there?'

'No. I was behind a bush.'

'And your camera looks a good one.'

'Cost me a lot of money.'

'Then of course he was intending to steal it. He must have thought he had dropped into a bit of good luck. Let me tell you about Wooster. The first time I met him was in an antique shop. I had gone there with Sir Watkyn Bassett, my future father-in-law. He collects old silver. And Sir Watkyn had propped his umbrella up against a piece of furniture. Wooster was there, but lurking, so we didn't see him.'

'In a dark corner, perhaps?'

'Or behind something. The first we saw of him, he was sneaking off with Sir Watkyn's umbrella.'

'Pretty cool.'

'Oh, he's cool all right. These fellows have to be.'

'I suppose so. Must take a nerve of ice.'

To say that I boiled with justifiable indignation would not be putting it too strongly. As I have recorded elsewhere, there was a ready explanation of my behaviour. I had come out without my umbrella that morning, and, completely forgetting that I had done so, I had grasped old Bassett's, obeying the primeval instinct which makes a man without an umbrella reach out for the nearest one in sight, like a flower groping towards the sun. Unconsciously, as it were.

Spode resumed. They had taken a moment off, no doubt in order to brood on my delinquency. His voice now was that of one about to come to the high spot in his narrative.

'You'll hardly believe this, but soon after that he turned up at Totleigh Towers, Sir Watkyn's house in Gloucestershire.'

'Incredible!'

'I thought you'd think so.'

'Disguised, of course? A wig? A false beard? His cheeks stained with walnut juice?'

'No, he came quite openly, invited by my future wife. She has a sort of sentimental pity for him. I think she hopes to reform him.'

'Girls will be girls.'

'Yes, but I wish they wouldn't.'

'Did you rebuke your future wife?'

'I wasn't in a position to then.'

'Probably a wise thing, anyway. I once rebuked the girl I wanted to marry, and she went off and teamed up with a stockbroker. So what happened?'

'He stole a valuable piece of silver. A sort of silver cream jug. A cow-creamer, they call it.'

'My doctor forbids me cream. You had him arrested, of course?'

'We couldn't. No evidence.'

'But you knew he had done it?'

'We were certain.'

'Well, that's how it goes. See any more of him after that?'

'This you will *not* believe. He came to Totleigh Towers *again*!'

'Impossible!'

'Once more invited by my future wife.'

'Would that be the Miss Bassett who arrived last night?'

'Yes, that was Madeline.'

'Lovely girl. I met her in the garden before breakfast. My doctor recommends a breath of fresh air in the early morning. Did you know she thinks those bits of mist you see on the grass are the elves' bridal veils?'

'She has a very whimsical fancy.'

'And nothing to be done about it, I suppose. But you were telling me about this second visit of Wooster's to Totleigh Towers. Did he steal anything this time?'

'An amber statuette worth a thousand pounds.'

'He certainly gets around,' said the camera chap with, I thought, a sort of grudging admiration. 'I hope you had him arrested?'

'We did. He spent the night in the local gaol. But next morning Sir Watkyn weakened and let him off.'

'Mistaken kindness.'

'So I thought.'

The camera chap didn't comment further on this, though he was probably thinking that of all the soppy families introduced to his notice the Bassetts took the biscuit.

'Well, I'm very much obliged to you,' he said, 'for telling me about this man Wooster and putting me on my guard. I've brought a very valuable bit of old silver with me. I am hoping to sell it to Mr Travers. If Wooster learns of this, he is bound to try to purloin it, and I can tell you, that if he does and I catch him, there will be none of this nonsense of a single night in gaol. He will get the stiffest sentence the law can provide. And now, how about a quick game of billiards before dinner? My doctor advises a little gentle exercise.'

'I should enjoy it.'

'Then let us be getting along.'

Having given them time to remove themselves, I went in and sank down on a sofa. I was profoundly stirred, for if you think fellows enjoy listening to the sort of thing Spode had been saying about me, you're wrong. My pulse was rapid and my brow wet with honest sweat, like the village blacksmith's. I was badly in need of alcoholic refreshment, and just as my tongue was beginning to stick out and blacken at the roots, shiver my timbers if Jeeves didn't enter left centre with a tray containing all the makings. St Bernard dogs, you probably know, behave in a similar way in the Alps and are well thought of in consequence.

Mingled with the ecstasy which the sight of him aroused in my bosom was a certain surprise that he should be acting as cup-bearer. It was a job that should rightly have fallen into the province of Seppings, Aunt Dahlia's butler.

'Hullo, Jeeves!' I ejaculated.

'Good evening, sir. I have unpacked your effects. Can I pour you a whisky and soda?'

'You can indeed. But what are you doing, buttling? This mystifies me greatly. Where's Seppings?'

'He has retired to bed, sir, with an attack of indigestion consequent upon a too liberal indulgence in Monsieur Anatole's cooking at lunch. I am undertaking his duties for the time being.'

'Very white of you, and very white of you to pop up at this particular moment. I have had a shock, Jeeves.'

'I am sorry to hear that, sir.'

'Did you know Spode was here?'

'Yes, sir.'

'And Miss Bassett?'

'Yes, sir.'

'We might as well be at Totleigh Towers.'

'I can appreciate your dismay, sir, but fellow guests are easily avoided.'

'Yes, and if you avoid them, what do they do? They go about telling men in Panama hats you're a sort of cross between Raffles and one of those fellows who pinch bags at railway stations,' I said, and in a few crisp words I gave him a résumé of Spode's remarks.

'Most disturbing, sir.'

'Very. You know and I know how sound my motives were for everything I did at Totleigh, but what if Spode tells Aunt Agatha?'

'An unlikely contingency, sir.'

'I suppose it is.'

'But I know just how you feel, sir. Who steals my purse steals trash; 'tis something, nothing; 'twas mine, 'tis his, and has been slave to thousands. But he who filches from me my good name robs me of that which not enriches him and makes me poor indeed.'

'Neat, that. Your own?'

'No, sir. Shakespeare's.'

'Shakespeare said some rather good things.'

'I understand that he has given uniform satisfaction, sir. Shall I mix you another?'

'Do just that thing, Jeeves, and with all convenient speed.'

He had completed his St Bernard act and withdrawn, and I was sipping my second rather more slowly than the first, when the door opened and Aunt Dahlia bounded in, all joviality and rosy complexion.

6

I never see this relative without thinking how odd it is that one
sister – call her Sister A – can be so unlike another sister, whom
we will call Sister B. My Aunt Agatha, for instance, is tall and
thin and looks rather like a vulture in the Gobi desert, while
Aunt Dahlia is short and solid, like a scrum half in the game
of Rugby football. In disposition, too, they differ widely. Aunt
Agatha is cold and haughty, though presumably unbending a
bit when conducting human sacrifices at the time of the full
moon, as she is widely rumoured to do, and her attitude towards
me has always been that of an austere governess, causing me to
feel as if I were six years old and she had just caught me stealing
jam from the jam cupboard; whereas Aunt Dahlia is as jovial
and bonhomous as a pantomime dame in a Christmas pantomime. Curious.

I welcomed her with a huge 'Hello', in both syllables of which
a nephew's love and esteem could be easily detected, and went
so far as to imprint an affectionate kiss on her brow. Later I
would take her roundly to task for filling the house with Spodes
and Madeline Bassetts and bulging bounders in Panama hats,
but that could wait.

She returned my greeting with one of her uncouth hunting
cries – 'Yoicks', if I remember correctly. Apparently, when
you've been with the Quorn and the Pytchley for some time,
you drop into the habit of departing from basic English.

'So here you are, young Bertie.'

'You never spoke a truer word. Up and doing, with a heart
for any fate.'

'As thirsty as ever, I observe. I thought I would find you
tucking into the drinks.'

'Purely medicinal. I've had a shock.'

'What gave you that?'

'Suddenly becoming apprised of the fact that the blighter
Spode was my fellow guest,' I said, feeling that I couldn't have

a better cue for getting down to my recriminations. 'What on earth was the idea of inviting a fiend in human shape like that here?' I said, for I knew she shared my opinion of the seventh Earl of Sidcup. 'You have told me many a time and oft that you consider him one of Nature's gravest blunders. And yet you go out of your way to court his society, if court his society is the expression I want. You must have been off your onion, old ancestor.'

It was a severe ticking-off, and you would have expected the blush of shame to have mantled her cheeks, not that you would have noticed it much, her complexion being what it was after all those winters in the hunting field, but she was apparently imp-something, impervious, that's the word, to remorse. She remained what Anatole would have called as cool as some cucumbers.

'Ginger asked me to. He wanted Spode to speak for him at this election. He knows him slightly.'

'Far the best way of knowing Spode.'

'He needs all the help he can get, and Spode's one of those silver-tongued orators you read about. Extraordinary gift of the gab he has. He could get into Parliament without straining a sinew.'

I dare say she was right, but I resented any praise of Spode. I made clear my displeasure by responding curtly:

'Then why doesn't he?'

'He can't, you poor chump. He's a lord.'

'Don't they allow lords in?'

'No, they don't.'

'I see,' I said, rather impressed by this proof that the House of Commons drew the line somewhere. 'Well, I suppose you aren't so much to blame as I had thought. How do you get on with him?'

'I avoid him as much as possible.'

'Very shrewd. I shall do the same. We now come to Madeline Bassett. She's here, too. Why?'

'Oh, Madeline came along for the ride. She wanted to be near Spode. An extraordinary thing to want, I agree. Morbid, you might call it. Florence Craye, of course, has come to help Ginger's campaign.'

I started visibly. In fact, I jumped about six inches, as if a skewer or knitting-needle had come through the seat of my chair.

'You don't mean Florence is here as well?'

'With bells on. You seem perturbed.'

'I'm all of a twitter. It never occurred to me that when I came here I would be getting into a sort of population explosion.'

'Who ever told you about population explosions?'

'Jeeves. They are rather a favourite subject of his. He says if something isn't done pretty soon—'

'I'll bet he said, If steps are not taken shortly through the proper channels.'

'He did, as a matter of fact. He said, If steps aren't taken shortly through the proper channels, half the world will soon be standing on the other half's shoulders.'

'All right if you're one of the top layer.'

'Yes, there's that, of course.'

'Though even then it would be uncomfortable. Tricky sort of balancing act.'

'True.'

'And difficult to go for a stroll if you wanted to stretch the legs. And one wouldn't get much hunting.'

'Not much.'

We mused for awhile on what lay before us, and I remember thinking that present conditions, even with Spode and Madeline and Florence on the premises, suited one better. From this to thinking of Uncle Tom was but a step. It seemed to me that the poor old buster must be on the verge of a nervous breakdown. Even a single guest is sometimes too much for him.

'How,' I asked, 'is Uncle Tom bearing up under this invasion of his cabin?'

She stared incredibly or rather incredulously.

'Did you expect to find him here playing his banjo? My poor halfwitted child, he was off to the south of France the moment he learned that danger threatened. I had a picture postcard from him yesterday. He's having a wonderful time and wishes I was there.'

'And don't you mind all these blighters overrunning the place?'

'I would prefer it if they went elsewhere, but I treat them with saintly forbearance because I feel it's all helping Ginger.'

'How do things look in that direction?'

'An even bet, I would say. The slightest thing might turn the scale. He and his opponent are having a debate in a day or two, and a good deal, you might say everything, depends on that.'

'Who's the opponent?'

'Local talent. A barrister.'

'Jeeves says Market Snodsbury is very straitlaced, and if the electors found out about Ginger's past they would heave him out without even handing him his hat.'

'Has he a past?'

'I wouldn't call it that. Pure routine, I'd describe it as. In the days before he fell under Florence's spell he was rather apt to get slung out of restaurants for throwing eggs at the electric fan, and he seldom escaped unjugged on Boat Race night for pinching policemen's helmets. Would that lose him votes?'

'Lose him votes? If it was brought to Market Snodsbury's attention, I doubt if he would get a single one. That sort of thing might be overlooked in the cities of the plain, but not in Market Snodsbury. So for heaven's sake don't go babbling about it to everyone you meet.'

'My dear old ancestor, am I likely to?'

'Very likely, I should say. You know how fat your head is.'

I would have what-d'you-call-it-ed this slur, and with vehemence, but the adjective she had used reminded me that we had been talking all this time and I hadn't enquired about the camera chap.

'By the way,' I said, 'who would a fat fellow be?'

'Someone fond of starchy foods who had omitted to watch his calories, I imagine. What on earth, if anything, are you talking about?'

I saw that my question had been too abrupt. I hastened to clarify it.

'Strolling in the grounds and messuages just now I encountered an obese bird in a Panama hat with a pink ribbon, and I was wondering who he was and how he came to be staying here. He didn't look the sort of bloke for whom you would be putting out mats with "Welcome" on them. He gave me the impression of being a thug of the first order.'

My words seemed to have touched a chord. Rising nimbly, she went to the door and opened it, then to the French window and looked out, plainly in order to ascertain that nobody – except me, of course – was listening. Spies in spy stories do the same kind of thing when about to make communications which are for your ears only.

'I suppose I'd better tell you about him,' she said.

I intimated that I would be an attentive audience.

'That's L. P. Runkle, and I want you to exercise your charm on him, such as it is. He has to be conciliated and sucked up to.'

'Why, is he someone special?'

'You bet he's someone special. He's a big financier, Runkle's Enterprises. Loaded with money.'

It seemed to me that these words could have but one significance.

'You're hoping to touch him?'

'Such is indeed my aim. But not for myself. I want to get a round sum out of him for Tuppy Glossop.'

Her allusion was to the nephew of Sir Roderick Glossop, the well-known nerve specialist and loony doctor, once a source of horror and concern to Bertram but now one of my leading pals. He calls me Bertie, I call him Roddy. Tuppy, too, is one of my immediate circle of buddies, in spite of the fact that he once betted me I couldn't swing myself from end to end of the swimming bath at the Drones, and when I came to the last ring I found he had looped it back, giving me no option but to drop into the water in faultless evening dress. This had been like a dagger in the bosom for a considerable period, but eventually Time the great healer had ironed things out and I had forgiven him. He has been betrothed to Aunt Dahlia's daughter Angela for ages, and I had never been able to understand why they hadn't got around to letting the wedding bells get cracking. I had been expecting every day for ever so long to be called on to weigh in with the silver fish-slice, but the summons never came.

Naturally I asked if Tuppy was hard up, and she said he wasn't begging his bread and nosing about in the gutters for cigarette ends, but he hadn't enough to marry on.

'Thanks to L. P. Runkle. I'll tell you the whole story.'

'Do.'

'Did you ever meet Tuppy's late father?'

'Once. I remember him as a dreamy old bird of the absent-minded professor type.'

'He was a chemical researcher or whatever they call it, employed by Runkle's Enterprises, one of those fellows you see in the movies who go about in white coats peering into test tubes. And one day he invented what were afterwards known as Runkle's Magic Midgets, small pills for curing headaches. You've probably come across them.'

'I know them well. Excellent for a hangover, though not of course to be compared with Jeeves's patent pick-me-up. They're very popular at the Drones. I know a dozen fellows who swear by them. There must be a fortune in them.'

'There was. They sell like warm winter woollies in Iceland.'

'Then why is Tuppy short of cash? Didn't he inherit them?'

'Not by a jugful.'

'I don't get it. You speak in riddles, aged relative,' I said, and there was a touch of annoyance in my voice, for if there is one thing that gives me the pip, it is an aunt speaking in riddles. 'If these ruddy midget things belonged to Tuppy's father—'

'L. P. Runkle claimed they didn't. Tuppy's father was working for him on a salary, and the small print in the contract read that all inventions made on Runkle's Enterprises' time became the property of Runkle's Enterprises. So when old Glossop died, he hadn't much to leave his son, while L. P. Runkle went on flourishing like a green bay tree.'

I had never seen a green bay tree, but I gathered what she meant.

'Couldn't Tuppy sue?'

'He would have been bound to lose. A contract is a contract.'

I saw what she meant. It was not unlike that time when she was running that weekly paper of hers, *Milady's Boudoir*, and I contributed to it an article, or piece as it is sometimes called, on What The Well-Dressed Man Is Wearing. She gave me a packet of cigarettes for it, and it then became her property. I didn't actually get offers for it from France, Germany, Italy, Canada and the United States, but if I had had I couldn't have accepted them. My pal Boko Littleworth, who makes a living by his pen, tells me I ought to have sold her only the first serial rights, but I didn't think of it at the time. One makes these mistakes. What one needs, of course, is an agent.

All the same, I considered that L. P. Runkle ought to have stretched a point and let Tuppy's father get something out of it. I put this to the ancestor, and she agreed with me.

'Of course he ought. Moral obligation.'

'It confirms one's view that this Runkle is a stinker.'

'The stinker supreme. And he tells me he has been tipped off that he's going to get a knighthood in the New Year's Honours.'

'How can they knight a chap like that?'

'Just the sort of chap they do knight. Prominent business man. Big deals. Services to Britain's export trade.'

'But a stinker.'

'Unquestionably a stinker.'

'Then what's he doing here? You usually don't go out of your way to entertain stinkers. Spode, yes. I can understand you letting him infest the premises, much as I disapprove of it. He's making speeches on Ginger's behalf, and according to you doing it rather well. But why Runkle?'

She said 'Ah!', and when I asked her reason for saying 'Ah!', she replied that she was thinking of her subtle cunning, and when I asked what she meant by subtle cunning, she said 'Ah!' again. It looked as if we might go on like this indefinitely, but a moment later, having toddled to the door and opened it and to the French window and peered out, she explained.

'Runkle came here hoping to sell Tom an old silver what-not for his collection, and as Tom had vanished and he had come a long way I had to put him up for the night, and at dinner I suddenly had an inspiration. I thought if I got him to stay on and plied him day and night with Anatole's cooking, he might get into mellowed mood.'

She had ceased to speak in riddles. This time I followed her.

'So that you would be able to talk him into slipping Tuppy some of his ill-gotten gains?'

'Exactly. I'm biding my time. When the moment comes, I shall act like lightning. I told him Tom would be back in a day or two, not that he will, because he won't come within fifty miles of the place till I blow the All Clear, so Runkle consented to stay on.'

'And how's it working out?'

'The prospects look good. He mellows more with every meal. Anatole gave us his Mignonette de poulet Petit Duc last night, and he tucked into it like a tapeworm that's been on a diet for weeks. There was no mistaking the gleam in his eyes as he downed the last mouthful. A few more dinners ought to do the trick.'

She left me shortly after this to go and dress for dinner. I, strong in the knowledge that I could get into the soup and fish in ten minutes, lingered on, plunged in thought.

Extraordinary how I kept doing that as of even date. It just shows what life is like now. I don't suppose in the old days I would have been plunged in thought more than about once a month.

7

I need scarcely say that Tuppy's hard case, as outlined by the old blood relation, had got right in amongst me. You might suppose that a fellow capable of betting you you couldn't swing yourself across the Drones swimming-bath by the rings and looping the last ring back deserved no consideration, but as I say the agony of that episode had long since abated and it pained me deeply to contemplate the spot he was in. For though I had affected to consider that the ancestor's scheme for melting L. P. Runkle was the goods, I didn't really believe it would work. You don't get anywhere filling with rich foods a bloke who wears a Panama hat like his: the only way of inducing the L. P. Runkle type of man to part with cash is to kidnap him, take him to the cellar beneath the lonely mill and stick lighted matches between his toes. And even then he would probably give you a dud cheque.

The revelation of Tuppy's hard-upness had come as quite a surprise. You know how it is with fellows you're seeing all the time; if you think about their finances at all, you sort of assume they must be all right. It had never occurred to me that Tuppy might be seriously short of doubloons, but I saw now why there had been all this delay in assembling the bishop and assistant clergy and getting the show on the road. I presumed Uncle Tom would brass up if given the green light, he having the stuff in heaping sackfuls, but Tuppy has his pride and would quite properly jib at the idea of being supported by a father-in-law. Of course he really oughtn't to have gone and signed Angela up with his bank balance in such a rocky condition, but love is love. Conquers all, as the fellow said.

Having mused on Tuppy for about five minutes, I changed gears and started musing on Angela, for whom I had always had a cousinly affection. A definitely nice young prune and just the sort to be a good wife, but of course the catch is that you can't be a good wife if the other half of the sketch hasn't enough money to marry you. Practically all you can do is hang around and twiddle your fingers and hope for the best. Weary waiting about sums it up, and the whole lay-out, I felt, must be g and wormwood for Angela, causing her to bedew her pillow with many a salty tear.

I always find when musing that the thing to do is to bury the face in the hands, because it seems to concentrate thought and keep the mind from wandering off elsewhere. I did this now, and was getting along fairly well, when I suddenly had that uncanny feeling that I was not alone. I sensed a presence, if you would prefer putting it that way, and I had not been mistaken. Removing the hands and looking up, I saw that Madeline Bassett was with me.

It was a nasty shock. I won't say she was the last person I wanted to see, Spode of course heading the list of starters with L. P. Runkle in close attendance, but I would willingly have dispensed with her company. However, I rose courteously, and I don't think there was anything in my manner to suggest that I would have liked to hit her with a brick, for I am pretty inscrutable at all times. Nevertheless, behind my calm front there lurked the uneasiness which always grips me when we meet.

Holding the mistaken view that I am hopelessly in love with her and more or less pining away into a decline, this Bassett never fails to look at me, when our paths cross, with a sort of tender pity, and she was letting me have it now. So melting indeed was her gaze that it was only by reminding myself that she was safely engaged to Spode that I was able to preserve my equanimity and sangfroid. When she had been betrothed to Gussie Fink-Nottle, the peril of her making a switch had always been present, Gussie being the sort of spectacled newt-collecting freak a girl might at any moment get second thoughts about, but there was something so reassuring in her being engaged to Spode. Because, whatever you might think of him, you couldn't get away from it that he was the seventh Earl of Sidcup, and no girl who has managed to hook a seventh Earl with a castle in Shropshire and an income of twenty thousand pounds per annum is lightly going to change her mind about him.

Having given me the look, she spoke, and her voice was like treacle pouring out of a jug.

'Oh, Bertie, how nice to see you again. How are you?'

'I'm fine. How are *you*?'

'I'm fine.'

'That's fine. How's your father?'

'He's fine.'

I was sorry to hear this. My relations with Sir Watkyn Bassett were such that a more welcome piece of news would have been that he had contracted bubonic plague and wasn't expected to recover.

'I heard you were here,' I said.

'Yes, I'm here.'

'So I heard. You're looking well.'

'Oh, I'm very, very well, and oh so happy.'

'That's good.'

'I wake up each morning to the new day, and I know it's going to be the best day that ever was. Today I danced on the lawn before breakfast, and then I went round the garden saying good morning to the flowers. There was a sweet black cat asleep on one of the flower beds. I picked it up and danced with it.'

I didn't tell her so, but she couldn't have made a worse social gaffe. If there is one thing Augustus, the cat to whom she referred, hates, it's having his sleep disturbed. He must have cursed freely, though probably in a drowsy undertone. I suppose she thought he was purring.

She had paused, seeming to expect some comment on her fatheaded behaviour, so I said:

'Euphoria.'

'I what?'

'That's what it's called, Jeeves tells me, feeling like that.'

'Oh, I see. I just call it being happy, happy, happy.'

Having said which, she gave a start, quivered and put a hand up to her face as if she were having a screen test and had been told to register remorse.

'Oh, Bertie!'

'Hullo?'

'I'm so sorry.'

'Eh?'

'It was so tactless of me to go on about my happiness. I should have remembered how different it was for you. I saw your face twist with pain as I came in and I can't tell you how sorry I am to think that it is I who have caused it. Life is not easy, is it?'

'Not very.'

'Difficult.'

'In spots.'

'The only thing is to be brave.'

'That's about it.'

'You must not lose courage. Who knows? Consolation may be waiting for you somewhere. Some day you will meet someone who will make you forget you ever loved me. No, not quite that. I think I shall always be a fragrant memory, always something deep in your heart that will be with you like a gentle, tender ghost as you watch the sunset on summer evenings while the little birds sing their off-to-bed songs in the shrubbery.'

'I wouldn't be surprised,' I said, for one simply has to say the civil thing. 'You look a bit damp,' I added, changing the subject. 'Was it raining when you were out?'

'A little, but I didn't mind. I was saying good-night to the flowers.'

'Oh, you say good-night to them, too?'

'Of course. Their poor little feelings would be so hurt if I didn't.'

'Wise of you to come in. Might have got lumbago.'

'That was not why I came in. I saw you through the window, and I had a question to ask you. A very, very serious question.'

'Oh, yes?'

'But it's so difficult to know how to put it. I shall have to ask it as they do in books. You know what they say in books.'

'What who say in books?'

'Detectives and people like that. Bertie, are you going straight now?'

'I beg your pardon?'

'You know what I mean. Have you given up stealing things?'

I laughed one of those gay debonair ones.

'Oh, absolutely.'

'I'm so glad. You don't feel the urge any more? You've conquered the craving? I told Daddy it was just a kind of illness. I said you couldn't help yourself.'

I remembered her submitting this theory to him ... I was hiding behind a sofa at the time, a thing I have been compelled to do rather oftener than I could wish ... and Sir Watkyn had replied in what I thought dubious taste that it was precisely my habit of helping myself to everything I could lay my hands on that he was criticizing.

Another girl might have left it at that, but not M. Bassett. She was all eager curiosity.

'Did you have psychiatric treatment? Or was it will power?'

'Just will power.'

'How splendid. I'm so proud of you. It must have been a terrible struggle.'

'Oh, so–so.'

'I shall write to Daddy and tell him—'

Here she paused and put a hand to her left eye, and it was easy for a man of my discernment to see what had happened. The French window being open, gnats in fairly large numbers had been coming through and flitting to and fro. It's a thing one always has to budget for in the English countryside. In America they have screens, of course, which make flying objects feel pretty nonplussed, but these have never caught on in England and the gnats have it more or less their own way. They horse around and now and then get into people's eyes. One of these, it was evident, had now got into Madeline's.

I would be the last to deny that Bertram Wooster has his limitations, but in one field of endeavour I am pre-eminent. In the matter of taking things out of eyes I yield to no one. I know what to say and what to do.

Counselling her not to rub it, I advanced handkerchief in hand.

I remember going into the technique of operations of this kind with Gussie Fink-Nottle at Totleigh when he had removed a fly from the eye of Stephanie Byng, now the Reverend Mrs Stinker Pinker, and we were in agreement that success could be achieved only by placing a hand under the patient's chin in order to steady the head. Omit this preliminary and your efforts are bootless. My first move, accordingly, was to do so and it was characteristic of Spode that he should have chosen this moment to join us, just when we twain were in what you might call close juxtaposition.

I confess that there have been times when I have felt more at my ease. Spode, in addition to being constructed on the lines of a rather oversized gorilla, has a disposition like that of a short-tempered tiger of the jungle and a nasty mind which leads him to fall a ready prey to what I have heard Jeeves call the green-eyed monster which doth mock the meat it feeds on – viz. jealousy. Such a man, finding you steadying the head of the girl he loves, is always extremely likely to start trying to ascertain the colour of your insides, and to avert this I greeted him with what nonchalance I could muster.

'Oh, hullo, Spode old chap, I mean Lord Sidcup old chap. Here we all are, what. Jeeves told me you were here, and Aunt Dahlia says you've been knocking the voting public base over apex with your oratory in the Conservative interest. Must be wonderful to be able to do that. It's a gift, of course. Some have it, some haven't. I couldn't address a political meeting to please a dying grandmother. I should stand there opening and shutting my mouth like a goldfish. You, on the other hand, just clear your throat and the golden words come pouring out like syrup. I admire you enormously.'

Conciliatory, I think you'll agree. I could hardly have given him the old salve with a more liberal hand, and one might have expected him to simper, shuffle his feet and mumble 'Awfully nice of you to say so' or something along those lines. Instead of which, all he did was come back at me with a guttural sound like an opera basso choking on a fishbone, and I had to sustain the burden of the conversation by myself.

'I've just been taking a gnat out of Madeline's eye.'

'Oh?'

'Dangerous devils, these gnats. Require skilled handling.'

'Oh?'

'Everything's back to normal now, I think.'

'Yes, thank you ever so much, Bertie.'

It was Madeline who said this, not Spode. He continued to gaze at me bleakly. She went on harping on the thing.

'Bertie's so clever.'

'Oh?'

'I don't know what I would have done without him.'

'Oh?'

'He showed wonderful presence of mind.'

'Oh?'

'I feel so sorry, though, for the poor little gnat.'

'It asked for it,' I pointed out. 'It was unquestionably the aggressor.'

'Yes, I suppose that's true, but . . . ' The clock on the mantelpiece caught her now de-gnatted eye, and she uttered an agitated squeak. 'Oh, my goodness, is that the time? I must rush.'

She buzzed off, and I was on the point of doing the same, when Spode detained me with a curt 'One moment'. There are all sorts of ways of saying 'One moment'. This was one of the nastier ones, spoken with an unpleasant rasping note in the voice.

'I want a word with you, Wooster.'

I am never anxious to chat with Spode, but if I had been sure that he merely wanted to go on saying 'Oh?', I would have been willing to listen. Something, however, seemed to tell me that he was about to give evidence of a wider vocabulary, and I edged towards the door.

'Some other time, don't you think?'

'Not some ruddy other time. Now.'

'I shall be late for dinner.'

'You can't be too late for me. And if you get your teeth knocked down your throat, as you will if you don't listen attentively to what I have to say, you won't be able to eat any dinner.'

This seemed plausible. I decided to lend him an ear, as the expression is. 'Say on,' I said, and he said on, lowering his voice to a sort of rumbling growl which made him difficult to follow. However, I caught the word 'read' and the word 'book' and perked up a bit. If this was going to be a literary discussion, I didn't mind exchanging views.

'Book?' I said.

'Book.'

'You want me to recommend you a good book? Well, of course, it depends on what you like. Jeeves, for instance, is never happier than when curled up with his Spinoza or his Shakespeare. I, on the other hand, go in mostly for who-dun-its and novels of suspense. For the who-dun-it Agatha Christie is always a safe bet. For the novel of suspense . . . '

Here I paused, for he had called me an opprobrious name and told me to stop babbling, and it is always my policy to stop babbling when a man eight foot six in height and broad in proportion tells me to. I went into the silence, and he continued to say on.

'I said that I could read you like a book, Wooster. I know what your game is.'

'I don't understand you, Lord Sidcup.'

'Then you must be as big an ass as you look, which is saying a good deal. I am referring to your behaviour towards my fiancée. I come into this room and I find you fondling her face.'

I had to correct him here. One likes to get these things straight.

'Only her chin.'

'Pah!' he said, or something that sounded like that.

'And I had to get a grip on it in order to extract the gnat from her eye. I was merely steadying it.'

'You were steadying it gloatingly.'

'I wasn't!'

'Pardon me. I have eyes and can see when a man is steadying a chin gloatingly and when he isn't. You were obviously delighted to have an excuse for soiling her chin with your foul fingers.'

'You are wrong, Lord Spodecup.'

'And, as I say, I know what your game is. You are trying to undermine me, to win her from me with your insidious guile, and what I want to impress upon you with all the emphasis at my disposal is that if anything of this sort is going to occur again, you would do well to take out an accident policy with some good insurance company at the earliest possible date. You probably think that being a guest in your aunt's house I would hesitate to butter you over the front lawn and dance on the fragments in hobnailed boots, but you are mistaken. It will be a genuine pleasure. By an odd coincidence I brought a pair of hobnailed boots with me!'

So saying, and recognizing a good exit line when he saw one, he strode out, and after an interval of tense meditation I followed him. Repairing to my bedroom, I found Jeeves there, looking reproachful. He knows I can dress for dinner in ten minutes, but regards haste askance, for he thinks it results in a tie which, even if adequate, falls short of the perfect butterfly effect.

I ignored the silent rebuke in his eyes. After meeting Spode's eyes, I was dashed if I was going to be intimidated by Jeeves's.

'Jeeves,' I said, 'you're fairly well up in Hymns Ancient and Modern, I should imagine. Who were the fellows in the hymn who used to prowl and prowl around?'

'The troops of Midian, sir.'

'That's right. Was Spode mentioned as one of them?'

'Sir?'

'I ask because he's prowling around as if Midian was his home town. Let me tell you all about it.'

'I fear it will not be feasible, sir. The gong is sounding.'

'So it is. Who's sounding it? You said Seppings was in bed.'

'The parlourmaid, sir, deputizing for Mr Seppings.'

'I like her wrist work. Well, I'll tell you later.'

'Very good, sir. Pardon me, your tie.'

'What's wrong with it?'

'Everything, sir. If you will allow me.'

'All right, go ahead. But I can't help asking myself if ties really matter at a time like this.'

'There is no time when ties do not matter, sir.'

My mood was sombre as I went down to dinner. Anatole, I was thinking, would no doubt give us of his best, possibly his Timbale de ris de veau Toulousaine or his Sylphides à la crème d'écrevisses, but Spode would be there and Madeline would be there and Florence would be there and L. P. Runkle would be there.

There was, I reflected, always something.

8

It has been well said of Bertram Wooster that when he sets his hand to the plough he does not stop to pick daisies and let the grass grow under his feet. Many men in my position, having undertaken to canvass for a friend anxious to get into Parliament, would have waited till after lunch next day to get rolling, saying to themselves Oh, what difference do a few hours make and going off to the billiard-room for a game or two of snooker. I, in sharp contradistinction as I have heard Jeeves call it, was on my way shortly after breakfast. It can't have been much more than a quarter to eleven when, fortified by a couple of kippers, toast, marmalade and three cups of coffee, I might have been observed approaching a row of houses down by the river to which someone with a flair for the *mot juste* had given the name of River Row. From long acquaintance with the town I knew that this was one of the posher parts of Market Snodsbury, stiff with householders likely to favour the Conservative cause, and it was for that reason that I was making it my first port of call. No sense, I mean, in starting off with the less highly priced localities where everybody was bound to vote Labour and would not only turn a deaf ear to one's reasoning but might even bung a brick at one. Ginger no doubt had a special posse of tough supporters, talking and spitting out of the side of their mouths, and they would attend to the brick-bunging portion of the electorate.

Jeeves was at my side, but whereas I had selected Number One as my objective, his intention was to push on to Number Two. I would then give Number Three the treatment, while he did the same to Number Four. Talking it over, we had decided that if we made it a double act and blew into a house together, it might give the occupant the impression that he was receiving a visit from the plain clothes police and excite him unduly. Many of the men who live in places like River Row have a tendency to apoplectic fits as the result of high living, and a voter expiring on the floor from shock means a voter less on the voting list. One has to think of these things.

'What beats me, Jeeves,' I said, for I was in thoughtful mood, 'is why people don't object to somebody they don't know from Adam muscling into their homes without a . . . without a what? It's on the tip of my tongue.'

'A With-your-leave or a By-your leave, sir?'

'That's right. Without a With-your-leave or a By-your-leave and telling them which way to vote. Taking a liberty, it strikes me as.'

'It is the custom at election time, sir. Custom reconciles us to everything, a wise man once said.'

'Shakespeare?'

'Burke, sir. You will find the apothegm in his *On The Sublime And Beautiful*. I think the electors, conditioned by many years of canvassing, would be disappointed if nobody called on them.'

'So we shall be bringing a ray of sunshine into their drab lives?'

'Something on that order, sir.'

'Well, you may be right. Have you ever done this sort of thing before?'

'Once or twice, sir, before I entered your employment.'

'What were your methods?'

'I outlined as briefly as possible the main facets of my argument, bade my auditors goodbye, and withdrew.'

'No preliminaries?'

'Sir?'

'You didn't make a speech of any sort before getting down to brass tacks? No mention of Burke or Shakespeare or the poet Burns?'

'No, sir. It might have caused exasperation.'

I disagreed with him. I felt that he was on the wrong track altogether and couldn't expect anything in the nature of a triumph at Number Two. There is probably nothing a voter enjoys more than hearing the latest about Burke and his *On The Sublime And Beautiful*, and here he was, deliberately chucking away the advantages his learning gave him. I had half a mind to draw his attention to the Parable of the Talents, with which I had become familiar when doing research for that Scripture Knowledge prize I won at school. Time, however, was getting along, so I passed it up. But I told him I thought he was mistaken. Preliminaries, I maintained, were of the essence.

Breaking the ice is what it's called. I mean, you can't just barge in on a perfect stranger and get off the mark with an abrupt 'Hoy there. I hope you're going to vote for my candidate!' How much better to say 'Good morning, sir. I can see at a glance that you are a man of culture, probably never happier than when reading your Burke. I wonder if you are familiar with his *On The Sublime And Beautiful?*' Then away you go, off to a nice start.

'You must have an approach,' I said. 'I myself am all for the jolly, genial. I propose, on meeting my householder, to begin with a jovial "Hullo there, Mr Whatever-it-is, hullo there", thus ingratiating myself with him from the kick-off. I shall then tell him a funny story. Then, and only then, will I get to the nub – waiting, of course, till he has stopped laughing. I can't fail.'

'I am sure you will not, sir. The system would not suit me, but it is merely a matter of personal taste.'

'The psychology of the individual, what?'

'Precisely, sir. By different methods different men excel.'

'Burke?'

'Charles Churchill, sir, a poet who flourished in the early eighteenth century. The words occur in his *Epistle To William Hogarth.*'

We halted. Cutting out a good pace, we had arrived at the door of Number One. I pressed the bell.

'Zero hour, Jeeves,' I said gravely.

'Yes, sir.'

'Carry on.'

'Very good, sir.'

'Heaven speed your canvassing.'

'Thank you, sir.'

'And mine.'

'Yes, sir.'

He pushed along and mounted the steps of Number Two, leaving me feeling rather as I had done in my younger days at a clergyman uncle's place in Kent when about to compete in the Choir Boys Bicycle Handicap open to all those whose voices had not broken by the first Sunday in Epiphany – nervous, but full of the will to win.

The door opened as I was running through the high spots of the laughable story I planned to unleash when I got inside. A maid was standing there, and conceive my emotion when I recognized her as one who had held office under Aunt Dahlia the last time I had enjoyed the latter's hospitality; the one with whom, the old sweats will recall, I had chewed the fat on the subject of the cat Augustus and his tendency to pass his days in sleep instead of bustling about and catching mice.

The sight of her friendly face was like a tonic. My morale, which had begun to sag a bit after Jeeves had left me, rose sharply, closing at nearly par. I felt that even if the fellow I was going to see kicked me downstairs, she would be there to show me out and tell me that these things are sent to try us, with the general idea of making us more spiritual.

'Why, hullo!' I said.

'Good morning, sir.'

'We meet again.'

'Yes, sir.'

'You remember me?'

'Oh yes, sir.'

'And you have not forgotten Augustus?'

'Oh no, sir.'

'He's still as lethargic as ever. He joined me at breakfast this morning. Just managed to keep awake while getting outside his portion of kipper, then fell into a dreamless sleep at the end of the bed with his head hanging down. So you have resigned your portfolio at Aunt Dahlia's since we last met. Too bad. We shall all miss you. Do you like it here?'

'Oh yes, sir.'

'That's the spirit. Well, getting down to business, I've come to see your boss on a matter of considerable importance. What sort of chap is he? Not too short-tempered? Not too apt to be cross with callers, I hope?'

'It isn't a gentleman, sir, it's a lady. Mrs McCorkadale.'

This chipped quite a bit off the euphoria I was feeling. I had been relying on the story I had prepared to put me over with a bang, carrying me safely through the first awkward moments when the fellow you've called on without an invitation is staring at you as if wondering to what he owes the honour of this visit, and now it would have to remain untold. It was one I had heard from Catsmeat Potter-Pirbright at the Drones and it was essentially a *conte* whose spiritual home was the smoking-room of a London club or the men's wash-room on an American train — in short, one by no means adapted to the ears of the gentler sex; especially a member of that sex who probably ran the local Watch Committee.

It was, consequently, a somewhat damped Bertram Wooster whom the maid ushered into the drawing-room, and my pep was in no way augmented by the first sight I had of mine hostess. Mrs McCorkadale was what I would call a grim woman. Not so grim as my Aunt Agatha, perhaps, for that could hardly be expected, but certainly well up in the class of Jael the wife of Heber and the Madame Whoever-it-was who used to sit and knit at the foot of the guillotine during the French Revolution. She had a beaky nose, tight thin lips, and her eye could have been used for splitting logs in the teak forests of Borneo. Seeing her steadily and seeing her whole, as the expression is, one marvelled at the intrepidity of Mr McCorkadale in marrying her – a man obviously whom nothing could daunt.

However, I had come there to be jolly and genial, and jolly and genial I was resolved to be. Actors will tell you that on these occasions, when the soul is a-twitter and the nervous system not like mother makes it, the thing to do is to take a deep breath. I took three, and immediately felt much better.

'Good morning, good morning, good morning,' I said. 'Good morning,' I added, rubbing it in, for it was my policy to let there be no stint.

'Good morning,' she replied, and one might have totted things up as so far, so good. But if I said she said it cordially, I would be deceiving my public. The impression I got was that the sight of me hurt her in some sensitive spot. The woman, it was plain, shared Spode's view of what was needed to make England a land fit for heroes to live in.

Not being able to uncork the story and finding the way her eye was going through me like a dose of salts more than a little trying to my already dented sangfroid, I might have had some difficulty in getting the conversation going, but fortunately I was full of good material just waiting to be decanted. Over an after-dinner smoke on the previous night Ginger had filled me in on what his crowd proposed to do when they got down to it. They were going, he said, to cut taxes to the bone, straighten out our foreign policy, double our export trade, have two cars in the garage and two chickens in the pot for everyone and give the pound the shot in the arm it had been clamouring for for years. Than which, we both agreed, nothing could be sweeter, and I saw no reason to suppose that the McCorkadale gargoyle would not feel the same. I began, therefore, by asking her if she had a vote, and she said Yes, of course, and I said Well, that was fine, because if she hadn't had, the point of my arguments would have been largely lost.

'An excellent thing, I've always thought, giving women the vote,' I proceeded heartily, and she said – rather nastily, it seemed to me – that she was glad I approved. 'When you cast yours, if cast is the word I want, I strongly advise you to cast it in favour of Ginger Winship.'

'On what do you base that advice?'

She couldn't have given me a better cue. She had handed it to me on a plate with watercress round it. Like a flash I went into my sales talk, mentioning Ginger's attitude towards taxes, our foreign policy, our export trade, cars in the garage, chickens in the pot and first aid for the poor old pound, and was shocked to observe an entire absence of enthusiasm on her part. Not a ripple appeared on the stern and rockbound coast of her map. She looked like Aunt Agatha listening to the boy Wooster trying to explain away a drawing-room window broken by a cricket ball.

I pressed her closely, or do I mean keenly.

'You want taxes cut, don't you?'

'I do.'

'And our foreign policy bumped up?'

'Certainly.'

'And our exports doubled and a stick of dynamite put under the pound? I'll bet you do. Then vote for Ginger Winship, the man who with his hand on the helm of the ship of state will steer England to prosperity and happiness, bringing back once more the spacious days of Good Queen Bess.' This was a line of talk that Jeeves had roughed out for my use. There was also some rather good stuff about this sceptred isle and this other Eden, demi-something, but I had forgotten it. 'You can't say that wouldn't be nice,' I said.

A moment before, I wouldn't have thought it possible that she could look more like Aunt Agatha than she had been doing, but she now achieved this breathtaking feat. She sniffed, if not snorted, and spoke as follows:

'Young man, don't be idiotic. Hand on the helm of the ship of state, indeed! If Mr Winship performs the miracle of winning this election, which he won't, he will be an ordinary humble back-bencher, doing nothing more notable than saying "Hear, hear" when his superiors are speaking and "Oh" and "Question" when the opposition have the floor. As,' she went on, 'I shall if I win this election, as I intend to.'

I blinked. A sharp 'Whatwasthatyousaid?' escaped my lips, and she proceeded to explain or, as Jeeves would say, elucidate.

'You are not very quick at noticing things, are you? I imagine not, or you would have seen that Market Snodsbury is liberally plastered with posters bearing the words "Vote for McCorkadale". An abrupt way of putting it, but one that is certainly successful in conveying its meaning.'

It was a blow, I confess, and I swayed beneath it like an aspen, if aspens are those things that sway. The Woosters can take a good deal, but only so much. My most coherent thought at the moment was that it was just like my luck, when I sallied forth as a canvasser, to collide first crack out of the box with the rival candidate. I also had the feeling that if Jeeves had taken on Number One instead of Number Two, he would probably have persuaded Ma McCorkadale to vote against herself.

I suppose if you had asked Napoleon how he had managed to get out of Moscow, he would have been a bit vague about it, and it was the same with me. I found myself on the front steps with only a sketchy notion of how I had got there, and I was in the poorest of shapes. To try to restore the shattered system I lit a cigarette and had begun to puff, when a cheery voice hailed me and I became aware that some foreign substance was sharing my doorstep. 'Hullo, Wooster old chap' it was saying and, the mists clearing from before my eyes, I saw that it was Bingley.

I gave the blighter a distant look. Knowing that this blot on the species resided in Market Snodsbury, I had foreseen that I might run into him sooner or later, so I was not surprised to see him. But I certainly wasn't pleased. The last thing I wanted in the delicate state to which the McCorkadale had reduced me was conversation with a man who set cottages on fire and chased the hand that fed him hither and thither with a carving knife.

He was as unduly intimate, forward, bold, intrusive and deficient in due respect as he had been at the Junior Ganymede. He gave my back a cordial slap and would, I think, have prodded me in the ribs if it had occurred to him. You wouldn't have thought that carving knives had ever come between us.

'And what are *you* doing in these parts, cocky?' he asked.

I said I was visiting my aunt Mrs Travers, who had a house in the vicinity, and he said he knew the place, though he had never met the old geezer to whom I referred.

'I've seen her around. Red-faced old girl, isn't she?'

'Fairly vermilion.'

'High blood pressure, probably.'

'Or caused by going in a lot for hunting. It chaps the cheeks.'

'Different from a barmaid. She cheeks the chaps.'

If he had supposed that his crude humour would get so much as a simper out of me, he was disappointed. I preserved the cold aloofness of a Wednesday matinée audience, and he proceeded.

'Yes, that might be it. She looks a sport. Making a long stay?'

'I don't know,' I said, for the length of my visits to the old ancestor is always uncertain. So much depends on whether she throws me out or not. 'Actually I'm here to canvass for the Conservative candidate. He's a pal of mine.'

He whistled sharply. He had been looking repulsive and cheerful; he now looked repulsive and grave. Seeming to realize that he had omitted a social gesture, he prodded me in the ribs.

'You're wasting your time, Wooster, old man,' he said. 'He hasn't an earthly.'

'No?' I quavered. It was simply one man's opinion, of course, but the earnestness with which he had spoken was unquestionably impressive. 'What makes you think that?'

'Never you mind what makes me think it. Take my word for it. If you're sensible, you'll phone your bookie and have a big bet on McCorkadale. You'll never regret it. You'll come to me later and thank me for the tip with tears in your—'

At some point in this formal interchange of thoughts by spoken word, as Jeeves's *Dictionary of Synonyms* puts it, he must have pressed the bell, for at this moment the door opened and my old buddy the maid appeared. Quickly adding the word 'eyes', he turned to her.

'Mrs McCorkadale in, dear?' he asked, and having been responded to in the affirmative he left me, and I headed for home. I ought, of course, to have carried on along River Row, taking the odd numbers while Jeeves attended to the even, but I didn't feel in the vein.

I was uneasy. You might say, if you happened to know the word, that the prognostications of a human wart like Bingley deserved little credence, but he had spoken with such conviction, so like someone who has heard something, that I couldn't pass them off with a light laugh.

Brooding tensely, I reached the old homestead and found the ancestor lying on a chaise longue, doing the *Observer* crossword puzzle.

9

There was a time when this worthy housewife, tackling the *Observer* crossword puzzle, would snort and tear her hair and fill the air with strange oaths picked up from cronies on the hunting field, but consistent inability to solve more than about an eighth of the clues has brought a sort of dull resignation and today she merely sits and stares at it, knowing that however much she licks the end of her pencil little or no business will result.

As I came in, I heard her mutter, soliloquizing like someone in Shakespeare, 'Measured tread of saint round St Paul's, for God's sake', seeming to indicate that she had come up against a hot one, and I think it was a relief to her to become aware that her favourite nephew was at her side and that she could conscientiously abandon her distasteful task, for she looked up and greeted me cheerily. She wears tortoiseshell-rimmed spectacles for reading which make her look like a fish in an aquarium. She peered at me through these.

'Hullo, my bounding Bertie.'

'Good morning, old ancestor.'

'Up already?'

'I have been up some time.'

'Then why aren't you out canvassing? And why are you looking like something the cat brought in?'

I winced. I had not intended to disclose the recent past, but with an aunt's perception she had somehow spotted that in some manner I had passed through the furnace and she would go on probing and questioning till I came clean. Any capable aunt can give Scotland Yard inspectors strokes and bisques in the matter of interrogating a suspect, and I knew that all attempts at concealment would be fruitless. Or is it bootless? I would have to check with Jeeves.

'I am looking like something the cat brought in because I am feeling like something the c b in,' I said. 'Aged relative, I have a strange story to relate. Do you know a local blister of the name of Mrs McCorkadale?'

'Who lives in River Row?'

'That's the one.'

'She's a barrister.'

'She looks it.'

'You've met her?'

'I've met her.'

'She's Ginger's opponent in this election.'

'I know. Is Mr McCorkadale still alive?'

'Died years ago. He got run over by a municipal tram.'

'I don't blame him. I'd have done the same myself in his place. It's the only course to pursue when you're married to a woman like that.'

'How did you meet her?'

'I called on her to urge her to vote for Ginger,' I said, and in a few broken words I related my strange story.

It went well. In fact, it went like a breeze. Myself, I was unable to see anything humorous in it, but there was no doubt about it entertaining the blood relation. She guffawed more liberally than I had ever heard a woman guffaw. If there had been an aisle, she would have rolled in it. I couldn't help feeling how ironical it was that, having failed so often to be well received when telling a funny story, I should have aroused such gales of mirth with one that was so essentially tragic.

While she was still giving her impersonation of a hyena which has just heard a good one from another hyena, Spode came in, choosing the wrong moment as usual. One never wants to see Spode, but least of all when someone is having a hearty laugh at your expense.

'I'm looking for the notes for my speech tomorrow,' he said. 'Hullo, what's the joke?'

Convulsed as she was, it was not easy for the ancestor to articulate, but she managed a couple of words.

'It's Bertie.'

'Oh?' said Spode, looking at me as if he found it difficult to believe that any word or act of mine could excite mirth and not horror and disgust.

'He's just been calling on Mrs McCorkadale.'

'Oh?'

'And asking her to vote for Ginger Winship.'

'Oh?' said Spode again. I have already indicated that he was a compulsive Oh-sayer. 'Well, it is what I would have expected of him,' and with another look in which scorn and animosity were nicely blended and a word to the effect that he might have left those notes in the summerhouse by the lake he removed his distasteful presence.

That he and I were not on Damon and Pythias terms seemed to have impressed itself on the aged relative. She switched off the hyena sound effects.

'Not a bonhomous type, Spode.'

'No.'

'He doesn't like you.'

'No.'

'And I don't think he likes me.'

'No,' I said, and it occurred to me, for the Woosters are essentially fairminded, that it was hardly for me to criticize Spode's Oh's when my No's were equally frequent. Why beholdest thou the mote that is in thy brother's eye, but considerest not the beam that is in thine own eye, Wooster? I found myself asking myself, it having been one of the many good things I had picked up in my researches when I won that Scripture Knowledge prize.

'Does he like anyone?' said the relative. 'Except, presumably, Madeline Bassett.'

'He seems fond of L. P. Runkle.'

'What makes you think that?'

'I overheard them exchanging confidences.'

'Oh?' said the relative, for these things are catching. 'Well, I suppose one ought not to be surprised. Birds of a feather—'

'Flock together?'

'Exactly. And even the dregs of pond life fraternize with other dregs of pond life. By the way, remind me to tell you something about L. P. Runkle.'

'Right ho.'

'We will come to L. P. Runkle later. This animosity of Spode's, is it just the memory of old Totleigh days, or have you done anything lately to incur his displeasure?'

This time I had no hesitation in telling her all. I felt she would be sympathetic. I laid the facts before her with every confidence that an aunt's condolences would result.

'There was this gnat.'

'I don't follow you.'

'I had to rally round.'

'You've still lost me.'

'Spode didn't like it.'

'So he doesn't like gnats either. Which gnat? What gnat? Will you get on with your story, curse you, starting at the beginning and carrying on to the end.'

'Certainly, if you wish. Here is the scenario.'

I told her about the gnat in Madeline's eye, the part I had played in restoring her vision to mid-season form and the exception Spode had taken to my well-meant efforts. She whistled. Everyone seemed to be whistling at me today. Even the recent maid on recognizing me had puckered up her lips as if about to.

'I wouldn't do that sort of thing again,' she said.

'If the necessity arose I would have no option.'

'Then you'd better get one as soon as possible. Because if you keep on taking things out of Madeline's eye, you may have to marry the girl.'

'But surely the peril has passed now that she's engaged to Spode.'

'I don't know so much. I think there's some trouble between Spode and Madeline.'

I would be surprised to learn that in the whole W.1 postal section of London there is a man more capable than Bertram Wooster of bearing up with a stiff upper lip under what I have heard Jeeves call the slings and arrows of outrageous fortune; but at these frightful words I confess that I went into my old aspen routine even more wholeheartedly than I had done during my get-together with the relict of the late McCorkadale.

And not without reason. My whole foreign policy was based on the supposition that the solidarity of these two consenting adults was something that couldn't be broken or even cracked. He, on his own statement, had worshipped her since she was so high, while she, as I have already recorded, would not lightly throw a man of his eligibility into the discard. If ever there was a union which you could have betted with perfect confidence would culminate in a golden wedding with all the trimmings, this was the one.

'Trouble?' I whispered hoarsely. 'You mean there's a what-d'you-call-it?'

'What would that be?'

'A rift within the lute which widens soon and makes the music mute. Not my own, Jeeves's.'

'The evidence points in that direction. At dinner last night I noticed that he was refusing Anatole's best, while she looked wan and saintlike and crumbled bread. And talking of Anatole's best, what I wanted to tell you about L. P. Runkle was that zero hour is approaching. I am crouching for my spring and have strong hopes that Tuppy will soon be in the money.'

I clicked the tongue. Nobody could be keener than I on seeing Tuppy dip into L. P. Runkle's millions, but this was no time to change the subject.

'Never mind about Tuppy for the moment. Concentrate on the sticky affairs of Bertram Wilberforce Wooster.'

'Wilberforce,' she murmured, as far as a woman of her outstanding lung power could murmur. 'Did I ever tell you how you got that label? It was your father's doing. The day before you were lugged to the font looking like a minor actor playing a bit part in a gangster film he won a packet on an outsider in the Grand National called that, and he insisted on you carrying on the name. Tough on you, but we all have our cross to bear. Your Uncle Tom's second name is Portarlington, and I came within an ace of being christened Phyllis.'

I rapped her sharply on the top-knot with a paper-knife of Oriental design, the sort that people in novels of suspense are always getting stabbed in the back with.

'Don't wander from the *res*. The fact that you nearly got christened Phyllis will, no doubt, figure in your autobiography, but we need not discuss it now. What we are talking about is the ghastly peril that confronts me if the Madeline-Spode axis blows a fuse.'

'You mean that if she breaks her engagement, you will have to fill the vacuum?'

'Exactly.'

'She won't. Not a chance.'

'But you said—'

'I only wanted to emphasize my warning to you not to keep on taking gnats out of Madeline's eyes. Perhaps I overdid it.'

'You chilled me to the marrow.'

'Sorry I was so dramatic. You needn't worry. They've only had a lovers' tiff such as occurs with the mushiest couples.'

'What about?'

'How do I know? Perhaps he queried her statement that the stars were God's daisy chain.'

I had to admit that there was something in this theory. Madeline's breach with Gussie Fink-Nottle had been caused by her drawing his attention to the sunset and saying sunsets always made her think of the Blessed Damozel leaning out from the gold bar of heaven, and he said, 'Who?' and she said, 'The Blessed Damozel', and he said, 'Never heard of her', adding that sunsets made him sick, and so did the Blessed Damozel. A girl with her outlook would be bound to be touchy about stars and daisy chains.

'It's probably over by now,' said the ancestor. 'All the same, you'd better keep away from the girl. Spode's an impulsive man. He might slosh you.'

'He said he would.'

'He used the word slosh?'

'No, but he assured me he would butter me over the front lawn and dance on the remains with hobnailed boots.'

'Much the same thing. So I would be careful if I were you. Treat her with distant civility. If you see any more gnats headed in her direction, hold their coats and wish them luck, but restrain the impulse to mix in.'

'I will.'

'I hope I have relieved your fears?'

'You have, old flesh and blood.'

'Then why the furrows in your brow?'

'Oh, those? It's Ginger.'

'What's Ginger?'

'He's why my brow is furrowed.'

It shows how profoundly the thought of Madeline Bassett possibly coming into circulation again had moved me that it was only now that I had remembered Bingley and what he had said about the certainty of Ginger finishing as an also-ran in the election. I burned with shame and remorse that I should have allowed my personal troubles to make me shove him down to the foot of the agenda paper in this scurvy manner. Long ere this I ought to have been inviting Aunt Dahlia's views on his prospects. Not doing so amounted to letting a pal down, a thing I pride myself on never being guilty of. Little wonder that I b'd with s and r.

I hastened to make amends, if those are what you make when you have done the dirty on a fellow you love like a brother.

'Did I ever mention a bloke called Bingley to you?'

'If you did, I've forgotten.'

'He was my personal attendant for a brief space when Jeeves and I differed about me playing the banjolele. That time when I had a cottage down at Chufnell Regis.'

'Oh yes, he set it on fire, didn't he?'

'While tight as an owl. It was burned to a cinder, as was my banjolele.'

'I've got him placed now. What about him?'

'He lives in Market Snodsbury. I met him this morning and happened to mention that I was canvassing for Ginger.'

'If you can call it canvassing.'

'And he told me I was wasting my time. He advised me to have a substantial bet on Ma McCorkadale. He said Ginger hadn't an earthly.'

'He's a fool.'

'I must say I've always thought so, but he spoke as if he had inside information.'

'What on earth information could he have? An election isn't a horse race where you get tips from the stable cat. I don't say it may not be a close thing, but Ginger ought to win all right. He has a secret weapon.'

'Repeat that, if you wouldn't mind. I don't think I got it.'

'Ginger defies competition because he has a secret weapon.'

'Which is?'

'Spode.'

'Spode?'

'My lord Sidcup. Have you ever heard him speak?'

'I did just now.'

'In public, fool.'

'Oh, in public. No, I haven't.'

'He's a terrific orator, as I told you, only you've probably forgotten.'

This seemed likely enough to me. Spode at one time had been one of those Dictators, going about at the head of a band of supporters in footer shorts shouting 'Heil Spode', and to succeed in that line you have to be able to make speeches.

'You aren't fond of him, nor am I, but nobody can deny that he's eloquent. Audiences hang on his every word, and when he's finished cheer him to the echo.'

I nodded. I had had the same experience myself when singing 'The Yeoman's Wedding Song' at village concerts. Two or three encores sometimes, even when I blew up in the words and had to fill in with 'Ding dong, ding dong, ding dong, I hurry along'. I began to feel easier in my mind. I told her this, and she said 'Your *what?*'

'You have put new heart into me, old blood relation,' I said, ignoring the crack. 'You see, it means everything to him to win this election.'

'Is he so bent on representing Market Snodsbury in the Westminster menagerie?'

'It isn't that so much. Left to himself, I imagine he could take Parliament or leave it alone. But he thinks Florence will give him the bum's rush if he loses.'

'He's probably right. She can't stand a loser.'

'So he told me. Remember what happened to Percy Gorringe.'

'And others. England is strewn with ex-fiancés whom she bounced because they didn't come up to her specifications. Dozens of them. I believe they form clubs and societies.'

'Perhaps calling themselves the Old Florentians.'

'And having an annual dinner!'

We mused on Florence for awhile; then she said she ought to be going to confer with Anatole about dinner tonight, urging him to dish up something special. It was vital, she said, that he should excel his always high standard.

'I was speaking, just now, when you interrupted me and turned my thoughts to the name Wilberforce, of L. P. Runkle.'

'You said you had an idea he might be going to cooperate.'

'Exactly. Have you ever seen a python after a series of hearty meals?'

'Not to my knowledge.'

'It gets all softened up. It becomes a kindlier, gentler, more lovable python. And if I am not greatly mistaken, the same thing is happening to L. P. Runkle as the result of Anatole's cooking. You saw him at dinner last night.'

'Sorry, no, I wasn't looking. Every fibre of my being was concentrated on the foodstuffs. He would have repaid inspection, would he? Worth seeing, eh?'

'He was positively beaming. He was too busy to utter, but it was plain that he had become all amiability and benevolence. He had the air of a man who would start scattering largesse if given a word of encouragement. It is for Anatole to see to it that this Christmas spirit does not evaporate but comes more and more to the boil. And I know that I can rely on him.'

'Good old Anatole,' I said, lighting a cigarette.

'Amen,' said the ancestor reverently; then, touching on another subject, 'Take that foul cigarette outside, you young hellhound. It smells like an escape of sewer gas.'

Always glad to indulge her lightest whim, I passed through the French window, in a far different mood from that in which I had entered the room. Optimism now reigned in the Wooster bosom. Ginger, I told myself, was going to be all right, Tuppy was going to be all right, and it would not be long before the laughing love god straightened things out between Madeline and Spode, even if he had talked out of turn about stars and daisy chains.

Having finished the gasper, I was about to return and resume conversation with the aged relative, when from within there came the voice of Seppings, now apparently restored to health, and what he was saying froze me in every limb. I couldn't have become stiffer if I had been Lot's wife, whose painful story I had had to read up when I won that Scripture Knowledge prize.

What he was saying ran as follows:

'Mrs McCorkadale, madam.'

10

Leaning against the side of the house, I breathed rather in the manner copyrighted by the hart which pants for cooling streams when heated in the chase. The realization of how narrowly I had missed having to mingle again with this blockbusting female barrister kept me Lot's-wifed for what seemed an hour or so, though I suppose it can't have been more than a few seconds. Then gradually I ceased to be a pillar of salt and was able to concentrate on finding out what on earth Ma McCorkadale's motive was in paying us this visit. The last place, I mean to say, where you would have expected to find her. Considering how she stood in regard to Ginger, it was as if Napoleon had dropped in for a chat with Wellington on the eve of Waterloo.

I have had occasion to mention earlier the advantages as a listening-post afforded by the just-outside-the-French-window spot where I was standing. Invisible to those within, I could take in all they were saying, as I had done with Spode and L. P. Runkle. Both had come through loud and clear, and neither had had a notion that Bertram Wooster was on the outskirts, hearing all.

As I could hardly step in and ask her to repeat any of her remarks which I didn't quite catch, it was fortunate that the McCorkadale's voice was so robust, while Aunt Dahlia's, of course, would be audible if you were at Hyde Park Corner and she in Piccadilly Circus. I have often thought that the deaf adder I read about when I won my Scripture Knowledge prize would have got the message right enough if the aged relative had been one of the charmers. I was able to continue leaning against the side of the house in full confidence that I shouldn't miss a syllable of either protagonist's words.

The proceedings started with a couple of Good mornings, Aunt Dahlia's the equivalent of 'What the hell?', and then the McCorkadale, as if aware that it was up to her to offer a word of explanation, said she had called to see Mr Winship on a matter of great importance.

'Is he in?'

Here was a chance for the ancestor to get one up by retorting that he jolly well would be after the votes had been counted, but she let it go, merely saying No, he had gone out, and the McCorkadale said she was sorry.

'I would have preferred to see him in person, but you, I take it, are his hostess, so I can tell you and you will tell him.'

This seemed fair enough to me, and I remember thinking that these barristers put things well, but it appeared to annoy the aged relative.

'I am afraid I do not understand you,' she said, and I knew she was getting steamed up, for if she had been her calm self, she would have said 'Sorry, I don't get you.'

'If you will allow me to explain. I can do so in a few simple words. I have just had a visit from a slimy slinking slug.'

I drew myself up haughtily. Not much good, of course, in the circs, but the gesture seemed called for. One does not object to fair criticism, but this was mere abuse. I could think of nothing in our relations which justified such a description of me. My views on barristers and their way of putting things changed sharply.

Whether or not Aunt Dahlia bridled, as the expression is, I couldn't say, but I think she must have done, for her next words were straight from the deep freeze.

'Are you referring to my nephew Bertram Wooster?'

The McCorkadale did much to remove the bad impression her previous words had made on me. She said her caller had not given his name, but she was sure he could not have been Mrs Travers's nephew.

'He was a very common man,' she said, and with the quickness which is so characteristic of me I suddenly got on to it that she must be alluding to Bingley, who had been ushered into her presence immediately after I had left. I could understand her applying those derogatory adjectives to Bingley. And the noun slug, just right. Once again I found myself thinking how well barristers put things.

The old ancestor, too, appeared – what's the word beginning with m and meaning less hot under the collar? Mollified, that's it. The suggestion that she could not have a nephew capable of being described as a common man mollified her. I don't say that even now she would have asked Ma McCorkadale to come on a long walking tour with her, but her voice was definitely matier.

'Why do you call him a slug?' she asked, and the McCorkadale had her answer to that.

'For the same reason that I call a spade a spade, because it is the best way of conveying a verbal image of him. He made me a disgraceful proposition.'

'WHAT?' said Aunt Dahlia rather tactlessly.

I could understand her being surprised. It was difficult to envisage a man so eager to collect girl friends as to make disgraceful propositions to Mrs McCorkadale. It amazed me that Bingley could have done it. I had never liked him, but I must confess to a certain admiration for his temerity. Our humble heroes, I felt.

'You're pulling my leg,' said the aged relative.

The McCorkadale came back at her briskly.

'I am doing nothing of the kind. I am telling you precisely what occurred. I was in my drawing-room going over the speech I have prepared for the debate tomorrow, when I was interrupted by the incursion of this man. Naturally annoyed, I asked him what his business was, and he said with a most offensive leer that he was Father Christmas bringing me manna in the wilderness and tidings of great joy. I was about to ring the bell to have him shown out, for of course I assumed that he was intoxicated, when he made me this extraordinary proposition. He had contrived to obtain information to the detriment of my opponent, and this he wished to sell to me. He said it would make my victory in the election certain. It would, as he phrased it, 'be a snip'.

I stirred on my base. If I hadn't been afraid I might be overheard, I would have said 'Aha!' Had circs been other than they were, I would have stepped into the room, tapped the ancestor on the shoulder and said 'Didn't I tell you Bingley had information? Perhaps another time you'll believe me'. But as this would have involved renewing my acquaintance with a woman of whom I had already seen sufficient to last a lifetime, it was not within the sphere of practical politics. I remained, accordingly, where I was, merely hitching my ears up another couple of notches in order not to miss the rest of the dialogue.

After the ancestor had said 'For heaven's sake!' or 'Gorblimey' or whatever it was, indicating that her visitor's story interested her strongly, the McCorkadale resumed. And what she resumed about unquestionably put the frosting on the cake. Words of doom is the only way I can think of to describe the words she spoke as.

'The man, it appeared, was a retired valet, and he belonged to a club for butlers and valets in London, one of the rules of which was that all members were obliged to record in the club book information about their employers. My visitor explained that he had been at one time in the employment of Mr Winship and had duly recorded a number of the latter's escapades which if made public, would be certain to make the worst impression on the voters of Market Snodsbury.'

This surprised me. I hadn't had a notion that Bingley had ever worked for Ginger. It just shows the truth of the old saying that half the world doesn't know how the other three-quarters live.

'He then told me without a blush of shame that on his latest visit to London he had purloined this book and now had it in his possession.'

I gasped with horror. I don't know why, but the thought that Bingley must have been pinching the thing at the very moment when Jeeves and I were sipping our snootfuls in the next room seemed to make it so particularly poignant. Not that it wouldn't have been pretty poignant anyway. For years I had been haunted by the fear that the Junior Ganymede club book, with all the dynamite it contained, would get into the wrong hands, and the hands it had got into couldn't have been more the sort of hands you would have wished it hadn't. I don't know if I make myself clear, but what I'm driving at is that if I had been picking a degraded character to get away with that book, Bingley was the last character I would have picked. I remember Jeeves speaking of someone who was fit for treasons, stratagems and spoils, and that was Bingley all over. The man was wholly without finer feelings, and when you come up against someone without finer feelings, you've had it.

The aged relative was not blind to the drama of the situation. She uttered an awed 'Lord love a duck!', and the McCorkadale said she might well say 'Lord love a duck', though it was not an expression she would have used herself.

'What did you do?' the ancestor asked, all agog, and the McCorkadale gave that sniffing snort of hers. It was partly like an escape of steam and partly like two or three cats unexpectedly encountering two or three dogs, with just a suggestion of a cobra waking up cross in the morning. I wondered how it had affected the late Mr McCorkadale. Probably made him feel that there are worse things than being run over by a municipal tram.

'I sent him away with a flea in his ear. I pride myself on being a fair fighter, and his proposition revolted me. If you want to have him arrested, though I am afraid I cannot see how it can be done, he lives at 5 Ormond Crescent. He appears to have asked my maid to look in and see his etchings on her afternoon off, and he gave her his address. But, as I say, there would seem not to be sufficient evidence for an arrest. Our conversation was without witnesses, and he would simply have to deny possession of the book. A pity. I would have enjoyed seeing a man like that hanged, drawn and quartered.'

She snorted again, and the ancestor, who always knows what the book of etiquette would advise, came across with the soothing syrup. She said Ma McCorkadale deserved a medal.

'Not at all.'

'It was splendid of you to turn the man down.'

'As I said, I am a fair fighter.'

'Apart from your revulsion at his proposition, it must have been very annoying for you to be interrupted when you were working on your speech.'

'Especially as a few moments before this person appeared I had been interrupted by an extraordinary young man who gave me the impression of being half-witted.'

'That would have been my nephew, Bertram Wooster.'

'Oh, I beg your pardon.'

'Quite all right.'

'I may have formed a wrong estimate of his mentality. Our interview was very brief. I just thought it odd that he should be trying to persuade me to vote for my opponent.'

'It's the sort of thing that would seem a bright idea to Bertie. He's like that. Whimsical. Moving in a mysterious way his wonders to perform. But he ought not to have butted in when you were busy with your speech. Is it coming out well?'

'I am satisfied with it.'

'Good for you. I suppose you're looking forward to the debate?'

'Very keenly. I am greatly in favour of it. It simplifies things so much if the two opponents face one another on the same platform and give the voters a chance to compare their views.

Provided, of course. that both observe the decencies of debate. But I really must be getting back to my work.'

'Just a moment.' No doubt it was the word 'observe' that had rung a bell with the ancestor. 'Do you do the *Observer* crossword puzzle by any chance?'

'I solve it at breakfast on Sunday mornings.'

'Not the whole lot?'

'Oh yes.'

'Every clue?'

'I have never failed yet. I find it ridiculously simple.'

'Then what's all that song and dance about the measured tread of saints round St Paul's?'

'Oh, I guessed that immediately. The answer, of course, is pedometer. You measure tread with a pedometer. Dome, meaning St Paul's, comes in the middle and Peter, for St Peter, round it. Very simple.'

'Oh, very. Well, thank you. You have taken a great weight off my mind,' said Aunt Dahlia, and they parted in complete amity, a thing I wouldn't have thought possible when Ma McCorkadale was one of the parters.

For perhaps a quarter of a minute after I had rejoined the human herd, as represented by my late father's sister Dahlia, I wasn't able to get a word in, the old ancestor being fully occupied with saying what she thought of the compiler of the *Observer* crossword puzzle, with particular reference to domes and pedometers. And when she had said her say on that subject she embarked on a rueful tribute to the McCorkadale, giving it as her opinion that against a woman with a brain like that Ginger hadn't the meagre chance of a toupee in a high wind. Though, she added in more hopeful vein, now that the menace of the Ganymede Club book had been squashed there was just a possibility that the eloquence of Spode might get his nose in front.

All this while I had been trying to cut in with my opening remark, which was to the effect that the current situation was a bit above the odds, but it was only when I had repeated this for the third time that I succeeded in obtaining her attention.

'This is a bit thick, what,' I said, varying my approach slightly.

She seemed surprised as if the idea had not occurred to her.

'Thick?'

'Well, isn't it?'

'Why? If you were listening, you heard her say that, being a fair fighter, she had scorned the tempter and sent him away with a flea in his ear, which must be a most uncomfortable thing to have. Bingley was baffled.'

'Only for the nonce.'

'Nonsense.'

'Not nonsense, nonce, which isn't at all the same thing. I feel that Bingley, though crushed to earth, will rise again. How about if he sells that book with all its ghastly contents to the *Market Snodsbury Argus-Reminder*?'

I was alluding to the powerful bi-weekly sheet which falls over itself in its efforts to do down the Conservative cause, omitting no word or act to make anyone with Conservative leanings feel like a piece of cheese. Coming out every Wednesday and Saturday with proofs of Ginger's past, I did not see how it could fail to give his candidature the sleeve across the windpipe.

I put this to the old blood relation in no uncertain terms. I might have added that that would wipe the silly smile off her face, but there was no necessity. She saw at once that I spoke sooth, and a crisp hunting-field expletive escaped her. She goggled at me with all the open dismay of an aunt who has inadvertently bitten into a bad oyster.

'I never thought of that!'

'Give it your attention now.'

'Those *Argus-Reminder* hounds stick at nothing.'

'The sky is notoriously their limit.'

'Did you tell me Ginger had done time?'

'I said he was always in the hands of the police on Boat Race night. And, of course, on Rugger night.'

'What's Rugger night?'

'The night of the annual Rugby football encounter between the universities of Oxford and Cambridge. Many blithe spirits get even more effervescent then than when celebrating the Boat Race. Ginger was one of them.'

'He really got jugged?'

'Invariably. His practice of pinching policemen's helmets ensured this. Released next morning on payment of a fine, but definitely after spending the night in a dungeon cell.'

There was no doubt that I had impressed on her the gravity of the situation. She gave a sharp cry like that of a stepped-on dachshund, and her face took on the purple tinge it always assumes in moments of strong emotion.

'This does it!'

'Fairly serious, I agree.'

'Fairly serious! The merest whisper of such goings-on will be enough to alienate every voter in the town. Ginger's done for.'

'You don't think they might excuse him because his blood was young at the time?'

'Not a hope. They won't be worrying about his ruddy blood. You don't know what these blighters here are like. Most of them are chapel folk with a moral code that would have struck Torquemada as too rigid.'

'Torquemada?'

'The Spanish Inquisition man.'

'Oh, that Torquemada.'

'How many Torquemadas did you think there were?'

I admitted that it was not a common name, and she carried on.

'We must act!'

'But how?'

'Or, rather, you must act. You must go to this man and reason with him.'

I h'med a bit at this. I doubted whether a fellow with Bingley's lust for gold would listen to reason.

'What shall I say?'

'You'll know what to say.'

'Oh, shall I?'

'Appeal to his better instincts.'

'He hasn't got any.'

'Now don't make difficulties, Bertie. That's your besetting sin, always arguing. You want to help Ginger, don't you?'

'Of course I do.'

'Very well, then.'

When an aunt has set her mind on a thing, it's no use trying to put in a *nolle prosequi*. I turned to the door.

Half-way there a thought occurred to me. I said:

'How about Jeeves?'

'What about him?'

'We ought to spare his feelings as far as possible. I repeatedly warned him that that club book was high-level explosive and ought not to be in existence. What if it fell into the wrong hands, I said, and he said it couldn't possibly fall into the wrong hands. And now it has fallen into about the wrongest hands it could have fallen into. I haven't the heart to say "I told you so" and watch him writhe with shame and confusion. You see, up till now Jeeves has always been right. His agony on finding that he has at last made a floater will be frightful. I shouldn't wonder if he might not swoon. I can't face him. You'll have to tell him.'

'Yes, I'll do it.'

'Try to break it gently.'

'I will. When you were listening outside, did you get this man Bingley's address?'

'I got it.'

'Then off you go.'

So off I went.

11

Considering how shaky was his moral outlook and how marked his tendency to weave low plots at the drop of a hat, you would have expected Bingley's headquarters to have been one of those sinister underground dens lit by stumps of candles stuck in the mouths of empty beer bottles such as abound, I believe, in places like Whitechapel and Limehouse. But no. Number 5 Ormond Crescent turned out to be quite an expensive-looking joint with a nice little bit of garden in front of it well supplied with geraniums, bird baths and terracotta gnomes, the sort of establishment that might have belonged to a blameless retired Colonel or a saintly stockbroker. Evidently his late uncle hadn't been just an ordinary small town grocer, weighing out potted meats and raisins to a public that had to watch the pennies, but something on a much more impressive scale. I learned later that he had owned a chain of shops, one of them as far afield as Birmingham, and why the ass had gone and left his money to a chap like Bingley is more than I can tell you, though the probability is that Bingley, before bumping him off with some little-known Asiatic poison, had taken the precaution of forging the will.

On the threshold I paused. I remember in my early days at the private school where I won my Scripture Knowledge prize, Arnold Abney M.A., the headmaster, would sometimes announce that he wished to see Wooster in his study after morning prayers, and I always halted at the study door, a prey to uneasiness and apprehension, not liking the shape of things to come. It was much the same now. I shrank from the impending interview. But whereas in the case of A. Abney my disinclination to get things moving had been due to the fear that the proceedings were going to lead up to six of the best from a cane that stung like an adder, with Bingley it was a natural reluctance to ask a favour of a fellow I couldn't stand the sight of. I wouldn't say the Woosters were particularly proud, but we do rather jib at having to grovel to the scum of the earth.

However, it had to be done, and, as I heard Jeeves say once, if it were done, then 'twere well 'twere done quickly. Stiffening the sinews and summoning up the blood, to quote another of his gags, I pressed the bell.

If I had any doubts as to Bingley now being in the chips, the sight of the butler who opened the door would have dispelled them. In assembling his domestic staff, Bingley had done himself proud, sparing no expense. I don't say his butler was quite in the class of Jeeves's Uncle Charlie Silversmith, but he came so near it that the breath was taken. And like Uncle Charlie he believed in pomp and ceremony when buttling. I asked him if I could see Mr Bingley, and he said coldly that the master was not receiving.

'I think he'll see me. I'm an old friend of his.'

'I will enquire. Your name, sir?'

'Mr Wooster.'

He pushed off, to return some moments later to say that Mr Bingley would be glad if I would join him in the library. Speaking in what seemed to me a disapproving voice, as though to suggest that, while he was compelled to carry out the master's orders however eccentric, he would never have admitted a chap like me if it had been left to him.

'If you would step this way, sir,' he said haughtily.

What with one thing and another I had rather got out of touch lately with that If-you-would-step-this-way-sir stuff, and it was in a somewhat rattled frame of mind that I entered the library and found Bingley in an armchair with his feet up on an occasional table. He greeted me cordially enough, but with that touch of the patronizing so noticeable at our two previous meetings.

'Ah, Wooster, my dear fellow, come in. I told Bastable to tell everyone I was not at home, but of course you're different. Always glad to see an old pal. And what can I do for you, Wooster?'

I had to say for him that he had made it easy for me to introduce the subject I was anxious to discuss. I was about to get going, when he asked me if I would like a drink. I said No, thanks, and he said in an insufferably smug way that I was probably wise.

'I often thought, when I was staying with you at Chuffnell Regis, that you drank too much, Wooster. Remember how you burned that cottage down? A sober man wouldn't have done that. You must have been stewed to the eyebrows, cocky.'

A hot denial trembled on my lips. I mean to say, it's a bit thick to be chided for burning cottages down by the very chap who put them to the flames. But I restrained myself. The man, I reminded myself, had to be kept in with. If that was how he remembered that night of terror at Chuffnell Regis, it was not for me to destroy his illusions. I refrained from comment, and he asked me if I would like a cigar. When I said I wouldn't, he nodded like a father pleased with a favourite son.

'I am glad to see this improvement in you, Wooster. I always thought you smoked too much. Moderation, moderation in all things, that's the only way. But you were going to tell me why you came here. Just for a chat about old times, was it?'

'It's with ref to that book you pinched from the Junior Ganymede.'

He had been drinking a whisky and soda as I spoke, and he drained his glass before replying.

'I wish you wouldn't use that word "pinch",' he said, looking puff-faced. It was plain that I had given offence. 'I simply borrowed it because I needed it in my business. They'll get it back all right.'

'Mrs McCorkadale told my aunt you tried to sell it to her.'

His annoyance increased. His air was that of a man compelled to listen to a tactless oaf who persisted in saying the wrong thing.

'Not sell. I would have had a clause in the agreement saying that she was to return it when she had done with it. The idea I had in mind was that she would have photostatic copies made of the pages dealing with young Winship without the book going out of my possession. But the deal didn't come off. She wouldn't cooperate. Fortunately I have other markets. It's the sort of property there'll be a lot of people bidding for. But why are you so interested, old man? Nothing to do with you, is it?'

'I'm a pal of Ginger Winship's.'

'And I've no objection to him myself. Nice enough young fellow he always seemed to me, though the wrong size.'

'Wrong size?' I said, not getting this.

'His shirts didn't fit me. Not that I hold that against him. These things are all a matter of luck. Don't run away with the idea that I'm a man with a grievance, trying to get back at him for something he did to me when I was staying at his place. Our relations were very pleasant. I quite liked him, and if it didn't matter to me one way or the other who won this election,

I'd just as soon he came out on top. But business is business. After studying form I did some pretty heavy betting on McCorkadale, and I've got to protect my investments, old man. That's only common sense, isn't it?'

He paused, apparently expecting a round of applause for his prudence. When I remained *sotto voce* and the silent tomb, he proceeded.

'If you want to get along in this world, Wooster old chap, you've got to grasp your opportunities. That's what I do. I examine each situation that crops up, and I ask myself "What is there in this for me? How," I ask myself, "can I handle this situation so as to do Rupert Bingley a bit of good?", and it's not often I don't find a way. This time I didn't even have to think. There was young Winship trying to get into Parliament, and here was I standing to win something like a couple of hundred quid if he lost the election, and there was the club book with all the stuff in it which would make it certain he did lose. I recognized it at once as money for jam. The only problem was how to get the book, and I soon solved that. I don't know if you noticed, that day we met at the Junior Ganymede, that I had a large briefcase with me? And that I said I'd got to see the secretary about something? Well, what I wanted to see him about was borrowing the book. And I wouldn't have to find some clever way of getting him looking the other way while I did it, because I knew he'd be out to lunch. So I popped in, popped the book in the briefcase and popped off. Nobody saw me go in. Nobody saw me come out. The whole operation was like taking candy from a kid.'

There are some stories which fill the man of sensibility with horror, repugnance, abhorrence and disgust. I don't mean anecdotes like the one Catsmeat Potter-Pirbright told me at the Drones, I am referring to loathsome revelations such as the bit of autobiography to which I had just been listening. To say that I felt as if the Wooster soul had been spattered with mud by a passing car would not be putting it at all too strongly. I also felt that nothing was to be gained by continuing this distasteful interview. I had had some idea of going into the possibility of Aunt Agatha reading the contents of the club book and touching on the doom, desolation and despair which must inevitably be my portion if she did, but I saw that it would be fruitless or bootless. The man was without something and pity . . . ruth, would it be? I know it begins with r . . . and would simply have given me the horse's laugh. I was now quite certain that he had murdered his uncle and forged the will. Such a performance to such a man would have been mere routine.

I turned, accordingly, to the door, but before I got there he stopped me, wanting to know if when coming to stay with Aunt Dahlia I had brought Reggie Jeeves with me. I said I had, and he said he would like to see old Reggie again.

'What a cough drop!' he said mirthfully. The word was strange to me, but weighing it and deciding that it was intended to be a compliment and a tribute to his many gifts, I agreed that Jeeves was in the deepest and truest sense a cough drop.

'Tell Bastable as you go out that if Reggie calls to send him up. But nobody else.'

'Right ho.'

'Good man, Bastable. He places my bets for me. Which reminds me. Have you done as I advised and put a bit on Ma McCorkadale for the Market Snodsbury stakes? No? Do it without fail, Wooster old man. You'll never regret it. It'll be like finding money in the street.'

I wasn't feeling any too good as I drove away. I have described my heart-bowed-down-ness on approaching the Arnold Abney study door after morning prayers in the days when I was *in statu pupillari*, as the expression is, and I was equally apprehensive now as I faced the prospect of telling the old ancestor of my failure to deliver the goods in the matter of Bingley. I didn't suppose that she would give me six of the best, as A. Abney was so prone to do, but she would certainly not hesitate to let me know she was displeased. Aunts as a class are like Napoleon, if it was Napoleon; they expect their orders to be carried out without a hitch and don't listen to excuses.

Nor was I mistaken. After lunching at a pub in order to postpone the meeting as long as possible, I returned to the old homestead and made my report, and was unfortunate enough to make it while she was engaged in reading a Rex Stout – in the hard cover, not a paperback. When she threw this at me with the accurate aim which years of practice have given her, its sharp edge took me on the tip of the nose, making me blink not a little.

'I might have known you would mess the whole thing up,' she boomed.

'Not my fault, aged relative,' I said. 'I did my best. Than which,' I added, 'no man can do more.'

I thought I had her there, but I was wrong. It was the sort of line which can generally be counted on to soothe the savage breast, but this time it laid an egg. She snorted. Her snorts are not the sniffing snorts snorted by Ma McCorkadale, they resemble more an explosion in the larger type of ammunition dump and send strong men rocking back on their heels as if struck by lightning.

'How do you mean you did your best? You don't seem to me to have done anything. Did you threaten to have him arrested?'

'No, I didn't do that.'

'Did you grasp him by the throat and shake him like a rat?'

I admitted that that had not occurred to me.

'In other words, you did absolutely nothing,' she said, and thinking it over I had to own that she was perfectly right. It's funny how one doesn't notice these things at the time. It was only now that I realized that I had let Bingley do all the talking, self offering practically nil in the way of a come-back. I could hardly have made less of a contribution to our conversation if I had been the deaf adder I mentioned earlier.

She heaved herself up from the chaise longue on which she was reclining. Her manner was peevish. In time, of course, she would get over her chagrin and start loving her Bertram again as of yore, but there was no getting away from it that an aunt's affection was, as of even date, at its lowest ebb. She said gloomily:

'I'll have to do it myself.'

'Are you going to see Bingley?'

'I am going to see Bingley, and I am going to talk to Bingley, and I am going, if necessary, to take Bingley by the throat and shake him—'

'Like a rat?'

'Yes, like a rat,' she said with the quiet confidence of a woman who had been shaking rats by the throat since she was a slip of a girl. 'Five Ormond Crescent, here I come!'

It shows to what an extent happenings in and about Market Snodsbury had affected my mental processes that she had been gone at least ten minutes before the thought of Bastable floated into my mind, and I wished I had been able to give her a word of warning. That zealous employee of Rupert Bingley had been instructed to see to it that no callers were admitted to the presence, and I saw no reason to suppose that he would fail in his duty when the old ancestor showed up. He would not use physical violence – indeed, with a woman of her physique he would be unwise to attempt it – but it would be the work of an instant with him not to ask her to step this way, thus ensuring her departure with what Ma McCorkadale would call a flea in her ear. I could see her returning in, say, about a quarter of an hour a baffled and defeated woman.

I was right. It was some twenty minutes later, as I sat reading the Rex Stout which she had used as a guided missile, that heavy breathing became audible without and shortly afterwards she became visible within, walking with the measured tread of a saint going round St Paul's. A far less discerning eye than mine could have spotted that she had been having Bastable trouble.

It would have been kinder, perhaps, not to have spoken, but it was one of those occasions when you feel you have to say something.

'Any luck?' I enquired.

She sank on to the chaise longue, simmering gently. She punched a cushion, and I could see she was wishing it could have been Bastable. He was essentially the sort of man who asks, nay clamours, to be treated in this manner.

'No,' she said. 'I couldn't get in.'

'Why was that?' I asked, wearing the mask.

'A beefy butler sort of bird slammed the door in my face.'

'Too bad.'

'And I was just too late to get my foot in.'

'Always necessary to work quick on these occasions. The most precise timing is called for. Odd that he should have admitted me. I suppose my air of quiet distinction was what turned the scale. What did you do?'

'I came away. What else could I have done?'

'No, I can see how difficult it must have been.'

'The maddening part of it is that I was all set to try to get that money out of L. P. Runkle this afternoon. I felt that today was the day. But if my luck's out, as it seems to be, perhaps I had better postpone it.'

'Not strike while the iron is hot?'

'It may not be hot enough.'

'Well, you're the judge. You know,' I said, getting back to the main issue, 'the ambassador to conduct the negotiations with Bingley is really Jeeves. It is he who should have been given the assignment. Where I am speechless in Bingley's presence and you can't even get into the house, he would be inside and talking a blue streak before you could say What ho. And he has the added advantage that Bingley seems fond of him. He thinks he's a cough drop.'

'What on earth's a cough drop?'

'I don't know, but it's something Bingley admires. When he spoke of him as one, it was with a genuine ring of enthusiasm in his voice. Did you tell Jeeves about Bingley having the book?'

'Yes, I told him.'

'How did he take it?'

'You know how Jeeves takes things. One of his eyebrows rose a little and he said he was shocked and astounded.'

'That's strong stuff for him. "Most disturbing" is as far as he goes usually.'

'It's a curious thing,' said the aged relative thoughtfully. 'As I was driving off in the car I thought I saw Jeeves coming away from Bingley's place. Though I couldn't be sure it was him.'

'It must have been. His first move on getting the low-down from you about the book would be to go and see Bingley. I wonder if he's back yet.'

'Not likely. I was driving, he was walking. There wouldn't be time.'

'I'll ring for Seppings and ask. Oh, Seppings,' I said, when he answered the bell, 'Is Jeeves downstairs?'

'No, sir. He went out and has not yet returned.'

'When he does, tell him to come and see me, will you.'

'Very good, sir.'

I thought of asking if Jeeves, when he left, had had the air of a man going to Number 5 Ormond Crescent, but decided that this might be trying Seppings too high, so let it go. He withdrew, and we sat for some time talking about Jeeves. Then, feeling that this wasn't going to get us anywhere and that nothing constructive could be accomplished till he returned, we took up again the matter of L. P. Runkle. At least, the aged relative took it up, and I put the question I had been wanting to put at an earlier stage.

'You say,' I said, 'that you felt today was the day for approaching him. What gave you that idea?'

'The way he tucked into his lunch and the way he talked about it afterwards. Lyrical was the only word for it, and I wasn't surprised. Anatole had surpassed himself.'

'The Suprême de Foie Gras au Champagne?'

'*And* the Neige aux Perles des Alpes.'

I heaved a silent sigh, thinking of what might have been. The garbage I had had to insult the Wooster stomach with at the pub had been of a particularly lethal nature. Generally these rural pubs are all right in the matter of browsing, but I had been so unfortunate as to pick one run by a branch of the Borgia family. The thought occurred to me as I ate that if Bingley had given his uncle lunch there one day, he wouldn't have had to go to all the bother and expense of buying little-known Asiatic poisons.

I would have told the old relative this, hoping for sympathy, but at this moment the door opened, and in came Jeeves. Opening the conversation with that gentle cough of his that sounds like a very old sheep clearing its throat on a misty mountain top, he said:

'You wished to see me, sir?'

He couldn't have had a warmer welcome if he had been the prodigal son whose life story I had had to bone up when I won that Scripture Knowledge prize. The welkin, what there was of it in the drawing-room, rang with our excited yappings.

'Come in, Jeeves,' bellowed the aged relative.

'Yes, come in, Jeeves, come in,' I cried. 'We were waiting for you with . . . with what?'

'Bated breath,' said the ancestor.

'That's right. With bated breath and—'

'Tense, quivering nerves. Not to mention twitching muscles and bitten finger nails. Tell me, Jeeves, was that you I saw coming away from 5 Ormond Crescent about an hour ago?'

'Yes, madam.'

'You had been seeing Bingley?'

'Yes, madam.'

'About the book?'

'Yes, madam.'

'Did you tell him he had jolly well got to return it?'

'No, madam.'

'Then why on earth did you go to see him?'

'To obtain the book, madam.'

'But you said you didn't tell him—'

'There was no necessity to broach the subject, madam. He had not yet recovered consciousness. If I might explain. On my arrival at his residence he offered me a drink, which I accepted. He took one himself. We talked for awhile of this and that.

Then I succeeded in diverting his attention for a moment, and while his scrutiny was elsewhere I was able to insert a chemical substance in his beverage which had the effect of rendering him temporarily insensible. I thus had ample time to make a search of the room. I had assumed that he would be keeping the book there, and I had not been in error. It was in a lower drawer of the desk. I secured it, and took my departure.'

Stunned by this latest revelation of his efficiency and do-it-yourself-ness, I was unable to utter, but the old ancestor gave the sort of cry or yowl which must have rung over many a hunting field, causing members of the Quorn and the Pytchley to leap in their saddles like Mexican jumping beans.

'You mean you slipped him a Mickey Finn?'

'I believe that is what they are termed in the argot, madam.'

'Do you always carry them about with you?'

'I am seldom without a small supply, madam.'

'Never know when they won't come in handy, eh?'

'Precisely, madam. Opportunities for their use are constantly arising.'

'Well, I can only say thank you. You have snatched victory from the jaws of defeat.'

'It is kind of you to say so, madam.'

'Much obliged, Jeeves.'

'Not at all, madam.'

I was expecting the aged relative to turn to me at this point and tick me off for not having had the sense to give Bingley a Mickey Finn myself, and I knew, for you cannot reason with aunts, that it would be no use pleading that I hadn't got any; but her jocund mood caused her to abstain. Returning to the subject of L. P. Runkle, she said this had made her realize that her luck was in, after all, and she was going to press it.

'I'll go and see him now,' she yipped, 'and I confidently expect to play on him as on a stringed instrument. Out of my way, young Bertie,' she cried, heading for the door, 'or I'll trample you to the dust. Yoicks!' she added, reverting to the patois of the old hunting days. 'Tally ho! Gone away! Hark forrard!'

Or words to that effect.

12

Her departure – at, I should estimate, some sixty m.p.h. – left behind it the sort of quivering stillness you get during hurricane time in America, when the howling gale, having shaken you to the back teeth, passes on to tickle up residents in spots further west. Kind of a dazed feeling it gives you. I turned to Jeeves, and found him, of course, as serene and unmoved as an oyster on the half shell. He might have been watching yowling aunts shoot out of rooms like bullets from early boyhood.

'What was that she said, Jeeves?'

'Yoicks, sir, if I am not mistaken. It seemed to me that Madam also added Tally-ho, Gone away and Hark forrard.'

'I suppose members of the Quorn and the Pytchley are saying that sort of thing all the time.'

'So I understand, sir. It encourages the hounds to renewed efforts. It must, of course, be trying for the fox.'

'I'd hate to be a fox, wouldn't you, Jeeves?'

'Certainly I can imagine more agreeable existences, sir.'

'Not only being chivvied for miles across difficult country but having to listen to men in top hats uttering those uncouth cries.'

'Precisely, sir. A very wearing life.'

I produced my cambric handkerchief and gave the brow a mop. Recent events had caused me to perspire in the manner popularized by the fountains at Versailles.

'Warm work, Jeeves.'

'Yes, sir.'

'Opens the pores a bit.'

'Yes, sir.'

'How quiet everything seems now.'

'Yes, sir. Silence like a poultice comes to heal the blows of sound.'

'Shakespeare?'

'No, sir. The American author Oliver Wendell Holmes. His

poem, "The Organ Grinders". An aunt of mine used to read it to me as a child.'

'I didn't know you had any aunts.'

'Three, sir.'

'Are they as jumpy as the one who has just left us?'

'No, sir. Their outlook on life is uniformly placid.'

I had begun to feel a bit more placid myself. Calmer, if you know what I mean. And with the calm had come more charitable thoughts.

'Well, I don't blame the aged relative for being jumpy,' I said. 'She's all tied up with an enterprise of pith and something.'

'Of great pith and moment, sir?'

'That's right.'

'Let us hope that its current will not turn awry and lose the name of action.'

'Yes, let's. Turn what?'

'Awry, sir.'

'Don't you mean agley?'

'No, sir.'

'Then it isn't the poet Burns?'

'No, sir. The words occur in Shakespeare's drama *Hamlet*.'

'Oh, I know *Hamlet*. Aunt Agatha once made me take her son Thos to it at the Old Vic. Not a bad show, I thought, though a bit highbrow. You're sure the poet Burns didn't write it?'

'Yes, sir. The fact, I understand, is well established.'

'Then that settles that. But we have wandered from the point, which is that Aunt Dahlia is up to her neck in this enterprise of great pith and moment. It's about Tuppy Glossop.'

'Indeed, sir?'

'It ought to interest you, because I know you've always liked Tuppy.'

'A very pleasant young gentleman, sir.'

'When he isn't looping back the last ring over the Drones swimming-pool, yes. Well, it's too long a story to tell you at the moment, but the gist of it is this. L. P. Runkle, taking advantage of a legal quibble . . . is it quibble?'

'Yes, sir.'

'Did down Tuppy's father over a business deal . . . no, not exactly a business deal, Tuppy's father was working for him, and he took advantage of the small print in their contract to rob him of the proceeds of something he had invented.'

'It is often the way, sir. The financier is apt to prosper at the expense of the inventor.'

'And Aunt Dahlia is hoping to get him to cough up a bit of cash and slip it to Tuppy.'

'Actuated by remorse, sir?'

'Not just by remorse. She's relying more on the fact that for quite a time he has been under the spell of Anatole's cooking, and she feels that this will have made him a softer and kindlier financier, readier to oblige and do the square thing. You look dubious, Jeeves. Don't you think it will work? She's sure it will.'

'I wish I could share Madam's confidence, but—'

'But, like me, you look on her chance of playing on L. P. Runkle as on a stringed instrument as . . . what? A hundred to eight shot?'

'A somewhat longer price than that, sir. We have to take into consideration the fact that Mr Runkle is . . .'

'Yes? You hesitate, Jeeves, Mr Runkle is what?'

'The expression I am trying to find eludes me, sir. It is one I have sometimes heard you use to indicate a deficiency of sweetness and light in some gentleman of your acquaintance. You have employed it of Mr Spode or, as I should say, Lord Sidcup and, in the days before your association with him took on its present cordiality, of Mr Glossop's uncle, Sir Roderick. It is on the tip of my tongue.'

'A stinker?'

No, he said, it wasn't a stinker.

'A tough baby?'

'No.'

'A twenty-minute egg?'

'That was it, sir. Mr Runkle is a twenty-minute egg.'

'But have you seen enough of him to judge? After all, you've only just met him.'

'Yes, sir, that is true, but Bingley, on learning that he was a guest of Madam's, told me a number of stories illustrative of his hardhearted and implacable character. Bingley was at one time in his employment.'

'Good lord, he seems to have been employed by everyone.'

'Yes, sir, he was inclined to flit. He never remained in one post for long.'

'I don't wonder.'

'But his relationship with Mr Runkle was of more extended

duration. He accompanied him to the United States of America some years ago and remained with him for several months.'

'During which period he found him a twenty-minute egg?'

'Precisely, sir. So I very much fear that Madam's efforts will produce no satisfactory results. Would it be a large sum of money that she is hoping to persuade Mr Runkle to part with?'

'Pretty substantial, I gather. You see, what Tuppy's father invented were those Magic Midget things, and Runkle must have made a packet out of them. I suppose she aims at a fifty-fifty split.'

'Then I am forced to the opinion that a hundred to one against is more the figure a level-headed turf accountant would place upon the likelihood of her achieving her objective.'

Not encouraging, you'll agree. In fact, you might describe it as definitely damping. I would have called him a pessimist, only I couldn't think of the word, and while I was trying to hit on something other than 'Gloomy Gus', which would scarcely have been a fitting way to address one of his dignity, Florence came in through the French window and he of course shimmered off. When our conversations are interrupted by the arrival of what you might call the quality, he always disappears like a family spectre vanishing at dawn.

Except at meals I hadn't seen anything of Florence till now, she, so to speak, having taken the high road while I took the low road. What I mean to say is that she was always in Market Snodsbury, bustling about on behalf of the Conservative candidate to whom she was betrothed, while I, after that nerve-racking encounter with the widow of the late McCorkadale, had given up canvassing in favour of curling up with a good book. I had apologized to Ginger for this ... is pusillanimity the word? ... and he had taken it extraordinarily well, telling me it was perfectly all right and he wished he could do the same.

She was looking as beautiful as ever, if not more so, and at least ninety-six per cent of the members of the Drones Club would have asked nothing better than to be closeted with her like this. I, however, would willingly have avoided the tête-à-tête, for my trained senses told me that she was in one of her tempers, and when this happens the instinct of all but the hardiest is to climb a tree and pull it up after them. The overbearing dishpotness to which I alluded earlier and which is so marked a feature of her make-up was plainly to the fore. She said, speaking abruptly:

'What are you doing in here on a lovely day like this, Bertie?'

I explained that I had been in conference with Aunt Dahlia, and she riposted that the conference was presumably over by now, Aunt D being conspicuous by her absence, so why wasn't I out getting fresh air and sunshine.

'You're much too fond of frowsting indoors. That's why you have that sallow look.'

'I didn't know I had a sallow look.'

'Of course you have a sallow look. What else did you expect? You look like the underside of a dead fish.'

My worst fears seemed to be confirmed. I had anticipated that she would work off her choler on the first innocent bystander she met, and it was just my luck that this happened to be me. With bowed head I prepared to face the storm, and then to my surprise she changed the subject.

'I'm looking for Harold,' she said.

'Oh, yes?'

'Have you seen him.'

'I don't think I know him.'

'Don't be a fool. Harold Winship.'

'Oh, Ginger,' I said, enlightened. 'No, he hasn't swum into my ken. What do you want to see him about? Something important?'

'It is important to me, and it ought to be to him. Unless he takes himself in hand, he is going to lose this election.'

'What makes you think that?'

'His behaviour at lunch today.'

'Oh, did he take you to lunch? Where did you go? I had mine at a pub, and the garbage there had to be chewed to be believed. But perhaps you went to a decent hotel?'

'It was the Chamber of Commerce luncheon at the Town Hall. A vitally important occasion, and he made the feeblest speech I have ever heard. A child with water on the brain could have done better. Even you could have done better.'

Well, I suppose placing me on a level of efficiency with a water-on-the-brained child was quite a stately compliment coming from Florence, so I didn't go further into the matter, and she carried on, puffs of flame emerging from both nostrils.

'Er, er, er!'

'I beg your pardon?'

'He kept saying Er. Er, er, er. I could have thrown a coffee spoon at him.'

Here, of course, was my chance to work in the old gag about to err being human, but it didn't seem to me the moment. Instead, I said:

'He was probably nervous.'

'That was his excuse. I told him he had no right to be nervous.'

'Then you've seen him?'

'I saw him.'

'After the lunch?'

'Immediately after the lunch.'

'But you want to see him again?'

'I do.'

'I'll go and look for him, shall I?'

'Yes, and tell him to meet me in Mr Travers's study. We shall not be interrupted there.'

'He's probably sitting in the summerhouse by the lake.'

'Well, tell him to stop sitting and come to the study,' she said, for all the world as if she had been Arnold Abney M.A. announcing that he would like to see Wooster after morning prayers. Quite took me back to the old days.

To get to the summerhouse you have to go across the lawn, the one Spode was toying with the idea of buttering me over, and the first thing I saw as I did so, apart from the birds, bees, butterflies, and what-not which put in their leisure hours there, was L. P. Runkle lying in the hammock wrapped in slumber, with Aunt Dahlia in a chair at his side. When she sighted me, she rose, headed in my direction and drew me away a yard or two, at the same time putting a finger to her lips.

'He's asleep,' she said.

A snore from the hammock bore out the truth of this, and I said I could see he was and what a revolting spectacle he presented, and she told me for heaven's sake not to bellow like that. Somewhat piqued at being accused of bellowing by a woman whose lightest whisper was like someone calling the cattle home across the sands of Dee, I said I wasn't bellowing, and she said 'Well, don't.'

'He may be in a nasty mood if he's woken suddenly.'

It was an astute piece of reasoning, speaking well for her grasp of strategy and tactics, but with my quick intelligence I spotted a flaw in it to which I proceeded to call her attention.

'On the other hand, if you don't wake him, how can you plead Tuppy's cause?'

'I said suddenly, ass. It'll be all right if I let Nature take its course.'

'Yes, you may have a point there. Will Nature be long about it, do you think?'

'How do I know?'

'I was only wondering. You can't sit there the rest of the afternoon.'

'I can if necessary.'

'Then I'll leave you to it. I've got to go and look for Ginger. Have you seen him?'

'He came by just now with his secretary on his way to the summerhouse. He told me he had some dictation to do. Why do you want him?'

'I don't particularly, though always glad of his company. Florence told me to find him. She has been giving him hell and is anxious to give him some more. Apparently—'

Here she interrupted me with a sharp 'Hist!', for L. P. Runkle had stirred in his sleep and it looked as if life was returning to the inert frame. But it proved to be a false alarm, and I resumed my remarks.

'Apparently he failed to wow the customers at the Chamber of Commerce lunch, where she had been counting on him being a regular . . . who was the Greek chap?'

'Bertie, if I wasn't afraid of waking Runkle, I'd strike you with a blunt instrument, if I had a blunt instrument. What Greek chap?'

'That's what I'm asking you. He chewed pebbles.'

'Do you mean Demosthenes?'

'You may be right. I'll take it up later with Jeeves. Florence was expecting Ginger to be a regular Demosthenes, if that was the name, which seems unlikely, though I was at school with a fellow called Gianbattista, and he let her down, and this has annoyed her. You know how she speaks her mind, when annoyed.'

'She speaks her mind much too much,' said the relative severely. 'I wonder Ginger stands it.'

It so happened that I was in a position to solve the problem that was perplexing her. The facts governing the relationship of guys and dolls had long been an open book to me. I had given deep thought to the matter, and when I give deep thought to a matter perplexities are speedily ironed out.

'He stands it, aged relative, because he loves her, and you wouldn't be far wrong in saying that love conquers all. I know what you mean, of course. It surprises you that a fellow of his thews and sinews should curl up in a ball when she looks squiggle-eyed at him and receive her strictures, if that's the word I want, with the meekness of a spaniel rebuked for bringing a decaying bone into the drawing-room. What you overlook is the fact that in the matter of finely chiselled profile, willowy figure and platinum-blonde hair she is well up among the top ten, and these things weigh with a man like Ginger. You and I, regarding Florence coolly, pencil her in as too bossy for human consumption, but he gets a different slant. It's the old business of what Jeeves calls the psychology of the individual. Very possibly the seeds of rebellion start to seethe within him when she speaks her mind, but he catches sight of her sideways or gets a glimpse of her hair, assuming for purposes of argument that she isn't wearing a hat, or notices once again that she has as many curves as a scenic railway, and he feels that it's worth putting up with a spot of mind-speaking in order to make her his own. His love, you see, is not wholly spiritual. There's a bit of the carnal mixed up in it.'

I would have spoken further, for the subject was one that always calls out the best in me, but at this point the old ancestor, who had been fidgeting for some time, asked me to go and drown myself in the lake. I buzzed off, accordingly, and she returned to her chair beside the hammock, brooding over L. P. Runkle like a mother over her sleeping child.

I don't suppose she had observed it, for aunts seldom give much attention to the play of expression on the faces of their nephews, but all through these exchanges I had been looking grave, making it pretty obvious that there was something on my mind. I was thinking of what Jeeves had said about the hundred to one which a level-headed bookie would wager against her chance of extracting money from a man so liberally equipped with one-way pockets as L. P. Runkle, and it pained me deeply to picture her dismay and disappointment when, waking from his slumbers, he refused to disgorge. It would be a blow calculated to take all the stuffing out of her, she having been so convinced that she was on a sure thing.

I was also, of course, greatly concerned about Ginger. Having been engaged to Florence myself, I knew what she could do in the way of ticking off the errant male, and the symptoms seemed to point to the probability that on the present occasion she would eclipse all previous performances. I had not failed to interpret the significance of that dark frown, that bitten lip and those flashing eyes, nor the way the willowy figure had quivered, indicating, unless she had caught a chill, that she was as sore as a sunburned neck. I marvelled at the depths to which my old friend must have sunk as an orator in order to get such stark emotions under way, and I intended – delicately, of course – to question him about this.

I had, however, no opportunity to do so, for on entering the summerhouse the first thing I saw was him and Magnolia Glendennon locked in an embrace so close that it seemed to me that only powerful machinery could unglue them.

13

In taking this view, however, I was in error, for scarcely had I uttered the first yip of astonishment when the Glendennon popsy, echoing it with a yip of her own such as might have proceeded from a nymph surprised while bathing, disentangled herself and came whizzing past me, disappearing into the great world outside at a speed which put her in the old ancestor's class as a sprinter on the flat. It was as though she had said 'Oh for the wings of a dove' and had got them.

I, meanwhile, stood rooted to the s, the mouth slightly ajar and the eyes bulging to their fullest extent. What's that word beginning with dis? Disembodied? No, not disembodied. Distemper? No, not distemper. Disconcerted, that's the one. I was disconcerted. I should imagine that if you happened to wander by accident into the steam room of a Turkish bath on Ladies' Night, you would have emotions very similar to those I was experiencing now.

Ginger, too, seemed not altogether at his ease. Indeed, I would describe him as definitely taken aback. He breathed heavily, as if suffering from asthma; the eye with which he regarded me contained practically none of the chumminess you would expect to see in the eye of an old friend; and his voice, when he spoke, resembled that of an annoyed cinnamon bear. Throaty, if you know what I mean, and on the peevish side. His opening words consisted of a well-phrased critique of my tactlessness in selecting that particular moment for entering the summerhouse. He wished, he said, that I wouldn't creep about like a ruddy detective. Had I, he asked, got my magnifying glass with me and did I propose to go around on all fours, picking up small objects and putting them away carefully in an envelope? What, he enquired, was I doing here, anyway?

To this I might have replied that I was perfectly entitled at all times to enter a summerhouse which was the property of my Aunt Dahlia and so related to me by ties of blood, but something told me that suavity would be the better policy. In rebuttal, therefore, I merely said that I wasn't creeping about like a ruddy detective, but navigating with a firm and manly stride, and had simply been looking for him because Florence had ordered me to and I had learned from a usually well-informed source that this was where he was.

My reasoning had the soothing effect I had hoped for. His manner changed, losing its cinnamon bear quality and taking on a welcome all-pals-together-ness. It bore out what I have always said, that there's nothing like suavity for pouring oil on the troubled w's. When he spoke again, it was plain that he regarded me as a friend and an ally.

'I suppose all this seems a bit odd to you, Bertie.'

'Not at all, old man, not at all.'

'But there is a simple explanation. I love Magnolia.'

'I thought you loved Florence.'

'So did I. But you know how apt one is to make mistakes.'

'Of course.'

'When you're looking for the ideal girl, I mean.'

'Quite.'

'I dare say you've had the same experience yourself.'

'From time to time.'

'Happens to everybody, I expect.'

'I shouldn't wonder.'

'Where one goes wrong when looking for the ideal girl is in making one's selection before walking the full length of the counter. You meet someone with a perfect profile, platinum-blonde hair and a willowy figure, and you think your search is over. "Bingo!" you say to yourself. "This is the one. Accept no substitutes." Little knowing that you are linking your lot with that of a female sergeant-major with strong views on the subject of discipline, and that if you'd only gone on a bit further you would have found the sweetest, kindest, gentlest girl that ever took down outgoing mail in shorthand, who would love you and cherish you and would never dream of giving you hell, no matter what the circumstances. I allude to Magnolia Glendennon.'

'I thought you did.'

'I can't tell you how I feel about her, Bertie.'

'Don't try.'

'Ever since we came down here I've had a lurking suspicion that she was the mate for me and that in signing on the dotted

line with Florence I had made the boner of a lifetime. Just now
my last doubts were dispelled.'

'What happened just now?'

'She rubbed the back of my neck. My interview with Florence,
coming on top of that ghastly Chamber of Commerce lunch,
had given me a splitting headache, and she rubbed the back of
my neck. Then I knew. As those soft fingers touched my skin
like dainty butterflies hovering over a flower—'

'Right ho.'

'It was a revelation, Bertie. I knew that I had come to
journey's end. I said to myself, "This is a good thing. Push it
along." I turned. I grasped her hand. I gazed into her eyes. She
gazed into mine. I told her I loved her. She said so she did
me. She fell into my arms. I grabbed her. We stood murmuring
endearments, and for a while everything was fine. Couldn't have
been better. Then a thought struck me. There was a snag.
You've probably spotted it.'

'Florence?'

'Exactly. Bossy though she is, plainspoken though she may
be when anything displeases her, and I wish you could have
heard her after that Chamber of Commerce lunch, I am still
engaged to her. And while girls can break engagements till the
cows come home, men can't.'

I followed his train of thought. It was evident that he, like
me, aimed at being a *preux chevalier*, and you simply can't be
preux or anything like it if you go about the place getting
betrothed and then telling the party of the second part it's all
off. It seemed to me that the snag which had raised its ugly
head was one of formidable – you might say king-size – dimensions, well calculated to make the current of whatever he
proposed to do about it turn awry and lose the name of action.
But when I put this to him with a sympathetic tremor in my
voice, and I'm not sure I didn't clasp his hand, he surprised
me by chuckling like a leaky radiator.

'That's all right,' he said. 'It would, I admit, appear to be a
tricky situation, but I can handle it. I'm going to get Florence
to break the engagement.'

He spoke with such a gay, confident ring in his voice, so like
the old ancestor predicting what she was going to do to L. P.
Runkle in the playing-on-a-stringed-instrument line, that I was
loth, if that's the word I want, to say anything to depress him,
but the question had to be asked.

'How?' I said, asking it.

'Quite simple. We agreed, I think, that she has no use for a loser. I propose to lose this election.'

Well, it was a thought of course, and I was in complete agreement with his supposition that if the McCorkadale nosed ahead of him in the voting, Florence would in all probability hand him the pink slip, but where it seemed to me that the current went awry was that he had no means of knowing that the electorate would put him in second place. Of course voters are like aunts, you never know what they will be up to from one day to the next, but it was a thing you couldn't count on.

I mentioned this to him, and he repeated his impersonation of a leaky radiator.

'Don't you worry, Bertie. I have the situation well in hand. Something happened in a dark corner of the Town Hall after lunch which justifies my confidence.'

'What happened in a dark corner of the Town Hall after lunch?'

'Well, the first thing that happened after lunch was that Florence got hold of me and became extremely personal. It was then that I realized that it would be the act of a fathead to marry her.'

I nodded adhesion to this sentiment. That time when she had broken her engagement with me my spirits had soared and I had gone about singing like a relieved nightingale.

One thing rather puzzled me and seemed to call for explanatory notes.

'Why did Florence draw you into a dark corner when planning to become personal?' I asked. 'I wouldn't have credited her with so much tact and consideration. As a rule, when she's telling people what she thinks of them, an audience seems to stimulate her. I recall one occasion when she ticked me off in the presence of seventeen Girl Guides, all listening with their ears flapping, and she had never spoken more fluently.'

He put me straight on the point I had raised. He said he had misled me.

'It wasn't Florence who drew me into the dark corner, it was Bingley.'

'Bingley?'

'A fellow who worked for me once.'

'He worked for me once.'

'Really? It's a small world, isn't it.'

'Pretty small. Did you know he'd come into money?'

'He'll soon be coming into some more.'

'But you were saying he drew you into the dark corner. Why did he do that?'

'Because he had a proposition to make to me which demanded privacy. He . . . but before going on I must lay a proper foundation. You know in those Perry Mason stories how whenever Perry says anything while cross-examining a witness, the District Attorney jumps up and yells "Objection, your honour. The S.O.B. has laid no proper foundation". Well, then, you must know that this man Bingley belongs to a butlers and valets club in London called the Junior Ganymede, and one of the rules there is that members have to record the doings of their employers in the club book.'

I would have told him I knew all too well about that, but he carried on before I could speak.

'Such a book, as you can imagine, contains a lot of damaging stuff, and he told me he had been obliged to contribute several pages about me which, if revealed, would lose me so many votes that the election would be a gift to my opponent. He added that some men in his place would have sold it to the opposition and made a lot of money, but he wouldn't do a thing like that because it would be low and in the short time we were together he had come to have a great affection for me. I had never realized before what an extraordinarily good chap he was. I had always thought him a bit of a squirt. Shows how wrong you can be about people.'

Again I would have spoken, but he rolled over me like a tidal wave.

'I should have explained that the committee of the Junior Ganymede, recognizing the importance of this book, had entrusted it to him with instructions to guard it with his life, and his constant fear was that bad men would get wind of this and try to steal it. So what would remove a great burden from his mind, he said, would be if I took it into my possession. Then I could be sure that its contents wouldn't be used against me. I could return it to him after the election and slip him a few quid, if I wished, as a token of my gratitude. You can picture me smiling my subtle smile as he said this. He little knew that my first act would be to send the thing by messenger to the offices of the *Market Snodsbury Argus-Reminder*, thereby handing the election on a plate to the McCorkadale and enabling me to free myself from my honourable obligations to Florence, who would of course, on reading the stuff, recoil from me in horror. Do you know the *Argus-Reminder*? Very far to the left. Can't stand Conservatives. It had a cartoon of me last week showing me with my hands dripping with the blood of the martyred proletariat. I don't know where they get these ideas. I've never spilled a drop of anybody's blood except when boxing, and then the other chap was spilling mine – wholesome give and take. So it wasn't long before Bingley and I had everything all fixed up. He couldn't give me the book then, as he had left it at home, and he wouldn't come and have a drink with me because he had to hurry back because he thought Jeeves might be calling and he didn't want to miss him. Apparently Jeeves is a pal of his – old club crony, that sort of thing. We're meeting tomorrow. I shall reward him with a purse of gold, he will give me the book, and five minutes later, if I can find some brown paper and string, it will be on its way to the *Argus-Reminder*. The material should be in print the day after tomorrow. Allow an hour or so for Florence to get hold of a copy and say twenty minutes for a chat with her after she's read it, and I ought to be a free man well before lunch. About how much gold do you think I should reward Bingley with? Figures were not named, but I thought at least a hundred quid, because he certainly deserves something substantial for his scrupulous high-mindedness. As he said, some men in his place would have sold the book to the opposition and cleaned up big.'

By what I have always thought an odd coincidence he paused at this point and asked me why I was looking like something the cat brought in, precisely as the aged relative had asked me after my interview with Ma McCorkadale. I don't know what cats bring into houses, but one assumes that it is something not very jaunty, and apparently, when in the grip of any strong emotion, I resemble their treasure trove. I could well understand that I was looking like that now. I find it distasteful to have to shatter a long-time buddy's hopes and dreams, and no doubt this shows on the surface.

There was no sense in beating about bushes. It was another of those cases of if it were done, then 'twere well 'twere done quickly.

'Ginger,' I said, 'I'm afraid I have a bit of bad news for you. 'That book is no longer among those present. Jeeves called on Bingley, gave him a Mickey Finn and got it away from him. He now has it among his archives.'

He didn't get it at first, and I had to explain.

'Bingley is not the man of integrity you think him. He is on the contrary a louse of the first water. You might describe him as a slimy slinking slug. He pinched that book from the Junior Ganymede and tried to sell it to the McCorkadale. She sent him away with a flea in his ear because she was a fair fighter, and he tried to sell it to you. But meanwhile Jeeves nipped in and obtained it.'

It took him perhaps a minute to absorb this, but to my surprise he wasn't a bit upset.

'Well, that's all right. Jeeves can take it to the *Argus-Reminder.*'

I shook the loaf sadly, for I knew that this time those hopes and dreams of his were really due for a sock in the eye.

'He wouldn't do it, Ginger. To Jeeves that club book is sacred. I've gone after him a dozen times, urging him to destroy the pages concerning me, but he always remains as uncooperative as Balaam's ass, who, you may remember, dug his feet in and firmly refused to play ball. He'll never let it out of his hands.'

He took it, as I had foreseen, big. He spluttered a good deal. He also kicked the table and would have splintered it if it hadn't been made of marble. It must have hurt like sin, but what disturbed him, I deduced, was not so much the pain of a bruised toe as spiritual anguish. His eyes glittered, his nose wiggled, and if he was not gnashing his teeth I don't know a gnashed tooth when I hear one.

'Oh, won't he?' he said, going back into the old cinnamon bear routine. 'He won't, won't he? We'll see about that. Pop off, Bertie. I want to think.'

I popped off, glad to do so. These displays of naked emotion take it out of one.

14

The shortest way to the house was across the lawn, but I didn't take it. Instead, I made for the back door. It was imperative, I felt, that I should see Jeeves without delay and tell him of the passions he had unchained and warn him, until the hot blood had had time to cool, to keep out of Ginger's way. I hadn't at all liked the sound of the latter's 'We'll see about that', nor the clashing of those gnashed teeth. I didn't of course suppose that, however much on the boil, he would inflict personal violence on Jeeves – sock him, if you prefer the expression – but he would certainly say things to him which would wound his feelings and cause their relations, so pleasant up to now, to deteriorate. And naturally I didn't want that to happen.

Jeeves was in a deck-chair outside the back door, reading Spinoza with the cat Augustus on his lap. I had given him the Spinoza at Christmas and he was constantly immersed in it. I hadn't dipped into it myself, but he tells me it is good ripe stuff, well worth perusal.

He would have risen at my approach, but I begged him to remain seated, for I knew that Augustus, like L. P. Runkle, resented being woken suddenly, and one always wants to consider a cat's feelings.

'Jeeves,' I said, 'a somewhat peculiar situation has popped up out of a trap, and I would be happy to have your comments on it. I am sorry to butt in when you are absorbed in your Spinoza and have probably just got to the part where the second corpse is discovered, but what I have to say is of great pith and moment, so listen attentively.'

'Very good, sir.'

'The facts are these,' I said, and without further preamble or whatever they call it I embarked on my narrative. 'Such,' I concluded some minutes later, 'is the position of affairs, and I think you will agree that the problem confronting us presents certain points of interest.'

'Undeniably, sir.'

'Somehow Ginger has got to lose the election.'

'Precisely, sir.'

'But how?'

'It is difficult to say on the spur of the moment, sir. The tide of popular opinion appears to be swaying in Mr Winship's direction. Lord Sidcup's eloquence is having a marked effect on the electorate and may well prove the deciding factor. Mr Seppings, who obliged as an extra waiter at the luncheon, reports that his lordship's address to the members of the Market Snodsbury Chamber of Commerce was sensational in its brilliance. He tells me that, owing entirely to his lordship, the odds to be obtained in the various public houses, which at one time favoured Mrs McCorkadale at ten to six, have now sunk to evens.'

'I don't like that, Jeeves.'

'No, sir, it is ominous.'

'Of course, if you were to release the club book . . .'

'I fear I cannot do that, sir.'

'No, I told Ginger you regarded it as a sacred trust. Then nothing can be done except to urge you to get the old brain working.'

'I will certainly do my utmost, sir.'

'No doubt something will eventually emerge. Keep eating lots of fish. And meanwhile stay away from Ginger as much as possible, for he is in ugly mood.'

'I quite understand, sir. Stockish, hard and full of rage.'

'Shakespeare?'

'Yes, sir. His *Merchant of Venice*.'

I left him then, pleased at having got one right for a change, and headed for the drawing-room, hoping for another quiet go at the Rex Stout which the swirling rush of events had forced me to abandon. I was, however, too late. The old ancestor was on the chaise longue with it in her grasp, and I knew that I had small chance of wresting it from her. No one who has got his or her hooks on a Rex Stout lightly lets it go.

Her presence there surprised me. I had supposed that she was still brooding over the hammock and its contents.

'Hullo,' I said, 'have you finished with Runkle?'

She looked up, and I noted a trace of annoyance in her demeanour. I assumed that Nero Wolfe had come down from the orchid room and told Archie Goodwin to phone Saul Panzar and Orrie what's his name and things were starting to warm up. In which event she would naturally resent the intrusion of even a loved nephew whom she had often dandled on her knee – not recently, I don't mean, but when I was a bit younger.

'Oh, it's you,' she said, which it was of course. 'No, I haven't finished with Runkle. I haven't even begun. He's still asleep.'

She gave me the impression of being not much in the mood for chit-chat, but one has to say something on these occasions. I brought up a subject which I felt presented certain points of interest.

'Have you ever noticed the remarkable resemblance between L. P. Runkle's daily habits and those of the cat Augustus? They seem to spend all their time sleeping. Do you think they've got traumatic symplegia?'

'What on earth's that?'

'I happened to come on it in a medical book I was reading. It's a disease that makes you sleep all the time. Has Runkle shown no signs of waking?'

'Yes, he did, and just as he was beginning to stir Madeline Bassett came along. She said could she speak to me, so I had to let her. It wasn't easy to follow what she was saying, because she was sobbing all the time, but I got it at last. It was all about the rift with Spode. I told you they had had a tiff. It turns out to be more serious than that. You remember me telling you he couldn't be a Member of Parliament because he was a peer. Well, he wants to give up his title so that he will be eligible.'

'Can a fellow with a title give it up? I thought he was stuck with it.'

'He couldn't at one time, at least only by being guilty of treason, but they've changed the rules and apparently it's quite the posh thing to do nowadays.'

'Sounds silly.'

'That's the view Madeline takes.'

'Did she say what put the idea into Spode's fat head?'

'No, but I can see what did. He has made such a smash hit with his speeches down here that he's saying to himself "Why am I sweating like this on behalf of somebody else? Why not go into business for myself?" Who was it said someone was intoxicated with the exuberance of his own verbosity?'

'I don't know.'

'Jeeves would. It was Bernard Shaw or Mark Twain or Jack Dempsey or somebody. Anyway, that's Spode. He's all puffed up and feels he needs a wider scope. He sees himself holding the House of Commons spellbound.'

'Why can't he hold the House of Lords spellbound?'

'It wouldn't be the same thing. It would be like playing in the Market Snodsbury tennis tournament instead of electrifying one and all on the centre court at Wimbledon. I can see his point.'

'I can't.'

'Nor can Madeline. She's all worked up about it, and I can understand how she feels. No joke for a girl who thinks she's going to be the Countess of Sidcup to have the fellow say "April fool, my little chickadee. What you're going to be is Mrs Spode." If I had been told at Madeline's age that Tom had been made a peer and I then learned that he was going to back out of it and I wouldn't be able to call myself Lady Market Snodsbury after all, I'd have kicked like a mule. Titles to a girl are like catnip to a cat.'

'Can nothing be done?'

'The best plan would be for you to go to him and tell him how much we all admire him for being Lord Sidcup and what a pity it would be for him to go back to a ghastly name like Spode.'

'What's the next best plan?'

'Ah, that wants thinking out.'

We fell into a thoughtful silence, on my part an uneasy one. I didn't at this juncture fully appreciate the peril that lurked, but anything in the nature of a rift within the lute between Spode and Madeline was always calculated to make me purse the lips to some extent. I was still trying to hit on some plan which would be more to my taste than telling Spode what a pity it would be for him to stop being the Earl of Sidcup and go back to a ghastly name like his, when my reverie was broken by the entry through the French window of the cat Augustus, for once awake and in full possession of his faculties, such as they were. No doubt in a misty dreamlike sort of way he had seen me when I was talking to Jeeves and had followed me on my departure, feeling, after those breakfasts of ours together, that association with me was pretty well bound to culminate in kippers. A vain hope, of course. The well-dressed man does not go around with kippered herrings in his pocket. But one of the lessons life teaches us is that cats will be cats.

As is my unvarying policy when closeted with one of these fauna, I made chirruping noises and bent down to tickle the back of the dumb chum's left ear, but my heart was not in the tickling. The more I mused on the recent conversation, the less I liked what the aged relative had revealed. Telling Augustus that I would be back with him in a moment, I straightened myself and was about to ask her for further details, when I discovered that she was no longer in my midst. She must suddenly have decided to have another pop at L. P. Runkle and was presumably even now putting Tuppy's case before him. Well, best of luck to her, of course, and nice to think she had a fine day for it, but I regretted her absence. When your mind is weighed down with matters of great pith and moment, it gives you a sort of sinking feeling to be alone. No doubt the boy who stood on the burning deck whence all but he had fled had this experience.

However, I wasn't alone for long. Scarcely had Augustus sprung on to my lap and started catching up with his sleep when the door opened and Spode came in.

I leaped to my feet, causing Augustus to fall to earth I knew not where, as the fellow said. I was a prey to the liveliest apprehensions. My relations with Spode had been for long so consistently strained that I never saw him nowadays without a lurking fear that he was going to sock me in the eye. Obviously I wasn't to be blamed if he and Madeline had been having trouble, but that wouldn't stop him blaming me. It was like the story of the chap who was in prison and a friend calls and asks him why and the chap tells him and the friend says But they can't put you in prison for that and the chap says I know they can't, but they have. Spode didn't have to have logical reasons for setting about people he wasn't fond of, and it might be that he was like Florence and would work off his grouch on the first available innocent bystander. Putting it in a nutshell, my frame of mind was approximately that of the fellows in the hymn who got such a start when they looked over their shoulders and saw the troops of Midian prowling and prowling around.

It was with profound relief, therefore, that I suddenly got on to it that his demeanour was free from hostility. He was looking like somebody who has just seen the horse on which he had put all his savings, plus whatever he had been able to lift from his employer's till, beaten by a short head. His face, nothing to write home about at the best of times, was drawn and contorted, but with pain rather than the urge to commit mayhem. And while one would always prefer him not to be present, a drawn-and-contorted-with-pain Spode was certainly the next best thing. My greeting, in consequence, had the real ring of cordiality in it.

'Oh, hullo, Spode, hullo. There you are, what? Splendid.'

'Can I have a word with you, Wooster?'

'Of course, of course. Have several.'

He did not speak for a minute or so, filling in the time by subjecting me to a close scrutiny. Then he gave a sigh and shook his head.

'I can't understand it,' he said.

'What can't you understand, Spode old man or rather Lord Sidcup old man?' I asked in a kind voice, for I was only too willing to help this new and improved Spode solve any little problem that was puzzling him.

'How Madeline can contemplate marrying a man like you. She has broken our engagement and says that's what she's going to do. She was quite definite about it. "All is over," she said. "Here is your ring," she said. "I shall marry Bertie Wooster and make him happy," she said. You can't want it plainer than that.'

I stiffened from head to f. Even with conditions what they were in this disturbed post-war world I hadn't been expecting to be turned into a pillar of salt again for some considerable time, but this had done it. I don't know how many of my public have ever been slapped between the eyes with a wet fish, but those who have will appreciate my emotions as the seventh Earl of Sidcup delivered this devastating bulletin. Everything started to go all wobbly, and through what is known as a murky mist I seemed to be watching a quivering-at-the-edges seventh Earl performing the sort of gyrations travelled friends have told me the Ouled Nail dancers do in Cairo.

I was stunned. It seemed to me incredible that Madeline Bassett should have blown the whistle on their engagement. Then I remembered that at the time when she had plighted her troth Spode was dangling a countess's coronet before her eyes, and the thing became more understandable. I mean, take away the coronet and what had you got? Just Spode. Not good enough, a girl would naturally feel.

He, meanwhile, was going on to explain why he found it so bizarre that Madeline should be contemplating marrying me, and almost immediately I saw that I had been mistaken in supposing that he was not hostile. He spoke from between clenched teeth, and that always tells the story.

'As far as I can see, Wooster, you are without attraction of any kind. Intelligence? No. Looks? No. Efficiency? No. You can't even steal an umbrella without getting caught. All that can be said for you is that you don't wear a moustache. They tell me you did grow one once, but mercifully shaved it off. That is to your credit, but it is a small thing to weigh in the balance against all your other defects. When one considers how numerous these are, one can only suppose that it is your shady record of stealing anything you can lay your hands on that appeals to Madeline's romantic soul. She is marrying you in the hope of reforming you, and let me tell you, Wooster, that if you disappoint that hope, you will be sorry. She may have rejected me, but I shall always love her as I have done since she was so high, and I shall do my utmost to see that her gentle heart is not broken by any sneaking son of a what-not who looks like a chorus boy in a touring revue playing the small towns and cannot see anything of value without pocketing it. You will probably think you are safe from me when you are doing your stretch in Wormwood Scrubs for larceny, but I shall be waiting for you when you come out and I shall tear you limb from limb. And,' he added, for his was a one-track mind, 'dance on the fragments in hob-nailed boots.'

He paused, produced his cigarette case, asked me if I had a match, thanked me when I gave him one, and withdrew.

He left behind him a Bertram Wooster whom the dullest eye could have spotted as not being at the peak of his form. The prospect of being linked for life to a girl who would come down to breakfast and put her hands over my eyes and say 'Guess who' had given my morale a sickening wallop, reducing me to the level of one of those wee sleekit timorous cowering beasties Jeeves tells me the poet Burns used to write about. It is always my policy in times of crisis to try to look on the bright side, but I make one proviso – viz. that there has to be a bright side to look on, and in the present case there wasn't even the sniff of one.

As I sat there draining the bitter cup, there were noises off stage and my meditations were interrupted by the return of the old ancestor. Well, when I say return, she came whizzing in but didn't stop, just whizzed through, and I saw, for I am pretty quick at noticing things, that she was upset about something. Reasoning closely, I deduced that her interview with L. P. Runkle must have gone awry or, as I much prefer to put it, agley.

And so it proved when she bobbed up again some little time later. Her first observation was that L. P. Runkle was an illegitimate offspring to end all illegitimate offsprings, and I hastened to commiserate with her. I could have done with a bit of commiseration myself, but Women and Children First is always the Wooster slogan.

'No luck?' I said.

'None.'

'Wouldn't part?'

'Not a penny.'

'You mentioned that without his cooperation Tuppy and Angela's wedding bells would not ring out?'

'Of course I did. And he said it was a great mistake for young people to marry before they knew their own minds.'

'You could have pointed out that Tuppy and Angela have been engaged for two years.'

'I did.'

'What did he say to that?'

'He said "Not nearly long enough".'

'So what are you going to do?'

'I've done it,' said the old ancestor. 'I pinched his porringer.'

15

I goggled at her, one hundred per cent nonplussed. She had spoken with the exuberance of an aunt busily engaged in patting herself between the shoulder-blades for having done something particularly clever, but I could make nothing of her statement. This habit of speaking in riddles seemed to be growing on her.

'You what?' I said. 'You pinched his what?'

'His porringer. I told you about it the day you got here. Don't you remember? That silver thing he came to try to sell to Tom.'

She had refreshed my memory. I recalled the conversation to which she referred. I had asked her why she was entertaining in her home a waste product like L. P. Runkle, and she had said that he had come hoping to sell Uncle Tom a silver something for his collection and she had got him to stay on in order to soften him up with Anatole's cooking and put to him, when softened up, her request for cash for Tuppy.

'When he turned me down just now, it suddenly occurred to me that if I got hold of the thing and told him he wouldn't get it back unless he made a satisfactory settlement, I would have a valuable bargaining point and we could discuss the matter further at any time that suited him.'

I was ap-what-is-it. Forget my own name next. Appalled, that's the word, though shocked to the core would be about as good; nothing much in it, really. I hadn't read any of those etiquette books you see all over the place, but I was prepared to bet that the leaders of Society who wrote them would raise an eyebrow or two at carrying-ons of this description. The chapter on Hints To Hostesses would be bound to have a couple of paragraphs warning them that it wasn't the done thing to invite people to the home and having got them settled in to pinch their porringers.

'But good Lord!' I ejaculated, appalled or, if you prefer it, shocked to the core.

'Now what?'

'The man is under your roof.'

'Did you expect him to be on it?'

'He has eaten your salt.'

'Very imprudent, with blood pressure like his. His doctor probably forbids it.'

'You can't do this.'

'I know I can't, but I have,' she said, just like the chap in the story, and I saw it would be fruitless or bootless to go on arguing. It rarely is with aunts – if you're their nephew, I mean, because they were at your side all through your formative years and know what an ass you were then and can't believe that anything that you may say later is worth listening to. I shouldn't be at all surprised if Jeeves's three aunts don't shut him up when he starts talking, remembering that at the age of six the child Jeeves didn't know the difference between the poet Burns and a hole in the ground.

Ceasing to expostulate, therefore, if expostulate is the word I want, I went to the bell and pressed it, and when she asked for footnotes throwing a light on why I did this, I told her I proposed to place the matter in the hands of a higher power.

'I'm ringing for Jeeves.'

'You'll only get Seppings.'

'Seppings will provide Jeeves.'

'And what do you think Jeeves can do?'

'Make you see reason.'

'I doubt it.'

'Well, it's worth a try.'

Further chit-chat was suspended till Jeeves arrived and silence fell except for the ancestor snorting from time to time and self breathing more heavily than usual, for I was much stirred. It always stirs a nephew to discover that a loved aunt does not know the difference between right and wrong. There *is* a difference . . . at my private school Arnold Abney M.A. used to rub it into the student body both Sundays and weekdays . . . but apparently nobody had told the aged relative about it, with the result that she could purloin people's porringers without a yip from her conscience. Shook me a bit, I confess.

When Jeeves blew in, it cheered me to see the way his head stuck out at the back, for that's where the brain is, and what was needed here was a man with plenty of the old grey matter who would put his points so that even a fermenting aunt would have to be guided by him.

'Well, here's Jeeves,' said the ancestor. 'Tell him the facts and I'll bet he says I've done the only possible thing and can carry on along the lines I sketched out.'

I might have risked a fiver on this at say twelve to eight, but it didn't seem fitting. But telling Jeeves the facts was a good idea, and I did so without delay, being careful to lay a proper foundation.

'Jeeves,' I said.

'Sir?' he responded.

'Sorry to interrupt you again. Were you reading Spinoza?'

'No, sir, I was writing a letter to my Uncle Charlie.'

'Charlie Silversmith,' I explained in an aside to the ancestor. 'Butler at Deverill Hall. One of the best.'

'Thank you, sir.'

'I know few men whom I esteem more highly than your Uncle Charlie. Well, we won't keep you long. It's just that another problem presenting certain points of interest has come up. In a recent conversation I revealed to you the situation relating to Tuppy Glossop and L. P. Runkle. You recall?'

'Yes, sir. Madam was hoping to extract a certain sum of money from Mr Runkle on Mr Glossop's behalf.'

'Exactly. Well, it didn't come off.'

'I am sorry to hear that, sir.'

'But not, I imagine, surprised. If I remember, you considered it a hundred to one shot.'

'Approximately that, sir.'

'Runkle being short of bowels of compassion.'

'Precisely, sir. A twenty-minute egg.'

Here the ancestor repeated her doubts with regard to L. P. Runkle's legitimacy, and would, I think, have developed the theme had I not shushed her down with a raised hand.

'She pleaded in vain,' I said. 'He sent her away with a flea in her ear. I wouldn't be surprised to learn that he laughed her to scorn.'

'The superfatted old son of a bachelor,' the ancestor interposed, and once more I shushed her down.

'Well, you know what happens when you do that sort of thing to a woman of spirit. Thoughts of reprisals fill her mind. And so, coming to the nub, she decided to purloin Runkle's porringer. But I mustn't mislead you. She did this not as an act of vengeance, if you know what I mean, but in order to have a bargaining point when she renewed her application. "Brass up," she would have said when once more urging him to scare the moths out of his pocketbook, "or you won't get back your porringer". Do I make myself clear?'

'Perfectly clear, sir. I find you very lucid.'

'Now first it will have to be explained to you what a porringer is, and here I am handicapped by not having the foggiest notion myself, except that it's silver and old and the sort of thing Uncle Tom has in his collection. Runkle was hoping to sell it to him. Could you supply any details?' I asked the aged relative.

She knitted the brows a bit, and said she couldn't do much in that direction.

'All I know is that it was made in the time of Charles the Second by some Dutchman or other.'

'Then I think I know the porringer to which you allude, sir,' said Jeeves, his face lighting up as much as it ever lights up, he for reasons of his own preferring at all times to preserve the impassivity of a waxwork at Madame Tussaud's. 'It was featured in a Sotheby's catalogue at which I happened to be glancing not long ago. Would it,' he asked the ancestor, 'be a silver-gilt porringer on a circular moulded foot, the lower part chased with acanthus foliage, with beaded scroll handles, the cover surmounted by a foliage on a rosette of swirling acanthus leaves, the stand of tazza form on circular detachable feet with acanthus border joined to a multifoil plate, the palin top with upcurved rim?'

He paused for a reply, but the ancestor did not speak immediately, her aspect that of one who has been run over by a municipal tram. Odd, really, because she must have been listening to that sort of thing from Uncle Tom for years. Finally she mumbled that she wouldn't be surprised or she wouldn't wonder or something like that.

'Your guess is as good as mine,' she said.

'I fancy it must be the same, madam. You mentioned a workman of Dutch origin. Would the name be Hans Conrael Brechtel of the Hague?'

'I couldn't tell you. I know it wasn't Smith or Jones or Robinson, and that's as far as I go. But what's all this in aid of? What does it matter if the stand is of tazza form or if the palin top has an upcurved rim?'

'Exactly,' I said, thoroughly concurring. 'Or if the credit for these tazza forms and palin tops has to be chalked up to Hans Conrael Brechtel of the Hague. The point, Jeeves, is not what particular porringer the ancestor has pinched, but how far she was justified in pinching any porringer at all when its owner was a guest of hers. I hold that it was a breach of hospitality and the thing must be returned. Am I right?'

'Well, sir . . .'

'Go on, Jeeves,' said the ancestor. 'Say I'm a crook who ought to be drummed out of the Market Snodsbury Ladies Social and Cultural Garden Club.'

'Not at all, madam.'

'Then what were you going to say when you hesitated?'

'Merely that in my opinion no useful end will be served by retaining the object.' ·

'I don't follow you. How about that bargaining point?'

'It will, I fear, avail you little, madam. As I understand Mr Wooster, the sum you are hoping to obtain from Mr Runkle amounts to a good many thousand pounds.'

'Fifty at least, if not a hundred.'

'Then I cannot envisage him complying with your demands. Mr Runkle is a shrewd financier—'

'Born out of wedlock.'

'Very possibly you are right, madam, nevertheless he is a man well versed in weighing profit and loss. According to Sotheby's catalogue the price at which the object was sold at the auction sale was nine thousand pounds. He will scarcely disburse a hundred or even fifty thousand in order to recover it.'

'Of course he won't,' I said, as enchanted with his lucidity as he had been with mine. It was the sort of thing you have to pay topnotchers at the Bar a king's ransom for. 'He'll simply say "Easy come, easy go" and write it off as a business loss, possibly consulting his legal adviser as to whether he can deduct it from his income tax. Thank you, Jeeves. You've straightened everything out in your customary masterly manner. You're a . . . what were you saying the other day about Daniel somebody?'

'A Daniel come to judgment, sir?'

'That was it. You're a Daniel come to judgment.'

'It is very kind of you to say so, sir.'

'Not at all. Well-deserved tribute.'

I shot a glance at the aged relative. It is notoriously difficult to change the trend of an aunt's mind when that mind is made up about this or that, but I could see at a g that Jeeves had done it. I hadn't expected her to look pleased, and she didn't, but it was evident that she had accepted what is sometimes called the inevitable. I would describe her as not having a word to say, had she not at this moment said one, suitable enough for the hunting field but on the strong side for mixed company. I registered it in my memory as something to say to Spode some time, always provided it was on the telephone.

'I suppose you're right, Jeeves,' she said, heavy-hearted, though bearing up stoutly. 'It seemed a good idea at the time, but I agree with you that it isn't as watertight as I thought it. It's so often that way with one's golden dreams. The—'

'—best-laid plans of mice and men gang aft agley,' I said helping her out. 'See the poet Burns. I've often wondered why Scotsmen say "gang". I asked you once, Jeeves, if you recall, and you said they had not confided in you. You were saying, ancestor?'

'I was about to say—'

'Or, for that matter, "agley".'

'I was about to say—'

'Or "aft" for "often".'

'I was about to say,' said the relative, having thrown her Rex Stout at me, fortunately with a less accurate aim than the other time, 'that there's nothing to be done but for me to put the thing back in Runkle's room where I took it from.'

'Whence I took it' would have been better, but it was not to comment on her prose style that I interposed. I was thinking that if she was allowed to do the putting back, she might quite possibly change her mind on the way to Runkle's room and decide to stick to the loot after all. Jeeves's arguments had been convincing to the last drop, but you can never be sure that the effect of convincing arguments won't wear off, especially with aunts who don't know the difference between right and wrong, and it might be that she would take the view that if she pocketed the porringer and kept it among her souvenirs, she would at least be saving something from the wreck. 'Always difficult to know what to give Tom for his birthday,' she might say to herself. 'This will be just the thing.'

'I'll do it,' I said. 'Unless you'd rather, Jeeves.'

'No, thank you, sir.'

'Only take a minute of your time.'

'No, thank you, sir.'

'Then you may leave us, Jeeves. Much obliged for your Daniel come to judgmenting.'

'A pleasure, sir.'

'Give Uncle Charlie my love.'

'I will indeed, sir.'

As the door closed behind him, I started to make my plans and dispositions, as I believe the word is, and I found the blood relation docile and helpful. Runkle's room, she told me, was the one known as the Blue Room, and the porringer should be inserted in the left top drawer of the chest of drawers, whence she had removed it. I asked if she was sure he was still in the hammock, and she said he must be, because on her departure he was bound to have gone to sleep again. Taking a line through the cat Augustus, I found this plausible. With these traumatic symplegia cases waking is never more than a temporary thing. I have known Augustus to resume his slumbers within fifteen seconds of having had a shopping bag containing tins of cat food fall on him. A stifled oath, and he was off to dreamland once more.

As I climbed the stairs, I was impressed by the fact that L. P. Runkle had been given the Blue Room, for in this house it amounted to getting star billing. It was the biggest and most luxurious of the rooms allotted to bachelors. I once suggested to the aged relative that I be put there, but all she said was '*You?*' and the conversation turned to other topics. Runkle having got it in spite of the presence on the premises of a seventh Earl showed how determined the a.r. had been that no stone should be left unturned and no avenue unexplored in her efforts to soften him up; and it seemed ironical that all her carefully thought-out plans should have gone agley. Just shows Burns knew what he was talking about. You can generally rely on these poets to hit the mark and entitle themselves to a cigar or coconut according to choice.

The old sweats will remember, though later arrivals will have to be told, that this was not the first time I had gone on a secret mission to the Blue Room. That other visit, the old sweats will recall, had ended in disaster and not knowing which way to look, for Mrs Homer Cream, the well-known writer of suspense novels, had found me on the floor with a chair round my neck, and it had not been easy to explain. This was no doubt why on the present occasion I approached the door with emotions somewhat similar to those I had had in the old days when approaching that of Arnold Abney M.A. at the conclusion of morning prayers. A voice seemed to whisper in my ear that beyond that door there lurked something that wasn't going to do me a bit of good.

The voice was perfectly right. It had got its facts correct first shot. What met my eyes as I entered was L. P. Runkle asleep on the bed, and with my customary quickness I divined what must have happened. After being cornered there by the old ancestor he must have come to the conclusion that a hammock out in the middle of a lawn, with access to it from all directions, was no place for a man who wanted peace and seclusion, and that these were to be obtained only in his bedroom. Thither, accordingly, he had gone, and there he was. *Voilà tout*, as one might say if one had made a study of the French language.

The sight of this sleeping beauty had, of course, given me a nasty start, causing my heart to collide rather violently with my front teeth, but it was only for a moment that I was unequal to what I have heard Jeeves call the intellectual pressure of the situation. It is pretty generally recognized in the circles in which I move that Bertram Wooster, though he may be down, is never out, the betting being odds on that, given time to collect his thoughts and stop his head spinning, he will rise on stepping stones of his dead self to higher things, as the fellow said, and it was so now. I would have preferred, of course, to operate in a room wholly free from the presence of L. P. Runkle, but I realized that as long as he remained asleep there was nothing to keep me from carrying on. All that was required was that my activities should be conducted in absolute silence. And it was thus that I was conducting them, more like a spectre or wraith than a chartered member of the Drones Club, when the air was rent, as the expression is, by a sharp yowl such as you hear when a cougar or a snow leopard stubs its toe on a rock, and I became aware that I had trodden on the cat Augustus, who had continued to follow me, still, I suppose, under the mistaken impression that I had kippered herrings on my person and might at any moment start loosening up.

In normal circumstances I would have hastened to make my apologies and to endeavour by tickling him behind the ear to apply balm to his wounded feelings, but at this moment L. P. Runkle sat up, said 'Wah-wah-wah', rubbed his eyes, gave me an unpleasant look with them and asked me what the devil I was doing in his room.

It was not an easy question to answer. There had been nothing in our relations since we first swam into each other's ken to make it seem likely that I had come to smooth his pillow or ask him if he would like a cooling drink, and I did not put forward these explanations. I was thinking how right the ancestor had been in predicting that, if aroused suddenly, he would wake up cross. His whole demeanour was that of a man who didn't much like the human race as a whole but was particularly allergic to Woosters. Not even Spode could have made his distaste for them plainer.

I decided to see what could be done with suavity. It had answered well in the case of Ginger, and there was no saying that it might not help to ease the current situation.

'I'm sorry,' I said with an enchanting smile, 'I'm afraid I woke you.'

'Yes, you did. And stop grinning at me like a half-witted ape.'

'Right ho,' I said. I removed the enchanting smile. It came off quite easily. 'I don't wonder you're annoyed. But I'm more to be pitied than censured. I inadvertently trod on the cat.'

A look of alarm spread over his face. It had a long way to go, but it spread all right.

'Hat?' he quavered, and I could see that he feared for the well-being of his Panama with the pink ribbon.

I lost no time in reassuring him.

'Not hat. Cat.'

'What cat?'

'Oh, haven't you met? Augustus his name is, though for purposes of conversation this is usually shortened to Gus. He and I have been buddies since he was a kitten. He must have been following me when I came in here.'

It was an unfortunate way of putting it, for it brought him back to his original theme.

'Why the devil did you come in here?'

A lesser man than Bertram Wooster would have been nonplussed, and I don't mind admitting that I was, too, for about a couple of ticks. But as I stood shuffling the feet and twiddling the fingers I caught sight of that camera of his standing on an adjacent table, and I got one of those inspirations you get occasionally. Shakespeare and Burns and even Oliver Wendell Holmes probably used to have them all the time, but self not so often. In fact, this was the first that had come my way for some weeks.

'Aunt Dahlia sent me to ask you if you would come and take a few photographs of her and the house and all that sort of thing, so that she'll have them to look at in the long winter evenings. You know how long the winter evenings get nowadays.'

The moment I had said it I found myself speculating as to whether the inspiration had been as hot as I had supposed. I mean, this man had just had a conference with the old ancestor which, unlike those between ministers of state, had not been conducted in an atmosphere of the utmost cordiality, and he might be thinking it odd that so soon after its conclusion she should be wanting him to take photographs of her. But all was well. No doubt he looked on her request as what is known as an olive branch. Anyway, he was all animation and eagerness to cooperate.

'I'll be right down,' he said. 'Tell her I'll be right down.'

Having hidden the porringer in my room and locked the door, I went back to the aged relative and found her with Jeeves. She expressed relief at seeing me.

'Oh, there you are, my beautiful bounding Bertie. Thank goodness you didn't go to Runkle's room. Jeeves tells me Seppings met Runkle on the stairs and he asked him to bring him a cup of tea in half an hour. He said he was going to lie down. You might have run right into him.'

I laughed one of those hollow, mirthless ones.

'Jeeves speaks too late, old ancestor. I did run into him.'

'You mean he was *there*?'

'With his hair in a braid.'

'What did you do?'

'I told him you had asked me to ask him to come and take some photographs.'

'Quick thinking.'

'I always think like lightning.'

'And did he swallow it?'

'He appeared to. He said he would be right down.'

'Well, I'm damned if I'm going to smile.'

Whether I would have pleaded with her to modify this stern resolve and at least show a portion of her front teeth when Runkle pressed the button, I cannot say, for as she spoke my thoughts were diverted. A sudden query presented itself. What, I asked myself, was keeping L. P. Runkle? He had said he would be right down, but quite a time had elapsed and no sign of him. I was toying with the idea that on a warm afternoon like this a man of his build might have had a fit of some kind, when there came from the stairs the sound of clumping feet, and he was with us.

But a very different L. P. Runkle from the man who had told

me he would be right down. Then he had been all sunny and beaming, the amateur photographer who was not only going to make a pest of himself by taking photographs but had actually been asked to make a pest of himself in this manner, which seldom happens to amateur photographers. Now he was cold and hard like a picnic egg, and he couldn't have looked at me with more loathing if I really had trodden on his Panama hat.

'Mrs Travers!'

His voice had rung out with the clarion note of a coster-monger seeking to draw the attention of the purchasing public to his blood oranges and Brussels sprouts. I saw the ancestor stiffen, and I knew she was about to go into her *grande dame* act. This relative, though in ordinary circs so genial and matey, can on occasion turn in a flash into a carbon copy of a Duchess of the old school reducing an underling to a spot of grease, and what is so remarkable is that she doesn't have to use a lorgnette, just does it all with the power of the human eye. I think girls in her day used to learn the trick at their finishing schools.

'Will you kindly not bellow at me, Mr Runkle. I am not deaf. What is it?'

The aristocratic ice in her tone sent a cold shiver down my spine, but in L. P. Runkle she had picked a tough customer to try to freeze. He apologized for having bellowed, but briefly and with no real contrition. He then proceeded to deal with her query as to what it was, and with a powerful effort forced himself to speak quite quietly. Not exactly like a cooing pigeon, but quietly.

'I wonder if you remember, Mrs Travers, a silver porringer I showed you on my arrival here.'

'I do.'

'Very valuable.'

'So you told me.'

'I kept it in the top left-hand drawer of the chest of drawers in my bedroom. It did not occur to me that there was any necessity to hide it. I took the honesty of everybody under your roof for granted.'

'Naturally.'

'Even when I found that Mr Wooster was one of my fellow guests I took no precautions. It was a fatal blunder. He has just stolen it.'

I suppose it's pretty much of a strain to keep up that *grande dame* stuff for any length of time, involving as it does rigidity of the facial muscles and the spinal column, for at these words the ancestor called it a day and reverted to the Quorn-and-Pytchleyness of her youth.

'Don't be a damned fool, Runkle. You're talking rot. Bertie would never dream of doing such a thing, would you, Bertie?'

'Not in a million years.'

'The man's an ass.'

'One might almost say a silly ass.'

'Comes of sleeping all the time.'

'I believe that's the trouble.'

'Addles the brain.'

'Must, I imagine. It's the same thing with Gus the cat. I love Gus like a brother, but after years of non-stop sleep he's got about as much genuine intelligence as a Cabinet minister.'

'I hope Runkle hasn't annoyed you with his preposterous allegations?'

'No, no, old ancestor, I'm not angry, just terribly terribly hurt.'

You'd have thought all this would have rendered Runkle a spent force and a mere shell of his former self, but his eye was not dimmed nor his natural force abated. Turning to the door, he paused there to add a few words.

'I disagree with you, Mrs Travers, in the view you take of your nephew's honesty. I prefer to be guided by Lord Sidcup, who assures me that Mr Wooster invariably steals anything that is not firmly fastened to the floor. It was only by the merest chance, Lord Sidcup tells me, that at their first meeting he did not make away with an umbrella belonging to Sir Watkyn Bassett, and from there he has, as one might put it, gone from strength to strength. Umbrellas, cow-creamers, amber statuettes, cameras, all are grist to his mill. I was unfortunately asleep when he crept into my room, and he had plenty of time before I woke to do what he had come for. It was only some minutes after he had slunk out that it occurred to me to look in the top left-hand drawer of my chest of drawers. My suspicions were confirmed. The drawer was empty. He had got away with the swag. But I am a man of action. I have sent your butler to the police station to bring a constable to search Wooster's room. I, until he arrives, propose to stand outside it, making sure that he does not go in and tamper with the evidence.'

Having said which in the most unpleasant of vocal deliveries, L. P. Runkle became conspic by his a, and the ancestor spoke with considerable eloquence on the subject of fat slobs of dubious parentage who had the immortal crust to send her butler on errands. I, too, was exercised by the concluding portion of his remarks.

'I don't like that,' I said, addressing Jeeves, who during the recent proceedings had been standing in the background giving a lifelike impersonation of somebody who wasn't there.

'Sir?'

'If the fuzz search my room, I'm sunk.'

'Have no anxiety, sir. A police officer is not permitted to enter private property without authority, nor do the regulations allow him to ask the owner of such property for permission to enter.'

'You're sure of that?'

'Yes, sir.'

Well, that was a crumb of comfort, but it would be deceiving my public if I said that Bertram Wooster was his usual nonchalant self. Too many things had been happening one on top of the other for him to be the carefree boulevardier one likes to see. If I hoped to clarify the various situations which were giving me the pip and erase the dark circles already beginning to form beneath the eyes, it would, I saw, be necessary for me to marshal my thoughts.

'Jeeves,' I said, leading him from the room, 'I must marshal my thoughts.'

'Certainly, sir, if you wish.'

'And I can't possibly do it here with crises turning handsprings on every side. Can you think of a good excuse for me to pop up to London for the night? A few hours alone in the peaceful surroundings of the flat are what I need. I must concentrate, concentrate.'

'But do you require an excuse, sir?'

'It's better to have one. Aunt Dahlia is on a sticky wicket and would be hurt if I deserted her now unless I had some good reason. I can't let her down.'

'The sentiment does you credit, sir.'

'Thank you, Jeeves. Can you think of anything?'

'You have been summoned for jury duty, sir.'

'Don't they let you have a longish notice for that?'

'Yes, sir, but when the post arrived containing the letter from the authorities, I forgot to give it to you, and only delivered it a moment ago. Fortunately it was not too late. Would you be intending to leave immediately?'

'If not sooner. I'll borrow Ginger's car.'

'You will miss the debate, sir.'

'The what?'

'The debate between Mr Winship and his opponent. It takes place tomorrow night.'

'What time?'

'It is scheduled for a quarter to seven.'

'Taking how long?'

'Perhaps an hour.'

'Then expect me back at about seven-thirty. The great thing in life, Jeeves, if we wish to be happy and prosperous, is to miss as many political debates as possible. You wouldn't care to come with me, would you?'

'No, thank you, sir. I am particularly anxious to hear Mr Winship's speech.'

'He'll probably only say "Er",' I riposted rather cleverly.

16

It was with a heart-definitely-bowed-down mood and the circles beneath my eyes darker than ever that I drove back next day in what is known as the quiet evenfall. I remember Jeeves saying something to me once about the heavy and the weary weight of this unintelligible world . . . not his own, I gathered, but from the works of somebody called Wordsworth, if I caught the name correctly . . . and it seemed to me rather a good way of describing the depressing feeling you get when the soup is about to close over you and no life-belt is in sight. I was conscious of this heavy and weary weight some years ago, that time when my cousins Eustace and Claude without notifying me inserted twenty-three cats in my bedroom, and I had it again, in spades, at the present juncture.

Consider the facts. I had gone up to London to wrestle in solitude with the following problems:

(a) How am I to get out of marrying Madeline Bassett?
(b) How am I to restore the porringer to L. P. Runkle before the constabulary come piling on the back of my neck?
(c) How is the ancestor to extract that money from Runkle?
(d) How is Ginger to marry Magnolia Glendennon while betrothed to Florence?

and I was returning with all four still in status quo. For a night and day I had been giving them the cream of the Wooster brain, and for all I had accomplished I might have been the aged relative trying to solve the *Observer* crossword puzzle.

Arriving at journey's end, I steered the car into the drive. About half-way along it there was a tricky right-hand turn, and I had slowed down to negotiate this, when a dim figure appeared before me, a voice said, 'Hoy!', and I saw that it was Ginger.

He seemed annoyed about something. His 'Hoy!' had had a note of reproach in it, as far as it is possible to get the note of reproach into a 'Hoy!', and as he drew near and shoved his torso through the window I received the distinct impression that he was displeased.

His opening words confirmed this.

'Bertie, you abysmal louse, what's kept you all this time? When I lent you my car, I didn't expect you'd come back at two o'clock in the morning.'

'It's only half-past seven.'

He seemed amazed.

'Is that all? I thought it was later. So much has been happening.'

'What has been happening?'

'No time to tell you now. I'm in a hurry.'

It was at this point that I noticed something in his appearance which I had overlooked. A trifle, but I'm rather observant.

'You've got egg in your hair,' I said.

'Of course I've got egg in my hair,' he said, his manner betraying impatience. 'What did you expect me to have in my hair, Chanel Number Five?'

'Did somebody throw an egg at you?'

'Everybody threw eggs at everybody. Correction. Some of them threw turnips and potatoes.'

'You mean the meeting broke up in disorder, as the expression is?'

'I don't suppose any meeting in the history of English politics has ever broken up in more disorder. Eggs flew hither and thither. The air was dark with vegetables of every description. Sidcup got a black eye. Somebody plugged him with a potato.'

I found myself in two minds. On the one hand I felt a pang of regret for having missed what had all the earmarks of having been a political meeting of the most rewarding kind: on the other, it was like rare and refreshing fruit to hear that Spode had got hit in the eye with a potato. I was conscious of an awed respect for the marksman who had accomplished this feat. A potato, being so nobbly in shape, can be aimed accurately only by a master hand.

'Tell me more,' I said, well pleased.

'Tell you more be blowed. I've got to get up to London. We want to be there bright and early tomorrow in order to inspect registrars and choose the best one.'

This didn't sound like Florence, who, if she ever gets through an engagement without breaking it, is sure to insist on a wedding with bishops, bridesmaids, full choral effects, and a reception afterwards. A sudden thought struck me, and I think I may have gasped. Somebody made a noise like a dying soda-water syphon and it was presumably me.

'When you say "we", do you mean you and M. Glendennon?'

'Who else?'

'But how?'

'Never mind how.'

'But I do mind how. You were Problem (d) on my list, and I want to know how you have been solved. I gather that Florence has remitted your sentence—'

'She has, in words of unmistakable clarity. Get out of that car.'

'But why?'

'Because if you aren't out of it in two seconds, I'm going to pull you out.'

'I mean why did she r your s?'

'Ask Jeeves,' he said, and attaching himself to the collar of my coat he removed me from the automobile like a stevedore hoisting a sack of grain. He took my place at the wheel, and disappeared down the drive to keep his tryst with the little woman, who presumably awaited him at some prearranged spot with the bags and baggage.

He left me in a condition which can best be described as befogged, bewildered, mystified, confused and perplexed. All I had got out of him was (a) that the debate had not been conducted in an atmosphere of the utmost cordiality, (b) that at its conclusion Florence had forbidden the banns and (c) that if I wanted further information Jeeves would supply it. A little more than the charmers got out of the deaf adder, but not much. I felt like a barrister, as it might be Ma McCorkadale, who has been baffled by an unsatisfactory witness.

However, he had spoken of Jeeves as a fount of information, so my first move on reaching the drawing-room and finding no one there was to put forefinger to bell button and push.

Seppings answered the summons. He and I have been buddies from boyhood – mine, of course, not his – and as a rule when we meet conversation flows like water, mainly on the subject of the weather and the state of his lumbago, but this was no time for idle chatter.

'Seppings,' I said, 'I want Jeeves. Where is he?'

'In the servants' hall, sir, comforting the parlourmaid.'

I took him to allude to the employee whose gong-work I had admired on my first evening, and, pressing though my business was, it seemed only humane to offer a word of sympathy for whatever her misfortunes might be.

'Had bad news, has she?'

'No, sir, she was struck by a turnip.'

'Where?'

'In the lower ribs, sir.'

'I mean where did this happen?'

'At the Town Hall, sir, in the later stages of the debate.'

I drew in the breath sharply. More and more I was beginning to realize that the meeting I had missed had been marked by passions which recalled the worst excesses of the French revolution.

'I myself, sir, narrowly escaped being hit by a tomato. It whizzed past my ear.'

'You shock me profoundly, Seppings. I don't wonder you're pale and trembling.' And indeed he was, like a badly set blancmange. 'What caused all this turmoil?'

'Mr Winship's speech, sir.'

This surprised me. I could readily believe that any speech of Ginger's would be well below the mark set by Demosthenes, if that really was the fellow's name, but surely not so supremely lousy as to start his audience throwing eggs and vegetables; and I was about to institute further enquiries, when Seppings sidled to the door, saying that he would inform Mr Jeeves of my desire to confer with him. And in due season the hour produced the man, as the expression is.

'You wished to see me, sir?' he said.

'You can put it even stronger, Jeeves. I yearned to see you.'

'Indeed, sir?'

'Just now I met Ginger in the drive.'

'Yes, sir, he informed me that he was going there to await your return.'

'He tells me he is no longer betrothed to Miss Craye, being now affianced to Miss Glendennon. And when I asked him how this switch had come about, he said that you would explain.'

'I shall be glad to do so, sir. You wish a complete report?'

'That's right. Omit no detail, however slight.'

He was silent for a space. Marshalling his thoughts, no doubt. Then he got down to it.

'The importance attached by the electorate to the debate,' he began, 'was very evident. An audience of considerable size had assembled in the Town Hall. The Mayor and Corporation were there, together with the flower of Market Snodsbury's aristo-cracy and a rougher element in cloth caps and turtleneck sweaters who should never have been admitted.'

I had to rebuke him at this point.

'Bit snobbish, that, Jeeves, what? You are a little too inclined to judge people by their clothes. Turtleneck sweaters are royal raiment when they're worn for virtue's sake, and a cloth cap may hide an honest heart. Probably frightfully good chaps, if one had got to know them.'

'I would prefer not to know them, sir. It was they who subsequently threw eggs, potatoes, tomatoes and turnips.'

I had to concede that he had a point there.

'True,' I said. 'I was forgetting that. All right, Jeeves. Carry on.'

'The proceedings opened with a rendering of the national anthem by the boys and girls of Market Snodsbury elementary school.'

'Pretty ghastly, I imagine?'

'Somewhat revolting, sir.'

'And then?'

'The Mayor made a short address, introducing the contest-ants, and Mrs McCorkadale rose to speak. She was wearing a smart coat in fine quality repp over a long-sleeved frock of figured marocain pleated at the sides and finished at the neck with—'

'Skip all that, Jeeves.'

'I am sorry, sir. I thought you wished every detail, however slight.'

'Only when they're . . . what's the word?'

'Pertinent, sir?'

'That's right. Take the McCorkadale's outer crust as read. How was her speech?'

'Extremely telling, in spite of a good deal of heckling.'

'That wouldn't put her off her stroke.'

'No, sir. She impressed me as being of a singularly forceful character.'

'Me, too.'

'You have met the lady, sir?'

'For a few minutes – which, however, were plenty. She spoke at some length?'

'Yes, sir. If you would care to read her remarks? I took down both speeches in shorthand.'

'Later on, perhaps.'

'At any time that suits you, sir.'

'And how was the applause? Hearty? Or sporadic?'

'On one side of the hall extremely hearty. The rougher element appeared to be composed in almost equal parts of her supporters and those of Mr Winship. They had been seated at opposite sides of the auditorium, no doubt by design. Her supporters cheered, Mr Winship's booed.'

'And when Ginger got up, I suppose her lot booed him?'

'No doubt they would have done so, had it not been for the tone of his address. His appearance was greeted with a certain modicum of hostility, but he had scarcely begun to speak when he was rapturously received.'

'By the opposition?'

'Yes, sir.'

'Strange.'

'Yes, sir.'

'Can you elucidate?'

'Yes, sir. If I might consult my notes for a moment. Ah, yes. Mr Winship's opening words were, "Ladies and gentlemen, I come before you a changed man." A Voice: "That's good news." A second Voice: "Shut up, you bleeder." A third Voice . . .'

'I think we might pass lightly over the Voices, Jeeves.'

'Very good, sir. Mr Winship then said, "I should like to begin with a word to the gentleman in the turtleneck sweater in that seat over there who kept calling my opponent a silly old geezer. If he will kindly step on to this platform. I shall be happy to knock his ugly block off. Mrs McCorkadale is *not* a silly old geezer." A Voice . . . Excuse me, sir, I was forgetting. "Mrs McCorkadale is *not* a silly old geezer," Mr Winship said, "but a lady of the greatest intelligence and grasp of affairs. I admire her intensely. Listening to her this evening has changed my political views completely. She has converted me to hers, and I propose, when the polls are opened, to cast my vote for her. I advise all of you to do the same. Thank you." He then resumed his seat.'

'Good Lord, Jeeves!'

'Yes, sir.'

'He really said that?'

'Yes, sir.'

'No wonder his engagement's off.'

'I must confess it occasioned me no surprise, sir.'

I continued amazed. It seemed incredible that Ginger, whose long suit was muscle rather than brain, should have had the ingenuity and know-how to think up such a scheme for freeing himself from Florence's clutches without forfeiting his standing as a fairly *preux chevalier*. It seemed to reveal him as possessed of snakiness of a high order, and I was just thinking that you never can tell about a fellow's hidden depths, when one of those sudden thoughts of mine came popping to the surface.

'Was this you, Jeeves?'

'Sir?'

'Did you put Ginger up to doing it?'

'It is conceivable that Mr Winship may have been influenced by something I said, sir. He was very much exercised with regard to his matrimonial entanglements and he did me the honour of consulting me. It is quite possible that I may have let fall some careless remark that turned his thoughts in the direction they took.'

'In other words, you told him to go to it?'

'Yes, sir.'

I was silent for a space. I was thinking how jolly it would be if he could dish up something equally effective with regard to me and M. Bassett. The thought also occurred to me that what had happened, while excellent for Ginger, wasn't so good for his backers and supporters and the Conservative cause in general.

I mentioned this.

'Tough on the fellows who betted on him.'

'Into each life some rain must fall, sir.'

'Though possibly a good thing. A warning to them in future to keep their money in the old oak chest and not risk it on wagers. May prove a turning point in their lives. What really saddens one is the thought that Bingley will now clean up. He'll make a packet.'

'He told me this afternoon that he was expecting to do so.'

'You mean you've seen him?'

'He came here at about five o'clock, sir.'

'Stockish, hard and full of rage, I suppose?'

'On the contrary, sir, extremely friendly. He made no allusion to the past. I gave him a cup of tea, and we chatted for perhaps half an hour.'

'Strange.'

'Yes, sir. I wondered if he might not have had an ulterior motive in approaching me.'

'Such as?'

'I must confess I cannot think of one. Unless he entertained some hope of inducing me to part with the club book, but that is hardly likely. Would there be anything further, sir?'

'You want to get back to the stricken parlourmaid?'

'Yes, sir. When you rang, I was about to see what a little weak brandy and water would do.'

I sped him on his errand of mercy and sat down to brood. You might have supposed that the singular behaviour of Bingley would have occupied my thoughts. I mean, when you hear that a chap of his well-established crookedness has been acting oddly, your natural impulse is to say 'Aha!' and wonder what his game is. And perhaps for a minute or two I did ponder on this. But I had so many other things to ponder on that Bingley soon got shoved into the discard. If I remember rightly, it was as I mused on Problem (b), the one about restoring the porringer to L. P. Runkle, and again drew a blank, that my reverie was interrupted by the entrance of the old ancestor.

She was wearing the unmistakable look of an aunt who has just been having the time of her life, and this did not surprise me. Hers since she sold the weekly paper she used to run, the one I did that piece on What The Well-Dressed Man Will Wear for, has been a quiet sort of existence, pleasant enough but lacking in incident and excitement. A really sensational event such as the egg-and-vegetable-throwing get-together she had just been present at must have bucked her up like a week at the seaside.

Her greeting could not have been more cordial. An aunt's love oozed out from every syllable.

'Hullo, you revolting object,' she said. 'So you're back.'

'Just arrived.'

'Too bad you had that jury job. You missed a gripping experience.'

'So Jeeves was telling me.'

'Ginger finally went off his rocker.'

With the inside information which had been placed at my disposal I was able to correct this view.

'It was no rocker that he went off, aged relative. His actions were motivated by the soundest good sense. He wanted to get Florence out of his hair without actually telling her to look elsewhere for a mate.'

'Don't be an ass. He loves her.'

'No longer. He's switched to Magnolia Glendennon.'

'You mean that secretary of his?'

'That identical secretary.'

'How do you know?'

'He told me so himself.'

'Well, I'll be blowed. He finally got fed up with Florence's bossiness, did he?'

'Yes, I think it must have been coming on for some time without him knowing it, subconsciously as Jeeves would say. Meeting Magnolia brought it to the surface.'

'She seems a nice girl.'

'Very nice, according to Ginger.'

'I must congratulate him.'

'You'll have to wait a bit. They've gone up to London.'

'So have Spode and Madeline. And Runkle ought to be leaving soon. It's like one of those great race movements of the Middle Ages I used to read about at school. Well, this is wonderful. Pretty soon it'll be safe for Tom to return to the nest. There's still Florence, of course, but I doubt if she will be staying on. My cup runneth over, young Bertie. I've missed Tom sorely. Home's not home without him messing about the place. Why are you staring at me like a halibut on a fishmonger's slab?'

I had not been aware that I was conveying this resemblance to the fish she mentioned, but my gaze had certainly been on the intent side, for her opening words had stirred me to my depths.

'Did you say,' I – yes, I suppose, vociferated would be the word, 'that Spode and Madeline Bassett had gone to London?'

'Left half an hour ago.'

'Together?'

'Yes, in his car.'

'But Spode told me she had given him the push.'

'She did, but everything's all right again. He's not going to give up his title and stand for Parliament. Getting hit in the eye with that potato changed his plans completely. It made him feel that if that was the sort of thing you have to go through to get elected to the House of Commons, he preferred to play it safe and stick to the House of Lords. And she, of course, assured that there was going to be no funny business and that she would become the Countess of Sidcup all right, withdrew her objections to marrying him. Now you're puffing like Tom when he goes upstairs too fast. Why is this?'

Actually, I had breathed deeply, not puffed, and certainly not like Uncle Tom when he goes upstairs too fast, but I suppose to an aunt there isn't much difference between a deep-breathing nephew and a puffing nephew, and anyway I was in no mood to discuss the point.

'You don't know who it was who threw that potato, do you?' I asked.

'The one that hit Spode? I don't. It sort of came out of the void. Why?'

'Because if I knew who it was, I would send camels bearing apes, ivory and peacocks to his address. He saved me from the fate that is worse than death. I allude to marriage with the Bassett disaster.'

'Was she going to marry you?'

'According to Spode.'

A look almost of awe came into the ancestor's face.

'How right you were,' she said, 'when you told me once that you had faith in your star. I've lost count of the number of times you've been definitely headed for the altar with apparently no hope of evading the firing squad, and every time something has happened which enabled you to wriggle out of it. It's uncanny.'

She would, I think, have gone deeper into the matter, for already she had begun to pay a marked tribute to my guardian angel, who, she said, plainly knew his job from soup to nuts, but at this moment Seppings appeared and asked her if she would have a word with Jeeves, and she went out to have it.

And I had just put my feet up on the chaise longue and was starting to muse ecstatically on the astounding bit of luck which had removed the Bassett menace from my life, when my mood of what the French call *bien être* was given the sleeve across the windpipe by the entrance of L. P. Runkle, the mere sight of whom, circs being what they were, was enough to freeze the blood and make each particular hair stand on end like quills upon the fretful porpentine, as I have heard Jeeves put it.

I wasn't glad to see him, but he seemed glad to see me.

'Oh, there you are,' he said. 'They told me you had skipped. Very sensible of you to come back. It's never any good going on the run, because the police are sure to get you sooner or later, and it makes it all the worse for you if you've done a bolt.'

With cold dignity I said I had had to go up to London on business. He paid no attention to this. He was scrutinizing me rather in the manner of the halibut on the fishmonger's slab to which the ancestor had referred in our recent conversation.

'The odd thing is,' he said, continuing to scan me closely, 'that you haven't a criminal face. It's a silly, fatuous face, but not criminal. You remind me of one of those fellows who do dances with the soubrette in musical comedy.'

Come, come, I said to myself, this is better. Spode had compared me to a member of the ensemble. In the view of L. P. Runkle I was at any rate one of the principals. Moving up in the world.

'Must be a great help to you in your business. Lulls people into a false security. They think there can't be any danger from someone who looks like you, they're off their guard, and *wham*! you've got away with their umbrellas and cameras. No doubt you owe all your successes to this. But you know the old saying about the pitcher going too often to the well. This time you're for it. This time—'

He broke off, not because he had come to an end of his very offensive remarks but because Florence had joined us, and her appearance immediately claimed his attention. She was far from being dapper. It was plain that she had been in the forefront of the late battle, for whereas Ginger had merely had egg in his hair, she was, as it were, festooned in egg. She had evidently been right in the centre of the barrage. In all political meetings of the stormier kind these things are largely a matter of luck. A escapes unscathed, B becomes a human omelette.

A more tactful man than L. P. Runkle would have affected not to notice this, but I don't suppose it ever occurred to him to affect not to notice things.

'Hullo!' he said. 'You've got egg all over you.'

Florence replied rather acidly that she was aware of this.

'Better change your dress.'

'I intend to. Would you mind, Mr Runkle, if I had a word with Mr Wooster alone?'

I think Runkle was on the point of saying 'What about?', but on catching her eye he had prudent second thoughts. He lumbered off, and she proceeded to have the word she had mentioned.

She kept it crisp. None of the 'Er' stuff which was such a feature of Ginger's oratory. Even Demosthenes would have been slower in coming to the nub, though he, of course, would have been handicapped by having to speak in Greek.

'I'm glad I found you, Bertie.'

A civil 'Oh, ah' was all the reply I could think of.

'I have been thinking things over, and I have made up my mind. Harold Winship is a mere lout, and I am having nothing more to do with him. I see now that I made a great mistake when I broke off my engagement to you. You have your faults, but they are easily corrected. I have decided to marry you, and I think we shall be very happy.'

'But not immediately,' said L. P. Runkle, rejoining us. I described him a moment ago as lumbering off, but a man like that never lumbers far if there is a chance of hearing what somebody has to say to somebody else in private. 'He'll first have to do a longish stretch in prison.'

His reappearance had caused Florence to stiffen. She now stiffened further, her aspect similar to that of the old ancestor when about to go into her *grande dame* act.

'Mr Runkle!'

'I'm here.'

'I thought you had gone.'

'I hadn't.'

'How dare you listen to a private conversation!'

'They're the only things worth listening to. I owe much of my large fortune to listening to private conversations.'

'What is this nonsense about prison?'

'Wooster won't find it nonsense. He has sneaked a valuable silver porringer of mine, a thing I paid nine thousand pounds for, and I am expecting a man any minute now who will produce the evidence necessary to convict. It's an open and shut case.'

'Is this true, Bertie?' said Florence with that touch of the prosecuting District Attorney I remembered so vividly, and all I could say was 'Well . . . I . . . er . . . well.'

With a guardian angel like mine working overtime, it was enough. She delivered judgment instantaneously.

'I shall not marry you,' she said, and went off haughtily to de-egg herself.

'Very sensible of her,' said L. P. Runkle. 'The right course to take. A man like you, bound to be in and out of prison, couldn't possibly be a good husband. How is a wife to make her plans . . . dinner parties, holidays, Christmas treats for the children, the hundred and one things a woman has to think of . . . when she doesn't know from one day to another whether the head of the house won't be telephoning to say he's been arrested again and no bail allowed? Yes?' said Runkle, and I saw that Seppings had appeared in the offing.

'A Mr Bingley has called to see you, sir.'

'Ah, yes, I was expecting him.'

He popped off, and scarcely had he ceased to pollute the atmosphere when the old ancestor blew in.

She was plainly agitated, the resemblance to a cat on hot bricks being very marked. She panted a good deal, and her face had taken on the rather pretty mauve colour it always does when the soul is not at rest.

'Bertie,' she boomed, 'when you went away yesterday, did you leave the door of your bedroom unlocked?'

'Of course I didn't.'

'Well, Jeeves says it's open now.'

'It can't be.'

'It is. He thinks Runkle or some minion of his has skeleton-keyed the lock. Don't yell like that, curse you.'

I might have retorted by asking her what she expected me to do when I suddenly saw all, but I was too busy seeing all to be diverted into arguments about my voice production. The awful truth had hit me as squarely between the eyes as if it had been an egg or a turnip hurled by one of the Market Snodsbury electorate.

'Bingley!' I ejaculated.

'And don't sing.'

'I was not singing, I was ejaculating "Bingley!", or vociferating "Bingley!" if you prefer it. You remember Bingley, the fellow who stole the club book, the chap you were going to take by the throat and shake like a rat. Aged relative, we are up against it in no uncertain manner. Bingley is the Runkle minion you alluded to. Jeeves says he dropped in to tea this afternoon. What simpler for him, having had his cuppa, than to nip upstairs and search my room? He used to be Runkle's personal attendant, so Runkle would turn to him naturally when he needed an accomplice. Yes, I don't wonder you're perturbed,' I added, for she had set the welkin ringing with one of those pungent monosyllables so often on her lips in the old Quorn-and-Pytchley days. 'And I'll tell you something else which will remove your last doubts, if you had any. He's just turned up again, and Runkle has gone out to confer with him. What do you suppose they're conferring about? Give you three guesses.'

The Quorn trains its daughters well. So does the Pytchley. She did not swoon, as many an aunt would have done in her place, merely repeated the monosyllable in a slightly lower tone – meditatively as it were, like some aristocrat of the French Revolution on being informed that the tumbril waited.

'This tears it,' she said, the very words such an aristocrat would have used, though speaking of course in French. 'I'll have to confess that I took his foul porringer.'

'No, no, you mustn't do that.'

'What else is there for me to do? I can't let you go to chokey.'

'I don't mind.'

'I do. I may have my faults—'

'No, no.'

'Yes, yes. I am quite aware that there are blemishes in my spiritual make-up which ought to have been corrected at my finishing school, but I draw the line at letting my nephew do a stretch for pinching porringers which I pinched myself. That's final.'

I saw what she meant, of course. *Noblesse oblige*, and all that. And very creditable, too. But I had a powerful argument to put forward, and I lost no time in putting it.

'But wait, old ancestor. There's another aspect of the matter. If it's . . . what's the expression? . . . if it's bruited abroad that I'm merely an as-pure-as-the-driven-snow innocent bystander, my engagement to Florence will be on again.'

'Your what to who?' It should have been 'whom', but I let it go. 'Are you telling me that you and Florence . . .'

'She proposed to me ten minutes ago and I had to accept her because one's either *preux* or one isn't, and then Runkle butted in and pointed out to her the disadvantages of marrying someone who would shortly be sewing mailbags in Wormwood Scrubs, and she broke it off.'

The relative seemed stunned, as if she had come on something abstruse in the *Observer* crossword puzzle.

'What is it about you that fascinates the girls? First Madeline Bassett, now Florence, and dozens of others in the past. You must have a magnetic personality.'

'That would seem to be the explanation,' I agreed. 'Anyway, there it is. One whisper that there isn't a stain on my character, and I haven't a hope. The Bishop will be notified, the assistant clergy and bridesmaids rounded up, the organist will start practising "The Voice That Breathed O'er Eden", and the limp figure you see drooping at the altar rails will be Bertram Wilberforce Wooster. I implore you, old blood relation, to be silent and let the law take its course. If it's a choice between serving a life sentence under Florence and sewing a mailbag or two, give me the mailbags every time.'

She nodded understandingly, and said she saw what I meant.

'I thought you would.'

'There is much in what you say.' She mused awhile. 'As a matter of fact, though, I doubt if it will get as far as mailbags. I'm pretty sure what's going to happen. Runkle will offer to drop the whole thing if I let him have Anatole.'

'Good God!'

'You may well say "Good God!" You know what Anatole means to Tom.'

She did not need to labour the point. Uncle Tom combines a passionate love of food with a singular difficulty in digesting it, and Anatole is the only chef yet discovered who can fill him up to the Plimsoll mark without causing the worst sort of upheaval in his gastric juices.

'But would Anatole go to Runkle?'

'He'd go to anyone if the price was right.'

'None of that faithful old retainer stuff?'

'None. His outlook is entirely practical. That's the French in him.'

'I wonder you've been able to keep him so long. He must have had other offers.'

'I've always topped them. If it was simply another case of outbidding the opposition, I wouldn't be worrying.'

'But when Uncle Tom comes back and finds Anatole conspicuous by his absence, won't the home be a bit in the melting pot?'

'I don't like to think of it.'

But she did think of it. So did I. And we were both thinking of it, when our musings were interrupted by the return of L. P. Runkle, who waddled in and fixed us with a bulging eye.

I suppose if he had been slenderer, one might have described him as a figure of doom, but even though so badly in need of a reducing diet he was near enough to being one to make my interior organs do a quick shuffle-off-to-Buffalo as if some muscular hand had stirred them up with an egg-whisk. And when he began to speak, he was certainly impressive. These fellows who have built up large commercial empires are always what I have heard Jeeves call orotund. They get that way from dominating meetings of shareholders. Having started off with 'Oh, there you are, Mrs Travers', he went into his speech, and it was about as orotund as anything that has ever come my way. It ran, as nearly as I can remember, as follows:

'I was hoping to see you, Mrs Travers. In a previous conversation, you will recall that I stated uncompromisingly that your nephew Mr Wooster had purloined the silver porringer which I brought here to sell to your husband, whose absence I greatly deplore. That this was no mere suspicion has now been fully substantiated. I have a witness who is prepared to testify on oath in court that he found it in the top drawer of the chest of drawers in Mr Wooster's bedroom, unskilfully concealed behind socks and handkerchiefs.'

Here if it had been a shareholders meeting, he would probably have been reminded of an amusing story which may be new to some of you present this afternoon, but I suppose in a private conversation he saw no need for it. He continued, still orotund.

'The moment I report this to the police and acquaint them with the evidence at my disposal, Wooster's arrest will follow automatically, and a sharp sentence will be the inevitable result.'

It was an unpleasant way of putting it, but I was compelled to admit that it covered the facts like a bedspread. Dust off that cell, Wormwood Scrubs, I was saying to myself, I shall soon be with you.

'Such is the position. But I am not a vindictive man, I have no wish, if it can be avoided, to give pain to a hostess who has been to such trouble to make my visit enjoyable.'

He paused for a moment to lick his lips, and I knew he was tasting again those master-dishes of Anatole's. And it was on Anatole that he now touched.

'While staying here as your guest, I have been greatly impressed by the skill and artistry of your chef. I will agree not to press charges against Mr Wooster provided you consent to let this gifted man leave your employment and enter mine.'

A snort rang through the room, one of the ancestor's finest. You might almost have called it orotund. Following it with the word 'Ha!', she turned to me with a spacious wave of the hand.

'Didn't I tell you, Bertie? Wasn't I right? Didn't I say the child of unmarried parents would blackmail me?'

A fellow with the excess weight of L. P. Runkle finds it difficult to stiffen all over when offended, but he stiffened as

far as he could. It was as if some shareholder at the meeting
had said the wrong thing.

'Blackmail?'

'That's what I said.'

'It is not blackmail. It is nothing of the sort.'

'He is quite right, madam,' said Jeeves, appearing from
nowhere. I'll swear he hadn't been there half a second before.
'Blackmail implies the extortion of money. Mr Runkle is merely
extorting a cook.'

'Exactly. A purely business transaction,' said Runkle, obviously
considering him a Daniel come to judgment.

'It would be very different,' said Jeeves, 'were somebody to try
to obtain money from him by threatening to reveal that while in
America he served a prison sentence for bribing a juror in a case
in which he was involved.'

A cry broke from L. P. Runkle's lips, somewhat similar to the
one the cat Gus had uttered when the bag of cat food fell on
him. He tottered and his face would, I think, have turned ashy
white if his blood pressure hadn't been the sort that makes it
pretty tough going for a face to turn ashy white. The best it
could manage was something Florence would have called sallow.

The ancestor, on the other hand, had revived like a floweret
beneath the watering-can. Not that she looks like a floweret,
but you know what I mean.

'What!' she ejaculated.

'Yes, madam, the details are all in the club book. Bingley
recorded them very fully. His views were very far to the left at
the time, and I think he derived considerable satisfaction from
penning an exposé of a gentleman of Mr Runkle's wealth. It is
also with manifest gusto that he relates how Mr Runkle, in
grave danger of a further prison sentence in connection with a
real estate fraud, forfeited the money he had deposited as
security for his appearance in court and disappeared.'

'Jumped his bail, you mean?'

'Precisely, madam. He escaped to Canada in a false beard.'

The ancestor drew a deep breath. Her eyes were glowing
more like twin stars than anything. Had not her dancing days
been long past, I think she might have gone into a brisk
buck-and-wing. The lower limbs twitched just as if she were
planning to.

'Well,' she said, 'a nice bit of news that'll be for the fellows
who dole out knighthoods. "Runkle?" they'll say. "That old lag?

If we made a man like that a knight, we'd never hear the last of it. The boys on the Opposition benches would kid the pants off us." We were discussing, Runkle, yesterday that little matter of the money you ought to have given Tuppy Glossop years ago. If you will step into my boudoir, we will go into it again at our leisure.'

17

The following day dawned bright and clear, at least I suppose it did, but I wasn't awake at the time. When eventually I came to life, the sun was shining, all Nature appeared to be smiling, and Jeeves was bringing in the breakfast tray. Gus the cat, who had been getting his eight hours on an adjacent armchair, stirred, opened an eye and did a sitting high jump on to the bed, eager not to miss anything that was going.

'Good morning, Jeeves.'

'Good morning, sir.'

'Weather looks all right.'

'Extremely clement, sir.'

'The snail's on the wing and the lark's on the thorn, or rather the other way round, as I've sometimes heard you say. Are those kippers I smell?'

'Yes, sir.'

'Detach a portion for Gus, will you. He will probably like to take it from the soap dish, reserving the saucer for milk.'

'Very good, sir.'

I sat up and eased the spine into the pillows. I was conscious of a profound peace.

'Jeeves,' I said, 'I am conscious of a profound peace. I wonder if you remember me telling you a few days ago that I was having a sharp attack of euphoria?'

'Yes, sir. I recall your words clearly. You said you were sitting on top of the world with a rainbow round your shoulder.'

'Similar conditions prevail this morning. I thought everything went off very well last night, didn't you?'

'Yes, sir.'

'Thanks to you.'

'It is very kind of you to say so, sir.'

'I take it the ancestor came to a satisfactory arrangement with Runkle?'

'Most satisfactory, sir. Madam has just informed me that Mr Runkle was entirely cooperative.'

'So Tuppy and Angela will be joined in holy wedlock, as the expression is?'

'Almost immediately, I understood from Madam.'

'And even now Ginger and M. Glendennon are probably in conference with the registrar of their choice.'

'Yes, sir.'

'And Spode has got a black eye, which one hopes is painful. In short, on every side one sees happy endings popping up out of traps. A pity that Bingley is flourishing like a green what-is-it, but one can't have everything.'

'No, sir. *Medio de fonte leporum surgit amari aliquid in ipsis floribus angat.*'

'I don't think I quite followed you there, Jeeves.'

'I was quoting from the Roman poet Lucretius, sir. A rough translation would be "From the heart of this fountain of delights wells up some bitter taste to choke them even among the flowers".'

'Who did you say wrote that?'

'Lucretius, sir, 99–55 B.C.'

'Gloomy sort of bird.'

'His outlook was perhaps somewhat sombre, sir.'

'Still, apart from Bingley, one might describe joy as reigning supreme.'

'A very colourful phrase, sir.'

'Not my own. I read it somewhere. Yes, I think we may say everything's more or less oojah-cum-spiff. With one exception, Jeeves,' I said, a graver note coming into my voice as I gave Gus his second helping of kipper. 'There remains a fly in the ointment, a familiar saying meaning . . . well, I don't quite know what it does mean. It seems to imply a state of affairs at which one is supposed to look askance, but why, I ask myself, shouldn't flies be in ointment? What harm do they do? And who wants ointment, anyway? But you get what I'm driving at. The Junior Ganymede club book is still in existence. That is what tempers my ecstasy with anxiety. We have seen how packed with trinitrotoluol it is, and we know how easily it can fall into the hands of the powers of darkness. Who can say that another Bingley may not come along and snitch it from the secretary's room? I know it is too much to ask you to burn the beastly thing, but couldn't you at least destroy the eighteen pages in which I figure?'

'I have already done so, sir.'

I leaped like a rising trout, to the annoyance of Gus, who had gone to sleep on my solar plexus. Words failed me, but in due season I managed three.

'Much obliged, Jeeves.'

'Not at all, sir.'

AUNTS AREN'T GENTLEMEN

1

My attention was drawn to the spots on my chest when I was in my bath, singing, if I remember rightly, the Toreador song from the opera *Carmen*. They were pink in colour, rather like the first faint flush of dawn, and I viewed them with concern. I am not a fussy man, but I do object to being freckled like a pard, as I once heard Jeeves describe it, a pard, I take it, being something in the order of one of those dogs beginning with d.

'Jeeves,' I said at the breakfast table, 'I've got spots on my chest.'

'Indeed, sir?'

'Pink.'

'Indeed, sir?'

'I don't like them.'

'A very understandable prejudice, sir. Might I enquire if they itch?'

'Sort of.'

'I would not advocate scratching them.'

'I disagree with you. You have to take a firm line with spots. Remember what the poet said.'

'Sir?'

'The poet Ogden Nash. The poem he wrote defending the practice of scratching. Who was Barbara Frietchie, Jeeves?'

'A lady of some prominence in the American war between the States, sir.'

'A woman of strong character? One you could rely on?'

'So I have always understood, sir.'

'Well, here's what the poet Nash wrote. "I'm greatly attached to Barbara Frietchie. I'll bet she scratched when she was itchy." But I shall not be content with scratching. I shall place myself in the hands of a competent doctor.'

'A very prudent decision, sir.'

The trouble was that, except for measles when I was just starting out, I've always been so fit that I didn't know any doctors. Then I remembered that my American pal, Tipton Plimsoll, with whom I had been dining last night to celebrate his betrothal to Veronica, only daughter of Colonel and Lady Hermione Wedge of Blandings Castle, Shropshire, had mentioned one who had once done him a bit of good. I went to the telephone to get his name and address.

Tipton did not answer my ring immediately, and when he did it was to reproach me for waking him at daybreak. But after he had got this off his chest and I had turned the conversation to mine he was most helpful. It was with the information I wanted that I returned to Jeeves.

'I've just been talking to Mr Plimsoll, Jeeves, and everything is straight now. He bids me lose no time in establishing contact with a medico of the name of E. Jimpson Murgatroyd. He says if I want a sunny practitioner who will prod me in the ribs with his stethoscope and tell me an anecdote about two Irishmen named Pat and Mike and then another about two Scotsmen named Mac and Sandy, E. Jimpson is not my man, but if what I'm after is someone to cure my spots, he unquestionably is, as he knows his spots from A to Z and has been treating them since he was so high. It seems that Tipton had the same trouble not long ago and Murgatroyd fixed him up in no time. So while I am getting out of these clothes into something more spectacular will you give him a buzz and make an appointment.'

When I had doffed the sweater and flannels in which I had breakfasted, Jeeves informed me that E. Jimpson could see me at eleven, and I thanked him and asked him to tell the garage to send the car round at ten-forty-five.

'Somewhat earlier than that, sir,' he said, 'if I might make the suggestion. The traffic. Would it not be better to take a cab?'

'No, and I'll tell you why. After I've seen the doc, I thought I might drive down to Brighton and get a spot of sea air. I don't suppose the traffic will be any worse than usual, will it?'

'I fear so, sir. A protest march is taking place this morning.'

'What, again? They seem to have them every hour on the hour these days, don't they?'

'They are certainly not infrequent, sir.'

'Any idea what they're protesting about?'

'I could not say, sir. It might be one thing or it might be another. Men are suspicious, prone to discontent. Subjects still loathe the present Government.'

'The poet Nash?'

'No, sir. The poet Herrick.'

'Pretty bitter.'

'Yes, sir.'

'I wonder what they had done to him to stir him up like that. Probably fined him five quid for failing to abate a smoky chimney.'

'As to that I have no information, sir.'

Seated in the old sports model some minutes later and driving to keep my tryst with E. Jimpson Murgatroyd, I was feeling singularly lighthearted for a man with spots on his chest. It was a beautiful morning, and it wouldn't have taken much to make me sing Tra-la as I bowled along. Then I came abaft of the protest march and found myself becalmed. I leaned back and sat observing the proceedings with a kindly eye.

2

Whatever these bimbos were protesting about, it was obviously something they were taking to heart rather. By the time I had got into their midst not a few of them had decided that animal cries were insufficient to meet the case and were saying it with bottles and brickbats, and the police who were present in considerable numbers seemed not to be liking it much. It must be rotten being a policeman on these occasions. Anyone who has got a bottle can throw it at you, but if you throw it back, the yell of police brutality goes up and there are editorials in the papers next day.

But the mildest cop can stand only so much, and it seemed to me, for I am pretty shrewd in these matters, that in about another shake of a duck's tail hell's foundations would be starting to quiver. I hoped nobody would scratch my paint.

Leading the procession, I saw with surprise, was a girl I knew. In fact, I had once asked her to marry me. Her name was Vanessa Cook, and I had met her at a cocktail party, and such was her radiant beauty that it was only a couple of minutes after I had brought her a martini and one of those little sausages on sticks that I was saying to myself, 'Bertram, this is a good thing. Push it along.' And in due season I suggested a merger. But apparently I was not the type, and no business resulted.

This naturally jarred the Wooster soul a good deal at the moment, but reviewing the dead past now I could see that my guardian angel had been on the job all right and had known what was good for me. I mean, radiant beauty is all very well, but it isn't everything. What sort of a married life would I have had with the little woman perpetually going on protest marches and expecting me to be at her side throwing bottles at the constabulary? It made me shudder to think what I might have let myself in for if I had been a shade more fascinating. Taught me a lesson, that did – viz. never to lose faith in your guardian angel, because these guardian angels are no fools.

Vanessa Cook was accompanied by a beefy bloke without a hat in whom I recognized another old acquaintance, O. J. (Orlo) Porter to wit, who had been on the same staircase with me at Oxford. Except for borrowing an occasional cup of sugar from one another and hulloing when we met on the stairs we had never been really close, he being a prominent figure at the Union, where I was told he made fiery far-to-the-left speeches, while I was more the sort that is content just to exist beautifully.

Nor did we get together in our hours of recreation, for his idea of a good time was to go off with a pair of binoculars and watch birds, a thing that has never appealed to me. I can't see any percentage in it. If I meet a bird, I wave a friendly hand at it, to let it know that I wish it well, but I don't want to crouch behind a bush observing its habits. So, as I say, Orlo Porter was in no sense a buddy of mine, but we had always got on all right and I still saw him every now and then.

Everybody at Oxford had predicted a pretty hot political future for him, but it hadn't got started yet. He was now in the employment of the London and Home Counties Insurance Company and earned the daily b. by talking poor saps – I was one of them – into taking out policies for larger amounts than they would have preferred. Making fiery far-to-the-left speeches naturally fits a man for selling insurance, enabling him to find the *mot juste* and enlarging the vocabulary. I for one had been corn before his sickle, as the expression is.

The bottle-throwing had now reached the height of its fever and I was becoming more than ever nervous about my paint, when all of a sudden there occurred an incident which took my mind off that subject. The door of the car opened and what the papers call a well-nourished body, male, leaped in and took a seat beside me. Gave me a bit of a start, I don't mind admitting, the Woosters not being accustomed to this sort of thing so soon after breakfast. I was about to ask to what I was indebted for the honour of this visit, when I saw that what I had drawn was Orlo Porter and I divined that after the front of the procession had passed from my view he must have said or done something which London's police force could not overlook, making instant flight a must. His whole demeanour was that of the hart that pants for cooling streams when heated in the chase.

Well, you don't get cooling streams in the middle of the metropolis, but there was something I could do to give his morale a shot in the arm. I directed his attention to the Drones Club scarf lying on the seat, at the same time handing him my hat. He put them on, and the rude disguise proved effective. Various rozzers came along, but they were looking for a man without a hat and he was definitely hatted, so they passed us by. Of course, I was bareheaded, but one look at me was enough to tell them that this polished boulevardier could not possibly be the dubious character they were after. And a few minutes later the crowd had melted.

'Drive on, Wooster,' said Orlo. 'Get a move on, blast you.'

He spoke irritably, and I remembered that he had always been an irritable chap, as who would not have been, having to go through life with a name like Orlo and peddling insurance when he had hoped to electrify the House of Commons with his molten eloquence. I took no umbrage, accordingly, if umbrage is the thing you take when people start ordering you about, making allowances for his state of mind. I drove on, and he said 'Phew' and removed a bead of persp. from the brow.

I hardly knew what to do for the best. He was still panting like a hart, and some fellows when panting like harts enjoy telling you all about it, while others prefer a tactful silence. I decided to take a chance.

'Spot of trouble?' I said.

'Yes.'

'Often the way during these protest marches. What happened?'

'I socked a cop.'

I could see why he was a bit emotional. Socking cops is a thing that should be done sparingly, if at all. I resumed the quiz.

'Any particular reason? Or did it just seem a good idea at the time?'

He gnashed a tooth or two. He was a red-headed chap, and my experience of the red-headed is that you can always expect high blood pressure from them in times of stress. The first Queen Elizabeth had red hair, and look what she did to Mary Queen of Scots.

'He was arresting the woman I love.'

I could understand how this might well have annoyed him. I have loved a fair number of women in my time, though it always seems to wear off after a while, and I should probably have drained the bitter cup a bit if I had seen any of them pinched by the police.

'What had she done?'

'She was heading the procession with me and shouting a good deal as always happens on these occasions when the emotions of a generous girl are stirred. He told her to stop shouting. She said this was a free country and she was entitled to shout as much as she pleased. He said not if she was shouting the sort of things she was shouting, and she called him a Cossack and socked him. Then he arrested her, and I socked him.'

A pang of pity for the stricken officer passed through me. Orlo, as I have said, was well nourished, and Vanessa was one of those large girls who pack a hefty punch. A cop socked by both of them would have entertained no doubt as to his having been in a fight.

But this was not what was occupying my thoughts. At the words 'she was heading the procession with me' I had started visibly. It seemed to me that, coupled with that 'woman I love' stuff, they could mean only one thing.

'Good Lord,' I said. 'Is Vanessa Cook the woman you love?'

'She is.'

'Nice girl,' I said, for there is never any harm in giving the old salve. 'And, of course, radiant-beauty-wise in the top ten.'

A moment later I was regretting that I had pitched it so strong, for the effect on Orlo was most unpleasant. His eyes bulged, at the same time flashing, as if he were on the verge of making a fiery far-to-the-left speech.

'You know her?' he said, and his voice was low and guttural, like that of a bull-dog which has attempted to swallow a chump chop and only got it down half-way.

I saw that I would do well to watch my step, for it was evident that what I have heard Jeeves call the green-eyed monster that doth mock the meat it feeds on was beginning to feel the rush of life beneath its keel. You never know what may happen when the g.-e.m. takes over.

'Slightly,' I said. 'Very slightly. We just met for a moment at some cocktail party or other.'

'That was all?'

'That was all.'

'You were not – how shall I put it? – in any sense intimate?'

'No, no. Simply on Good-morning-good-morning-lovely-morning-is-it-not terms if I happened to run into her in the street.'

'Nothing more?'

'Nothing more.'

I had said the right thing. He went off the boil, and when he next spoke, it was without bull-dog and chump chop effects.

'You call her a nice girl. That puts in a nutshell my own opinion of her.'

'And she, I imagine, thinks highly of you?'

'Correct.'

'You're engaged, possibly?'

'Yes.'

'Many happy returns.'

'But we can't get married because of her father.'

'He objects?'

'Strongly.'

'But surely you don't have to have Father's consent in these enlightened days?'

A look of pain came into his face and he writhed like an electric fan. It was plain that my words had touched a sore s.

'You do if he is trustee for your money and you don't make enough at your job to marry on. My Uncle Joe left me enough to get married to twenty girls. He was Vanessa's father's partner in one of those big provision businesses. But I can't touch it because he made old Cook my trustee, and Cook refuses to part.'

'Why?'

'He disapproves of my political views. He says he has no intention of encouraging any damned Communists.'

I think at this juncture I may have looked askance at him a bit. I hadn't realized that that was what he was, and it rather shocked me, because I'm not any too keen on Communists. However, he was my guest, so to speak, so I merely said that that must have been unpleasant, and he said Yes, very unpleasant, adding that only Cook's grey hairs had saved him from getting plugged in the eye, which shows that it's not such a bad thing to let your hair go grey.

'And in addition to disliking my political views he considers that I have led Vanessa astray. He has heard about her going on these protest marches, and he considers me responsible. But for me, he says, she would never have done such a thing, and that if she ever made herself conspicuous and got her name in the papers, she would come straight home and stay there. He has a big house in the country with a stable of racehorses, as he can well afford to after his years of grinding the faces of the widow and the orphan.'

I could have corrected him here, pointing out that you don't grind people's faces by selling them pressed beef and potato chips at a lower price than they would be charged elsewhere, but, as I say, he was my guest, so I refrained. I was conscious of a passing thought that Vanessa Cook would not be remaining long in London now that she had developed this habit of socking policemen, but I did not share this with Orlo Porter, not wishing to rub salt into the wound.

'But let's not talk about it any more,' he said, closing the subject with a bang. 'You can drop me anywhere round here. Thanks for the ride.'

'Don't mention it.'

'Where are you going?'

'Harley Street, to see a doctor. I've got spots on my chest.'

The effect of this disclosure was rather remarkable. A keen go-getter look came into his face, and I could see that Orlo Porter the lover had been put in storage for the time being, his place taken by Orlo Porter the zealous employee of the London and Home Counties Insurance Company.

'Spots?' he said.

'Pink,' I said.

'Pink spots,' he said. 'That's serious. You'd better take out a policy with me.'

I reminded him that I had already done so. He shook his head.

'Yes, yes, yes, but that was only for accidents. What you must have now is a life policy, and most fortunately,' he said, drawing papers from his pocket like a conjuror taking rabbits from a hat, 'I happen to have one on me. Sign here, Wooster,' he said, this time producing a fountain pen.

And such was his magnetism that I signed there.

He registered approval.

'You have done the wise thing, Wooster. Whatever the doctor may tell you when you see him, however brief your span of life, it will be a comfort to you to know that your widow and the little ones are provided for. Drop me here, Wooster.'

I dropped him, and drove on to Harley Street.

3

In spite of being held up by the protest march I was a bit early for my appointment, and was informed on arrival that the medicine man was tied up for the moment with another gentleman. I took a seat and was flitting idly through the pages of an *Illustrated London News* of the previous December when the door of E. Jimpson Murgatroyd's private lair opened and there emerged an elderly character with one of those square, empire-building faces, much tanned as if he was accustomed to sitting out in the sun without his parasol. Seeing me, he drank me in for a while and then said 'Hullo', and conceive my emotion when I recognized him as Major Plank the explorer and Rugby football aficionado, whom I had last seen at his house in Gloucestershire when he was accusing me of trying to get five quid out of him under false pretences. A groundless charge, I need scarcely say, self being as pure as the driven snow, if not purer, but things had got a bit difficult and the betting was that they would become difficult now. I sat waiting for him to denounce me and was wondering what the harvest would be, when he spoke, to my astonishment, in the most bonhomous way, as if we were old buddies.

'We've met before. I never forget a face. Isn't your name Allen or Allenby or Alexander or something?'

'Wooster,' I said, relieved to the core. I had been anticipating a painful scene.

He clicked his tongue.

'I could have sworn it was something beginning with Al. It's this malaria of mine. Picked it up in Equatorial Africa, and it affects my memory. So you've changed your name, have you? Secret enemies after you?'

'No, no secret enemies.'

'That's generally why one changes one's name. I had to change mine that time I shot the chief of the 'Mgombis. In self-defence, of course, but that made no difference to his

widows and surviving relatives who were looking for me. If they
had caught me, they would have roasted me alive over a slow
fire, which is a thing one always wants to avoid. But I baffled
them. Plank was the man they were trying to contact, and it
never occurred to them that somebody called George Bernard
Shaw could be the chap they were after. They are not very
bright in those parts. Well, Wooster, how have you been since
we last met? Pretty bobbish?'

'Oh, fine, thanks, except that I've got spots on my chest.'

'Spots? That's bad. How many?'

I said I had not actually taken a census, but there were quite
a few, and he shook his head gravely.

'Might be bubonic plague or possibly sprue or schistosomiasis.
One of my native bearers got spots on his chest, and we buried
him before sundown. Had to. Delicate fellows, these native
bearers, though you wouldn't think so to look at them. Catch
everything that's going around – sprue, bubonic plague, schistosomiasis, jungle fever, colds in the head – the lot. Well,
Wooster, it's been nice seeing you again. I would ask you to
lunch, but I have a train to catch. I'm off to the country.'

He left me, as you may imagine, in something of a twitter.
Bertram Wooster, as is well known, is intrepid and it takes a
lot to scare the pants off him. But his talk of native bearers
who had to be buried before sundown had caused me not a
little anxiety. Nor did the first sight of E. Jimpson Murgatroyd
do anything to put me at my ease. Tipton had warned me that
he was a gloomy old buster, and a gloomy old buster was what
he proved to be. He had sad, brooding eyes and long whiskers,
and his resemblance to a frog which had been looking on the
dark side since it was a slip of a tadpole sent my spirits right
down into the basement.

However, as so often happens when you get to know a fellow
better, he turned out to be not nearly as pessimistic a Gawd-
help-us as he appeared to be at first sight. By the time he had
weighed me and tied that rubber thing round my biceps and
felt my pulse and tapped me all over like a whiskered wood-
pecker he had quite brightened up and words of good cheer
were pouring out of him like ginger beer from a bottle.

'I don't think you have much to worry about,' he said.

'You don't?' I said, considerably bucked up. 'Then it isn't
sprue or schistosomiasis?'

'Of course it is not. What gave you the idea it might be?'

'Major Plank said it might. The chap who was in here before me.'

'You shouldn't listen to people, especially Plank. We were at school together. Barmy Plank we used to call him. No, the spots are of no importance. They will disappear in a few days.'

'Well, that's a relief,' I said, and he said he was glad I was pleased.

'But,' he added.

This chipped a bit off my *joie de vivre*.

'But what?'

He was looking like a minor prophet about to rebuke the sins of the people – it was the whiskers that did it mostly, though the eyebrows helped. I forgot to mention that he had bushy eyebrows – and I could see that this was where I got the bad news.

'Mr Wooster,' he said, 'you are a typical young man about town.'

'Oh, thanks,' I responded, for it sounded like a compliment, and one always likes to say the civil thing.

'And like all young men of your type you pay no attention to your health. You drink too much.'

'Only at times of special revelry. Last night, for instance, I was helping a pal to celebrate the happy conclusion of love's young dream, and it may be that I became a mite polluted, but that rarely happens. One Martini Wooster, some people call me.'

He paid no attention to my frank manly statement, but carried on regardless.

'You smoke too much. You stay up too late at night. You don't get enough exercise. At your age you ought to be playing Rugby football for the old boys of your school.'

'I didn't go to a Rugger school.'

'Where did you go?'

'Eton.'

'Oh,' he said, and he said it as if he didn't think much of Eton. 'Well, there you are. You do all the things I have said. You abuse your health in a hundred ways. Total collapse may come at any moment.'

'At any moment?' I quavered.

'At any moment. Unless—'

'Unless?' Now, I felt, he was talking.

'Unless you give up this unwholesome London life. Go to

the country. Breathe pure air. Go to bed early. And get plenty of exercise. If you do not do this, I cannot answer for the consequences.'

He had shaken me. When a doctor, even if whiskered, tells you he cannot answer for the consequences, that's strong stuff. But I was not dismayed, because I had spotted a way of following his advice without anguish. Bertram Wooster is like that. He thinks on his feet.

'Would it be all right,' I asked, 'if I went to stay with my aunt in Worcestershire?'

He weighed the question, scratching his nose with his stethoscope. He had been doing this at intervals during our get-together, being evidently one of the scratchers, like Barbara Frietchie. The poet Nash would have taken to him.

'I see no objection to your staying with your aunt, provided the conditions are right. Whereabouts in Worcestershire does she live?'

'Near a town called Market Snodsbury.'

'Is the air pure there?'

'Excursion trains are run for people to breathe it.'

'Your life would be quiet?'

'Practically unconscious.'

'No late hours?'

'None. The early dinner, the restful spell with a good book or the crossword puzzle and so to bed.'

'Then by all means do as you suggest.'

'Splendid. I'll ring her up right away.'

The aunt to whom I alluded was my good and deserving Aunt Dahlia, not to be confused with my Aunt Agatha who eats broken bottles and is strongly suspected of turning into a werewolf at the time of the full moon. Aunt Dahlia is as good a sort as ever said 'Tally Ho' to a fox, which she frequently did in her younger days when out with the Quorn or Pytchley. If she ever turned into a werewolf, it would be one of those jolly breezy werewolves whom it is a pleasure to know.

It was very satisfactory that he had given me the green light without probing further, for an extended quiz might have revealed that Aunt Dahlia has a French cook who defies competition, and I need scarcely explain that the first thing a doctor does when you tell him you are going to a house where there's a French cook is to put you on a diet.

'Then that's that,' I said, all buck and joviality. 'Many thanks for your sympathetic cooperation. Lovely weather we are having, are we not? Good morning, good morning, good morning.'

And I slipped him a purse of gold and went off to phone Aunt Dahlia. I had given up all idea of driving to Brighton for lunch. I had stern work before me – viz. cadging an invitation from this aunt, sometimes a tricky task. In her darker moods, when some domestic upheaval is troubling her, she has been known to ask me if I have a home of my own and, if I have, why the hell I don't stay in it.

I got her after the delays inseparable from telephoning a remote hamlet like Market Snodsbury, where the operators are recruited exclusively from the Worcestershire branch of the Jukes family.

'Hullo, aged relative,' I began, as suavely as I could manage.

'Hullo to you, you young blot on Western civilization,' she responded in the ringing tones with which she had once rebuked hounds for taking time off to chase rabbits. 'What's on your mind, if any? Talk quick, because I'm packing.'

I didn't like the sound of this.

'Packing?' I said. 'Are you going somewhere?'

'Yes, to Somerset, to stay with friends of mine, the Briscoes.'

'Oh, curses.'

'Why?'

'I was hoping I might come to you for a short visit.'

'Well, sucks to you, young Bertie, you can't. Unless you'd like to rally round and keep Tom company.'

I h'm-ed at this. I am very fond of Uncle Tom, but the idea of being cooped up alone with him in his cabin didn't appeal to me. He collects old silver and is apt to hold you with a glittering eye and talk your head off about sconces and foliations and gadroon borders, and my interest in these is what you might call tepid. 'No,' I said. 'Thanks for the kind invitation, but I think I'll take a cottage somewhere.'

Her next words showed that she had failed to grasp the gist.

'What is all this?' she queried. 'I don't get it. Why have you got to go anywhere? Are you on the run from the police?'

'Doctor's orders.'

'What are you talking about? You've always been as fit as ten fiddles.'

'Until this morning, when spots appeared on my chest.'

'Spots?'

'Pink.'

'Probably leprosy.'

'The doc thinks not. His view is that they are caused by my being a typical young man about town who doesn't go to bed early enough. He says I must leg it to the country and breathe pure air, so I shall need a cottage.'

'With honeysuckle climbing over the door and old Mister Moon peeping in through the window?'

'That sort of thing. Any idea how one sets about getting a cottage of that description?'

'I'll find you one. Jimmy Briscoe has dozens. And Maiden Eggesford, where he lives, is not far from the popular seaside resort of Bridmouth-on-Sea, notorious for its invigorating air. Corpses at Bridmouth-on-Sea leap from their biers and dance round the maypole.'

'Sounds good.'

'I'll drop you a line when I've got the cottage. You'll like Maiden Eggesford. Jimmy has a racing stable, and there's a big meeting coming on soon at Bridmouth; so you'll have not only pure air but entertainment. One of Jimmy's horses is running, and most of the wise money is on it, though there is a school of thought that maintains that danger is to be expected from a horse belonging to a Mr Cook. And now for heaven's sake get off the wire. I'm busy.'

So far, I said to myself as I put back the receiver, so g. I would have preferred, of course, to be going to the aged relative's home, where Anatole her superb chef dished up his mouth-waterers, but we Woosters can rough it, and life in a country cottage with the aged r just around the corner would be a very different thing from a country c without her to come through with conversation calculated to instruct, elevate and amuse.

All that remained now was to break the news to Jeeves, and I rather shrank from the prospect.

You see, we had practically settled on a visit to New York, and I knew he was looking forward to it. I don't know what he does in New York, but whatever it is it's something he gets a big kick out of, and disappointment, I feared, would be inevitable.

'Jeeves,' I said when I had returned to the Wooster G.H.Q., 'I'm afraid I have bad news.'

'Indeed, sir? I am sorry to hear that.'

One of his eyebrows had risen about an eighth of an inch, and I knew he was deeply stirred, because I had rarely seen him raise an eyebrow more than a sixteenth of an inch. He had, of course, leaped to the conclusion that I was about to tell him that the medicine man had given me three months to live, or possibly two. 'Mr Murgatroyd's diagnosis was not encouraging?'

I hastened to relieve his apprehensions.

'Yes, as a matter of fact it was. Most encouraging. He said the spots *qua* spots . . . Is it *qua*?'

'Perfectly correct, sir.'

'His verdict was that the spots *qua* spots didn't amount to a row of beans and could be disregarded. They will pass by me like the idle wind which I respect not.'

'Extremely gratifying, sir.'

'Extremely, as you say. But pause before you go out and dance in the streets, because there's more to come. It was to this that I was alluding when I said I had bad news. I've got to withdraw to the country and lead a quiet life. He says if I don't, he cannot answer for the consequences. So I'm afraid New York is off.'

It must have been a severe blow, but he bore it with the easy nonchalance of a Red Indian at the stake. Not a cry escaped him, merely an 'Indeed, sir?', and I tried to point out the bright side.

'It's a disappointment for you, but it's probably an excellent thing. Everybody in New York is getting mugged these days or shot by youths, and being mugged and shot by youths doesn't do a fellow any good. We shall avoid all that sort of thing at Maiden Eggesford.'

'Sir?'

'Down in Somerset. Aunt Dahlia is visiting friends there and is going to get me a cottage. It's near Bridmouth-on-Sea. Have you ever been to Bridmouth?'

'Frequently, sir, in my boyhood, and I know Maiden Eggesford well. An aunt of mine lives there.'

'And an aunt of mine is going there. What a coincidence.'

I spoke blithely, for this obviously made everything hotsy-totsy. He had probably been looking on beetling off to the country as going into the wilderness, and the ecstasy of finding that the first thing he would set eyes on would be a loved aunt must have been terrific.

So that was that. And having got the bad news broken, I felt at liberty to turn the conversation to other topics, and I thought he would be interested in hearing about my encounter with Plank.

'I got a shock at the doc's, Jeeves.'

'Indeed, sir?'

'Do you remember Major Plank?'

'The name seems vaguely familiar, sir, but only vaguely.'

'Throw the mind back. The explorer bloke who accused me of trying to chisel him out of five quid and was going to call the police, and you came along and said you were Inspector Witherspoon of Scotland Yard and that I was a notorious crook whom you had been after for ages, and I was known as Alpine Joe because I always wore an Alpine hat. And you took me away.'

'Ah, yes, sir, I remember now.'

'I ran into him this morning. He remembered my face, but nothing more except that he said he knew my name began with Al.'

'A most unnerving experience, sir.'

'Yes, it rattled me more than somewhat. It's a great relief to think that I shall never see him again.'

'I can readily understand your feelings, sir.'

In due course Aunt Dahlia rang to say that she had got a cottage for me and to let her know what day I would be arriving.

And so began what I suppose my biographers will refer to as The Maiden Eggesford Horror – or possibly The Curious Case Of The Cat Which Kept Popping Up When Least Expected.

4

I left for Maiden Eggesford a couple of days later in the old two-seater. Jeeves had gone on ahead with the luggage and would be there to greet me on my arrival, no doubt all braced and refreshed from communing with his aunt.

It was in jocund mood that I set forth. There were rather more astigmatic loonies sharing the road with me than I could have wished, but that did nothing to diminish my euphoria, as I have heard it called. The weather couldn't have been better, blue skies and sunshine all over the place, and to put the frosting on the cake E. Jimpson Murgatroyd had been one hundred per cent right about the spots. They had completely disappeared, leaving not a wrack behind, and the skin on my chest was back to its normal alabaster.

I reached journey's end at about the hour of the evening cocktail and got my first glimpse of the rural haven which was to be the Wooster home for I didn't know how long.

Well, I had had a sort of idea that there would be what they call subtle but well-marked differences between Maiden Eggesford and such resorts as Paris and Monte Carlo, and a glance told me I had not erred. It was one of those villages where there isn't much to do except walk down the main street and look at the Jubilee watering-trough and then walk up the main street and look at the Jubilee watering-trough from the other side. E. Jimpson Murgatroyd would have been all for it. 'Oh, boy,' I could hear him saying, 'this is the stuff to give the typical young man about town.' The air, as far as I could tell from the first few puffs, seemed about as pure as could be expected, and I looked forward to a healthy and invigorating stay.

The only thing wrong with the place was that it appeared to be haunted, for as I alighted from the car I distinctly saw the phantasm or wraith of Major Plank. It was coming out of the local inn, the Goose and Grasshopper, and as I gazed at it with bulging eyes it vanished round a corner, leaving me, I need scarcely say, in something of a twitter. I am not, as I mentioned earlier, a fussy man, but nobody likes to have spectres horsing around, and for a while my jocund mood became a bit blue about the edges.

I speedily pulled myself together. 'Twas but a momentary illusion, I said to myself. I reasoned the thing out. If Plank had come to a sticky end since I had seen him last and had started on a haunting career, I said to myself, why should he be haunting Maiden Eggesford when the whole of equatorial Africa was open to him? He would be much happier scaring the daylights out of natives whom he had cause to dislike – the widows and surviving relatives of the late chief of the 'Mgombis, for instance.

Fortified by these reflections, I went into the cottage.

A glance told me it was all right. I think it must have been built for an artist or somebody like that, for it had all the modern cons including electric light and the telephone, being in fact more a desirable bijou residence than a cottage.

Jeeves was there, and he brought me a much-needed refresher – in deference to E. Jimpson Murgatroyd a dry ginger ale. Sipping it, I decided to confide in him, for in spite of the clarity with which I had reasoned with myself I was still not altogether convinced that what I had seen had not been a phantom. True, it had looked solid enough, but I believe the best ghosts often do.

'Most extraordinary thing, Jeeves,' I said, 'I could have sworn I saw Major Plank coming out of the pub just now.'

'No doubt you did, sir. Major Plank would be quite likely to come to the village. He is the guest of Mr Cook of Eggesford Court.'

You could have knocked me down with a cheese straw.

'You mean he's *here*?'

'Yes, sir.'

I was astounded. When he had told me he was off to the country, I had naturally assumed that he meant he was returning to his home in Gloucestershire. Not, of course, that there's any reason why someone who lives in Gloucestershire shouldn't visit Somerset. Aunt Dahlia lives in Worcestershire, and she was visiting Somerset. You have to look at these things from every angle.

Nevertheless, I was perturbed.

'I'm not sure I like this, Jeeves.'

'No, sir?'

'He may remember what our last meeting was all about.'

'It should not be difficult to avoid him, sir.'

'Something in that. Still, what you say has given me a shock. Plank is the last person I want in my neighbourhood. I think, as my nervous system has rather taken the knock, we might discard this ginger ale and substitute for it a dry Martini.'

'Very good, sir.'

'Murgatroyd will never know.'

'Precisely, sir.'

And so, having breathed considerable quantities of pure air and taken a couple of refreshing looks at the Jubilee watering-trough, to bed early, as recommended by E. Jimpson Murgatroyd.

The result of this following of doctor's orders was sensational. Say what you might about his whiskers and his habit of looking as if he had been attending the funeral of a dear friend, E. Jimpson knew his job. After about ten hours of restful sleep I sprang from between the sheets, leaped to the bathroom, dressed with a song on my lips and headed for the breakfast table like a two-year-old. I had cleaned up the eggs and b., and got the toast and marmalade down the hatch to the last crumb with all the enthusiasm of a tiger of the jungle tucking into its ration of coolie, and was smoking a soothing cigarette, when the telephone rang and Aunt Dahlia's voice came booming over the wire.

'Hullo, old ancestor,' I said, and it was a treat to hear me, so full of ginger and loving-kindness was my diction. 'A very hearty good morning to you, aged relative.'

'You've got here, have you?'

'In person.'

'So you're still alive. The spots didn't turn out to be fatal.'

'They've entirely disappeared,' I assured her. 'Gone with the wind.'

'That's good. I wouldn't have liked introducing a piebald nephew to the Briscoes, and they want you to come to lunch today.'

'Vastly civil of them.'

'Have you a clean collar?'

'Several, with immaculate shirts attached.'

'Don't wear that Drones Club tie.'

'Certainly not,' I agreed. If the Drones Club tie has a fault, it is a little on the loud side and should not be sprung suddenly on nervous people and invalids, and I had no means of knowing if Mrs Briscoe was one of these. 'What time is the binge?'

'One-thirty.'

'Expect me then with my hair in a braid.'

The invitation showed a neighbourly spirit which I applauded, and I said as much to Jeeves.

'They sound good eggs, these Briscoes.'

'I believe they give uniform satisfaction, sir.'

'Aunt Dahlia didn't say where they lived.'

'At Eggesford Hall, sir.'

'How does one get there?'

'One proceeds up the main street of the village to the high road, where one turns to the left. You cannot miss the house. It is large and stands in extensive grounds. It is a walk of about a mile and a half, if you were intending to walk.'

'I think I'd better. Murgatroyd would advise it. You, I take it, in my absence will go and hobnob with your aunt. Have you seen her yet?'

'No, sir. I learn from the lady behind the bar of the Goose and Grasshopper, where I looked in on the night of my arrival, that she has gone to Liverpool for her annual holiday.'

Liverpool, egad! Sometimes one feels that aunts live for pleasure alone.

I made an early start. If these Briscoes were courting my society, I wanted to give them as much of it as possible.

Reaching the high road, where Jeeves had told me to turn to the left, I thought I had better make sure. He had spoken confidently, but it is always well to get a second opinion. And by jove I found that he had goofed. I accosted a passing centenarian – everybody in Maiden Eggesford seemed to be about a hundred and fifty, no doubt owing to the pure air – and asked which way I turned for Eggesford Court, and he said to the right. It just showed how even Jeeves can be mistaken.

On one point, however, he had been correct. A large house, he had said, standing in extensive grounds, and I had been walking what must have been a mile and a half when I came in sight of just such a residence, standing in grounds such as he had described. There were gates opening on a long drive, and I was starting to walk up this, when it occurred to me that I could save time by cutting across country, because the house I could see through the trees was a good deal to the nor'-nor'-east. They make these drives winding so as to impress visitors.

Bless my soul, the visitor says, this drive must be three-quarters of a mile long; shows how rich the chap is.

Whether I was singing or not I can't remember – more probably whistling – but be that as it may I made good progress, and I had just come abreast of what looked like stables when there appeared from nowhere a cat.

It was a cat of rather individual appearance, being black in its general colour scheme but with splashes of white about the ribs and also on the tip of its nose. I chirruped and twiddled my fingers, as is my custom on these occasions, and it advanced with its tail up and rubbed its nose against my leg in a manner that indicated clearly that in Bertram Wooster it was convinced that it had found a kindred soul and one of the boys.

Nor had its intuition led it astray. One of the first poems I ever learned – I don't know who wrote it, probably Shakespeare – ran:

> I love little pussy; her coat is so warm;
> And if I don't hurt her, she'll do me no harm;

and that is how I have been all my life. Ask any cat with whom I have had dealings what sort of a chap I am cat-wise, and it will tell you that I am a thoroughly good egg in whom complete confidence can safely be placed. Cats who know me well, like Aunt Dahlia's Augustus, will probably allude to my skill at scratching them behind the ear.

I scratched this one behind the ear, and it received the attention with obvious gratification, purring like the rumble of distant thunder. Cordial relations having now been established, I was proceeding to what you might call Phase Two – viz. picking it up in my arms in order to tickle its stomach – when the welkin was split by a stentorian 'Hi'.

There are many ways of saying 'Hi'. In America it is a pleasant form of greeting, often employed as a substitute for 'Good morning'. Two friends meet. One of them says 'Hi, Bill.' The other replies 'Hi, George.' Then Bill says 'Is this hot enough for you?', and George says that what he minds is not the heat but the humidity, and they go on their way.

But this 'Hi' was something very different. I believe the sort of untamed savages Major Plank mixes with do not go into battle shouting 'Hi', but if they did the sound would be just like the uncouth roar which had nearly shattered my ear drums.

Turning, I perceived a red-faced little half-portion brandishing a hunting crop I didn't much like the look of. I have never been fond of hunting crops since at an early age I was chased for a mile across difficult country by an uncle armed with one, who had found me smoking one of his cigars. In frosty weather I can still feel the old wounds.

But now I wasn't really perturbed. This, I took it, was the Colonel Briscoe who had asked me to lunch, and though at the moment he had the air of one who would be glad to dissect me with a blunt knife, better conditions would be bound to prevail as soon as I mentioned my name. I mean, you don't ask a fellow to lunch and start assaulting and battering him as soon as he clocks in.

I mentioned it, accordingly, rather surprised by his size, for I had thought they made colonels somewhat larger. Still, I suppose they come in all sizes, like potatoes or, for the matter of that, girls. Vanessa Cook, for instance, was definitely on the substantial side, whereas others who had turned me down from time to time were practically midgets.

'Wooster, Bertram,' I said, tapping my chest.

I had anticipated an instant cooling of the baser passions, possibly a joyful cry and a 'How are you, my dear fellow, how are you?' accompanied by a sunny smile of welcome, but nothing of the sort occurred. He continued to effervesce, his face now a rather pretty purple.

'What are you doing with that cat?' he demanded hoarsely.

I preserved a dignified calm. I didn't like his tone, but then one often doesn't like people's tones.

'Merely passing the time of day,' I replied with a suavity that became me well.

'You were making away with it.'

'Making a what?'

'Stealing it.'

I drew myself up to my full height, and I shouldn't be surprised if my eyes didn't flash. I have been accused of a good many things in my time, notably by my Aunt Agatha, but never of stealing cats, and the charge gave deep offence to the Wooster pride. Heated words were on the tip of my tongue, but I kept them in status quo, as the expression is. After all, the man was my host.

With an effort to soothe, I said:

'You wrong me, Colonel. I wouldn't dream such a thing.'

'Yes you would, yes you would, yes you would. And don't call me Colonel.'

It was hardly an encouraging start, but I tried again.

'Nice day.'

'Damn the day.'

'Crops coming on nicely?'

'Curse the crops.'

'How's my aunt?'

'How the devil should I know how your aunt is?'

I thought this odd. When you've got an aunt staying with you, you ought to be able to supply enquirers with a bulletin, if only a sketchy one, of her state of health. I began to wonder if the little shrimp I was chatting with wasn't a bit fuzzy in the upper storey. Certainly, as far as the conversation had gone at present, he would have aroused the professional interest of any qualified brain specialist.

But I didn't give up. We Woosters don't. I tried another tack altogether.

'It was awfully kind of you to ask me to lunch,' I said.

I don't say he actually frothed at the mouth. There was no question, however, that my words had displeased him:

'Ask you to lunch? Ask you to *lunch*? I wouldn't ask you to lunch—'

I think he was about to add 'with a ten-foot pole', but at this moment from off-stage there came the sound of a robust tenor voice singing what sounded like the song hit from some equatorial African musical comedy, and the next moment Major Plank appeared, and the scales fell from my eyes. Plank being on the premises meant that this wasn't the Briscoe residence by a damn sight. By losing faith in Jeeves and turning to the right on reaching the high road, instead of to the left as he had told me to, I had come to the wrong house. For an instant I felt like blaming the centenarian, but we Woosters are fairminded and I remembered that I had asked him the way to Eggesford Court, which this joint presumably was, and if you say Court when you mean Hall, there's bound to be confusion.

'Good Lord,' I said, suffused with embarrassment, 'aren't you Colonel Briscoe?'

He didn't deign to answer that one, and Plank started talking.

'Why, hullo, Wooster,' he said. 'Who would ever have thought of seeing you here? I didn't know you knew Cook.'

'Do *you* know him?' said the purple chap, evidently stunned by the idea that I could have a respectable acquaintance.

'Of course I know him. Met him at my place in Gloucestershire, though under what circumstances I've forgotten. It'll come back, but at the moment all I know is that he has changed his name. It used to be something beginning with Al, and now it's Wooster. I suppose the original name was something ghastly which he couldn't stand any longer. I knew a man at the United Explorers who changed his name from Buggins to Westmacote-Trevelyan. I thought it very sensible of him, but it didn't do him much good, poor chap, because he had scarcely got used to signing his I.O.U.s Gilbert Westmacote-Trevelyan when he was torn asunder by a lion. Still, that's the way it goes. How did you come out with the doctor, Wooster? Was it bubonic plague?'

I said No, not bubonic plague, and he said he was glad to hear it, because bubonic plague was no joke, ask anyone.

'You staying in these parts?'

'No, I have a cottage in the village.'

'Pity. You could have come here. Been company for Vanessa. But you'll join us at lunch?' said Plank, who seemed to think that a guest is entitled to issue invitations to his host's house, which any good etiquette book would have told him is not the case.

'I'm sorry,' I said. 'I'm lunching at Eggesford Hall with the Briscoes.'

This caused Cook, who had been silent for some time, probably having trouble with his vocal cords, to snort visibly.

'I knew it! I was right! I knew you were Briscoe's hireling!'

'What are you talking about, Cook?' asked Plank, not abreast.

'Never mind what I'm talking about. I know what I'm talking about. This man is in the pay of Briscoe, and he came here to steal my cat.'

'Why would he steal your cat?'

'You know why he would steal my cat. You know as well as I do that Briscoe stops at nothing. Look at this man. Look at his face. Guilt written all over it. I caught him with the cat in his arms. Hold him there, Plank, while I go and telephone the police.'

And so saying he legged it.

I confess to being a little uneasy when I heard him tell Plank to hold me, because I had had experience of Plank's methods of holding people. I believe I mentioned earlier that at our previous meeting he had proposed to detain me with the assistance of his Zulu knob-kerrie, and he had in his grasp now a stout stick, which, if it wasn't a Zulu knob-kerrie, was unquestionably the next best thing.

Fortunately he was in a friendly mood.

'You mustn't mind Cook, Wooster. He's upset. He's been having a spot of domestic trouble. That's why he asked me to come and stay. He thought I might have advice to offer. He allowed his daughter Vanessa to go to London to study Art at the Slade, if that's the name of the place, and she got in with the wrong crowd, got pinched by the police and so on and so forth, upon which Cook did the heavy father and jerked her home and told her she had got to stay there till she learned a bit of sense. She doesn't like it, poor girl, but I tell her she's lucky not to be in equatorial Africa, because there if a daughter blots her copybook, her father chops her head off and buries her in the back garden. Well, I hate to see you go, Wooster, but I think you had better be off. I don't say Cook will be back with a shot-gun, but you never know. I'd leave, if I were you.'

His advice struck me as good. I took it.

I headed for the cottage, where I had left the car. By the time I got there I should have done three miles of foot-slogging and I proposed to give the leg muscles a bit of time off, and if E. Jimpson Murgatroyd didn't like it, let him eat cake.

I was particularly anxious to get together with Jeeves and hear what he had to say about the strange experience through which I had just passed, as strange an e. as had come my way in what you might call a month of Sundays.

I could make nothing of the attitude Cook had taken up. Plank's theory that his asperity had been due to the fact that Vanessa had got into the wrong crowd in London seemed to me pure apple sauce. I mean, if your daughter picks her social circle unwisely and starts clobbering the police, you don't necessarily accuse the first person you meet of stealing cats. The two things don't go together.

'Jeeves,' I said, reaching the finish line and sinking into an armchair, 'answer what I am about to ask you frankly. You have known me a good time.'

'Yes, sir.'

'You have had every opportunity of studying my psychology.'

'Yes, sir.'

'Well, would you say I was a fellow who stole cats?'

'No, sir.'

His ready response pleased me not a little. No hesitation, no humming and hawing, just 'No, sir'.

'Exactly what I expected you to say. Just what anyone at the Drones or elsewhere would say. And yet cat-stealing is what I have been accused of.'

'Indeed, sir?'

'By a scarlet-faced blighter named Cook.'

And forthwith, if that's the expression, I told him about my strange e., passing lightly over my not having trusted his directions on reaching the high road. He listened attentively, and when I had finished came as near to smiling as he ever does. That is to say, a muscle at the corner of his mouth twitched slightly as if some flying object such as a mosquito had settled there momentarily.

'I think I can explain, sir.'

It seemed incredible. I felt like Doctor Watson hearing Sherlock Holmes talking about the one hundred and forty-seven varieties of tobacco ash and the time it takes parsley to settle in the butter dish.

'This is astounding, Jeeves,' I said. 'Professor Moriarty wouldn't have lasted a minute with you. You really mean the pieces of the jig-saw puzzle have come together and fallen into their place?'

'Yes, sir.'

'You know all?'

'Yes, sir.'

'Amazing!'

'Elementary, sir. I found the habitués of the Goose and Grasshopper a ready source of information.'

'Oh, you asked the boys in the back room?'

'Yes, sir.'

'And what did they tell you?'

'It appears that bad blood exists between Mr Cook and Colonel Briscoe.'

'They don't like each other, you mean?'

'Precisely, sir.'

'I suppose it's often that way in the country. Not much to do except think what a tick your neighbour is.'

'It may be as you say, sir, but in the present case there is more solid ground for hostility, at least on Mr Cook's part. Colonel Briscoe is chairman of the board of magistrates and in that capacity recently imposed a substantial fine on Mr Cook for moving pigs without a permit.'

I nodded intelligently. I could see how this must have rankled. I do not keep pigs myself, but if I did I should strongly resent not being allowed to give them a change of air and scenery without getting permission from a board of magistrates. Are we in Russia?

'Furthermore—'

'Oh, that wasn't all?'

'No, sir. Furthermore, they are rival owners of race horses, and that provides another source of friction.'

'Why?'

'Sir?'

'I don't see why. Most of the big owners are very chummy. They love one another like brothers.'

'The big owners, yes, sir. It is different with those whose activities are confined to small local meetings. There the rivalry is more personal and acute. In the forthcoming contest at Bridmouth-on-Sea the race, in the opinion of my informants at the Goose and Grasshopper, will be a duel between Colonel Briscoe's Simla and Mr Cook's Potato Chip. All the other entries are negligible. There is consequently no little friction between the two gentlemen as the date of the contest approaches, and it is of vital importance to both of them that nothing shall go wrong with the training of their respective horses. Rigid attention to training is essential.'

Well, he didn't need to tell me that. An old hand like myself knows how vital rigid training is for success on the turf. I have not forgotten the time at Aunt Dahlia's place in Worcestershire when I had a heavy bet on Marlene Cooper, the gardener's niece, in the Girls' Under Fifteen Egg and Spoon race on Village Sports Day, and on the eve of the meeting she broke training, ate pounds of unripe gooseberries, and got abdominal pains which prevented her showing up at the starting-post.

'But, Jeeves,' I said, 'while all this is of absorbing interest, what I want to know is why Cook got into such a frenzy about this cat. You ought to have seen his blood pressure. It shot up like a rocket. He couldn't have been more emotional if he had been a big shot in the Foreign Office and I a heavily veiled woman diffusing a strange exotic scent whom he had caught getting away with the Naval Treaty.'

'Fortunately I am in a position to elucidate the mystery, sir. One of the habitués with whom I fraternized at the Goose and Grasshopper chances to be an employee of Mr Cook, and he furnished me with the facts in the case. The cat was a stray which appeared one morning in the stable yard, and Potato Chip took an instant fancy to it. This, I understand, is not unusual with highly bred horses, though more often it is a goat or a sheep which engages their affection.'

This was quite new stuff to me. First I'd ever heard of it.

'Goat?' I said.

'Yes, sir.'

'Or a sheep?'

'Yes, sir.'

'You mean love at first sight?'

'One might so describe it, sir.'

'What asses horses are, Jeeves.'

'Certainly their mentality is open to criticism, sir.'

'Though I suppose if for weeks you've seen nothing but Cook and stable boys, a cat comes as a nice change. I take it that the friendship ripened?'

'Yes, sir. The cat now sleeps nightly in the horse's stall and is there to meet him when he returns from his daily exercise.'

'The welcome guest?'

'Extremely welcome, sir.'

'They've put down the red carpet for it, you might say. Strange. I'd have thought a human vampire bat like Cook would have had a stray cat off the premises with a single kick.'

'Something of that nature did occur, my informant tells me, and the result was disastrous. Potato Chip became listless and refused his food. Then one day the cat returned, and the horse immediately recovered both vivacity and appetite.'

'Golly!'

'Yes, sir, the story surprised me when I heard it.'

I rose. Time was getting on, and I had a vision of the Briscoes with their noses pressed to the drawing-room window, looking out and telling each other that surely their Wooster ought to have shown up by now.

'Well, many thanks, Jeeves,' I said. 'With your customary what-d'you-call-it you have cast light on what might have remained a permanent brain-teaser. But for you I should have passed sleepless nights wondering what on earth Cook thought he was playing at. I now feel kindlier towards him. I still wouldn't care to have to go on a long walking tour with the son of a what-not, and if he ever gets himself put up for the Drones, I shall certainly blackball him, but I can see his point of view. He finds me clutching his cat, learns that I am on pally terms with his deadly rival the Colonel, and naturally assumes that there is dirty work afoot. No wonder he yelled like a soul in torment and brandished his hunting crop. He deserves considerable credit for not having given me six of the best with it.'

'Your broadminded view is to be applauded, sir.'

'One must always strive to put oneself in the other fellow's place and remember . . . remember what?'

'*Tout comprendre c'est tout pardonner.*'

'Thank you, Jeeves.'

'Not at all, sir.'

'And now Ho for Eggesford Hall.'

If you ask about me in circles which I frequent, you will be told that I am a good mixer who is always glad to shake hands with new faces, and it ought to have been in merry mood that I braked the car at the front door of Eggesford Hall. But it wasn't. Not that there was anything about the new faces on the other side to give me the pip. Colonel Briscoe proved to be a genial host, Mrs B a genial hostess. There were also present, besides Aunt Dahlia, the Rev Ambrose Briscoe, the Colonel's brother, and the latter's daughter Angelica, a very personable wench with whom, had I not been so preoccupied, I should probably have fallen in love. In short, as pleasant a bunch as you could wish to meet.

But that was the trouble. I *was* preoccupied. It wasn't so much finding myself practically next door to Vanessa Cook that worried me. It would be pretty difficult for me to go anywhere in England where there wasn't somebody who had turned me down at one time or another. I have run across them in spots as widely separated as Bude, Cornwall, and Sedbergh, Yorks. No, what was occupying the Wooster mind was the thought of Pop Cook and his hunting crop. It was not agreeable to feel that one was on bad terms with a man who might run amok at any moment and who, if he did, would probably make a beeline for Bertram.

The result was that I did not shine at the festive b. The lunch was excellent and the port with which it concluded definitely super, and I tucked in with a zest which would have made E. Jimpson Murgatroyd draw in a sharp breath, but as far as sprightly conversation went I was a total loss, and the suspicion must have crossed the minds of my host and hostess fairly soon in the proceedings that they were entertaining a Trappist monk with a good appetite.

That this had not failed to cross the mind of Aunt Dahlia was made abundantly clear to me when the meal was over and she took me for a tour of what Jeeves had called the extensive grounds. She ticked me off with her habitual non-mincing of words. All through my life she has been my best friend and severest critic, and when she rebukes a nephew she rebukes him good.

She spoke as follows, her manner and diction similar to those of a sergeant-major addressing recruits.

'What's the matter with you, you poor reptile? I told Jimmy and Elsa that my nephew might look like a half-witted halibut, but wait till he starts talking, I said, he'll have you in stitches. And what occurs? Quips? Sallies? Diverting anecdotes? No, sir. You sit there stupefying yourself with food, and scarcely a sound out of you except the steady champing of your jaws. I felt like an impresario of performing fleas who has given his star artist a big build-up, only to have him forget his lines on the opening night.'

I bowed my head in shame, knowing how justified was the rebuke. My contribution to what I have heard called the feast of reason and flow of soul had been, as I have indicated, about what you might have expected from a strong silent Englishman with tonsilitis.

'And the way you waded into that port. Like a camel arriving at an oasis after a long journey through desert sands. It was as if you had received private word from Jimmy that he wanted his cellar emptied quick so that he could turn it into a games room. If that's the way you carry on in London, no wonder you come out all over in spots. I'm surprised you can walk.'

She was right. I had to admit it.

'Did you ever see a play called *Ten Nights in a Bar Room*?'

I could bear no more. Weakly I tried to plead my case.

'I am sorry, aged relative. What you say is true. But I am not myself today.'

'Well, that's a bit of luck for everybody.'

'I'm what you could call distraught.'

'You're what I could call a mess.'

'I passed through a strange experience this morning.'

And with no further ado – or is it to-do? I never can remember – I told her my cat-Cook story.

I told it well, and there was no mistaking her interest when I came to the part where Jeeves elucidated the mystery of the cat's importance in the scheme of things.

'Do you mean to say,' she yipped, 'that if you had got away with that cat—'

I had to pull her up here with a touch of austerity. In spite of the clearness with which I had been at pains to tell the story just right she seemed to have got the wrong angle on the thing.

'There was no question, old ancestor, of my getting away with the cat. I was merely doing the civil thing by tickling its stomach.'

'But do you really mean that if someone were to get away with it, it would be all up with Potato Chip's training?'

'So Jeeves informs me, and he had it from a reliable source at the Goose and Grasshopper.'

'H'm.'

'Why do you say H'm?'

'Ha.'

'Why do you say Ha?'

'Never mind.'

But I did mind. When an aunt says 'H'm' and 'Ha', it means something, and I was filled with a nameless fear.

However, I had no time to go into it, for at this moment we were joined by the Rev Briscoe and his daughter. And shortly afterwards I left.

6

The afternoon had now hotted up to quite a marked extent, and what with a substantial lunch and several beakers of port I was more or less in the condition a python gets into after its mid-day meal. A certain drowsiness had stolen over me, so much so that twice in the course of my narrative the aged r. had felt compelled to notify me that if I didn't stop yawning in her face, she would let me have one on the side of my fat head with the parasol with which she was shielding herself from the rays of the sun.

There had been no diminution of this drowsiness since last heard of, and as I bowled along the high road I was practically in dreamland, and it occurred to me that if I didn't pause somewhere and sleep it off, I should shortly become a menace to pedestrians and traffic. The last thing I wanted was to come before my late host in his magisterial capacity, charged with having struck some citizen amidships while under the influence of his port. Colonel Briscoe's port, I mean, not the citizen's. Embarrassing for both of us, though in a way a compliment to the excellence of his cellar.

The high road, like most high roads, was flanked on either side by fields, some with cows, some without, so, the day being as warm as it was, just dropping anchor over here or over there meant getting as cooked to a crisp as Major Plank would have been, had the widows and surviving relatives of the late chief of the 'Mgombis established connection with him. What I wanted was shade, and by great good fortune I came on a little turning leading to wooded country, just what I needed. I drove into this wooded country, stopped the machinery, and it wasn't long before sleep poured over me in a healing wave, as the expression is.

It started off by being one of those dreamless sleeps, but after a while a nightmare took over. It seemed to me that I was out fishing with E. Jimpson Murgatroyd in what appeared to be tropical waters, and he caught a shark and I was having a look at it, when it suddenly got hold of my arm. This of course gave me a start, and I woke. And as I opened my eyes I saw that there was something attached to my port-side biceps, but it wasn't a shark, it was Orlo Porter.

'I beg your pardon, sir,' he was saying, 'for interrupting your doze, but I am a bird-watcher. I was watching a Clarkson's warbler in that thicket over there, and I was afraid your snoring might frighten it away, so might I beg you to go easy on the sound effects. Clarkson's warblers are very sensitive to loud noises, and you were making yourself audible a mile off.'

Or words to that general import.

I would have replied 'Oh, hullo', or something like that, but I was too astonished to speak, partly because I had never suspected that Orlo Porter could be so polite, but principally because he was there at all. I had looked on Maiden Eggesford as somewhere where I would be free from all human society, a haven where I would have peace perfect peace with loved ones far away, as the hymnbook says, and it was turning out to be a sort of meeting place of the nations. First Plank, then Vanessa Cook, and now Orlo Porter. If this sort of thing was going to go on, I told myself, I wouldn't be surprised to see my Aunt Agatha come round the corner arm in arm with E. J. Murgatroyd.

Orlo Porter seemed now to recognize me, for he started like a native of India who sees a scorpion in his path, and went on to say:

'Wooster, you blasted slimy creeping crawling serpent, I might have expected this!'

It was plain that he was not glad to see me, for there was nothing affectionate in what he said or the way he said it, but apart from that I was unable to follow him. He had me at a loss.

'Expected what?' I asked, hoping for footnotes.

'That you would have followed Vanessa here, your object to steal her from me.'

This struck me as so absurd that I laughed a light laugh, and he asked me to stop cackling like a hen whose union had been blest – or laying a blasted egg, as he preferred to put it.

'I haven't followed anyone anywhere,' I said, trying to pour oil on the troubled w.'s. I debated with myself whether to add 'old man', and decided not. I doubt if it would have had much effect, anyway.

'Then why are you here?' he demanded in a voice so fortissimo that it was obvious that he didn't give a damn if Clarkson's warbler heard him and legged it in a panic.

I continued suave.

'The matter is susceptible of a ready explanation,' I said. 'You remember those spots of mine.'

'Don't change the subject.'

'I wasn't. Having inspected the spots, the doc advised me to retire to the country.'

'There are plenty of other places in the country to retire to.'

'Ah,' I said, 'but my Aunt Dahlia is staying with some people here, and I knew it would make all the difference if I had her to exchange ideas with. Very entertaining woman, my Aunt Dahlia. Never a dull moment when she's around.'

This, as I had foreseen, had him stymied. Something of his belligerence left him, and I could see that he was saying to himself, 'Can it be that I have wronged Bertram?' Then he clouded over again.

'All this is very plausible,' he said, 'but it does not explain why you were slinking round Eggesford Court this morning.'

I was amazed. When I was a child, my nurse told me that there was One who was always beside me, spying out all my ways, and that if I refused to eat my spinach I would hear about it on Judgment Day, but it never occurred to me that she was referring to Orlo Porter.

'How on earth do you know that?' I said – or perhaps 'gasped' would be a better word, or even 'gurgled'.

'I was watching the place through my bird-watching binoculars, hoping to get a glimpse of the woman I love.'

This gave me the opportunity to steer the conversation into less controversial topics.

'I had forgotten you were a bird-watcher till you reminded me just now. You went in for it at Oxford, I remember. It isn't a thing I would care to do myself. Not,' I hastened to add, 'that I've anything against bird-watching. Must be most interesting, besides keeping you' – I was about to say 'out of the public houses' but thought it better to change it to 'out in the open air'. 'What's the procedure?' I said. 'I suppose you lurk in a bush till a bird comes along, and then you out with the glasses and watch it.'

I had more to say, notably a question as to who Clarkson was and how he came to have a warbler, but he interrupted me.

'I will tell you why you were sneaking round Eggesford Court this morning. It was in the hope of seeing Vanessa.'

I no-noed, but he paid no attention.

'And I would like to say for your guidance, Wooster, that if I catch you trying to inflict your beastly society on her again, I shall have no hesitation in tearing your insides out.'

He started to walk away, paused, added over his shoulder the words 'With my bare hands' and was gone, whether or not to resume watching Clarkson's warbler, I had no means of knowing. My own feeling was that any level-headed bird with sensitive ears would have removed itself almost immediately after he had begun to speak.

7

These parting remarks of O. Porter gave me, as may readily be imagined, considerable food for thought. There happened at the moment to be no passers-by, but if any passers had been by, they would have noticed that my brow was knitted and the eyes a bit glazed. This always happens when you are turning things over in your mind and not liking the look of them. You see the same thing in Cabinet ministers when they are asked awkward questions in Parliament.

It was not, of course, the first time an acquaintance had expressed a desire to delve into my interior and remove its contents. Roderick Spode, now going about under the alias of Lord Sidcup, had done so frequently when in the grip of the illusion that I was trying to steal Madeline Bassett from him, little knowing that she gave me a pain in the gizzard and that I would willingly have run a mile in tight shoes to avoid her.

But I had never before had such a sense of imminent peril as now. Spode might talk airily – or is it glibly? – of buttering me over the lawn and jumping on the remains with hobnailed boots, but it was always possible to buoy oneself up with the thought that his bark was worse than his b. I mean to say, a fellow like Spode has a position to keep up. He can't afford to indulge every passing whim. If he goes buttering people over lawns, he's in for trouble. *Debrett's Peerage* tut-tuts, *Burke's Landed Gentry* raises its eyebrows, and as likely as not he gets cut by the County and has to emigrate.

But Orlo Porter was under no such restraint. Being a Communist, he was probably on palsy-walsy terms with half the big shots at the Kremlin, and the more of the bourgeoisie he disembowelled, the better they would be pleased. 'A young man with the right stuff in him, this Comrade Porter. Got nice ideas,' they would say when reading about the late Wooster. 'We must keep an eye on him with a view to further advancement.'

Obviously, then, the above Porter having expressed himself

as he had done about Vanessa Cook, the shrewd thing for me to do was to keep away from her. I put this up to Jeeves when I returned, and he saw eye to eye with me.

'What are those things circumstances have, Jeeves?' I said.

'Sir?'

'You know what I mean. You talk of a something of circumstances which leads to something. Cats enter into it, if I'm not wrong.'

'Would concatenation be the word you are seeking?'

'That's right. It was on the tip of my tongue. Do concatenations of circumstances arise?'

'Yes, sir.'

'Well, one has arisen now. The facts are these. When we were in London, I formed a slight acquaintance with a Miss Cook who turns out to be the daughter of the chap who owns the horse which thinks so highly of that cat. She had a spot of trouble with the police, and her father summoned her home to see that she didn't get into more. So she is now at Eggesford Court. Got the scenario so far?'

'Yes, sir.'

'This caused her betrothed, a man named Porter, to follow her here in order to give her aid and comfort. Got that?'

'Yes, sir. This frequently happens when two young hearts are sundered.'

'Well, I met him this morning, and my presence in Maiden Eggesford came as a surprise to him.'

'One can readily imagine it, sir.'

'He took it for granted that I had come in pursuit of Miss Cook.'

'Like young Lochinvar, when he came out of the West.'

The name was new to me, but I didn't ask for further details. I saw that he was following the plot, and it never does, when you're telling a story, to wander off into side issues.

'And he said if I didn't desist, he would tear my insides out with his bare hands.'

'Indeed, sir?'

'You don't know Porter, do you?'

'No, sir.'

'Well, you know Spode. Porter is Spode plus. Hasty temper. Quick to take offence. And the muscles of his brawny arms are strong as iron bands, as the fellow said. The last chap you'd want to annoy. So what do you suggest?'

'I think it would be advisable to avoid the society of Miss Cook.'

'Exactly the idea which occurred to me. And it ought not to be difficult. The chances of Pop Cook asking me to drop in are very slim. So if I take the high road and she takes the low road . . . Answer that, will you, Jeeves,' I said as the telephone rang in the hall. 'It's probably Aunt Dahlia, but it may be Porter, and I do not wish to have speech with him.'

He went out, to return a few moments later.

'It was Miss Cook, sir, speaking from the post office. She desired me to inform you that she would be calling on you immediately.'

A sharp 'Lord-love-a-duck' escaped me, and I eyed him with reproach.

'You didn't think to say I was out?'

'The lady gave me no opportunity of doing so, sir. She delivered her message and rang off without waiting for me to speak.'

My brow got all knitted again.

'This isn't too good, Jeeves.'

'No, sir.'

'Calling at my home address like this.'

'Yes, sir.'

'Who's to say that Orlo Porter is not lurking outside with his bird-watching binoculars?' I said.

But before I could go into the matter in depth, the door bell had rung, and Vanessa Cook was in my midst. Jeeves, I need scarcely say, had vanished like a family spectre at the crack of dawn. He always does when company arrives. I hadn't seen him go, and I doubted if Vanessa had, but he had gone.

As I stood gazing at Vanessa, I was conscious of the uneasiness you feel when you run up against something particularly hot and are wondering when it is going to explode. It was more than a year since I had seen her, except in the distance when about to be scooped in by the police, and the change in her appearance was calculated to curdle the blood a bit. Her outer aspect was still that of a girl who would have drawn whistles from susceptible members of America's armed forces, but there was something sort of formidable about her which had not been there before, something kind of imperious and defiant, if you know what I mean. Due no doubt to the life she had been leading. You can't go heading protest marches and socking the constabulary without it showing.

Hard, that's the word I was trying for. She had always been what they call a proud beauty, but now she was a hard one. Her lips were tightly glued together, her chin protruding, her whole lay-out that of a girl who intended to stand no ranny-gazoo. Except that the latter was way down in Class D as a looker, while she, as I have indicated, was the pin-up girl to end all pin-up girls, she reminded me of my childhood dancing mistress. The thought occurred to me that in another thirty years or so she would look just like my Aunt Agatha, before whose glare, as is well known, strong men curl up like rabbits.

Nor was there anything in her greeting to put me at my ease. Having given me a nasty look as if I ranked in her esteem in one of the lowest brackets, she said:

'I am very angry with you, Bertie.'

I didn't like the sound of this at all. It is never agreeable to incur the displeasure of a girl with a punch like hers. I said I was sorry to hear that, and asked what seemed to be the trouble.

'Following me here!'

There is nothing that braces one up like being accused of something to which you can find a ready answer. I laughed merrily, and her reaction to my mirth was much the same as Orlo Porter's had been, though where he had spoken of hens laying eggs she preferred the simile of a hyena with a bone stuck in its throat. I said I hadn't had a notion that she was in these parts, and this time she laughed, one of those metallic ones that are no good to man or beast.

'Oh, come!' she said. 'Oddly enough,' she added, 'although I am furious, I can't help admiring you in a way. I am surprised to find that you have so much initiative. It is abominable, but it does show spirit. It makes me feel that if I had married you, I could have made something of you.'

I shuddered from hair-do to shoe-sole. I was even more thankful than before that she had given me the bum's rush. I know what making something of me meant. Ten minutes after the Bishop and colleague had done their stuff she would have been starting to mould me and jack up my soul, and I like my soul the way it is. It may not be the sort of soul that gets crowds cheering in the streets, but it suits me and I don't want people fooling about with it.

'But it is quite impossible, Bertie. I love Orlo and can love no one else.'

'That's all right. Entirely up to you. I must put you straight on one thing, though. I really didn't know you were here.'

'Are you trying to make me believe that it was a pure coincidence—'

'No, not that. More what I would call a concatenation of circumstances. My doctor ordered me a quiet life in the country, and I chose Maiden Eggesford because my aunt is staying with some people here and I thought it would be nice being near her. A quiet life in the country can be a bit too quiet if you don't know anybody. She got me this cottage.'

You might have thought that that would have cleaned everything up and made life one grand sweet song, as the fellow said, but no, she went on looking puff-faced. No pleasing some girls.

'So I was wrong in thinking that you had initiative,' she said, and if her lip didn't curl scornfully, I don't know a scornfully curling lip when I see one. 'You are just an ordinary footling member of the bourgeoisie that Orlo dislikes so much.'

'A typical young man about town, some authorities say.'

'I don't suppose you have ever done anything worthwhile in your life.'

I could have made her look pretty silly at this juncture by revealing that I had won a Scripture Knowledge prize at my private school, a handsomely bound copy of a devotional work whose name has escaped me, and that when Aunt Dahlia was running that *Milady's Boudoir* paper of hers I contributed to it an article, or piece as we writers call it, on What The Well-Dressed Man Is Wearing, but I let it go, principally because she had gone on speaking and it is practically impossible to cut in on a woman who has gone on speaking. They get the stuff out so damn quick that the slower male hasn't a hope.

'But the matter of your wasted life is beside the point. God made you, and presumably he knew what he was doing, so we need not go into that. What you will want to hear is my reason for coming to see you.'

'Any time you're passing,' I said in my polished way, but she took no notice and continued.

'Father's friend, Major Plank, who is staying with us, was talking at lunch about someone named Wooster who had called this morning, and when Father turned purple and choked on his lamb cutlet I knew it must be you. You are the sort of young man he dislikes most.'

'Do young men dislike him?'

'Invariably. Father is and always has been a cross between Attila the Hun and a snapping turtle. Well, having found that you were in Maiden Eggesford I came to ask you to do something for me.'

'Anything I can.'

'It's quite simple. I shall of course be writing to Orlo, but I don't want him to send his letters to the Court because Father, in addition to resembling a snapping turtle, is a man of low cunning who wouldn't hesitate to intercept and destroy them, and he always gets down to breakfast before I do, which gives him a strategical advantage. By the time I got to the table the cream of my correspondence would be in his trouser pocket. So I am going to tell Orlo to address his letters care of you, and I will call for them every afternoon.'

I never heard a proposition I liked the sound of less. The idea of her calling at the cottage daily, with Orlo Porter, already heated to boiling point, watching its every move, froze my young blood and made my two eyes, like stars, start from their spheres, as I have heard Jeeves put it. It was with infinite relief that I realized a moment later that my fears were groundless, there being no need for correspondence between the parties of the first and second part.

'But he's here,' I said.

'*Here?* In Maiden Eggesford?'

'Right plump spang in Maiden Eggesford.'

'Are you being funny, Bertie?'

'Of course I'm not being funny. If I were being funny, I'd have had you in convulsions from the outset. I tell you he's here. I met him this afternoon. He was watching a Clarkson's warbler. Arising from which, you don't happen to have any data relating to Clarkson, do you? I've been wondering who he was and how he got a warbler.'

She ignored my observation. This generally happens with me. Show me a woman, I sometimes say, and I will show you someone who is going to ignore my observations.

Looking at her closely, I noted a change in her aspect. I have said that her face had hardened as the result of going about the place socking policemen, but now it had got all soft. And while her two eyes didn't actually start from their spheres, they widened to about the size of regulation golf balls, and a tender smile lit up her map. She said, 'Well, strike me pink!' or words to that effect.

'So he has come! He has followed me!' She spoke as if it had given her no end of a kick that he had done this. Apparently it wasn't being followed that she objected to; it just had to be the right chap. 'Like some knight in shining armour riding up on his white horse.'

Here would have been a chance to give Jeeves's friend who came out of the west a plug by saying that Orlo reminded me of him, but I had to give it a miss because I couldn't remember the fellow's name.

'I wonder how he managed to get away from his job,' I said.

'He was on his annual two weeks' holiday. That is how he came to be at that protest march. He and I were heading the procession.'

'I know. I was watching from afar.'

'I have not found out yet what happened to him that day. After he knocked the policeman down he suddenly disappeared.'

'Always the best thing to do if you knock a policeman down. He jumped into my car and I drove him to safety.'

'Oh, I see.'

I must say I thought she might have put it a bit stronger. One does not desire thanks for these little kindnesses one does here and there, but considering that on his behalf I had inter-fered with the police in the execution of their duty, if that's how the script reads, thereby rendering myself liable to a sizeable sojourn in chokey, a little enthusiasm would not have been amiss. Nothing to be done about it except give her a reproachful look. I did this. It made no impression whatever, and she proceeded.

'Is he staying at the Goose and Grasshopper?'

'I couldn't say,' I said, and if I spoke with a touch of what-d'you-call-it in my voice, who can blame me? 'When I met him, we talked mostly about my interior organs.'

'What's wrong with your interior organs?'

'Nothing so far, but he thought there might be something later on.'

'He has a wonderfully sympathetic nature.'

'Yes, hasn't he.'

'Did he recommend anything that would be good for you?'

'As a matter of fact he did.'

'How like him!'

She was silent for a while, no doubt pondering on all Orlo's lovable qualities, many of which I had missed. At length she spoke.

'He must be at the Goose and Grasshopper. It's the only decent inn in the place. Go there and tell him to meet me here at three o'clock tomorrow afternoon.'

'Here?'

'Yes.'

'You mean at this cottage?'

'Why not?'

'I thought you might want to see him alone.'

'Oh, that's all right. You can go for a walk.'

Once more I sent up a silent vote of thanks to my guardian angel for having fixed it that this proud beauty should not become Mrs Bertram Wooster. Her cool assumption that she had only got to state her wishes and all and sundry would jump to fulfil them gave me the pip. So stung was the Wooster pride by the thought of being slung out at her bidding from my personal cottage that it is not too much to say that my blood boiled, and I would probably have said something biting like 'Oh, yes?', only I felt that a *preux chevalier*, which I always aim to be, ought not to crush the gentler sex beneath the iron heel, no matter what the provocation.

So I changed it to 'Right-ho', and went off to the Goose and Grasshopper to give Orlo the low-down.

8

I found him in the private bar having a gin and ginger ale. His face, never much to write home about, was rendered even less of a feast for the eye by a dark scowl. His spirits were plainly at their lowest ebb, as so often happens when Sundered Heart A is feeling that the odds against his clicking with Sundered Heart B cannot be quoted at better than a hundred to eight.

Of course he may have been brooding because he had just heard that a pal of his in Moscow had been liquidated that morning, or he had murdered a capitalist and couldn't think of a way of getting rid of the body, but I preferred to attribute his malaise to frustrated love, and I couldn't help feeling a pang of pity for him.

He looked at me as I entered in a manner which made me realize how little chance there was of our exchanging presents at Christmas, and I remember thinking what a lot of him there was and all of it anti-Wooster. I had often felt the same about Spode. It seemed that there was something about me that aroused the baser passions in men who were eight feet tall and six across. I took this up with Jeeves once, and he agreed that it was singular.

His eye as I approached was what I have heard described as lacklustre. Whatever it was that was causing this V-shaped depression, seeing me had not brought the sunshine into his life. His demeanour was that of any member of a Wednesday matinée audience or, let us say, a dead fish on a fishmonger's slab. Nor did he brighten when I had delivered my message. After I had done so there was a long silence, broken only by the gurgling of ginger ale as it slid down his throat.

Eventually he spoke, his voice rather like that of a living corpse in one of those horror films where the fellow takes the lid off the tomb in the vault beneath the ruined chapel and blowed if the occupant doesn't start a conversation with him.

'I don't understand this.'

'What don't you understand?' I said, adding 'Comrade', for there is never anything lost by being civil. 'Any assistance I can give in the way of solving any little problems you may have will be freely given. I am only here to help.'

The amount of sunny charm I had put into these words ought to have melted the reserve of a brass monkey, but they got absolutely nowhere with him. He continued to eye me in an Aunt Agathaesque manner.

'It seems odd, if as you say you are the merest acquaintance, that she should be paying you clandestine visits at your cottage. Taken in conjunction with your surreptitious appearance at Eggesford Court, it cannot but invite suspicion.'

When someone talks like that, using words like 'clandestine' and 'surreptitious' and saying that something cannot but invite suspicion, the prudent man watches his step. It was a great relief to me that I had a watertight explanation. I gave it with a winning frankness which I felt could scarcely fail to bring home the bacon.

'My appearance at Eggesford Court wasn't surreptitious. I was there because I had come to the wrong house. And Miss Cook's visit to my cottage had to be clandestine because her father watches her as closely as the paper on the wall. And she visited my cottage because there was no other way of getting in touch with you. She didn't know you were in Maiden Eggesford, and she thought if you wrote her a letter that Pop would intercept it, he being a man who would intercept a daughter's letter at the drop of a hat.'

It sounded absolutely copper-bottomed to me, but he went on giving me the eye.

'All the same,' he said, 'I find it curious that she should have confided in you. It suggests an intimacy.'

'Oh, I wouldn't call it that. Girls I hardly know confide in me. They look upon me as a father figure.'

'Father figure my foot. Any girl who takes you for a father figure ought to have her head examined.'

'Well, let us say a brother figure. They know their secrets are safe with good old Bertie.'

'I'm not so sure you are good old Bertie. More like a snake who goes about the place robbing men of the women they love, if you ask me.'

'Certainly not,' I protested, learning for the first time that this was what snakes did.

'Well, it looks fishy to me,' he said. Then to my relief he changed the subject. 'Do you know a man named Spofforth?'

I said No, I didn't think so.

'P. B. Spofforth. Big fellow with a clipped moustache.'

'No, I've never met him.'

'And you won't for some time. He's in hospital.'

'Too bad. What sent him there?'

'I did. He kissed the woman I love at the annual picnic of the Slade Social and Outing Club. Have you ever kissed the woman I love, Wooster?'

'Good Lord, no.'

'Be careful not to. Did she make a long stay at your cottage?'

'No, very short. In and out like a flash. Just had time to say you were like a knight in shining armour riding up on a white horse and to tell me to tell you to show up at my address tomorrow at three on the dot, and she was off.'

This seemed to soothe him. He went on brooding but now not so much like Jack the Ripper getting up steam for his next murder. He was not, however, quite satisfied.

'I don't call it much of an idea meeting at your cottage,' he said.

'Why not?'

'We shall have you underfoot all the time.'

'Oh, that's all right, Comrade. I shall be going for a walk.'

'Ah,' he said, brightening visibly. 'Going for a walk, eh? Just the thing to do. Capital exercise. Bring the roses to your cheeks. Take your time. Don't hurry back. They tell me there are beauty spots around here well worth seeing.'

And on this cordial note we parted, he to go to the bar for another gin and ginger, I to go back and tell Vanessa that the *pourparlers* had been completed and that he would be at the starting post at three pip-emma on the morrow.

'How did he look?' she asked, all eagerness.

It was a little difficult to answer this, because he had looked like a small-time gangster with a painful gumboil, but I threw together a tactful word or two which, as Jeeves would say, gave satisfaction, and she buzzed off.

Jeeves came shimmering in shortly after she had left. He seemed a shade perturbed.

'We were interrupted in our recent conversation, sir.'

'We were, Jeeves, and I am glad to say that I no longer need your advice. During your absence the situation has become clarified. A meeting has been arranged and will shortly take place, in fact here at this cottage at three o'clock tomorrow afternoon. I, not wishing to intrude, shall be going for a walk.'

'Extremely gratifying, sir,' he said, and I agreed with him that he had tetigisti-ed the rem acu.

At five minutes to three on the following afternoon I had girded my loins and was preparing to iris out, when Vanessa Cook arrived. The sight of me appeared to displease her. She frowned as if I were something that didn't smell just right, and said:

'Haven't you gone yet?'

I considered this a shade brusque, even for a proud beauty, but, true to my resolve to be *preux*, I responded suavely:

'Just going.'

'Well, go,' she said, and I went.

The street outside was as usual, offering little entertainment to the sightseer. A few centenarians were dotted about, exchanging reminiscences of the Boer War, and the eye detected a dog which had interested itself in something it had found in the gutter, but otherwise it was empty. I walked down it and had a look at the Jubilee watering-trough and was walking back on the other side, thinking how pleased E. J. Murgatroyd would be if he could see me, when I caught sight of the shop which acted as a post office and remembered that Jeeves had told me that in addition to selling stamps, picture postcards, socks, boots, overalls, pink sweets, yellow sweets, string, cigarettes and stationery it ran a small lending library.

I went in. I had come away rather short of reading matter, and it never does to neglect one's intellectual side.

Like all village lending libraries, this one had not bothered much about keeping itself up to date, and I was hesitating between *By Order Of The Czar* and *The Mystery Of A Hansom Cab*, which seemed the best bets, when the door opened to Angelica Briscoe, the personable wench I had met at lunch. The vicar's daughter, if you remember.

Her behaviour on seeing me was peculiar. She suddenly became all conspiratorial, as if she had been a Nihilist in *By Order Of The Czar* meeting another Nihilist. I had not yet read that opus, but I assumed that it was full of Nihilists who were always meeting other Nihilists and plotting dark plots with them. She clutched my arm and lowering her voice to a sinister whisper said:

'Has he brought it yet?'

I missed her drift by a wide margin. I like to think of myself as a polished man of the world who can kid back and forth with a pretty girl as well as the next chap, but I must confess that my only response to this query was a silent goggle. It struck me as unusual that a vicar's daughter should be a member of a secret society, but I could think of no other explanation for her words. They had sounded like a secret code, the sort of thing you haven't a hope of making sense of if you aren't a unit of The Uncanny Seven in good standing with all your dues paid up.

Eventually I found speech. Not much of it, but some.

'Eh?' I said.

She seemed to feel that her question had been answered. Her manner changed completely. She dropped the *By Order Of The Czar* stuff and became the nice girl who in all probability played the organ in her father's church.

'I see he hasn't. But of course one has to give him time for a job like that.'

'Like what?'

'I can't explain. Here's Father.'

And the Reverend Briscoe ambled in, his purpose, as it appeared immediately, to purchase half a pound of the pink sweets and half a pound of the yellow as a present for the more deserving of his choir boys. His presence choked the personable wench off from further revelations, and the only conversation that followed had to do with the weather, the condition of the church roof and how-well-your-aunt-is-looking-it-was-such-a-pleasure-seeing-her-again. And after a few desultory exchanges I left them and resumed my walk.

It is always difficult to estimate the time two sundered hearts, unexpectedly reunited, will require for picking up the threads. To be on the safe side I gave Orlo and Vanessa about an hour and a half, and when I returned to the cottage I found I had called my shots correctly. Both had legged it.

I was still much perplexed by that utterance of Angelica Briscoe's. The more I brooded on it, the more cryptic, if that's the word, it became. 'Has he brought it yet?', I mean to say. Has who? Brought what? I called Jeeves in, to see what he made of it.

'Tell me, Jeeves,' I said. 'Suppose you were in a shop taking *By Order Of The Czar* out of the lending library and a clergyman's daughter came in and without so much as a preliminary "Hullo, there", said to you, "Has he brought it yet?", what interpretation would you place on those words?'

He pondered, this way and that dividing the swift mind, as I have heard him put it.

' "Has he brought it yet", sir?'

'Just that.'

'I should reach the conclusion that the lady was expecting a male acquaintance to have arrived or to be arriving shortly bearing some unidentified object.'

'Exactly what I thought. What unidentified object we shall presumably learn in God's good time.'

'No doubt, sir.'

'We must wait patiently till all is revealed.'

'Yes, sir.'

'In the meantime, pigeonholing that for the moment, did Miss Cook and Mr Porter have their conference all right?'

'Yes, sir, they conversed for some time.'

'In low, throbbing voices?'

'No, sir, the voices of both lady and gentleman became noticeably raised.'

'Odd. I thought lovers generally whispered.'

'Not when an argument is in progress, sir.'

'Good Lord. Did they have an argument?'

'A somewhat acrimonious one, sir, plainly audible in the kitchen, where I was reading the volume of Spinoza which you so kindly gave me for Christmas. The door happened to be ajar.'

'So you were an ear-witness?'

'Throughout, sir.'

'Tell me all, Jeeves.'

'Very good, sir. I must begin by explaining that Mr Cook is trustee for a sum of money left to Mr Porter by his late uncle, who appears to have been a partner of Mr Cook in various commercial enterprises.'

'Yes, I know about that. Porter told me.'

'Until Mr Cook releases this money Mr Porter is in no position to marry. I gathered that his present occupation is not generously paid.'

'He's an insurance salesman. Didn't I tell you that I had taken out an accident policy with him?'

'Not that I recall, sir.'

'And a life policy as well, both for sums beyond the dreams of avarice. He talked me into it. But I mustn't interrupt you. Go on telling me all.'

'Very good, sir. Miss Cook was urging Mr Porter to demand an interview with her father.'

'In order to make him cough up?'

'Precisely, sir. "Be firm", I heard her say. "Throw your weight about. Look him in the eye and thump the table." '

'She specified that?'

'Yes, sir.'

'To which he replied?'

'That any time he started thumping tables in the presence of Mr Cook you could certify him as mentally unbalanced and ship him off to the nearest home for the insane – or loony-bin, as he phrased it.'

'Strange.'

'Sir?'

'I wouldn't have thought Porter would have shown such what-is-it.'

'Would pusillanimity be the word for which you are groping, sir?'

'Quite possibly. I know it begins with pu. I said it was strange because I hadn't supposed these knights in shining armour were afraid of anything.'

'Apparently they make an exception in the case of Mr Cook. I gathered from your account of your visit to Eggesford Court that he is a gentleman of somewhat formidable personality.'

'You gathered right. Ever hear of Captain Bligh of the Bounty?'

'Yes, sir. I read the book.'

'I saw the movie. Ever hear of Jack the Ripper?'

'Yes, sir.'

'Put them together and what have you got? Cook. It's that hunting crop of his chiefly. You can face a man with fortitude if he has simply got the disposition of a dyspeptic rattlesnake and confines himself to coarse abuse, but put a hunting crop in his hand and that spells trouble. It was a miracle that I escaped from Eggesford Court with my trouser seat unscathed. But go on, Jeeves. What happened then?'

'May I marshal my thoughts, sir?'

'Certainly. Marshal them all you want.'

'Thank you, sir. One aims at coherence.'

Marshalling his thoughts took between twenty and thirty seconds. At the end of that period he resumed his blow-by-blow report of the dust-up between Vanessa Cook and O. J. Porter, which was beginning to look like the biggest thing that had happened since Gene Tunney and Jack Dempsey had their dispute at Chicago.

'It was almost immediately after Mr Porter's refusal to go to Mr Cook and thump tables that Miss Cook introduced the cat into the conversation.'

'Cat? What cat?'

'The one you met at Eggesford Court, with which the horse Potato Chip formed such a durable friendship. Miss Cook was urging Mr Porter to purloin it.'

'Golly!'

'Yes, sir. The female of the species is more deadly than the male.'

Neatly put, I thought.

'Your own?' I said.

'No, sir. A quotation.'

'Well, carry on,' I said, thinking what a lot of good things Shakespeare had said in his time. Female of species deadlier than male. You had only to think of my Aunt Agatha and spouse to realize the truth of this. 'I get the idea, Jeeves. Porter, in possession of the cat, would have a bargaining point with Cook when it came to discussing trust funds.'

'Precisely, sir. *Rem acu tetigisti*.'

'So I take it that he is now at Eggesford Court putting the bite on old Captain Bligh.'

'No, sir. His refusal to do as Miss Cook asked was unequivocal. "Not in a million years" was the expression he used.'

'Not a very cooperative bloke, this O. J. Porter.'

'No, sir.'

'A bit like Balaam's ass,' I said, referring to one of the dramatis personae who had figured in the examination paper the time I won the Scripture Knowledge prize at my private school. 'If you recall, it too dug in its feet and refused to play ball.'

'Yes, sir.'

'That must have made Miss Cook as sore as a sunburned neck.'

'I did gather from her remarks that she was displeased. She

accused Mr Porter of being a lily-livered poltroon, and said that she never wished to speak to him again or hear from him by letter, telegram or carrier pigeon.'

'Pretty final.'

'Yes, sir.'

I didn't actually heave a sigh, but I sort of half-heaved one.

To a man of sensibility there is always something sort of sad about young love coming a stinker on the rocks. Myself, I couldn't imagine anyone wanting to marry Orlo Porter and it would have jarred me to the soles of my socks if I had had to marry Vanessa Cook, but they had unquestionably been all for teaming up, and it seemed a shame that harsh words had come between them and the altar rails.

However, there was this to be said in favour of the rift, that it would do Vanessa all the good in the world to find that she had come up against someone she couldn't say 'Go' to and he goeth, as the fellow said. I mentioned this to Jeeves, and he agreed that there was that aspect to the matter.

'Show her that she isn't Cleopatra or somebody.'

'Very true, sir.'

I would gladly have continued our conversation, but I knew he must be wanting to get back to his Spinoza. No doubt I had interrupted him just as Spinoza was on the point of solving the mystery of the headless body on the library floor.

'Right ho, Jeeves,' I said. 'That'll be all for the moment.'

'Thank you, sir.'

'If any solution of that "Has he brought it yet?" thing occurs to you, send me an inter-office memo.'

I spoke lightly, but I wasn't feeling so dashed light. Those cryptic words of Angelica Briscoe had shaken me. They seemed to suggest that things were going on behind my back which weren't likely to do me any good. I had suffered so much in the past from girls of Angelica's age starting something – Stiffy Byng is a name that springs to the mind – that I have become wary and suspicious, like a fox that had had the Pytchley after it for years.

By speaking in riddles, as the expression is, A. Briscoe had given me a mystery to chew on; and while mysteries are fine in books – I am never happier than when curled up with the latest Agatha Christie – you don't want them in your private life, for that's how you get headaches.

I was beginning to get one now, when my mind was taken

off the throbbing which had started. The front door was open, and through it came Vanessa Cook.

She bore traces of the recent set-to. The cheeks were flushed, the eyes glittering, and looking at the teeth one was left in no doubt that they had been well gnashed in the not too distant past. Her whole demeanour was that of a girl whose emotional nature had been stirred up as if a cyclone had hit it.

'Bertie,' she said.

'Hullo?' I said.

'Bertie,' she said, 'I will be your wife.'

10

You would have expected this to have drawn some comment from me such as 'Oh, my God!' or 'You'll be my *what*?', but I remained *sotto voce* and the silent tomb, my eyes bulging like those of the fellows I've heard Jeeves mention, who looked at each other with a wild surmise, silent upon a peak in Darien.

The thing had come on me as such a complete surprise. Her rejection of my addresses at the time when I proposed to her had been so definite that it had seemed to me that all danger from that quarter had passed and that from now on we wouldn't even be just good friends. Certainly she had given no indication that she would not prefer to be dead in a ditch rather than married to me. And now this. Is any man safe, one asked oneself. No wonder words failed me, as the expression is.

She, on the other hand, became chatty. Getting the thing off her chest seemed to have done her good. The glitter of her eyes was practically switched off, and she was not clenching her teeth any more. I don't say that even now I would have cared to meet her down a dark alley, but there was a distinct general improvement.

'We shall have quite a quiet wedding,' she said. 'Just a few people I know in London. And it may have to be even quieter than that. It all depends on Father. Your standing with him is roughly what that of a Public Enemy Number One would be at the annual Policeman's Ball. What you did to him I don't know, but I have never seen him a brighter mauve than when your name came up at the luncheon table. If he persists in this attitude, we shall have to elope. That will be perfectly all right with me. I suppose many people would say I was being rash, but I am prepared to take the chance. I know very little of you, true, but anyone the mention of whose name can make Father swallow his lunch the wrong way cannot be wholly bad.'

At last managing to free my tongue from the uvula with which it had become entangled, I found speech, as I dare say those Darien fellows did eventually.

'But I don't understand!'

'What don't you understand?'

'I thought you were going to marry Orlo Porter.'

She uttered a sound rather like an elephant taking its foot out of a mud hole in a Burmese teak forest. The name appeared to have touched an exposed nerve.

'You did, did you? You were mistaken. Would any girl with an ounce of sense marry a man who refuses to do the least little thing she asks him because he is afraid of her father? I shall always be glad to see Orlo Porter fall downstairs and break his neck. Nothing would give me greater pleasure than to read his name in *The Times* obituary column. But marry him? What an idea! No, I am quite content with you, Bertie. By the way, I do dislike that name Bertie. I think I shall call you Harold. Yes, I am perfectly satisfied with you. You have many faults, of course. I shall be pointing some of them out when I am at leisure. For one thing,' she said, not waiting till she was at leisure, 'you smoke too much. You must give that up when we are married. Smoking is just a habit. Tolstoy,' she said, mentioning someone I had not met, 'says that just as much pleasure can be got from twirling the fingers.'

My impulse was to tell her Tolstoy was off his onion, but I choked down the heated words. For all I knew, the man might be a bosom pal of hers and she might resent criticism of him, however justified. And one knew what happened to people, policemen for instance, whose criticism she resented.

'And that silly laugh of yours, you must correct that. If you are amused, a quiet smile is ample. Lord Chesterfield said that since he had had the full use of his reason nobody had ever heard him laugh. I don't suppose you have read Lord Chesterfield's *Letters To His Son*?'

. . . Well, of course I hadn't. Bertram Wooster does not read other people's letters. If I were employed in the post office, I wouldn't even read the postcards.

'I will draft out a whole course of reading for you.'

She would probably have gone on to name a few of the authors she had in mind, but at this moment Angelica Briscoe came bursting in.

'Has he brought it yet?' she yipped.

Then she saw Vanessa, added the word 'Golly', and disappeared like an eel into mud. Vanessa followed her with an indulgent eye.

'Eccentric child,' she said.

I agreed that Angelica Briscoe moved in a mysterious way her wonders to perform, and shortly after Vanessa went off, leaving me to totter to a chair and bury my face in my hands.

I was doing this, and very natural, too, considering that I had just become engaged to a girl who was going to try to make me stop smoking, when from outside the front door there came the unmistakable sound of an aunt tripping over a door mat. The next moment, my late father's sister Dahlia staggered in, pirouetted awhile, cursed a bit, recovered her equilibrium and said:

'Has he brought it yet?'

11

I am not, I think, an irascible man, particularly in my dealings with the gentler sex, but when every ruddy female you meet bellows 'Has he brought it yet?' at you, it does something to your aplomb. I gave her a look which I suppose no nephew should have given an aunt, and it was with no little asperity that I said:

'If some of you girls would stop talking as if you were characters in *By Order Of The Czar*, the world would be a better place. Brought what?'

'The cat, of course, you poor dumb-bell,' she responded in the breezy manner which had made her the popular toast of both the Quorn and the Pytchley fox-hunting organizations. 'Cook's cat. I'm kidnapping it. Or, rather, my agent is acting for me. I told him to bring it here.'

I was reft, as they say, of speech. If there is one thing that affects a nephew's vocal cords, it is the discovery that a loved aunt is all foggy about the difference between right and wrong. Experience over the years ought to have taught me that where this aunt was concerned anything went and the sky was the limit, but nevertheless I was . . . I know there's a word that just describes it . . . Ah, yes, I thought I'd get it . . . I was dumbfounded.

Well, of course, what every woman wants when she has a tale to tell is a dumbfounded audience, and it did not surprise me when she took advantage of my silence to carry on. Naturally aware that her goings-on required a bit of explanation, she made quite a production number of it. I won't say that she omitted no detail however slight, but she certainly didn't condense. She started off at 75 m.p.h. thus:

'I must begin by making clear to the meanest intelligence – yours, to take an instance at random – how extremely sticky my position was on coming to stay with the Briscoes. Jimmy, when inviting me to Eggesford Hall, had written in the most enthusiastic terms of his horse Simla's chances in the forthcoming race. He said he was a snip and putting a large bet on him would be like finding money in the street. And I, poor weak woman, allowed myself to be persuaded. I wagered everything I possessed, down to my more intimate garments. It was only after I got here and canvassed local opinion that I realized that Simla was not a snip or anything like a snip. Cook's Potato Chip was just as fast and had just as much staying power. In fact, the thing would probably end in a dead-heat unless, get this, Bertie, unless one of the two animals blew up in its training. And then you came along with your special information about Potato Chip not being able to keep his mind on the race without this cat there to egg him on, and a bright light shone on me. "Out of the mouths of babes and sucklings!" I said to myself. "Out of the mouths of babes and sucklings!" '

I could have wished that she had phrased it differently, but there was no chance of telling her so. When the aged relative collars the conversation, she collars it.

'I was saying,' she proceeded, 'that I wagered on Simla everything I possessed. Correction. Change that to considerably more than I possessed. If I lost, it would mean touching Tom for a goodish bit before I could brass up, and you know how parting with money always gives him indigestion. You can picture my state of mind. If it hadn't been for Angelica Briscoe, I think I would have had a nervous breakdown. There were moments when only my iron will kept me from shooting up to the ceiling, shrieking like a banshee. The suspense was so terrific.'

I was still dumbfounded, but I managed to say 'Angelica Briscoe?', at a loss to see where she got into the act, and the speaker spoke on.

'Don't tell me you've forgotten her. I would have thought by this time you would have asked her to marry you, which seems to be your normal practice five minutes after you've met any girl who isn't actually repulsive. But I suppose you couldn't see straight after all that port. Angelica, daughter of the Rev Briscoe. I had a long talk with her after you had left, and I found that she, too, had betted heavily on Simla and was wondering how she could pay up if he lost. I told her about the cat and she was enthusiastically in favour of stealing it, and she solved the problem which had been bothering me, the question of how it could be done. You see, it's not a job that's up everybody's street. Mine, for instance. You have to be like one of those Red Indians I used to read about in Fenimore Cooper's books when I was a child, the fellows who never let a twig snap beneath their feet, and I'm not built for that.'

There was justice in this. I believe the old relative was sylphlike in her youth, but the years have brought with them a certain solidity, and any twig trodden on by her in the evening of her life would go off like the explosion of a gas main.

'But Angelica pointed the way. There's a girl, that Angelica. Only a clergyman's daughter, but with all the executive qualities of a great statesman. She didn't hesitate a moment. Her face lighting up and her eyes sparkling. She said:

' "This is a job for Billy Graham." '

I could not follow her here. The name was familiar to me, but I never associated it with proficiency in the art of removing cats from Spot A to Spot B, especially cats belonging to someone else. Indeed, I should have thought that that was the sort of activity Mr Graham would rather have frowned on, being in his particular line of business.

I mentioned this to the old ancestor, and she told me I had fallen into a natural error.

'His real name is Herbert Graham, but everyone calls him Billy.'

'Why?'

'Rustic humour. There's a lot of that around here. He's the king of the local poachers, and you don't find any twigs snapping beneath *his* feet. All the gamekeepers for miles around have been trying for years to catch him with the goods, but they haven't a hope. It is estimated that seventy-six point eight per cent of the beer sold in the Goose and Grasshopper is bought by haggard gamekeepers trying to drown their sorrows after being baffled by Billy. I have this on the authority of Angelica, who is a great buddy of his. She told him about our anxiety, and he said he would attend to the matter immediately. He is particularly well situated to carry out operations at the Court, as his niece Marlene is the scullery maid there, so it arouses no suspicion if he is caught hanging around. He can always say he has come to see if she's getting on all right. Really, the whole thing has worked out so smoothly that one feels one is being watched over by Providence.'

I went on being appalled. Her scheme of engaging the services of a hired bravo who would probably blackmail her for the rest of her life shook me to the core. As for Angelica Briscoe, one asked oneself what clergymen's daughters were coming to.

I tried to reason with her.

'You can't do this, old blood relation. It's as bad as nobbling a horse.'

If you think that caused the blush of shame to mantle her cheek, you don't know much about aunts.

'Well, isn't nobbling a horse an ordinary business precaution everyone would take if only they could manage it?' she riposted.

The Woosters never give up. I tried again.

'How about the purity of the turf?'

'No good to me. I like my turf impure. More genuine excitement.'

'What would the Quorn say of this? Or, for the matter of that, the Pytchley?'

'They would send me a telegram wishing me luck. You don't understand these small country meetings. It's not like Epsom or Ascot. A little finesse from time to time is taken for granted. It's expected of you. A couple of years ago Jimmy had a horse called Poonah running at Bridmouth, and a minion of Cook's got hold of the jockey on the eve of the race, lured him into the Goose and Grasshopper and filled him up with strong drink, sending him to the starting post next day with such a hangover that all he wanted to do was sit down and cry. He came in fifth, sobbing bitterly, and went to sleep before he was out of the saddle. Of course Jimmy guessed what had happened, but nothing was ever said about it. No hard feelings on either side. It wasn't till Jimmy fined Cook for moving pigs without a permit that relations became strained.'

I put another point, a shrewd one.

'What happens if this fellow of yours does get caught? His first move will be to give you away, blackening your reputation in Maiden Eggesford beyond repair.'

'He's never caught. He's the local Scarlet Pimpernel. And nothing could blacken my reputation in Maiden Eggesford. I'm much too much the popular pet ever since I sang "Every Nice Girl Loves A Sailor" at the village concert last year. I had them rolling in the aisles. Three encores, and so many bows that I got a crick in the back.'

'Spare me the tale of your excesses,' I said distantly.

'I wore a sailor suit.'

'Please,' I said, revolted.

'And you ought to have seen the notice I got in the *Bridmouth Argus*, with which is incorporated the *Somerset Farmer* and the *South Country Intelligencer*. But I can't stop here all day listening to you. Elsa's got some bores coming to tea and wants me to rally round. Entertain the cat when it arrives. I gather that it is rather the Bohemian type and probably prefers whisky, but try it with a spot of milk.'

And with these words she exited left centre, as full of beans as any aunt that ever stepped.

Jeeves entered. He had his arms full.

'We appear to have this cat, sir,' he said.

I gave him a look, lacklustre to the last drop.

'So he brought it?'

'Yes, sir. A few moments ago.'

'To the back door?'

'Yes, sir. He showed a proper feeling in that.'

'Is he here now?'

'No, sir. He has gone to the Goose and Grasshopper.'

I got down to the *res*. This was no time for beating about the bush. I needed his advice, and I needed it quick.

'I take it, Jeeves,' I said, 'that seeing the cat at this address you have put two and two together, as the expression is, and realize that there has been dirty work at the crossroads?'

'Yes, sir. I had the advantage of hearing Mrs Travers's observations. She is a lady with a very carrying voice.'

'That expresses it to a nicety. I believe that when hunting in her younger days she could make herself heard in several adjoining counties.'

'I can readily credit it, sir.'

'Well, if you know all about it, there's no need to explain the situation. The problem that confronts us now is where do we go from here?'

'Sir?'

'You know what I mean. I can't just sit here . . . what's the word?'

'Supinely, sir?'

'That's it. I can't just sit here supinely and allow the rannygazoo to proceed unchecked. The honour of the Woosters is at stake.'

'You are blameless, sir. You did not purloin the cat.'

'No, but a member of my family did. By the way, could she get jugged if the crime were brought home to her?'

'It is difficult to say without consulting a competent legal authority. But an unpleasant scandal would inevitably result.'

'You mean her name would become a hissing and a byword?'

'Substantially that, sir.'

'With disastrous effects on Uncle Tom's digestion. That's bad, Jeeves. We can't have that. You know how he is after the mildest lobster. We must return this cat to Cook.'

'It would seem advisable, sir.'

'You wouldn't care to do it?'

'No, sir.'

'It would be the feudal thing to do.'

'No doubt, sir.'

'One of those vassals in the Middle Ages would have jumped to it.'

'Very possibly, sir.'

'It would take you ten minutes. You could go in the car.'

'I fear that I must continue to plead a *nolle prosequi*, sir.'

'Then I shall have to see what I can do. Leave me, Jeeves, I want to think.'

'Very good, sir. Would a whisky and soda be of assistance?'

'*Rem acu tetigisti*,' I said.

Left alone, I gave my problem the cream of the Wooster brain for some time, but without avail, as they say. Try as I would I couldn't seem to hit on a method of getting the cat back to square one which didn't involve a meeting with Pop Cook and his hunting crop, and I didn't want that whistling about my legs. Courageous though the Woosters are, there are things from which they shrink.

I was still thinking when there was a cheery cry from without and the blood froze in my veins as Plank came bounding in.

12

The reason why the blood froze in my v. needs little explanation. The dullest eye could have perceived the delicacy of my position. With the cat practically *vis-à-vis* as you might say and Plank among those present, my predicament was that of a member of the criminal classes who has got away with the Maharajah's ruby and after stashing it among his effects sees a high official of Scotland Yard walk in at the door. Worse, as a matter of fact, because rubies don't talk, whereas cats do. This one had struck me during our brief acquaintance as the taciturn type, content merely to purr, but who knew that, finding itself in unfamiliar surroundings and missing its pal Potato Chip, it would not utter a yowl or two? And a single mew would be enough to plunge me in the soup.

I remember my Aunt Agatha once making me take her revolting son, young Thos, to a play at the Old Vic by the name of *Macbeth*. Thos slept throughout, but I thought it rather good, and the reason I bring it up is because there was a scene in it where Macbeth is giving a big dinner party and the ghost of a fellow called Banquo, whom he has recently murdered, crashes the gate all covered with blood. Macbeth took it big, and the point I'm trying to make is that my feelings on seeing Plank were much the same as his on that occasion. I goggled at him as he would have goggled at a scorpion or tarantula or whatever they have in Africa if on going to bed one night he had found it nestling in his pyjamas.

Plank was very merry and bright.

'I thought I'd come and tell you,' he said, 'that I'm getting my memory back. Pretty soon I'll be remembering every detail of that first meeting of ours. Wrapped in mist at the moment, but light is beginning to seep through. It's often that way with malaria.'

I didn't like the sound of this at all. As I explained earlier, the meeting to which he referred had been one fraught with embarrassment for me, and I would have preferred to let the dead past bury its dead as the fellow said. Well, when I remind you that it concluded with a suggestion on his part that he hit me over the head with a Zulu knob-kerrie, you will probably gather that it had not been conducted throughout in an atmosphere of the utmost cordiality.

'One thing I remember,' he proceeded, 'is that you were very keen on Rugby football, which of course is the great interest of my life, and I told you my village team was shaping well and showed great promise. And by an extraordinary stroke of luck I've got a new vicar, chap called Pinker, who was an international prop forward. Played for Oxford four years and got I don't know how many English caps. He pulls the whole side together, besides preaching an excellent sermon.'

Nothing could have pleased me more than to hear that my old friend Stinker Pinker was giving satisfaction, and if it had not been for the dark shadow of the cat brooding over us I might quite have enjoyed this little get-together. For he was an entertaining companion, as these far-flung chaps so often are, and told me a lot I hadn't known before about tsetse flies and what to do if cornered by a charging rhinoceros. But in the middle of one of his best stories – he had just got to where the natives seemed friendly, so he decided to stay the night – he broke off, cocked his head sideways, and said:

'What was that?'

I had heard it, too, of course. But I preserved my poise.

'What was what?' I said.

'I heard a cat.'

I continued to wear the mask. I laughed a light laugh.

'Oh, that was my man Jeeves. He imitates cats.'

'He does, eh?'

'It gives him a passing pleasure.'

'And, I suppose, gets a laugh if he does it at the pub near closing time when everyone's fairly tight. I had a native bearer once who could imitate the mating call of the male puma.'

'Really?'

'So that even female pumas were deceived. They used to come flocking round the camp in dozens, and were as sick as mud when they found it was only a native bearer. He was the one I was telling you we had to bury before sundown. Which reminds me. How are those spots of yours?'

'Completely disappeared.'

'Not always a good sign. It's bad if they work inward and get mixed up with the blood stream.'

'Doctor Murgatroyd expected them to disappear.'

'He ought to know.'

'I have great confidence in him.'

'So have I, in spite of those whiskers.' He paused, and laughed amusedly. 'Odd, the passage of time.'

'Pretty odd,' I conceded.

'Old Jimpy Murgatroyd. You'd never think, to look at him now, that when I knew him as a boy he was about the best wing-three we ever had at Haileybury. Fast as a streak and never failed to give the reverse pass. He scored two tries against Bedford, one of them from our twenty-five, and dropped a goal against Tonbridge.'

Though not having a clue to what he was talking about, I said 'Really?' and he said 'Absolutely', and I think we should have had a lot more about E. Jimpson Murgatroyd the boy, but at this moment the cat came on the air again and he changed the subject.

'Listen. Wouldn't you swear that was a cat? That man of yours certainly makes it lifelike.'

'Just a knack.'

'A gift, I'd call it. Good animal-impersonators don't grow on every bush. I never had another bearer like the puma chap. Plenty of fellows who could do you a passable screech owl, but that's not the same thing. It's lucky Cook isn't here.'

'Why do you say that?'

'Because he would insist on being confronted by what he imagined to be his cat and would tear the place apart to get at it. He wouldn't believe for a moment that it was your man practising his art. You see, a very valuable cat belonging to Cook has vanished, and he is convinced that rival interests have stolen it. He talked of calling Scotland Yard in. But I must be getting along. I only stopped by to tell you about the remarkable improvement in my memory. It's all coming back. It won't be long before I shall be remembering why I thought your name was something that began with Al. Could it have been a nickname of some sort?'

'I don't think so.'

'Not short for Alka-Seltzer, or something like that? Well, no good worrying about it now. It'll come. It'll come.'

I couldn't imagine what had given him this idea that my name began with Al, but it was a small point and I didn't linger on it. No sooner had he beetled off than I was calling Jeeves in for a conference.

When he came, he was full of apologies. He seemed to think he had let the young master down.

'I fear you will have thought me remiss, sir, but I found it impossible to stifle the animal's cries completely. I trust they were not overheard by your visitor.'

'They were, and the visitor was none other than Major Plank, from whom you saved me so adroitly at Totleigh-in-the-Wold. He is closely allied to Pop Cook, and I don't mind telling you that when he blew in I was as badly rattled as Macbeth, if you know what I mean, that time he was sitting down to dinner and the ghost turned up.'

'I know the scene well, sir. "Never shake thy gory locks at me," he said.'

'And I don't blame him. Plank heard those yowls.'

'I am extremely sorry, sir.'

'Not your fault. Cats will be cats. I was taken aback at the moment, like Macbeth, but I kept my head. I told him you were a cat-imitator brushing up your cat-imitating.'

'A very ingenious ruse, sir.'

'Yes, I didn't think it was too bad.'

'Did it satisfy the gentleman?'

'It seemed to. But what of Pop Cook?'

'Sir?'

'What's worrying me is the possibility of Cook being less inclined to swallow the story and coming here to search the premises. And when I say the possibility, I mean the certainty. Figure it out for yourself. He finds me up at Eggesford Court apparently swiping the cat. He learns that I am lunching at Eggesford Hall. "Ha!" he says to himself, "one of the Briscoe gang, is he? And I caught him with the cat actually on his person." Do you suppose that when Plank gets back and tells him he heard someone imitating cats *chez* me, he is going to believe that what Plank heard was a human voice? I doubt it, Jeeves. He will be at my door in ten seconds flat, probably accompanied by the entire local police force.'

My remorseless reasoning had its effect. A slight wiggling of the nose showed that. Nothing could ever make Jeeves say 'Gorblimey!', but I could see that was the word that would have sprung to his lips if he hadn't stopped it half-way. His comment on my *obiter dicta* was brief and to the point.

'We must act, sir!'

'And without stopping to pick daisies by the wayside. Are you still resolved not to return this cat to *status quo*?'

'Yes, sir.'

'Sam Weller would have done it like a shot to oblige Mr Pickwick.'

'It is not my place to return cats, sir. But if I might make a suggestion.'

'Speak on, Jeeves.'

'Why should we not place the matter in the hands of the man Graham?'

'Of course! I never thought of that.'

'He is a poacher of established reputation, and a competent poacher is what we need.'

'I see what you mean. His experience enables him to move around without letting a twig snap beneath his feet, which is the first essential when you are returning cats.'

'Precisely, sir. With your permission I will go to the Goose and Grasshopper and tell him that you wish to see him.'

'Do so, Jeeves,' I said, and only a few minutes later I found myself closeted with Herbert (Billy) Graham.

The first thing that impressed itself on me as I gave him the once-over was his air of respectability. I had always supposed that poachers were tough-looking eggs who wore whatever they could borrow from the nearest scarecrow and shaved only once a week. He, to the contrary, was neatly clad in form-fitting tweeds and was shaven to the bone. His eyes were frank and blue, his hair a becoming grey. I have seen more raffish Cabinet ministers. He looked like someone who might have sung in the sainted Briscoe's church choir, as I was informed later he did, being the possessor of a musical tenor voice which came in handy for the anthem and when they were doing those 'miserable sinner' bits in the Litany.

He was about the height and tonnage of Fred Astaire, and he had the lissomness which is such an asset in his chosen profession. One could readily imagine him flitting silently through the undergrowth with a couple of rabbits in his grasp, always two jumps ahead of the gamekeepers who were trying to locate him. The old ancestor had compared him to the Scarlet Pimpernel, and a glance was enough to tell me that the tribute was well deserved. I thought how wise Jeeves had been in suggesting that I entrust to him the delicate mission which I had in mind. When it comes to returning cats that have been snitched from their lawful homes, you need a specialist. Where Lloyd George or Winston Churchill would have failed, this Graham, I knew would succeed.

'Good afternoon, sir,' he said, 'you wished to see me?'

I got down without delay to the nub. No sense in humming or, for the matter of that, hawing.

'It's about this cat.'

'I delivered it according to instructions.'

'And now I want you to take it back.'

He seemed perplexed.

'Back, sir?'

'To where you got it.'

'I do not quite understand, sir.'

'I'll explain.'

I think I outlined the position of affairs rather well, making it abundantly clear that a Wooster could not countenance what was virtually tantamount, if tantamount is the word I want, to nobbling a horse and that the cat under advisement must be restored to its proprietor with all possible slippiness, and he listened attentively. But when I had finished, he shook his head.

'Out of the question, sir.'

'Out of the question? Why? You purloined it.'

'Yes, sir.'

'Then you can put it back.'

'No, sir. You are overlooking certain vital facts.'

'Such as?'

'The theft to which you refer was perpetrated as a personal favour to Miss Briscoe, whom I have known from childhood, and a sweet child she was.'

I thought of trying to move him by saying that I had been a sweet child, too, but I knew that this was not the case, having frequently been informed to that effect by my Aunt Agatha, so I let it go. There was not much chance, of course, that he had ever met my Aunt Agatha and discussed me with her, but it was not worth risking.

'Furthermore,' he proceeded, and I was impressed, as I had been from the start, by the purity of his diction. He had evidently had a good education, though I doubted if he was an

Oxford man. 'Furthermore,' he said, 'I have five pounds on Potato Chip with the landlord of the Goose and Grasshopper.'

'Aha!' I said to myself, and I'll tell you why I said 'Aha' to myself. I said it because the scales had fallen from my eyes and I saw all. Plainly that stuff about personal favours to sweet children had been the merest bobbledy-gook. He had been actuated throughout entirely by commercial motives. When Angelica Briscoe had come to him, he would have started with a regretful *nolle prosequi* on the ground that he had this fiver on Potato Chip and was obliged to protect his investment. She had said, would he do it for ten quid, which would leave him with a nice profit? He had right-hoed. Angelica had then touched Aunt Dahlia for ten and the deal had gone through. I have often thought I would have made a good detective. I can reason and deduce.

Everything was simple now that the matter could be put on a business basis. All that remained was to arrange terms. It would have to be a ready-money transaction, he being the shrewd man he was, and fortunately I had brought wads of cash with me for betting-on-the-course-at-Bridmouth purposes, so there was no problem.

'How much do you want?' I said.

'Sir?'

'To de-cat my premises and restore this feline to the strength.'

A sort of film came over his frank blue eyes, as I suppose it always did when he talked business, though not when singing in the choir. Fellows at the Drones have told me they notice the same thing in Oofy Prosser, the club millionaire, when they try to float a small loan with him to see them through till next Wednesday.

'How much do I want, sir?'

'Yes. Give it a name. We won't haggle.'

He pursed his lips.

'I'm afraid,' he said, having unpursed them, 'I couldn't do it as cheap as I'd like, sir. You see, what with them having discovered the animal's absence by this time, the hue and cry, as you might say, will be up and everybody at Mr Cook's residence on the *qui vive* or alert. I'd be in the position of a spy in wartime carrying secret dispatches through the enemy's lines with every eye on the look-out for him. I'd have to make it twenty pounds.'

I was relieved. I had been expecting something higher. He,

too, seemed to feel that he had erred on the side of moderation, for he immediately added:

'Or, rather, thirty.'

'Thirty!'

'Thirty, sir.'

'Let's haggle,' I said.

But when I suggested twenty-five, a nicer-looking sort of number than thirty, he shook his grey head regretfully, so we went on haggling, and he haggled better than me, so that eventually we settled on thirty-five.

It wasn't one of my best haggling days.

13

One of the questions put to me when I won that Scripture Knowledge prize at my private school was, I recall, 'What do you know of the deaf adder?', and my grip on Holy Writ enabled me to reply correctly that it stopped its ears and would not hear the voice of the charmer, charm he never so wisely, and after my session with Herbert Graham I knew how that charmer must have felt. If I had been in a position to compare notes with him, we would have agreed that the less we saw of adders in the future the better it would be for us.

Nobody could have charmed more wisely than me as I urged Herbert Graham to lower his price, and nobody could have stopped his ears more firmly than did that human serpent. Talk about someone not meeting you half-way; he didn't go an inch in the direction of coming to a peaceful settlement. Thirty-five quid, I mean to say. Absolutely monstrous. But that's what happens when you're up against it and the other fellow holds all the cards.

Haggling is a thing that takes it out of you, and it was a limp Bertram Wooster who after Graham and cat had set forth on their journey sat skimming listlessly through the opening pages of *By Order Of The Czar*. And I had read enough to make me wish I had taken out *The Mystery Of A Hansom Cab* instead, when the telephone rang.

It was, as I had feared, Aunt Dahlia. Sooner or later, I had of course realized, exchanges with the aged relative were inevitable, but I could have faced them better if they could have been postponed for a while. In my enfeebled condition I was in no shape to cope with aunts. A man who has just become engaged to a girl whose whole personality gives him a sinking feeling and who has had to pay thirty-five quid to a bloodsucker and another twopence to a lending library for a dud book is seldom in mid-season form.

The old ancestor, on the other hand, little knowing that she was about to get a sock on the jaw which would shake her to her foundation garments, was all lightheartedness and joviality.

'Hullo, fathead,' she said. 'What news on the Rialto?'

'What, what, where?' I responded, not getting it.

'The cat. Has he brought it?'

'Yes.'

'Is it in your bosom?'

I saw the time had come. Shrink though I might from revealing the awful truth, it had to be done. I took a deep breath. It was some small comfort to feel that she was at the end of the telephone wire a mile and a half away. You can never be certain what aunts will do when at close quarters. Far less provocation in my earlier days had led this one to buffet me soundly on the side of the head.

'No,' I said, 'it's gone.'

'Gone? Gone where?'

'Billy Graham has taken it back.'

'Taken it *back*?'

'To Eggesford Court. I told him to.'

'You *told* him to?'

'Yes. You see—'

That concluded for a considerable space of time my share in the duologue, for she got into high with the promptness which I had anticipated. She spoke as follows:

'Hell's bells! Ye gods! Angels and ministers of grace defend us! He brought the cat, and you deliberately turned it from your door, though you knew what it meant to me. Letting the side down! Failing me in my hour of need! Bringing my grey hairs in sorrow to the grave! And after all I've done for you, you miserable ungrateful worm. Do you remember me telling you that when you were a babe and suckling and looking, I may add in passing, like a badly poached egg, you nearly swallowed your rubber comforter, and if I hadn't jerked it out in time, you would have choked to death? It would go hard for you if you swallowed your rubber comforter now. I wouldn't stir a finger. Do you remember when you had measles and I gave up hours of my valuable time to playing tiddlywinks with you and letting you beat me without a murmur?'

I could have disputed that. My victories had been due entirely to skill. I haven't played much tiddlywinks lately, but in those boyhood days I was pretty hot stuff at the pastime. I did not mention this, however, because she was proceeding and I didn't like to interrupt the flow.

'Do you remember when you were at that private school of yours I used to send you parcels of food at enormous expense because you said you were about to expire from starvation? Do you remember when you were at Oxford—'

'Stop, aged r.,' I cried, for she had touched me deeply with these reminiscences of the young Wooster. 'You're breaking my heart.'

'You haven't got a heart. If you had, you wouldn't have driven that poor defenceless cat out into the snow. All I asked of you was to give it a bed in the spare room for a few days and so place my financial affairs on a sound basis, but you wouldn't do a trifling service for me which would have cost you nothing except a bob or two for milk and fish. What, I ask myself, has become of the old-fashioned nephew to whom his aunt's wishes were law? They don't seem to be making them nowadays.'

At this point Nature took its toll. She had to pause to take in breath, and I was enabled to speak.

'Old blood relation,' I said, 'you are under a what-is-it.'

'What is what?'

'The thing people get under. It's on the tip of my tongue. Begins with mis. Ah, I've got it, misapprehension. I've heard Jeeves use the word. Your view of my behaviour with the above cat is all cockeyed. I disapproved of your pinching it, because I felt that such an action stained the escutcheon of the Woosters, but I would have given it bed and board, however reluctantly, had it not been for Plank.'

'Plank?'

'Major Plank the explorer.'

'What's he got to do with it?'

'Everything. You've probably heard of Major Plank.'

'I haven't.'

'Well, he's one of those chaps who have native bearers and things and go exploring. Who was it out in Africa somewhere who met the other fellow and presumed he was Doctor something? Plank is, or was, in the same line of business.'

A snort came over the wire, nearly fusing it.

'Bertie,' said the blood relation, now having taken aboard an adequate supply of air, 'I am hampered by being at the other end of the telephone, but were I within reach of you I would give you one on the side of the head which you wouldn't forget in a hurry. Tell me in a few simple words what you think you're talking about.'

'I'm talking about Plank. And what I'm trying to establish is that Plank, though an explorer, is not exploring now. He is staying with Cook at Eggesford Court.'

'So what?'

'So jolly well this. He dropped in on me shortly after Billy Graham had clocked in and left the cat. It was with Jeeves in the kitchen, having one for the tonsils. And while Plank was there it yowled, and Plank of course heard it. You don't need to be told the upshot. Plank goes back to Cook, tells him he thought he heard a cat at Wooster's address, and Cook, already suspicious of me after our unfortunate encounter, comes down here like a wolf on the fold, his cohorts all gleaming with purple and gold. I ought to add that I told Plank that the cat he heard was not a cat but Jeeves imitating cats, and he believed it all right because explorers are simple-minded bozos who believe everything they're told, but will the story get over with Cook? Not a hope. There was nothing for me to do but tell Billy Graham to return the cat.'

I suppose one of the top-notch barristers could have put it more clearly, but not much more. She was silent for a space. Musing, no doubt, and weighing this against that. Finally she spoke.

'I see.'

'Good.'

'You appear not to have been such a non-cooperative hell-hound as I thought you were.'

'Excellent.'

'Sorry I ticked you off with such vigour.'

'Quite all right, aged relative. *Tout comprendre c'est tout pardonner.*'

'Yes, I suppose it was the only thing you could do. But don't expect any hallelujahs from me. My whole plan of campaign has gone phut.'

'Oh, I don't know. Perhaps everything will be all right. Simla may win anyway.'

'Yes, but one did like to feel that one was betting on a certainty. It's no good trying to cheer me up. I feel awful.'

'Me, too.'

'What's wrong with you?'

'I'm engaged to be married to a girl I can't stand the sight of.'

'What, another? Who is it this time?'

'Vanessa Cook.'

'Any relation to old Cook?'

'His daughter.'

'How did it happen?'

'I proposed to her a year ago, and she turned me down, and just now she blew in and said she had changed her mind and would marry me. Came as a nasty shock.'

'You should have told her to go and boil her head.'

'I couldn't.'

'Why couldn't you?'

'Not *preux*.'

'Not what?'

'*Preux*. P for potted meat, r for rissole, e for egg nog, and so on. You've heard of a *preux chevalier*? It is my aim to be one.'

'Oh, well, if you go about being *preux*, you must expect to get into trouble. But I wouldn't worry. You're bound to wriggle out of it somehow. You told me once that you had faith in your star. The girls you've been engaged to and have escaped from would reach, if placed end to end, from Piccadilly to Hyde Park Corner. I won't believe you're married till I see the bishop and assistant clergy mopping their foreheads and saying, "Well, that's that. We've really got the young blighter off at last." '

And with these words of cheer she rang off.

You would rather have expected that it would have been with a light heart that I returned to *By Order Of The Czar*. Such, however, was not the case. I had squared myself with the old flesh and blood and so had put a stopper on her wrath, a continuance of which might have resulted in her barring me from her table for an indefinite period, thus depriving me of the masterpieces of her French chef Anatole, God's gift to the gastric juices, but, as I say, the h. was not l. I could not but mourn for the collapse of the aged relative's hopes and dreams, a collapse for which I, though a mere toy in the hands of Fate, was bound to consider myself responsible.

I said as much to Jeeves when he came in with the materials for the pre-dinner cocktail.

'My heart is heavy, Jeeves,' I said, after expressing gratification at the sight of the fixings.

'Indeed, sir? Why is that?'

'I have just been having a painful scene with Aunt Dahlia. Well, when I say scene that's not quite the right word, the conversation having been conducted over the telephone. Did Graham get off all right?'

'Yes, sir.'

'Accompanied by cat?'

'Yes, sir.'

'That's what I was telling her, and she became a bit emotional. You never hunted with the Quorn or the Pytchley, did you, Jeeves? It seems to do something to the vocabulary. Lends a speaker eloquence. The old flesh and blood didn't have to pause to pick her words, they came out like bullets from a machine-gun. I was thankful we weren't talking face to face. Goodness knows what might have happened if we had been.'

'You should have told Mrs Travers the facts relating to Major Plank, sir.'

'I did, the moment I could get a word in edgeways, and it was that that acted like . . . like what?'

'Balm in Gilead, sir?'

'Exactly. I was going to say manna in the wilderness, but balm in Gilead hits it off better. She calmed down and admitted that I couldn't have done anything else but return the cat.'

'Most satisfactory, sir.'

'Yes, that part of it is all pretty smooth, but there's one other thing that's weighing on me a bit. I'm engaged to be married.'

14

As always when I tell him I'm engaged to be married, he betrayed no emotion, continuing to look as if he had been stuffed by a good taxidermist. It is not his place, he would say if you asked him, to go beyond the basic formalities on these occasions.

'Indeed, sir?' he said.

Usually this about covers it, and I don't discuss my predicament with him. I feel it wouldn't be seemly, if that's the word, and I know he would feel it wouldn't be seemly, so with both of us feeling it wouldn't be seemly we talk of other matters.

But this was a special occasion. Never before had I become betrothed to someone who would make me cut out smoking and cocktails, and in my opinion this made the subject a legitimate one for debate. When you're up against it as I was, it is essential to exchange views with a mastermind, if you can get hold of one, however unseemly it may be.

So when he added, 'May I offer my congratulations, sir,' I replied with lines which were not on the routine.

'No, Jeeves, you may not, not by a jugful. You see before you a man who is as near to being what is known as a toad at Harrow as a man can be who was educated at Eton. I'm in sore straits, Jeeves.'

'I am sorry to hear that, sir.'

'You'll be sorrier when I explain further. Have you ever seen a garrison besieged by howling savages, with their ammunition down to the last box of cartridges, the water supply giving out and the United States Marines nowhere in sight?'

'Not to my recollection, sir.'

'Well, my position is roughly that of such a garrison, except that compared with me they're sitting pretty. Compared with me they haven't a thing to worry about.'

'You fill me with alarm, sir.'

'I bet I do, and I haven't even started yet. I will begin by saying that Miss Cook, to whom I'm engaged, is a lady for whom I have the utmost esteem and respect, but on certain matters we do not . . . what's the expression?'

'See eye to eye, sir?'

'That's right. And unfortunately those matters are the what-d'you-call-it of my whole policy. What is it that policies have?'

'I think the word for which you are groping, sir, may possibly be cornerstone.'

'Thank you, Jeeves. She disapproves of a variety of things which are the cornerstone of my policy. Marriage with her must inevitably mean that I shall have to cast them from my life, for she has a will of iron and will have no difficulty in making her husband jump through hoops and snap sugar off his nose. You get what I mean?'

'I do, sir. A very colourful image.'

'Cocktails, for instance, will be barred. She says they are bad for the liver. Have you noticed, by the way, how frightfully lax everything's getting now? In Queen Victoria's day a girl would never have dreamed of mentioning livers in mixed company.'

'Very true, sir. *Tempora mutanter, nos et mutamar in illis.*'

'That, however, is not the worst.'

'You horrify me, sir.'

'At a pinch I could do without cocktails. It would be agony, but we Woosters can rough it. But she says I must give up smoking.'

'This was indeed the most unkindest cut of all, sir.'

'Give up smoking, Jeeves!'

'Yes, sir. You will notice that I am shuddering.'

'The trouble is that she is greatly under the influence of a pal of hers called Tolstoy. I've never met him, but he seems to have the most extraordinary ideas. You won't believe this, Jeeves, but he says that no one needs to smoke, as equal pleasure can be obtained by twirling the fingers. The man must be an ass. Imagine a posh public dinner – one of those "decorations will be worn" things. The royal toast has been drunk, strong men are licking their lips at the thought of cigars, and the toastmaster bellows "Gentlemen, you may twirl your fingers." Don't tell me there wouldn't be a flat feeling, a sense of disappointment. Do you know anything about this fellow Tolstoy? You ever heard of him?'

'Oh, yes, sir. He was a very famous Russian novelist.'

'Russian, eh? Well, there you are. And a novelist? He didn't write *By Order Of The Czar*, did he?'

'I believe not, sir.'

'I thought he might have under another name. You say "was". Is he no longer with us?'

'No, sir. He died some years ago.'

'Good for him. Twirl your fingers! Too absurd. I'd laugh only she says I mustn't laugh because another pal of hers, called Chesterfield, didn't. Well, she needn't worry. The way things are shaping I haven't anything to laugh about. For I've not mentioned the principal objection to the marriage. Don't jump to the hasty conclusion that I mean because a father-in-law like Cook is included in the package deal. I grant you that that's enough by itself to darken the horizon, but what's on my mind is the thought of Orlo Porter.'

'Ah, yes, sir.'

I gave him an austere look.

'If you can't say anything better than "Ah, yes", Jeeves, say nothing.'

'Very good, sir.'

'The thought, as I was saying, of Orlo Porter. We have already touched on his testy disposition, the iron-bandlike muscles of his brawny arms, and his jealousy. The mere suspicion that I was inflicting my beastly society, as he put it, on Miss Cook was enough to make him tell me that he would tear out my insides with his bare hands. What'll he do when he finds I'm engaged to her?'

'Surely, sir, the lady having so unequivocally rejected him, he can scarcely blame you—'

'For filling the vacant spot? Don't you believe it. He'll take it for granted that I persuaded her to give him the pink slip. Nothing will drive it out of his nut. The belief that I'm a Grade A snake in the grass, and we all know what to expect from snakes in the g. No, we have got to be frightfully subtle and think of some plan for drawing his fangs. Otherwise my insides won't be worth a moment's purchase.'

I was about to go on to ask him if he still had the cosh – or blackjack, to use the American term – which he had taken away from Aunt Dahlia's son Bonzo some months previously. Bonzo had bought it to use on a schoolmate he disliked, and we all thought he would be better without it. It was, of course, precisely what I needed to ease the tenseness of the O. Porter situation. Armed with this weapon, I could defy O. Porter without a qualm. But before I could speak the telephone tootled in the hall. I waved a hand in its direction.

'Answer that, would you mind, Jeeves, and say I've gone for a brisk walk, as recommended by my medical adviser. It'll be Aunt Dahlia, and though she was in a reasonable frame of mind at the conclusion of our recent talk, there's no telling how long these reasonable frames of mind will last.'

'Very good, sir.'

'You know what women are.'

'I do, indeed, sir.'

'Especially aunts.'

'Yes, sir. My aunt—'

'Tell me all about her later.'

'Any time you wish, sir.'

I remember Jeeves once saying of my friend Catsmeat Potter-Pirbright – it was when a long shot he had backed had come in first by a head, only to be disqualified owing to some infringement of the rules by its jockey – that melancholy had marked him for her own, and it was the same with me now as I sat totting up the score and realizing how extraordinarily deeply I had been plunged in the soup.

Compared with other items on the list of my troubles it was perhaps a minor cause for melancholy that the old ancestor should be trying to get me on the telephone. Nevertheless, it added one more thing to worry about. It could only mean, I felt, that she had come out of the amiable mood she had been in when last heard from and had thought of a lot more nasty cracks to make on the subject of my failure to reach the standard which she considered adequate in a nephew. And I was in no shape to listen to destructive criticism when we next met, especially when delivered by a voice trained by years of shouting 'Gone away' at foxes to reduce the hearer's nervous system to pulp.

When, therefore, Jeeves returned, my first observation was:

'What did she say?'

'It was not Mrs Travers, sir, it was Mr Porter.'

I was more thankful than ever that I had got him to answer the phone.

'Well, what did *he* say?' I asked, though I could have made a rough guess.

'I regret that I am not able to report the entire conversation verbatim, sir. I found the gentleman incoherent at the outset.

I gathered that he was under the impression that he was addressing you, and emotion interfered with the clarity of his diction. I informed him of my identity, and he moderated his verbal speed. I was thus enabled to follow him. He gave me several messages to give to you.'

'Messages?'

'Yes, sir, embodying what he proposed to do to you when next you met. His remarks were in the main of a crudely surgical nature, and many of the plans he outlined would be extremely difficult to put into practice. His threat, for instance, to pull off your head and make you swallow it.'

'He said that?'

'Among other things more or less on the same trend. But you need have no apprehension, sir.'

It shows the state to which the slings and arrows of outrageous fortune, as somebody called them, had reduced me that I didn't laugh a hacking laugh at this. I didn't even utter a sardonic 'Oh, yeah' or 'Says you'. I merely buried the face in the hands, and he continued:

'Before I left the room you were speaking of the necessity of drawing Mr Porter's fangs, as you very aptly put it. It gives me great pleasure to say that I have succeeded in doing this.'

I thought I couldn't have heard him correctly, and asked him to repeat his amazing statement. He did so, and I looked at him astounded. You might suppose that I would have been used by this time to seeing him pull rabbits out of a hat with a flick of the wrist and solve in a flash problems which had defied the best efforts of the finest minds, but it always comes fresh to me, depriving me of breath and causing the eyeballs to rotate in the parent sockets.

Then I saw what must be behind the easy confidence with which he had spoken.

'So you remembered the cosh?' I said.

'Sir?'

'And you have it in your possession.'

'I do not quite understand you, sir.'

'I thought you meant that you still had that cosh which you took away from Aunt Dahlia's Bonzo and were going to give it to me so that I would be armed when Porter made his spring.'

'Oh, no, sir. The instrument to which you refer is among my effects at our London residence.'

'Then how did you draw his fangs?'

'By reminding him that you have taken out an accident policy with him and drawing his attention to the inevitable displeasure of his employers if through him they were mulcted in a substantial sum of money. I had little difficulty in persuading the gentleman that anything in the nature of aggressive action on his part would be a mistake.'

I repeated the stare. His resource and ingenuity had stunned me.

'Jeeves,' I said, 'your resource and ingenuity have stunned me. Porter is baffled.'

'Yes, sir.'

'Unless you would prefer "thwarted".'

'Baffled I think is stronger.'

'Talk of drawing his fangs. His dentist will have to fit him with a completely new set.'

'Yes, sir, but we must not forget that the removal of Mr Porter as a menace is only half a battle. I hesitate to touch on a delicate subject . . .'

'Touch on, Jeeves.'

'But I gathered, partly from what you were saying and partly from the tone of your voice as you said it when you were speaking of her plans for your future, that the idea of marriage with Miss Cook is not wholly agreeable to you, and it occurred to me that much unpleasantness would be avoided, were the lady and Mr Porter to be reconciled.'

'It would indeed. But—'

'You were about to say, sir, that in your opinion the rift is too serious for that?'

'Well, isn't it?'

'I think not.'

'Your blow by blow description of the hostilities certainly gave me the impression that they had parted brass rags pretty finally. How about that lily-livered poltroon?'

'You have placed your finger on the real trouble, sir. Miss Cook applied that term to Mr Porter because of his refusal to approach her father and demand the money which the latter is holding in trust for him.'

'Well, according to you he said he wouldn't approach her father in a million years.'

'The situation has been changed by your becoming affianced to the woman he loves. To restore himself to Miss Cook's esteem he would face perils from which formerly he shrank.'

I got what he meant, but I didn't buy the idea. I still saw Orlo shrinking.

'Furthermore, sir, if you were to go to Mr Porter and point out to him that success might crown his efforts if he were to choose a moment shortly after dinner to approach Mr Cook, he would take the risk. A gentleman mellowed by a good dinner is always more amenable to overtures of any kind than one who is waiting for his food, as I understood from his conversation that Mr Cook was when Mr Porter discussed business with him on a former occasion.'

I started visibly. He had electrified me.

'Jeeves,' I said, 'I believe you've got something.'

'I think so, sir.'

'I'll go and see Porter at once. He's probably at the Goose and Grasshopper drowning his sorrows in gin and ginger ale. And let me say once more that you stand alone. You have made my day. I wish there was something I could do for you by way of return.'

'There is, sir.'

'It's yours, even unto half my kingdom. Give me a name.'

'I should be extremely grateful if you would allow me to spend the night at my aunt's.'

'You want to go to Liverpool? A long journey.'

'No, sir. My aunt returned this morning and is at her home in the village.'

'Then go to her, Jeeves, and heaven smile upon your reunion.'

'Thank you very much, sir. Should you have need of my services, the address is Balmoral, Mafeking Road, care of Mrs P. B. Pigott.'

'Oh, she isn't a Jeeves?'

'No, sir.'

He shimmered out, to return a moment later with the information that Mr Graham was in the kitchen and would be glad of a word with me. And it shows the extent to which the strain and rush of life at Maiden Eggesford had taken its toll that for a moment the name conveyed nothing to me. Then memory returned to its throne, and I felt as anxious to see Mr Graham as he apparently was to see me. Such was my confidence in him as a returner of cats that I could not imagine him failing in his mission, but I was naturally anxious to have the full details.

'In the kitchen, you say?'

'Yes, sir.'

'Then bung him in, Jeeves. There is no one I'd rather give audience to.'

And the hour, which was getting on for six o'clock, produced the man.

I was struck, as before, by the intense respectability of his appearance. He looked as though no rabbit or pheasant need entertain the slightest tremors in his presence, and one could readily picture him as the backbone of the choir when anthem time came along. His gentle 'Good evening, sir' was a treat to listen to.

'Good evening,' I said in my turn. 'Well? You accomplished your mission? The cat is back at the old stand?'

His eyes darkened, as if I had brought to the surface a secret sorrow.

'Well, yes and no, sir.'

'How do you mean, yes and no?'

'To the first of your questions the answer is in the affirmative. I did accomplish my mission. But unfortunately the cat is not at the old stand.'

'I don't get you.'

'It is here, sir, in your kitchen. I took it to Eggesford Court as per contract and released it near the stables and started on my homeward journey, happy to have earned the money which you so generously paid me for my services. Picture my astonishment and dismay when on reaching the village I discovered that the cat had followed me. It is a very affectionate animal, and we had become great friends. Would you wish me to take it back again? Of course I should not feel justified in charging my full fee, so shall we say ten pounds?'

If you want to know how this proposition affected me, I can put it in a nutshell by saying that I read him like a book. Many people are led by my frank and open countenance into thinking that I am one of the mugs, but I know a twister when I see one and I was in no doubt that one of these stood before me now.

What stopped me drawing myself to my full height and denouncing him was the reflection that the blighter had me in a cleft stick. Refusal to come across would mean him going to Pop Cook and getting a handsome fee from him for revealing that the aged relative had paid him to purloin the cat, and in spite of what she had said about her popularity in Maiden

Eggesford, resulting from her rendering 'Every Nice Girl Loves A Sailor' in a sailor suit, I knew that her name would be mud. I still wasn't sure she couldn't even be jugged, and what a sock in the eye that would give Uncle Tom's digestion.

I disbursed the tenner. Not blithely, but I disbursed it, and he went on his way.

For some little time after he had left I sat wrapped in thought. And then, just as I was getting up to go and see Orlo, in came Vanessa Cook.

15

She was accompanied by a dog of about the size of a young elephant, yellow in colour and with large ears sticking up, with whom I would willingly have fraternized, but after drinking in the delicious scent of my trouser legs for a brief moment it saw something out in the street which aroused its interest and left us.

Vanessa, meanwhile, had picked up my *By Order Of The Czar*, and I could see by the way she sniffed that she was about to become critical. There had always been a strong strain of book-reviewer blood in her.

'Trash,' she said. 'It really is time you began reading something worth while. I don't expect you to start off with Turgenev and Dostoievski,' she said, evidently alluding to a couple of Russian exiles she had met in London who did a bit of writing on the side, 'but there are plenty of good books which are easier and at the same time educational. I have brought one with me,' she went on, and I saw that she was holding a slim volume bound in limp purple leather with some sort of decoration in gold on the cover, and I shuddered strongly. To a man who has seen as much of life as I have there is always something sinister in a book bound in limp purple leather. 'It is a collection of whimsical essays, *The Prose Ramblings Of A Rhymester*, by Reginald Sprockett, a brilliant young poet from whom the critics expect great things. His style has been much praised, but it is the thought in these little gems to which I particularly call your attention. I will leave them here. I must be off. I only came to bring you the book . . .'

You probably think I reeled beneath this blow, but actually my heart was not so heavy as it might have been, for my quick brain had perceived how this would do me a bit of good. The revolting object would make an admirable Christmas present for my Aunt Agatha, always a difficult person to find Yuletide gifts for. I was warming myself with this thought, when Vanessa continued.

'Be very careful not to lose it. It has Reginald's autograph in it,' and glancing at the title page I saw that this was indeed so, which would have bucked Aunt Agatha up no little, but in addition to inscribing the slim volume with his own foul name the blighter had inscribed Vanessa's. 'To Vanessa, the fairest of the fair, from a devoted admirer,' he had written, dishing my plans completely. That was when my heart got heavy again. For though she hadn't definitely said so, something told me that later on I would be expected to pass an examination on the little opus, and failure would have the worst effects.

Having said she must be off, she naturally stayed on for another half-hour, much of which time was devoted to pointing out additional defects in my spiritual make-up which had occurred to her since our last meeting. It just showed how strong the missionary spirit can be in women that she could contemplate the idea of teaming up with a dubious character like B. Wooster. Her best friends would have warned her against it. 'Cast him into outer darkness where there is weeping and gnashing of teeth,' they would have said. 'No good trying to patch him up, he's hopeless.'

It was my membership of the Drones Club that now formed the basis of her observations. She didn't like the Drones Club, and she made it quite clear that at the conclusion of the honeymoon I would cross its threshold only over her dead body.

So, reckoning up the final score, the Bertram Wooster who signed the charge sheet in the vestry after the wedding ceremony would be a non-smoker, a teetotaller (for I knew it would come to that) and an ex-member of the Drones, in other words a mere shell of his former self. Little wonder that, as I listened to her, I gulped as Plank's native bearer must have done when they were getting ready to bury him before sundown.

The prospect appalled me, and while it was appalling me Vanessa moved to the door, this time apparently really intending to be off. And she had opened the door, Bertram much too much of a shell of his former self to open it for her, when she started back with a gasping cry.

'Father!' she cried gaspingly. 'He's coming up the garden path.'

'He's coming up the garden *path*?' I said. I was at a loss to imagine why Pop Cook should be calling on me. I mean to say we weren't on those terms.

'He's stopped to tie his boot lace,' she cried, gaspingly as before, and that concluded her share of the dialogue. With no further words she bounded into the kitchen like a fox pursued by both the Quorn and the Pytchley, slamming the door behind her.

I could appreciate her emotion. She was aware of her parent's distaste for the last of the Woosters, a distaste so marked that he turned mauve and swallowed his lunch the wrong way at the mention of my name, and *chez* me was the last place he would wish to find her. Orlo Porter had thought the worst on learning of what he called her clandestine visits to the Wooster home, and a father would, of course, think worse than Orlo. Pure though I was as the driven s., a fat chance I had of persuading him that I wasn't a modern Casa something. Not Casabianca. That was the chap who stood on the burning deck. Casanova. I knew I'd get it.

And what he would do to Vanessa in his wrath would be plenty. She was, as I have made clear, a proud beauty, but a father of the calibre of Pop Cook can make even a proud beauty wish she had thought twice before blotting her copy-book. He may not be able any longer to whale the tar out of her with his walking stick as in the good old days, but he can cut off her pocket money and send her to stay with her grandmother at Tunbridge Wells, where she will have to look after seven cats and attend divine service three times on Sunday. Yes, one could understand her being perturbed on seeing him tying up his boot lace outside Wee Nooke, which, I forgot to mention earlier, was the name of my G.H.Q. (It had been built, I learned subsequently, for a female cousin of Mrs Briscoe's who painted water colours.)

And if she was perturbed, I was on the perturbed side, too. It was with some trepidation – in fact, quite a lot of it – that I awaited my visitor's arrival, a trepidation that was not diminished when I saw that he had brought his hunting crop with him.

I hadn't taken to him much at our previous meeting, and I had the feeling that I wasn't going to get very fond of him now, but I will say this for him, that he didn't waste time. He was a man of quick, decisive speech who had no use for tedious preliminaries but came to the point at once. I suppose you have to in order to run a big business successfully.

'Well, Mr Wooster, as I understand you are calling yourself now, it may interest you to know that Major Plank, who had lost his memory, recovered it last night, and he told me all about you.'

It was a nasty knock, and the fact that I had been expecting it didn't make it any better. Oddly enough, I felt no animosity towards Cook, holding Plank the bloke responsible for this awkward situation. Roaming through Africa knee-deep in poisonous snakes of every description and with more man-eating pumas around than you could shake a stick at, he could so easily have passed away, regretted by all. Instead of which, he survived and went about making life tough for harmless typical young men about town who simply wanted to be left alone to restore their delicate health.

Cook was continuing, and getting nastier every moment.

'You are a notorious crook, known to your associates as Alpine Joe, and your latest crime was to try to sell Major Plank a valuable statuette which you had stolen from Sir Watkyn Bassett of Totleigh Towers. You were arrested by Inspector Witherspoon of Scotland Yard, fortunately before you had accomplished your nefarious ends. I presume from the fact that you are at large that you have served your sentence, and you are now in the pay of Colonel Briscoe, who has employed you to steal my cat. Have you anything to say?'

'Yes,' I said.

'No, you haven't,' he said.

'I can explain everything,' I said.

'No, you can't,' he said.

And, by Jove, I suddenly realized I couldn't. It would have involved a long character analysis of Sir Watkyn Bassett, another of my Uncle Tom, a third of Stephanie (Stiffy) Byng, now Mrs Stinker Pinker, a fourth of Jeeves, and would have taken about two hours and a quarter, provided he listened attentively and didn't interrupt, which of course he would have done.

Matters, therefore, seemed to be at what you might call a deadlock, and the thought had suggested itself to me that my best plan would be to leave his presence and start running and keep on running till I reached the northern fringe of Scotland, when a noise like an explosion in a gas works broke in on my reverie, and I saw that he was holding the slim volume which Vanessa, the silly ass, had omitted to take off-stage with her.

'This book!' he yowled.

I did my best.

'Ah, yes,' I said, 'Reggie Sprockett's latest. I always keep up with his work. A brilliant young poet of whom the critics expect great things. These, in case you are interested, are whimsical essays. They are superb. Not only the style, but the thought in these little gems . . .'

My voice died away. I had been about to urge him to buy a copy, but I saw that he was not in the mood. He was staring at the opening page with its inscription, and I knew that words would be wasted, as the expression is.

He gave the hunting crop a twitch.

'My daughter has been here.'

'She did look in.'

'Ha!'

I knew what that 'Ha!' meant. It was short for 'I shall now thrash you within an inch of your life.' A moment later he used the longer version, as if in doubt as to whether he had made himself clear.

If you were to come to me and say 'Wooster, to settle a bet, which would you estimate is to be preferred, having your insides torn out by somebody's bare hands or being thrashed within an inch of your life?', I would find it difficult to decide. Both are things you'd rather have happen to another chap. But I think I would give my vote in favour of the last-named, always provided the other fellow was doing it in a small room, for there he would find that he had set himself a testing task. The dimensions of the sitting-room of Wee Nooke did not permit of a full swing. Cook had to confine himself to chip shots, which an agile person like myself had little difficulty in eluding.

I eluded them, therefore, with no great expenditure of physical effort, but I would be deceiving my public if I said that I was enjoying the episode. It offends one's pride when one has to leap like a lamb in Springtime at the bidding of an elderly little gawd-help-us with whom it is impossible to reason. And it was plain that Cook in his present frame of mind wouldn't recognize reason if you served it up to him in an individual plate with watercress round it.

That, of course, was what prevented me fulfilling myself in the encounter, the fact that he *was* an elderly little gawd-help-us. It was the combination of age and size that kept me from giving of my best. I might – indeed I would – have dotted in the eye a small young gawd-help-us or a gawd-help-us of riper years of the large economy size, but I couldn't possibly get tough with an undersized little squirt who would never see fifty-five again. The chivalry of the Woosters couldn't ever contemplate such an action.

I thought once or twice of adopting the policy which had occurred to me at the outset – viz. running up to the north of Scotland. I had often wondered, when I read about fellows getting horsewhipped on the steps of their club, why they didn't just go up the steps and into the club, knowing that the chap behind the horsewhip wasn't a member and wouldn't have a chance of getting past the hall porter.

But the catch was that running up to Scotland would mean turning my back, a fatal move. So we just carried on with our rhythmic dance till my guardian angel, who until now had just been sitting there, decided – and about time, too – to take a hand in the proceedings. As might have been expected in a cottage called Wee Nooke, there was a grandfather clock over against the wall, and he now arranged that Cook should bump into this and come a purler. And while he was still on the floor I acted with the true Wooster resource.

I have stated that the previous owner of Wee Nooke expressed herself as a rule in water colours, but on one occasion she had changed her act. Over the mantelpiece there hung a large oil painting depicting a bloke in a three-cornered hat and riding breeches in conference with a girl in a bonnet and what looked like muslin, and as it caught my eye I suddenly remembered Gussie Fink-Nottle and the portrait at Aunt Dahlia's place in Worcestershire.

Gussie – stop me if you've heard this before – while closely pursued by Spode, now Lord Sidcup, who, if memory serves me aright, wanted to break his neck, had taken refuge in my bedroom and was on the point of having his neck broken when he plucked a picture from the wall and brought it down on Spode's head. The head came through the canvas, and Spode, momentarily bewildered at finding himself wearing a portrait of one of Uncle Tom's ancestors round his neck like an Elizabethan ruff, gave me the opportunity of snatching a sheet from the bed and enveloping him in it, rendering him null and void, as the expression is.

I went through a precisely similar routine now, first applying the picture and then the tablecloth. After which I withdrew and went off to the Goose and Grasshopper to see Orlo.

16

Anybody not in possession of the facts would probably have been appalled at my rashness in placing myself within disembowelling range of Orlo Porter, feeling that I was tempting fate, and in about two ticks would be wishing I hadn't.

But I, strong in the knowledge that Orlo P. had been reduced to the level of a fifth-rate power, was able to approach the coming interview in a bumps-a-daisy spirit which might quite easily have led to my bursting into song.

Orlo, as I had predicted, was in the bar having a gin and ginger. He lowered the beaker as I drew near and regarded me in a squiggle-eyed manner like a fastidious luncher observing a caterpillar in his salad.

'Oh, it's you,' he said.

I conceded this, for he was right. No argument about it. Assured that he wasn't looking squiggle-eyed at the wrong chap, he proceeded.

'What do you want?'

'A word with you.'

'So you have come to gloat?'

'Certainly not, Porter,' I said, 'when you hear what I have to say, you will start skipping like the high hills, not that I've ever seen high hills skip, or low hills for that matter. Porter, what would you say if I told you all your troubles, all the little odds and ends that are bothering you now, would be over 'ere yonder sun had set?'

'It has set.'

'Oh, has it? I didn't notice.'

'And it is getting on for dinner time. So if you will kindly get the hell out of here—'

'Not till I have spoken.'

'Are you going to speak some *more*?'

'Lots more. Let us examine the position you and I are in calmly, and in a judicial spirit. Vanessa Cook has told me she will marry me, and you are probably looking on me as a snake in the grass. Well, let me tell you that any resemblance between me and a snake in the grass is purely coincidental. I couldn't issue a *nolle prosequi*, could I, when she said that? Of course not. But all the while I was right-hoing I felt I was behaving like a louse.'

'You are a louse.'

'No, that's where you make your error, Porter. I am a man of sensibility, and a man of sensibility does not marry a girl who's in love with somebody else. He gives her up.'

He finished his gin and ginger, and choked on it as he suddenly got the gist.

'You would give her up to me?'

'Absolutely.'

'But, Wooster, this is noble. I'm sorry I said you were a louse.'

'Quite all right. Sort of mistake anyone might make.'

'You remind me of Cyrano de Bergerac.'

'One has one's code.'

He had been all smiles – or pretty nearly all smiles – up to this point, but now melancholy marked him for her own again. He heaved a sigh, as if he had found a dead mouse at the bottom of his tankard.

'It would be useless for you to make this sacrifice, Wooster. Vanessa would never marry me.'

'Of course she would.'

'You weren't there when she broke the engagement.'

'My representative was. At least he was listening at the door.'

'Then you know the general run of the thing.'

'He gave me a full report.'

'And you say she still loves me?'

'Like a ton of bricks. Love cannot be extinguished by a potty little lovers' quarrel.'

'Potty little lovers' quarrel my left eyeball. She called me a lily-livered poltroon. And a sleekit timorous cowering beastie. One wonders where she picks up such expressions. And all because I refused to go to old Cook and demand my money. I'd been to him once and asked him in the most civil manner to cough up, and she wanted me to go again and this time to thump the table and generally throw my weight about.'

'You should, Orlo. That's just what you ought to do. What happened last time?'

'He flatly refused.'

'How flatly?'

'Very flatly. And it would be the same if I went again.'

He had given me the cue I wanted. I had been wondering how best to introduce what I had in mind. I smiled one of my subtle smiles, and he asked me what I was grinning about.

'Not if you select your time properly,' I said. 'What time was it you made your other try?'

'About five in the afternoon.'

'As I suspected. No wonder he gave you the bum's rush. Five in the afternoon is when a man's sunny disposition is down in the lowest brackets. Lunch wore off hours ago, and cocktails are not yet in sight. He isn't in the mood to oblige anyone about anything. Cook may be a hard-boiled egg, but dinner softens the hardest. Approach him when he is full to the brim, and you'll be surprised. Fellows at the Drones have told me that, applying after he had tucked into the evening meal, they have got substantial loans out of Oofy Prosser.'

'Who is Oofy Prosser?'

'The club millionaire, a man who by daylight watches his disbursement like a hawk. Cook is probably just the same. Tails up, Porter. Get cracking. Be bloody, bold and resolute,' I said, remembering a gag from that play *Macbeth*, which I was mentioning some while back.

He was impressed, as who would not have been. His face lit up as if someone had pressed a button.

'Wooster,' he said, 'you're right. You have shown me the way. You have made my path straight. Thank you, Wooster, old man.'

'Not at all, Porter, old chap.'

'It's an extraordinary thing; anyone looking at you would write you off as a brainless nincompoop with about as much intelligence as a dead rabbit.'

'Thank you, Porter, old chap.'

'Not at all, Wooster, old man. Whereas all the time you have this amazing insight into human psychology.'

'I have hidden depths, would you say?'

'You bet you have, Wooster, old horse.'

And in another jiffy he was pressing a gin and ginger on me as if we had been bosom pals for years and the subject of my insides had never come up between us.

Returning to Wee Nooke some twenty minutes later after what had practically amounted to a love-feast, I had that jolly feeling you don't often get nowadays that God was in his heaven and all right with the world, as the fellow said. I counted my blessings one by one and found the sum total most satisfactory. All was quiet on the Porter front, Billy Graham was even now returning the cat to its little circle at Eggesford Court, Porter and Vanessa Cook would soon be sweethearts again, and if my popularity with Pop Cook was at a low ebb, rendering unlikely any chance of a present from him next Christmas, that was a small flaw in the ointment. Or is it fly? I never can remember. Everything, in short, was just like Mother makes it, and it was a blithe B. Wooster who, hearing the telephone tootle, went to answer it with, as you might say, a song on his lips.

It was the aged relative, and the dullest ear could have spotted that she was in something of a doodah. For some moments after we had established connection she confined herself to gasps and gurgles such as might have proceeded from some strong swimmer in his agony.

'Hullo,' I said. 'Is something up?'

In the course of this narrative I have had occasion to mention several hacking laughs, but for sheer rasp and explosiveness the one the old ancestor emitted at these words topped the lot.

'Something up?' she boomed. 'You would say a thing like that when I'm nearly off my rocker. Has that cat been returned to store yet?'

'Billy Graham is in full control.'

'You mean he hasn't started yet?'

'Yes, and come back. But unfortunately the cat followed him. So he says. Anyway, he arrived here with it in close attendance, and he has now taken it off again. He's probably decanting the animal at this moment. But why the agitation?'

'I'll tell you why the agitation. If that cat is not back where it belongs immediately, if not sooner, ruin stares me in the eyeball and Tom is in for the worst attack of indigestion he has had since the time he ate all that lobster at his club. And only myself to blame.'

'Did you say you were to blame?'

'Yes. Why?'

'I only wondered if I had heard you correctly.'

I have become so accustomed to being blamed for everything that goes wrong that her words had touched me deeply. You don't often find an aunt taking the rap when she has a nephew at her disposal to shove the thing on to. It is pretty universally agreed that that is what nephews are for. My voice shook a bit as I applied for further details.

'What seems to be the trouble?' I asked.

Aunts as a class are seldom good listeners. She did not answer the question, but embarked on what sounded as if it was going to be a lecture on conditions in her native land.

'I'll tell you what's wrong with the England of today, Bertie. There are too many people around with scruples and high principles and all that sort of guff. You can't do the simplest thing without somebody jumping on the back of your neck because you've offended against his blasted code of ethics. You'd think a man like Jimmy Briscoe would be broadminded, but no. He couldn't have been more puff-faced if he'd been the Archbishop of Canterbury. You probably put the blame on his brother the vicar, but I don't agree. I can excuse him because it's his job to be finicky about things. But Jimmy! He made me feel as if I'd shot a fox or something. And it wasn't as if I was getting anything out of it. It was a pure act of kindness because I could see he had the interests of the organ at heart and was really worried about it. Dammit, St Francis of Assisi would have done the same and everybody would have said what a splendid chap he was and what a pity there weren't more like him, whereas the way Jimmy went on . . .'

I could see that if not checked with a firm hand this would continue for a goodish time.

'I'm sorry if I seem slow in the uptake, aged r.,' I said, 'but, if so, put it down to the fact that you appear to me to be delirious. Your words are like the crackling of thorns under the pot, as the fellow said. What on earth do you think you're talking about?'

'Haven't you been listening?'

'I have been listening, yes, but without coming within a mile and a quarter of getting the gist.'

'Oh, heavens, I might have known I would have to tell you in words of one syllable. Here's what's happened in simple language which even you can understand. I happened to be talking to the vicar, and he told me what a weight on his mind the church organ was, it being at its last gasp and no money to pay the vet., because he'd already touched Jimmy for quite a bit to mend the church roof, and if he tried to bite his ear again so soon after that, there would, he said, be hell to pay. So what the devil to do, he said, he didn't know.

'Well, you know me, Bertie. Being a woman with a heart like butter and always anxious to spread a little happiness as I pass by, I told him that if he wanted a bit of easy money, to put his shirt on Jimmy's Simla for the big race. And I told him about the cat, just to make it quite clear to him that he would be betting on a sure thing.'

'But—'

'Put a sock in it and listen. Can't you stop talking for half a second? I know what you were going to say – that you were returning the cat. But this was before you told me. So I went ahead, fearing nothing, just thinking of the happiness I was bringing into his life. I ought to have known that a clergyman was bound to have scruples, but it didn't occur to me at the time and to cut a long story short he went to Jimmy and spilled the beans, and Jimmy blew his top. "Take that cat back where it belongs," he said, and a lot of stuff about being shocked and horrified. Which wouldn't have mattered if he had confined himself to telling me what he thought of me, but he didn't. He said that if that cat wasn't back at Cook's within the hour he would scratch Simla's nomination. Yessir, he said Simla would not be among those present at the starting post, which meant that bang would go the vast sum I had put on his nose.'

'But—'

'Yes, I know you had told me you were sending the cat back, but how was I to be sure that, on thinking it over and realizing what a good thing you would be passing up, you hadn't changed your mind?'

I could see what she meant. A nephew with a lust for gold and lacking the Wooster play-the-game spirit might quite well have done as she said. No wonder she had been all of a doodah. It was a pleasure to set her mind at rest.

'It's quite all right, old ancestor,' I said. 'Billy Graham is already en route for the Cookeries, and ought to have got there by now.'

'Complete with cat?'

'To the last drop.'

'Not to worry?'

'Not as far as Simla getting scratched is concerned.'

'Well, that's a weight off my mind, though it's disappointing to feel that my bit of stuff isn't on a cert.'

'Teach you not to nobble horses.'

'Yes, there's that, I suppose.'

Some further talk followed, for an aunt who has got hold of a telephone receiver does not lightly relinquish it, but eventually she rang off, and I picked up *Daffodil Days* and gave it a casual glance.

Its contents proved even less fit for human consumption than I had expected. I turned away with rising nausea, and was thus enabled to get a good view of Herbert Graham, who was coming in from the kitchen.

The suddenness of his appearance, coupled with the fact that I had supposed him to be up at Eggesford Court, had made me bite my tongue, but in my concern I ignored the anguish.

'Good Lord!' I ejaculated, if that's the word.

'Sir?'

'Haven't you gone yet? You should have been there and back by this time.'

'Very true, sir, but something occurred which prevented me making the immediate start which I had intended.'

'What was that? Did they keep you a long time at the bank, counting your money?'

Bitter, yes, but I thought justified. Wasted, however, for he did not wince beneath my sarcasm.

'No, sir,' he replied. 'I bank in Bridmouth-on-Sea, and it is long past office hours. The occurrence to which I refer took place on these premises, in fact in this very room. I had gone to the kitchen to get the cat, which I had left there in its little basket, and I heard sounds proceeding from in here and assuming that you were not at home I went in to investigate, fearing that a burglar might have effected an entry, and there on the floor was a human form enveloped in a tablecloth. I raised this, and there underneath it was Mr Cook with a picture round his neck, vociferating something chronic.'

He paused, and I decided not to put him abreast. Never does to take fellows like Graham too fully into one's confidence.

'Wrapped in a tablecloth, was he?' I said nonchalantly. 'I suppose chaps like Cook are bound to get wrapped in tablecloths sooner or later.'

'The sight affected me profoundly.'

'I bet it did. Sights like that do give one a start. But you soon got over it, eh?'

'No, sir, I did not, and I'll tell you why I was what you might call stupefied. It was his language that did it chiefly. As I was saying, he expressed himself in a very violent manner, and I

260 The Jeeves Omnibus 5

saw that it would be madness to proceed to Eggesford Court and possibly encounter him in this dangerous mood. I am a married man and have others to think of. So if you want that cat re-established in its former quarters, you'll have to get another operative to do it for you or else nip up to the Court and do it yourself.'

And while I looked at him with a wild surmise, silent upon a sitting-room carpet in Maiden Eggesford, Somerset, he withdrew.

I was still gazing at the spot where he had been and thinking how crazy I must have been to let Jeeves wander off, frittering away his time whooping it up with aunts, when I might have known I was bound to need his advice and moral support at any moment, and it was only after a bit that I realized that the telephone was ringing.

It was, as I had rather expected it would be, my late father's sister Dahlia, and it was made clear immediately that she had just been hearing from Billy Graham and getting the bad news. In a moving passage in which she referred to him as a double-crossing rat she said that he had formally refused to fulfil his sacred obligations.

'He had some extraordinary story about finding Cook in your cottage with a picture round his neck and a tablecloth over him and of being scared of going near him. Sounded like raving to me.'

'No, it was quite true.'

'You mean he really did have the picture round his neck and the tablecloth over him?'

'Yes.'

'How did he get that way?'

'We had a little argument, and that was how it worked out.'

She snorted in a rather febrile manner.

'Are you telling me that *you* are responsible for the man Graham's cold feet?'

'In a measure, yes. Let me give you a brief account of the episode,' I said, and did so. When I had finished, she spoke again, and her manner was almost calm.

'I might have known that if there was a chance of mucking up these very delicate negotiations, you would spring to the task. Well, as you are the cause of Graham walking out on us, you'll have to take his place.'

I was expecting this. Graham himself, it will be remembered, had made the same suggestion. I was resolved to discourage it from the outset.

'No!' I cried.

'Did you say No?'

'Yes, a thousand times no.'

'Scared, eh?'

'I am not ashamed to admit it.'

'You wouldn't be ashamed to admit practically anything. Where's your pride? Have you forgotten your illustrious ancestors? There was a Wooster at the time of the Crusades who would have won the Battle of Joppa singlehanded, if he hadn't fallen off his horse.'

'I daresay, but—'

'And the one in the Peninsular War. Wellington always used to say he was the best spy he ever had.'

'Quite possible. Nevertheless—'

'You don't want to show yourself worthy of those splendid fellows?'

'Not if it involves crossing Cook's path again.'

'Well, if you won't, you won't. Poor old Tom, how he will have to suffer. And talking of Tom, I had a letter from him this morning. It was all about the superb dinner Anatole had dished up on the previous night. He was absolutely lyrical. I must give it you to read. Apparently Anatole has struck one of these veins of perfection which French chefs do occasionally strike. Tom says in a postscript "How dear Bertie would have enjoyed this".'

I'm pretty shrewd, and I didn't miss the hideous unspoken threat behind her words. She was switching from the iron hand to the hand in the velvet glove, or rather the other way round, and letting me know without being crude about it that if I didn't allow myself to be bent to her will she would put sanctions on me and bar me from Anatole's cooking.

I made the great decision.

'Say no more, old flesh and blood,' I said. 'I will return the cat to store. And if while I am doing so Cook jumps out from behind a bush and tears me into a hundred fragments, what of it? It will be merely one more grave among the hills. What did you say?'

'Just "My Hero",' said the aged relative.

17

I was more to be pitied than censured, mind you, for quailing a bit in the circs. A touch of the wee sleekit cowering beastie is unavoidable when you're up against it as I was. I remember once when I was faced with the task of defying my Aunt Agatha and stoutly refusing to put up her son Thos at my flat for his mid-term holiday from his school and take him (*a*) to the British Museum (*b*) to the National Gallery and (*c*) to a play at the Old Vic by a bloke of the name of Chekhov, Jeeves, in whom I had confided the uneasiness I felt when contemplating the shape of things to come, told me my agitation was quite normal.

'Between the acting of a dreadful thing and the first motion,' he said, 'all the interim is like a phantasma or a hideous dream. The genius and the mortal instruments are then in council and the state of man, like to a little kingdom, suffers the nature of an insurrection.'

I could have put it better myself, but I saw what he meant. At these times your feet are bound to get chilly, and there's nothing you can do about it.

I hid my tremors. A lifetime of getting socks on the jaw from the fist of Fate has made Bertram Wooster's face an inscrutable mask, and no one would have suspected that I was not as calm as an oyster on the half-shell as I started out for Eggesford Court with the cat. But actually, behind those granite features I was far from being tranquil. Indeed, you wouldn't have been wrong in saying that I was as jumpy as the above cat would have been if on hot bricks.

I never know when I'm telling a tale of peril and suspense whether to charge straight ahead or whether to pause from time to time and bung in what is called atmosphere. Some prefer the first way, others the second. For the benefit of the latter I will state that it was a nice evening with gentle breezes blowing and stars peeping out and the scent of growing things and all that, and then I can get down to the *res*.

It was dark when I reached the Cook premises, which suited me, for I had dark work to do. I halted the car about halfway up the drive and took the short cut across country. My best friends would have warned me that I was asking for trouble, and they would have been right. The visibility being poor, the terrain lumpy and the cat wriggling, it was a pretty safe bet that sooner or later I would come a purler. This I did as I approached the stables. I struck a wet patch, my feet slid from under me, the cat shot from my arms, falling to earth I know not where, and I found myself face down in what was unquestionably mud which had been there some time and had had a number of unpleasant substances thrown into it. I remember thinking as I extracted myself that it was lucky I wasn't on my way to mix in company, as that mud must have taken at least eighty per cent off my glamour. It was not Bertram Wooster, the natty boulevardier, who started to return to the car but one of the dregs of society who had got his clothes off a handy scarecrow and had slept in them.

I say 'started to return', for I had not gone more than a yard or two when something solid bumped against my leg and I became aware that I had been joined by a dog of formidable physique, none other than the one I had exchanged civilities with at Wee Nooke. I recognized him by his ears.

At our former meeting, overcome by having found what he instantly recognized as one of the right sort, he had made the welkin ring in his enthusiasm. I urged him in an undertone to preserve a tactful silence now, for you never knew what minions of Pop Cook might be abroad in the night, and my presence would be difficult to explain, but there was no reasoning with him. At Wee Nooke he had found the Wooster aroma roughly equivalent to Chanel Number Five, and it was as if he were trying now to assure me that he was not the dog to be put off a pal just because the pal's scent had deteriorated somewhat. It's the soul that counts, you could hear him saying to himself between barks.

Well, I appreciated the compliment, of course, but I was not my usual debonair self, for I feared the worst. Barking like this, I felt, could not go unheard unless Cook's outdoor staff had been recruited entirely from deaf adders. And I was right. Somewhere off-stage a voice shouted 'Hey', making it clear that Bertram, as so often before, was about to cop it amidships.

I gave the dog a reproachful look. Not much good in that light, of course. I was recalling the story they used to read to me in my childhood, the one about the fellow who had written a book and his dog Diamond chewed up the manuscript; the point being what a decent chap the fellow was, because all he said was 'Ah, Diamond, Diamond, you little know what you have done'. It ought to be 'thou little knowest' and 'what thou hast done', but I can't do the dialect.

I feature the story because I was equally restrained. 'I *told* you not to bark, you silly ass,' was my only comment, and as I spoke the shouter who had shouted 'Hey' came up.

He had not made a good impression on me from the start because his voice had reminded me of the Sergeant-Major who used to come twice a week to drill us at the private school where I won the Scripture Knowledge prize which I may have mentioned once or twice. The Sergeant-Major's voice had been like a vehicle full of tin cans going over gravel, and so was the Hey chap's. Some relation, perhaps.

It was pretty dark, of course, by now, but the visibility was good enough to enable me to see that there was something else I didn't like about this creature of the night – viz. that he was shoving a whacking great shot-gun against my midriff. Taken all in all, a bloke to be conciliated with soft speech rather than struck in the mazzard. I tried speech, keeping it as soft as I could manage with my teeth chattering.

'Nice evening,' I said. 'I wonder if you could direct me to the village of Maiden Eggesford,' and would have gone on to explain that I had been for a country ramble and had lost my way, but I don't think he was listening, because all he did was bellow ' 'Enry', presumably addressing a colleague called Henry something, and a voice that might have been that of the Sergeant-Major's son replied 'Yus?'

'Cummere.'

'Where?'

'Here. Wanteher.'

'I'm having me supper.'

'Well, stop having it and cummere. I've cotched a chap after the horses.'

He had found the right talking-point. Henry was plainly a man who let nothing stand between him and his duty. When d. called he abandoned his eggs and bacon or whatever it was and hastened to answer the summons. In next to no time he was with us. The dog had disappeared. It was a dog, no doubt, with all sorts of interests and could give only a certain amount of its attention to each. Having sniffed my trouser legs and put his front paws on my chest, if felt that the time had come to seek other fields of endeavour.

Henry had a torch with him. He let it play on me.

'Coo,' he said. 'Is this him?'

'R.'

'Nasty slinking-looking bleeder.'

'R.'

'He don't half niff.'

'R.'

'Brings to mind that old song "It ain't all violets".'

'Lavender.'

'Violets, I always thought.'

'No, lavender.'

'Well, have it your own way. What are you going to do with him?'

'Take him to Mr Cook.'

The prospect of another meeting with Pop Cook under such conditions and after what had occurred between us was naturally distasteful to me, but there seemed little I could do about it, for at this moment Henry attached himself to my collar and we moved off, his associate prodding me in the back with his gun.

They took me to the house, where we were ill received by a butler annoyed at being interrupted while smoking an off-duty pipe. He further resented being confronted with what he called tramps who smelled like something gone wrong with the drains. I didn't know what I had fallen into, but it was becoming abundantly evident that it had been something rather special. The whole tone of the public's reaction to my society emphasized this.

The butler was very definite about everything. No, he said, they couldn't see Mr Cook. Were they under the impression, he asked, that Mr Cook was wearing a gas mask? In any case, he added, even if I had been smelling like new-mown hay, Mr Cook could not be disturbed, because he had a gentleman with him. Shut the fellow up in one of the stables why don't you, the butler said, and this was what my proposer and seconder decided to do.

I cannot too strongly recommend those of my readers who are thinking of getting shut up in stables to abandon the idea, for there is no percentage in it. It's stuffy, it's dark and there's nowhere to sit except the floor. Odd squeaking noises and sinister scratching noises making themselves heard from time to time, suggesting that rats are getting up an appetite before starting to chew you to the bone. After my escort had left me I shuffled about a good deal, with a view to finding some way of removing myself from as morale-testing a position as I had been in since I was so high, but the only method which occurred to me was to catch a rat and train it to gnaw through the door, but that would take time and I was anxious to get home and go to bed.

I had groped my way to the door as I was weighing the pros and cons of this rat sequence, and automatically, my mind on other things, I gave the handle a twiddle, more by way of something to do than because I expected anything to come of it, and shiver my timbers if the door didn't come open.

I thought at first that my guardian angel, who had been noticeably lethargic up to this point, had taken a stiff shot of vitamin something and had become the ball of fire he ought to have been right along, but reflection told me what must have happened. There had been confusion between the two principals, arising from inadequate planning. Each had thought the other had turned the key, with the result that it had remained unturned. It just showed how foolish it is to embark on any enterprise without first having a frank round-table conference conducted in an atmosphere of the utmost cordiality. It was difficult to think which of the two would kick himself harder when it was drawn to their attention that they had lost their Bertram.

But though I was now as free as the air, as you might say, I could see that it behooved me, if behooved is the word I want, to watch my step with the utmost vigilance. It would be too silly to run into Henry and the other bloke again and get bunged into durance-whatever-it's-called once more. I wanted complete freedom from both of them. Probably quite decent chaps when you got to know them, but definitely not for me.

Their sphere of influence was no doubt confined to the stable yard and neighbourhood, so it would be safe to leave by the route I had come by, but I shrank from doing that because I might meet that mud again. The thing to do was to roam about till I found the drive and go down it to where I had left the car. This I proceeded to do, and I had rounded the house and was crossing a lawn of sorts, when something gleamed in front of me and before I could stop myself I was stepping into a swimming-pool.

It was with mixed emotions that I rose to the surface. Surprise was one of them, for I hadn't thought that Cook was the sort of fellow to have a swimming-pool. Another was annoyance. I am not accustomed to bathing with all my clothes on, though there was that occasion at the Drones when Tuppy Glossop betted me I couldn't swing across the pool by the rings and I was reaching the last one when I found he had roped it back, causing me to fall into the fluid in correct evening costume.

But oddly enough, the emotion which stood out from the mixture was one of pleasure. Left to myself, I wouldn't have indulged in these aquatic sports, but now that I was in I was quite enjoying my dip. And there was the agreeable thought that this would do much to reduce the bouquet I had been giving out. What I had needed to enable me to rejoin the human herd without exciting adverse comment had been a good rinsing.

So I did not hurry to leave the pool, but floated there like a water-lily, or perhaps it would be better to say like a dead fish. And I had been doing so for some minutes, when there was that old familiar sound of barking in the night, and I gathered that my friend the dog had found another soul-mate.

I paused in my floating. I didn't like this. It suggested that Henry and his pal the man behind the gun were on the prowl again. What more likely than that they had got together and compared notes about locking the door and rushed to the stable and found me conspic. by my absence? I stiffened till my resemblance to a dead fish was even more striking than it had been, and I was still rigid when I heard the sound of galloping feet, as if somebody in a hurry were coming my way, and a human form splashed into the pool beside me.

That this had not been an intentional move on the human form's part was made clear by his opening remark on rising to the surface. It was the word 'Help!', and I had no difficulty in recognizing the voice of Orlo Porter.

'Help!' he repeated.

'Oh, hullo, Porter,' I said. 'Did you say "Help!"?'

'Yes.'

'Can't you swim?'

'No.'

'Then . . .' I was about to say 'Then surely it was rash to come bathing!', but I refrained, feeling that it would not be tactful. 'Then you could probably do with a helping hand,' I said.

He said he could, and I gave him one. We were at the deep end, and I hauled him into the shallow end, where he immediately became more at his ease. Spitting out perhaps a couple of pints of water, he thanked me – brokenly, as you might say – and I begged him not to mention it.

'Quite a surprise, meeting you like this,' I said. 'What are you doing in these parts, Porter?'

'Call me Orlo.'

'What are you doing in these parts, Orlo? Watching owls?'

'I came to see that blasted Cook, Wooster.'

'Call me Bertie.'

'I came to see that blasted Cook, Bertie. You remember your advice. Approach the old child of unmarried parents after he has had dinner, you said, and the more I thought about it, the sounder the idea seemed. You really have an extraordinary flair, Bertie. You read your fellow man like a book.'

'Oh, thanks. Just a matter of studying the psychology of the individual.'

'Unfortunately you can't judge someone like Cook by ordinary standards. Do you know why this is, Bertie?'

'No, Orlo. Why?'

'Because he's a hellhound, and there's no telling what a hellhound will do. Planning strategy is hopeless when you're dealing with hellhounds.'

'I gather that things did not go altogether as planned.'

'And how right you are, Bertie. The thing was a flop. It couldn't have been a worse flop if I had been trying to get money out of a combination of Scrooge and Gaspard the Miser.'

'Tell me all, Orlo.'

'If you have a moment, Bertie.'

'All the time in the world, Orlo.'

'You don't want to hurry away anywhere?'

'No, I like it here.'

'So do I. Pleasantly cool, is it not. Well, then, I arrived and told the butler I wanted to see Mr Cook on a matter of importance, and the butler took me to the library, where I found Cook smoking a fat cigar. I was confident when I saw it that I had chosen my time right. The cigar was plainly an after-dinner cigar, and he was drinking brandy. There could be no doubt that the man was full to the back teeth. You are following me, Bertie?'

'I get the picture, Orlo.'

'There was another man there. Some sort of African explorer, I gathered.'

'Major Plank.'

'His presence was an embarrassment because he would insist on telling us all about the fertility rites of the natives of Bongo on the Congo, which, take it from me, are too improper for words, but he left us after a while and I was able to get down to business. And a lot of good it did me. Cook refused to part with a penny.'

I put a question which had been in my mind for some time. I don't say I had actually been worrying about Orlo's financial position, but it had seemed to me to need explaining.

'What exactly is the arrangement about your money? Surely Cook can't just hang on to it?'

'He can till I'm thirty.'

'How old are you?'

'Twenty-seven.'

'Then in another three years——'

For the first time he showed a flash of the old Orlo Porter who had been so anxious to tear out my insides with his bare hands. He didn't actually foam at the mouth, but I could see that he missed it by the closest of margins.

'But I don't want to wait another three years, dammit. Do you know what my insurance company pays me? A pittance. Barely enough to keep body and soul together on. And I am a man who likes nice things. I want to branch out.'

'A Mayfair flat?'

'Yes.'

'Champagne with every meal?'

'Exactly.'

'Rolls-Royces?'

'Those, too.'

'Leaving something over, of course, to slip to the hard-up proletariat? You'd like them to have what you don't need.'

'There won't be anything I don't need.'

It was a little difficult to know what to say. I had never talked things over with a Communist before, and it came as something of a shock to find that he wasn't so fond of the hard-up proletariat as I had supposed. I thought of advising him not to let the boys at the Kremlin hear him expressing such views, but decided that it was none of my business. I changed the subject.

'By the way, Orlo,' I said, 'what brought you here?'

'Haven't you been listening? I came to see Cook.'

'I mean how did you come to fall into the pool?'

'I didn't know it was there.'

'You seemed to be running very fast. What was your hurry?'

'I was escaping from a dog which was attacking me.'

'A large dog with stand-up ears?'

'Yes. You know it?'

'We've met. But it wasn't attacking you.'

'It sprang on me.'

'In a purely friendly spirit. It springs on everyone. It's its way of being matey.'

He drew a long breath of relief. It would have been longer, had he not lost his footing and disappeared into the depths. I reached about for him and hauled him up, and he thanked me.

'A pleasure,' I said.

'You have taken a weight off my mind, Bertie. I was wondering how I could get back in safety to the inn.'

'I'll give you a lift in my car.'

'No, thanks. Now that you have explained the purity of that dog's motives I'd rather walk. I don't want to catch cold. By the way, Bertie, there's just one point I'd like you to clarify for me. What are *you* doing here?'

'Just strolling around.'

'It struck me as odd that you should have been in the pool.'

'Oh, no. Just cooling off, Orlo, just cooling off.'

'I see. Well, good night, Bertie.'

'Good night, Orlo.'

'I can rely on the accuracy of your information about the dog?'

'Completely, Orlo. His life is gentle, and the elements mixed in him just right,' I said, remembering a gag of Jeeves's.

It was with water dripping from my person in all directions but with a song in my heart, as the expression is, that some minutes later I climbed from the pool and started to where I had left the car. In addition to having a song in it my heart ought of course to have been bleeding for Orlo, for I realized how long it was going to take him to get all those nice things we had been talking about, but the ecstasy of having parted from the cat left little room for sympathy for other people's troubles. My concern for Orlo was, I regret to say, about equal to his for the hard-up proletariat.

All was quiet on the Cook front. No sign of Henry and his pal. The dog after fraternizing with Orlo had apparently curled up somewhere and was getting his eight hours.

I drove on. The song in my heart rose to fortissimo as I got out of the car at the door of Wee Nooke, only to die away in a gurgle as something soft and furry brushed against my leg and looking down I saw the familiar form of the cat.

18

I should have to check with Jeeves, but I think the word to describe the way I slept that night is 'fitfully'. I turned and twisted like an adagio dancer, and no wonder, for what I have heard Jeeves call 'the fell clutch of circumstance' which was clutching me was not the ordinary fell clutch which can be wriggled out of by some simple ruse such as going on a voyage round the world and not showing up again till things have blown over.

I had the option, of course, of disassociating myself entirely from the cat sequence and refusing to have anything more to do with the ruddy animal, but this would mean Colonel Briscoe scratching Simla's nomination, which would mean that a loved aunt would lose a packet and have to touch Uncle Tom to make up the deficit, which would mean upsetting the latter's gastric juices for one didn't know how long, which would mean him pushing his plate away untasted night after night, which would mean Anatole, temperamental like all geniuses, getting deeply offended and handing in his resignation. Ruin, desolation and despair all round, in short.

Manifestly, I think it's manifestly, the chivalry of the Woosters could not permit all that to happen. Somehow, whatever the perils involved, the cat had to be decanted somewhere where it could find its way back to its G.H.Q. But who was to do the decanting? Billy Graham had made it plain that no purse of gold, however substantial, could persuade him to brave the horrors of Eggesford Court, that sinister house. Jeeves had formally declared himself a non-starter. And Aunt Dahlia was disqualified by her unfortunate inability to move from spot to spot without having twigs snap beneath her feet.

This put the issue squarely up to Bertram. And no chance for him to do a *nolle prosequi*, because if he did bang went his hopes, for quite a time at least, of enjoying Anatole's cooking.

It was consequently in sombre mood that I went across to the Goose and Grasshopper for breakfast. I do not as a rule take the morning meal at six-thirty, but I had been awake since four, and the pangs of hunger could be resisted no longer.

If there was one thing I had taken for granted, it was that I would be breakfasting alone. My surprise, therefore, at finding Orlo in the dining-room, tucking into eggs and bacon, was considerable. I couldn't imagine how he came to be in circulation at such an hour. Bird-watchers, of course, are irregular in their habits, but even if he had an appointment with a Clarkson's warbler you would have expected him to have made it for much nearer lunch.

'Oh, hullo, Bertie,' he said. 'Glad to see you.'

'You're up early, Orlo.'

'A little before my usual time. I don't want to keep Vanessa waiting.'

'You've asked her to breakfast?'

'No, she will have had breakfast. Our date was for half-past seven. She may, of course, be late. It depends on how soon she can find the key of the garage.'

'Why does she want the key of the garage?'

'To get the Bentley.'

'Why does she want the Bentley?'

'My dear Bertie, we've got to elope in *something*.'

'Elope?'

'I ought to have explained that earlier. Yes, we're eloping, and thank goodness we've got a fine day for it. Ah, here are your eggs. You'll enjoy them. They're very good at the Goose and Grasshopper. Come, no doubt, from contented hens.'

On seating myself at the table I had ordered eggs, and, as he justly observed, they were excellent. But I dug into them listlessly. I was too bewildered to give them the detached thought they deserved.

'Do you mean to say,' I said, 'that you and Vanessa are e-*lop*-ing?'

'The only sober sensible course to pursue. This comes as a surprise?'

'You could knock me down with a ham sandwich.'

'What seems to be puzzling you?'

'I thought you weren't on speaking terms.'

His response was a hyenaesque guffaw. It was plain that he was feeling his oats to no little extent – quite naturally, of course, Vanessa being the tree on which the fruit of his life hung, as I have heard it described. It made me reflect on the extraordinary extent to which tastes can differ. I, as I have shown, though momentarily attracted by her radiant beauty, had frozen in every limb at the prospect of linking my lot with hers, whereas he was obviously all for it. In just the same way my Uncle Tom dances round in circles if he can get hold at enormous expense of a silver oviform chocolate pot of the Queen Anne period which I wouldn't be seen in public with. Curious.

He continued to guffaw.

'You aren't up to the minute with your society gossip, Bertie. That's all a thing of the past. Admittedly relations were at one time strained and harsh words spoken about the colour of my liver, but we had a complete reconciliation last night.'

'Oh, you met her last night?'

'Shortly after I left you. She was taking a stroll preparatory to going to bed and bedewing her pillow with salt tears.'

'Why should she do that?'

'Because she thought she was going to marry you.'

'I see. The fate that is worse than death, you might say.'

'Exactly.'

'Sorry she was troubled.'

'Quite all right. She soon got over it when I told her I had been seeing Cook and demanding my money. When she heard that I had several times thumped the table, her remorse for having called me a sleekit cowering beastie was pitiful. She compared me with heroes of old Greek legend, to their disadvantage, and, to cut a long story short, flung herself into my arms.'

'She must have got wet.'

'Very wet. But she didn't mind that. An emotional girl wouldn't.'

'I suppose not.'

'We then decided to elope. You may be wondering what we're going to live on, but with my salary and a bit of money she has from the will of an aunt we shall be all right. So it was arranged that she should have an early breakfast, go to the garage, pinch the Bentley and put the other cars out of action, leaving Cook for pursuing purposes only the gardener's Ford.'

'That ought to fix him.'

'I think so. It is an excellent car for its purpose, but scarcely adapted to chasing daughters across country. Cook will never catch up with us.'

'Though I don't see what he could do, even if he did catch up with you.'

'You don't? What about that hunting crop of his?'

'Ah, yes, I see what you mean.'

I don't know if he would have developed this theme, but before he could speak there came from the street a musical tooting.

'There she is,' he said, and went out.

So did I. I had no wish to meet Vanessa. I slid out of the back door and returned to Wee Nooke. And I had picked up *By Order Of The Czar* and was hoping to discover what it was that he had ordered, my bet being that a lot of characters with names ending in 'sky' would be off to Siberia before they knew what had hit them, when who should enter hurriedly but Orlo.

He had an envelope in his hand.

'Oh, there you are, Bertie,' he said. 'I can only stop a minute. Vanessa's out there in the car.'

'Ask her to come in.'

'She won't come in. She says it would be too painful for you.'

'What would?'

'Meeting her, you ass. Gazing on her when you knew she is another's.'

'Oh, I see.'

'No sense in giving yourself a lot of agony if you don't have to.'

'Quite.'

'I wouldn't have disturbed you, only I wanted to give you this letter. It's a note I've written to Cook in place of the one Vanessa wrote last night.'

'Oh, she wrote him a note?'

'Yes.'

'To be pinned to her pincushion?'

'That was the idea. But she dropped it somewhere and couldn't be bothered to hunt around for it. So I thought I had better send him a line. If you're running away with a man's daughter, it's only civil to let him know. And I would put the facts before him much better than she would. Girls are apt not to stick to the point when writing letters. With the best intentions in the world they ramble and embroider. A University-trained man like myself who contributes to the *New Statesman* does not fall into this blunder. He is concise. He is lucid.'

'I didn't know you wrote for the *New Statesman*.'

'Occasional letters to the editor. And I rarely fail to enter for the weekly competitions.'

'Absorbing work.'

'Very.'

'I'm a writer of sorts myself. When my Aunt Dahlia was running that paper of hers, *Milady's Boudoir*, I did a piece for it on What The Well-Dressed Man Is Wearing.'

'Did you indeed? Next time we meet you must tell me all about it. Can't stop now. Vanessa's waiting and,' he added as the tooting of a horn broke the morning stillness, 'getting impatient. Here's the letter.'

'You want me to take it to Cook?'

'What do you think I want you to do with it? Get it framed?'

And so saying he legged it like a nymph surprised while bathing, and I picked up my *By Order Of The Czar*.

As I did so I was thinking bitterly that I wished the general public would stop regarding me as an uncomplaining Hey-You on whom all the unpleasant jobs could be shovelled off. Whenever something sticky was afoot and action had to be taken the cry was sure to go up, 'Let Wooster do it'. I have already touched on my Aunt Agatha's tendency to unload her foul son Thos on me at all seasons. My Aunt Dahlia had blotted the sunshine from my life in the matter of the cat. And here was Orlo Porter coolly telling me to take the letter to Cook, as if entering Cook's presence in his present difficult mood wasn't much the same as joining Shadrach, Meshach and Abednego, of whom I had read when I won that Scripture Knowledge prize at my private school, on their way to the burning fiery furnace. What, I asked myself, was to be done?

It was a dilemma which might well have baffled a lesser man, but the whole point about the Woosters is that they are not lesser men. I don't suppose it was more than three-quarters of an hour before the solution flashed on me – viz. to write Cook's name and address on the envelope, stick a stamp on it and post it. Having decided to do this, I returned to my reading.

But everything seemed to conspire today to prevent me making any real progress with *By Order Of The Czar*. Scarcely had I perused a paragraph when the door burst open and I found that I was seeing Cook after all. He was standing on the threshold looking like the Demon King in a pantomime.

With him was Major Plank.

19

I have always rather prided myself on being a good host, putting visitors at their ease with debonair smiles and courteous wise-cracks, but I am compelled to admit that at the sight of these two I didn't come within a mile of doing so, and the best I could do in the way of wisecracks was a hoarse cry like that of a Pekinese with laryngitis. It was left to Plank to get the conversation going.

'We're in luck, Cook,' he said. 'They haven't started yet. Because if they had,' he added, reasoning closely, 'the bounder wouldn't be here, would he?'

'You're right,' said Cook. Then, addressing me, 'Where is my daughter, you scoundrel?'

'Yes, where is she, rat?' said Plank, and I suddenly came over all calm. From being a Pekinese with throat trouble I turned in a flash into one of those fellows in historical novels who flick a speck of dust from the irreproachable mechlin lace at their wrists preparatory to making the bad guys feel like pieces of cheese. Because with my quick intelligence I had spotted that the parties of the second part had got all muddled up and that I was in a position to score off them as few parties of the second part had ever been scored off.

'Fill me in on two points, Messrs Plank and Cook, if you will be so good,' I said. '(*a*) Why are you taking up space in my cottage which I require for other purposes, and (*b*) What the hell are you talking about? What is all this song and dance about daughters?'

'Trying to brazen it out,' said Plank. 'I told you he would. He reminds me of a man I knew in East Africa, who always tried to brazen things out. If you caught him with his fingers in your cigar box, he would say he was just tidying the cigars. Fellow named Abercrombie-Smith, eventually eaten by a crocodile on the Lower Zambesi. But even he had to give up when confronted with overwhelming evidence. Confront this blighter with the overwhelming evidence, Cook.'

'I will,' said Cook, producing an envelope from his pocket. 'I have here a letter from my daughter. Signed "Vanessa".'

'A very important point,' said Plank.

'I will read it to you. "Dear Father. I am going away with the man I love." '

'Let's see him wriggle out of that,' said Plank.

'Yes,' said Cook. 'What have you to say?'

'Merely this,' I riposted. I was thinking how mistaken Orlo had been in asserting that girls rambled when writing letters. Anything more lucid and concise than this one I had never come across. Possibly, I felt, Vanessa, too, was a contributor to the *New Statesman*. 'Cook,' I said, 'you are labouring under a what-d'you-call-it.'

'See!' said Plank. 'Didn't I say he would try to brazen it out?'

'That letter does not refer to me.'

'Are you denying that you are the man my daughter loves?'

'That's just what I am denying.'

'In spite of the fact that she is always in and out of this beastly cottage and is probably at this moment hiding under the bed in the spare room,' said Plank, continuing to shove his oar in in the most unnecessary manner. These African explorers have no tact, no reticence.

'May I explain,' I said. 'The chap you're looking for is Orlo Porter. They fell for each other when she was in London and love has been burgeoning ever since, if burgeoning means what I think it means, until they felt they could bear being separated no longer. So she pinched your car and they've driven off together to the registrar's.'

It didn't go well. Cook said I was lying, and Plank said of course I was, adding that the more he saw of me the more I reminded him of Abercrombie-Smith, who, he said, would undoubtedly have done a long stretch in chokey if the crocodile hadn't taken things into its own hands.

I should have mentioned that in the course of these exchanges Cook's complexion had been steadily deepening. It now looked like a Drone Club tie, which is a rich purple. There was talk at one time of having it crimson with white spots, but the supporters of that view were outvoted.

'How dare you have the insolence to suppose that I am fool enough to believe this story of my daughter being in love with Orlo Porter?' he thundered. 'As if any girl in her senses would love Orlo Porter.'

'Ridiculous,' said Plank.

'Vanessa would turn from him in disgust.'

'On her heel,' said Plank.

'What she can see in *you* I cannot imagine.'

'Nor can I,' said Plank. 'He's got a beard like one of those Victorian novelists. Revolting spectacle.'

It was true that I hadn't shaved this morning, but this was going too far. I don't mind criticism, but I will not endure vulgar abuse.

'Pfui,' I said. It is an expression I don't often use, but Nero Wolfe is always saying it with excellent results, and it seemed to fit in rather well here. 'Enough of this back-chat. Read this,' I said, handing Cook Orlo's letter.

I must say his reception of what Plank would have called the overwhelming evidence was all that could be desired. His jaw fell. He snorted. His face crumpled up like a sheet of carbon paper.

'Good God!' he gurgled.

'What is it?' asked Plank. 'What's the matter?'

'This is from Porter, saying that he has eloped with Vanessa.'

'Probably a forgery.'

'No. Porter's writing is unmistakable . . .' He choked. 'Mr Wooster—'

'Don't call him Mister Wooster as if he were a respectable member of society,' said Plank. 'He's a desperate criminal who once came within an ace of stinging me for five pounds. He is known to the police as Alpine Joe. Address him as that. Wooster is only a pen name.'

Cook did not seem to have listened – and I didn't blame him.

'Mr Wooster, I owe you an apology.'

I decided to temper justice with m. No sense in grinding the poor old buster beneath the iron heel. True, he had been extremely offensive, but to a man who has lost his daughter and his cat within a day or two of each other much must be excused.

'Don't give it another thought, my dear fellow,' I said. 'We all make mistakes. I forgive you freely. If this little misunderstanding has taught you not to speak till you are sure of your facts, it will have been time well spent.'

I had paused, speculating as to whether I wasn't being a bit too patronising, when somebody said 'Miaow' in a low voice, and looking down I saw that the cat had strolled in. And if ever a cat chose the wrong moment for getting the party spirit and wanting to mix with the boys, this cat was that cat. I looked at it with a wild surmise, as silent as those bimbos on the peak in Darien. With both hands pressed to the top of my head to prevent it taking to itself the wings of a dove and soaring to the ceiling, I was asking myself what the harvest would be.

I was speedily informed on this point.

'Ha!' said Cook, scooping up the animal and pressing it to his bosom. He seemed to have lost all interest in eloping daughters.

'I told you it must have been Alpine Joe who was the kidnapper,' said Plank. 'That was why he was hanging about the stables that day. He was waiting his chance.'

'Biding his time.'

'And he hasn't a word to say for himself.'

He was right. I was unable to utter. I couldn't clear myself by exposing the aged relative at the bar of world opinion. I couldn't make them believe that I was going to return the cat. You might have described me as being trapped in the net of fate if you had happened to think of the expression, and when that happens to you, it is no use saying anything. Ask the boys in Dartmoor or Pentonville. I could only trust that joy at recovering his lost one might soften Cook's heart and make him let me off lightly.

Not a hope.

'I shall insist on an exemplary sentence,' he said.

'And meanwhile,' said Plank in that offensively officious way of his, 'shall I be hitting him on the head with my stick? The Zulu knob-kerrie would be better, but I left it up at the house.'

'I was going to ask you to go for a policeman.'

'While you do what?'

'While I take the cat back to Potato Chip.'

'Suppose while we're both gone he does a bunk?'

'You have a point there.'

'When anyone is caught stealing in Bongo on the Congo, they tie him down on an ant-hill until they can get hold of the walla-walla, as judges are called in the native dialect. Makes it awkward for the accused if he isn't fond of ants and the walla-walla is away for the week-end, but into each life some rain must fall and he ought to have thought of that before he started pinching things. We're short of ants, of course, but we can tie him to the sofa. It only means pulling down a couple of curtain cords.'

'Then by all means let us do as you suggest.'

'Better gag him. We don't want him yelling for help.'
'My dear Plank, you think of everything.'

I am a great reader of novels of suspense, and I had often wondered how the heroes of them felt when the heavy tied them up, as he generally did about half-way through. I was now in a position to get a rough idea, but of course only a rough one, for they were pretty nearly always attached to a barrel of gunpowder with a lighted candle on top of it, which must have made the whole thing considerably more poignant.

I had been spared this what you might call added attraction, but even so I was far from being in sunny mood. I think it was the gag which contributed most to the lowering of my spirits. Plank had inserted his tobacco pouch between my upper and lower teeth, and it tasted far too strongly of African explorer to be agreeable. It was a great relief when I heard a footstep and realized that Jeeves had returned from revelling with Mrs P. B. Pigott of Balmoral, Mafeking Road.

'Good morning, sir,' he said.

He expressed no surprise at seeing me tied to a sofa with curtain cords, just as he would have e. no s. if he had seen me being eaten by a crocodile like the late Abercrombie-Smith, though in the latter case he might have heaved a regretful sigh.

Assuming that I would prefer to be without them, he removed the gag and unfastened my bonds.

'Have you breakfasted, sir?' he asked. I told him I had.

'Perhaps some coffee, sir?'

'A great idea. And make it strong,' I said, hoping that it would wash the taste of Plank's tobacco pouch away. 'And when you return, I shall a tale unfold which will make you jump as if you'd sat on a fretful porpentine.'

I was quite wrong, of course. I doubt if he would do much more than raise an eyebrow if, when entering his pantry, he found one of those peculiar fauna from the Book of Revelations in the sink. When he returned with the steaming pot and I unfolded my tale, he listened attentively, but gave no indication that he recognized that what he was listening to was front page stuff. Only when I told him of the clicking of Orlo and Vanessa, releasing me from my honourable obligations to the latter, did a flicker of interest disturb his frozen features. I think he might have unbent to the extent of offering me respectful congratulations, had not Plank come bounding in.

He was alone. I could have told him it was hopeless to try to get hold of the Maiden Eggesford Police Force at that time of day. There was only one of it and in the morning he does his rounds on his bicycle.

Seeing Jeeves, he registered astonishment.

'Inspector Witherspoon!' he cried. 'Amazing how you Scotland Yard fellows always get your man. I suppose you've been on Alpine Joe's trail for weeks like a stoat and a rabbit. Little did he know that Inspector Witherspoon, the man who never sleeps, was watching his every move. Well, you couldn't have come up with him at a better moment, for in addition to whatever the police want him for he has stolen a valuable cat belonging to my friend Cook. We caught him redhanded, or as redhanded as it is possible to be when stealing cats. But I'm surprised that you should have untied him from the sofa. I always thought the one thing the police were fussy about was the necessity of leaving everything untouched.'

I must say I was what is called at a loss of words, but luckily Jeeves had plenty.

'I fail to understand you,' he said, his voice and manner so chilly that Plank must have been wishing he was wearing his winter woollies. 'And may I ask why you address me as Inspector Witherspoon? I am not Inspector Witherspoon.'

Plank clicked his tongue impatiently.

'Of course you are,' he said. 'I remember you distinctly. You'll be telling me next that you didn't arrest this man at my place in Gloucestershire for trying to obtain five pounds from me by false pretences.'

Jeeves had no irreproachable mechlin lace at his wrist, or he would unquestionably have flicked a speck of dust off it. He increased the coldness of his manner.

'You are mistaken in every respect,' he said. 'Mr Wooster has ample means. It seems scarcely likely, therefore, that he would have attempted to obtain a mere five pounds from you. I can speak with authority as to Mr Wooster's financial standing, for I am his solicitor and prepare his annual income tax return.'

'So there you are, Plank,' I said. 'It must be obvious to every thinking man that you have been having hallucinations, possibly the result of getting a touch of the sun while making a pest of yourself to the natives of Equatorial Africa. If I were you, I'd pop straight back to E. J. Murgatroyd and have him give you something for it. You don't want that sort of thing to spread. You'll look silly if it goes too far and we have to bury you before sundown.'

Plank was plainly shaken. He could not pale beneath his tan because he had so much tan that it was impossible to pale beneath it. I'm not sure I have put that exactly right. What I mean is that he may have paled, but you couldn't see it because of his sunburn.

But he was looking very thoughtful, and I knew what was passing in his mind. He was wondering how he was going to explain to Cook, whom by tying people to sofas he had rendered liable for heavy damages for assault and battery and all sorts of things.

These African explorers think quick. It took him about five seconds flat to decide not to stay and explain to Cook. Then he was out of the room in a flash, his destination presumably Bongo on the Congo or somewhere similar where the arm of the law couldn't touch him. I don't suppose he had shown a brisker turn of speed since the last time he had thought the natives seemed friendly and had decided to stay the night, only to have them come after him with assegais.

My first move after he had left us was, of course, to pay a marked tribute to Jeeves for his services and cooperation. This done, we struck the more social note.

'Did you have a good time last night, Jeeves?'

'Extremely enjoyable, thank you, sir.'

'How was your aunt?'

'At first somewhat dispirited.'

'Why was that?'

'She had lost her cat, sir. On leaving for her holiday she placed it in the charge of a friend, and it had strayed.'

I gasped. A sudden idea had struck me. We Woosters are like that. We are always getting struck by sudden ideas.

'Jeeves! Could it be . . . Do you think it's possible . . . ?'

'Yes, sir. She described the animal to me in minute detail, and there can be no doubt that it is the one now in residence at Eggesford Court.'

I danced a carefree dance step. I know a happy ending when I see one.

'Then we've got Cook cold!'

'So it would seem, sir.'

'We go to him and tell him he can carry on plus cat till the race is over, paying, of course, a suitable sum to your aunt. Lend-lease, isn't it called?'

'Yes, sir.'

'And in addition we make it a proviso . . . It is proviso?'

'Yes, sir.'

'That he gives Orlo Porter his money. I'd like to see Orlo fixed up. He can't refuse, because he must have the cat, and if he tries any *nolle prosequi* as regards Orlo we slap an assault and battery suit on him. Am I right, Jeeves?'

'Indubitably, sir.'

'And another thing. I have thought for some time that the hectic rush and swirl of life in Maiden Eggesford can scarcely be what E. Jimpson Murgatroyd had in mind when he sent me to the country to get a complete rest. What I need is something quieter, more peaceful, as it might be in New York. And if I am mugged, what of it? It is probably all right getting mugged, when you are used to it. Do you agree, Jeeves?'

'Yes, sir.'

'And you are in favour of bearding Pop Cook?'

'Yes, sir.'

'Then let's go. My car is outside. Next stop, Eggesford Court.'

20

It was about a week after we had fetched up in New York that coming to the breakfast table one morning, rejoicing in my youth if I remember rightly, I found a letter with an English stamp lying by my plate. Not recognizing the writing, I pushed it aside, intending to get at it later after I had fortified myself with a square meal. I generally do this with the letters I get at breakfast time, because if they're stinkers and you read them on an empty stomach, you start your day all wrong. And in these disturbed times you don't often find people writing anything but stinkers.

Some half-hour later, refreshed and strengthened, I opened the envelope, and no wonder the writing had seemed unfamiliar, for it was from Uncle Tom, and he hadn't written to me since I was at my private school, when, to do him credit, he had always enclosed a postal order for five or ten bob.

He hauled up his slacks thus:

Dear Bertie.

You will doubtless be surprised at hearing from me. I am writing for your aunt, who has met with an unfortunate accident and is compelled to wear her arm in a sling. This occurred during the concluding days of her visit to some friends of hers in Somerset named Briscoe. If I understand her rightly, a party was in progress to celebrate the victory of Colonel Briscoe's horse Simla in an important race, and a cork, extracted from a bottle of champagne, struck her so sharply on the tip of the nose that she lost her balance and fell, injuring her wrist.

Then came three pages about the weather, the income tax (which he dislikes) and the recent purchases he had made for his collection of old silver, and finally a postscript:

P.S. Your aunt asks me to enclose this newspaper clipping.

I couldn't find any newspaper clipping, and I supposed he must have forgotten to enclose it. Then I saw it lying on the floor.

I picked it up. It was from the *Bridmouth Argus*, with which is incorporated the *Somerset Farmer* and the *South Country Intelligencer*, the organ, if you remember, whose dramatic critic gave the old ancestor such a rave notice when she sang 'Every Nice Girl Loves A Sailor' in her sailor suit at the Maiden Eggesford village concert.

It ran as follows:

JUBILEE STAKES SENSATION

JUDGES' DECISION

Yesterday the Judges, Major Welsh, Admiral Sharpe and Sir Everard Boot, after prolonged consideration, gave their decision in the Jubilee Stakes incident which has led to so much controversy in Bridmouth-on-Sea sporting circles. The race was awarded to Colonel Briscoe's Simla. Bets will accordingly be settled in accordance with this fiat. Rumour whispers that large sums will change hands.

Here I paused, for letter and clipping had given me much food for thought.

Naturally it was with the deepest concern that I pictured the tragic scene of Aunt Dahlia and the champagne cork. Something similar happened to me once during some rout or revelry at the Drones, and I can testify that it calls for all that one has of fortitude. But against this must be set the fact that she had won a substantial chunk of money and would not be faced with the awful necessity of getting into Uncle Tom's ribs in order to keep the budget balanced.

But this aspect of the matter ceased to enchain my interest. What I wanted was to probe to the heart of the mystery that had presented itself. Apparently Cook's Potato Chip had finished first but had been disqualified. Why? Bumping?

That's usually what you get disqualified for.

I read on.

The facts will of course be fresh in the minds of our

readers. Rounding into the straight, Simla and his rival were neck and neck, far ahead of the field, and it was plain that one of the two must be the ultimate winner. Nearing the finish, Simla took the lead and was a full length ahead, when a cat with black and white markings suddenly ran on to the course, causing him to shy and unseat his jockey.

It was then discovered that the cat was the property of Mr Cook and had actually been brought to the course in his horse's horse box. It was this that decided the judges, who, as we say, yesterday awarded the race to Colonel Briscoe's entrant. Sympathy has been expressed for Mr Cook.

Not by me, I hasten to say. I felt it served the old blighter jolly well right. He ought to have known that you can't go about the place for years making a hellhound of yourself without eventually paying the price. Remember what the fellow said about the mills of the gods.

I was in philosophical mood as I smoked the after-breakfast cigarette. Jeeves came in to clear away the debris, and I told him the news.

'Simla won, Jeeves.'

'Indeed, sir? That is most gratifying.'

'And Aunt Dahlia got hit on the tip of the nose with a champagne cork.'

'Sir?'

'At the subsequent celebrations at the Briscoe home.'

'Ah, yes, sir. A painful experience, but no doubt satisfaction at her financial gains would enable Mrs Travers to bear it with fortitude. Was the tone of her communication cheerful?'

'The letter wasn't from her, it was from Uncle Tom. He enclosed this.'

I handed him the clipping, and I could see how deeply it interested him. One of his eyebrows rose at least a sixteenth of an inch.

'Dramatic, Jeeves.'

'Exceedingly, sir. But I am not sure that I altogether agree with the verdict of the judges.'

'You don't?'

'I should have been inclined to regard the episode as an Act of God.'

'Well, thank goodness the decision wasn't up to you. The imagination boggles at the thought of how Aunt Dahlia would have reacted if it had gone the other way. One pictures her putting hedgehogs in Major Welsh's bed and getting fourteen days without the option for pouring buckets of water out of windows on the heads of Admiral Sharpe and Sir Everard Boot. I should have got nervous prostration in the first couple of days. And it was difficult enough to avoid nervous prostration in Maiden Eggesford as it was, Jeeves,' I said, my philosophical mood now buzzing along on all twelve cylinders. 'Do you ever brood on life?'

'Occasionally, sir, when at leisure.'

'What do you make of it? Pretty odd in spots, don't you think?'

'It might be so described, sir.'

'This business of such-and-such seeming to be so-and-so, when it really isn't so-and-so at all. You follow me?'

'Not entirely, sir.'

'Well, take a simple instance. At first sight Maiden Eggesford had all the indications of being a haven of peace. You agreed with me?'

'Yes, sir.'

'As calm and quiet as you could wish, with honeysuckle-covered cottages and apple-cheeked villagers wherever you looked. Then it tore off its whiskers and revealed itself as an inferno. To obtain calm and quiet we had to come to New York, and there we got it in full measure. Life saunters along on an even keel. Nothing happens. Have we been mugged?'

'No, sir.'

'Or shot by youths?'

'No, sir.'

'No, sir, is right. We are tranquil. And I'll tell you why. There are no aunts here. And in particular we are three thousand miles away from Mrs Dahlia Travers of Brinkley Manor, Market Snodsbury, Worcestershire. Don't get me wrong, Jeeves, I love the old flesh and blood. In fact I revere her. Nobody can say she isn't good company. But her moral code is lax. She cannot distinguish between what is according to Hoyle and what is not according to Hoyle. If she wants to do anything, she doesn't ask herself "Would Emily Post approve of this?", she goes ahead and does it, as she did in this matter of the cat. Do you know what is the trouble with aunts as a class?'

'No, sir.'

'They are not gentlemen,' I said gravely.

'EXTRICATING YOUNG GUSSIE'

She sprang it on me before breakfast. There in seven words you have a complete character sketch of my Aunt Agatha. I could go on indefinitely about brutality and lack of consideration. I merely say that she routed me out of bed to listen to her painful story somewhere in the small hours. It can't have been half-past eleven when Jeeves, my man, woke me out of the dreamless and broke the news:

'Mrs Gregson to see you, sir.'

I thought she must be walking in her sleep, but I crawled out of bed and got into a dressing-gown. I knew Aunt Agatha well enough to know that, if she had come to see me, she was going to see me. That's the sort of woman she is.

She was sitting bolt upright in a chair, staring into space. When I came in she looked at me in that darn critical way that always makes me feel as if I had gelatine where my spine ought to be. Aunt Agatha is one of those strong-minded women. I should think Queen Elizabeth must have been something like her. She bosses her husband, Spencer Gregson, a battered little chappie on the Stock Exchange. She bosses my cousin, Gussie Mannering-Phipps. She bosses her sister-in-law, Gussie's mother. And, worst of all, she bosses me. She has an eye like a man-eating fish, and she has got moral suasion down to a fine point.

I dare say there are fellows in the world – men of blood and iron, don't you know, and all that sort of thing – whom she couldn't intimidate; but if you're a chappie like me, fond of a quiet life, you simply curl into a ball when you see her coming, and hope for the best. My experience is that when Aunt Agatha wants you to do a thing you do it, or else you find yourself wondering why those fellows in the olden days made such a fuss when they had trouble with the Spanish Inquisition.

'Halloa, Aunt Agatha!' I said.

'Bertie,' she said, 'you look a sight. You look perfectly dissipated.'

I was feeling like a badly wrapped brown-paper parcel. I'm never at my best in the early morning. I said so.

'Early morning! I had breakfast three hours ago, and have been walking in the park ever since, trying to compose my thoughts.'

If I ever breakfasted at half-past eight I should walk on the Embankment, trying to end it all in a watery grave.

'I am extremely worried, Bertie. That is why I have come to you.'

And then I saw she was going to start something, and I bleated weakly to Jeeves to bring me tea. But she had begun before I could get it.

'What are your immediate plans, Bertie?'

'Well, I rather thought of tottering out for a bite of lunch later on, and then possibly staggering round to the club, and after that, if I felt strong enough, I might trickle off to Walton Heath for a round of golf.'

'I am not interested in your totterings and tricklings. I mean, have you got any important engagements in the next week or so?'

I scented danger.

'Rather,' I said. 'Heaps! Millions! Booked solid!'

'What are they?'

'I . . . er . . . well, I don't quite know.'

'I thought as much. You have no engagements. Very well, then, I want you to start immediately for America.'

'America!'

Do not lose sight of the fact that all this was taking place on an empty stomach, shortly after the rising of the lark.

'Yes, America. I suppose even you have heard of America?'

'But why America?'

'Because that is where your Cousin Gussie is. He is in New York, and I can't get at him.'

'What's Gussie been doing?'

'Gussie is making a perfect idiot of himself.'

To one who knew young Gussie as well as I did, the words opened up a wide field for speculation.

'In what way?'

'He has lost his head over a creature.'

On past performances this rang true. Ever since he arrived at man's estate Gussie had been losing his head over creatures. He's that sort of chap. But, as the creatures never seemed to lose their heads over him, it had never amounted to very much.

'I imagine you know perfectly well why Gussie went to America, Bertie. You know how wickedly extravagant your Uncle Cuthbert was.'

She alluded to Gussie's governor, the late head of the family, and I am bound to say she spoke the truth. Nobody was fonder of old Uncle Cuthbert than I was, but everybody knows that, where money was concerned, he was the most complete chump in the annals of the nation. He had an expensive thirst. He never backed a horse that didn't get housemaid's knee in the middle of the race. He had a system of beating the bank at Monte Carlo which used to make the administration hang out the bunting and ring the joy-bells when he was sighted in the offing. Take him for all in all, dear old Uncle Cuthbert was as willing a spender as ever called the family lawyer a bloodsucking vampire because he wouldn't let Uncle Cuthbert cut down the timber to raise another thousand.

'He left your Aunt Julia very little money for a woman in her position. Beechwood requires a great deal of keeping up, and poor dear Spencer, though he does his best to help, has not unlimited resources. It was clearly understood why Gussie went to America. He is not clever, but he is very good-looking, and, though he has no title, the Mannering-Phippses are one of the best and oldest families in England. He had some excellent letters of introduction, and when he wrote home to say that he had met the most charming and beautiful girl in the world I felt quite happy. He continued to rave about her for several mails, and then this morning a letter has come from him in which he says, quite casually as a sort of afterthought, that he knows we are broad-minded enough not to think any the worse of her because she is on the vaudeville stage.'

'Oh, I say!'

'It was like a thunderbolt. The girl's name, it seems, is Ray Denison, and according to Gussie she does something which he describes as a single on the big time. What this degraded performance may be I have not the least notion. As a further recommendation he states that she lifted them out of their seats at Mosenstein's last week. Who she may be, and how or why, and who or what Mr Mosenstein may be, I cannot tell you.'

'By Jove,' 'I said, 'it's like a sort of thingummybob, isn't it? A sort of fate, what?'

'I fail to understand you.'

'Well, Aunt Julia, you know, don't you know? Heredity, and

so forth. What's bred in the bone will come out in the wash, and all that kind of thing, you know.'

'Don't be absurd, Bertie.'

That was all very well, but it was a coincidence for all that. Nobody ever mentions it, and the family have been trying to forget it for twenty-five years, but it's a known fact that my Aunt Julia, Gussie's mother, was a vaudeville artist once, and a very good one, too, I'm told. She was playing in pantomine at Drury Lane when Uncle Cuthbert saw her first. It was before my time, of course, and long before I was old enough to take notice the family had made the best of it, and Aunt Agatha had pulled up her socks and put in a lot of educative work, and with a microscope you couldn't tell Aunt Julia from a genuine dyed-in-the-wool aristocrat. Women adapt themselves so quickly!

I have a pal who married Daisy Trimble of the Gaiety, and when I meet her now I feel like walking out of her presence backwards. But there the thing was, and you couldn't get away from it. Gussie had vaudeville blood in him, and it looked as if he were reverting to type, or whatever they call it.

'By Jove,' I said, for I am interested in this heredity stuff, 'perhaps the thing is going to be a regular family tradition, like you read about in books – a sort of Curse of the Mannering-Phippses, as it were. Perhaps each head of the family's going to marry into vaudeville for ever and ever. Unto the what-d'you-call-it generation, don't you know?'

'Please do not be quite idiotic, Bertie. There is one head of the family who is certainly not going to do it, and that is Gussie. And you are going to America to stop him.'

'Yes, but why me?'

'Why you? You are too vexing, Bertie. Have you no sort of feeling for the family? You are too lazy to try to be a credit to yourself, but at least you can exert yourself to prevent Gussie's disgracing us. You are going to America because you are Gussie's cousin, because you have always been his closest friend, because you are the only one of the family who has absolutely nothing to occupy his time except golf and night clubs.'

'I play a lot of auction.'

'And, as you say, idiotic gambling in low dens. If you require another reason, you are going because I ask you as a personal favour.'

What she meant was that, if I refused, she would exert the full bent of her natural genius to make life a Hades for me. She held me with her glittering eye. I have never met anyone who can give a better imitation of the Ancient Mariner.

'So you will start at once, won't you, Bertie?'

I didn't hesitate.

'Rather!' I said. 'Of course I will.'

Jeeves came in with the tea.

'Jeeves,' I said, 'we start for America on Saturday.'

'Very good, sir,' he said; 'which suit will you wear?'

New York is a large city conveniently situated on the edge of America, so that you step off the liner right on to it without an effort. You can't lose your way. You go out of a barn and down some stairs, and there you are, right in among it. The only possible objection any reasonable chappie could find to the place is that they loose you into it from the boat at such an ungodly hour.

I left Jeeves to get my baggage safely past an aggregation of suspicious-minded pirates who were digging for buried treasures among my shirts, and drove to Gussie's hotel, where I requested the squad of gentlemanly clerks behind the desk to produce him.

That's where I got my first shock. He wasn't there. I pleaded with them to think again, and they thought again, but it was no good. No Augustus Mannering-Phipps on the premises.

I admit I was hard hit. There I was alone in a strange city and no signs of Gussie. What was the next step? I am never one of the master minds in the early morning; the old bean doesn't somehow seem to get into its stride till pretty late in the p.m.'s, and I couldn't think what to do. However, some instinct took me through a door at the back of the lobby, and I found myself in a large room with an enormous picture stretching across the whole of one wall, and under the picture a counter, and behind the counter divers chappies in white, serving drinks. They have barmen, don't you know, in New York, not barmaids. Rum idea!

I put myself unreservedly into the hands of one of the white chappies. He was a friendly soul, and I told him the whole state of affairs. I asked him what he thought would meet the case.

He said that in a situation of that sort he usually prescribed a 'lightning whizzer', an invention of his own. He said this was what rabbits trained on when they were matched against grizzly bears, and there was only one instance on record of the bear having lasted three rounds. So I tried a couple, and, by Jove! the man was perfectly right. As I drained the second a great load seemed to fall from my heart, and I went out in quite a braced way to have a look at the city.

I was surprised to find the streets quite full. People were bustling along as if it were some reasonable hour and not the grey dawn. In the tramcars they were absolutely standing on each other's necks. Going to business or something, I take it. Wonderful johnnies!

The odd part of it was that after the first shock of seeing all this frightful energy the thing didn't seem so strange. I've spoken to fellows since who have been to New York, and they tell me they found it just the same. Apparently there's something in the air, either the ozone or the phosphates or something, which makes you sit up and take notice. A kind of zip, as it were. A sort of bally freedom if you know what I mean, that gets into your blood and bucks you up, and makes you feel that:

> God's in His Heaven:
> All's right with the world,

and you don't care if you've got odd socks on. I can't express it better than by saying that the thought uppermost in my mind, as I walked about the place they call Times Square, was that there were three thousand miles of deep water between me and my Aunt Agatha.

It's a funny thing about looking for things. If you hunt for a needle in a haystack you don't find it. If you don't give a darn whether you ever see the needle or not it runs into you the first time you lean against the stack. By the time I had strolled up and down once or twice, seeing the sights and letting the white chappie's corrective permeate my system, I was feeling that I wouldn't care if Gussie and I never met again, and I'm dashed if I didn't suddenly catch sight of the old lad, as large as life, just turning in at a doorway down the street.

I called after him, but he didn't hear me, so I legged it in pursuit and caught him going into an office on the first floor. The name on the door was Abe Riesbitter, Vaudeville Agent, and from the other side of the door came the sound of many voices.

He turned and stared at me.

'Bertie! What on earth are you doing? Where have you sprung from? When did you arrive?'

'Landed this morning. I went round to your hotel, but they said you weren't there. They had never heard of you.'

'I've changed my name. I call myself George Wilson.'

'Why on earth?'

'Well, you try calling yourself Augustus Mannering-Phipps over here, and see how it strikes you. You feel a perfect ass. I don't know what it is about America, but the broad fact is that it's not a place where you can call yourself Augustus Mannering-Phipps. And there's another reason. I'll tell you later. Bertie, I've fallen in love with the dearest girl in the world.'

The poor old nut looked at me in such a deuced cat-like way, standing with his mouth open, waiting to be congratulated, that I simply hadn't the heart to tell him that I knew all about that already, and had come over to the country for the express purpose of laying him a stymie.

So I congratulated him.

'Thanks awfully, old man,' he said. 'It's a bit premature, but I fancy it's going to be all right. Come along in here, and I'll tell you about it.'

'What do you want in this place? It looks a rummy spot?'

'Oh, that's part of the story. I'll tell you the whole thing.'

We opened the door marked 'Waiting Room'. I never saw such a crowded place in my life. The room was packed till the walls bulged.

Gussie explained.

'Pros,' he said, 'music-hall artistes, you know, waiting to see old Abe Riesbitter. This is September the first, vaudeville's opening day. The early fall,' said Gussie, who is a bit of a poet in his way, 'is vaudeville's springtime. All over the country, as August wanes, sparkling comediennes burst into bloom, the sap stirs in the veins of tramp cyclists, and last year's contortionists, waking from their summer sleep, tie themselves tentatively into knots. What I mean is, this is the beginning of the new season, and everybody's out hunting for bookings.'

'But what do you want here?'

'Oh, I've just got to see Abe about something. If you see a fat man with about fifty-seven chins come out of that door grab him, for that'll be Abe. He's one of those fellows who advertise each step up they take in the world by growing another chin. I'm told that way back in the nineties he only had two. If you do grab Abe, remember that he knows me as George Wilson.'

'You said that you were going to explain that George Wilson business to me, Gussie, old man.'

'Well, it's this way—'

At this juncture dear old Gussie broke off short, rose from his seat, and sprang with indescribable vim at an extraordinarily stout chappie who had suddenly appeared. There was the deuce of a rush for him, but Gussie had got away to a good start, and the rest of the singers, dancers, jugglers, acrobats, and refined sketch teams seemed to recognize that he had won the trick, for they ebbed back into their places again, and Gussie and I went into the inner room.

Mr Riesbitter lit a cigar, and looked at us solemnly over his zareba of chins.

'Now, let me tell ya something,' he said to Gussie. 'You lizzun t' me.'

Gussie registered respectful attention. Mr Riesbitter mused for a moment and shelled the cuspidor with indirect fire over the edge of the desk.

'Lizzun t' me,' he said again. 'I seen you rehearse, as I promised Miss Denison I would. You ain't bad for an amateur. You gotta lot to learn, but it's in you. What it comes to is that I can fix you up in the four-a-day, if you'll take thirty-five per. I can't do better than that, and I wouldn't have done that if the little lady hadn't of kep' after me. Take it or leave it. What do you say?'

'I'll take it,' said Gussie, huskily. 'Thank you.'

In the passage outside, Gussie gurgled with joy and slapped me on the back. 'Bertie, old man, it's all right. I'm the happiest man in New York.'

'Now what?'

'Well, you see, as I was telling you when Abe came in, Ray's father used to be in the profession. He was before our time, but I remember hearing about him – Joe Danby. He used to be well known in London before he came over to America. Well, he's a fine old boy, but as obstinate as a mule, and he didn't like the idea of Ray marrying me because I wasn't in the profession. Wouldn't hear of it. Well, you remember at Oxford I could always sing a song pretty well; so Ray got hold of old Riesbitter and made him promise to come and hear me rehearse and get me bookings if he liked my work. She stands high with him. She coached me for weeks, the darling. And now, as you heard him say, he's booked me in the small time a thirty-five dollars a week.'

I steadied myself against the wall. The effects of the restoratives supplied by my pal at the hotel bar were beginning to work off, and I felt a little weak. Through a sort of mist I seemed to have a vision of Aunt Agatha hearing that the head of the Mannering-Phippses was about to appear on the vaudeville stage. Aunt Agatha's worship of the family name amounts to an obsession. The Mannering-Phippses were an old-established clan when William the Conqueror was a small boy going round with bare legs and a catapult. For centuries they have called kings by their first names and helped dukes with their weekly rent; and there's practically nothing a Mannering-Phipps can do that doesn't blot his escutcheon. So what Aunt Agatha would say – beyond saying that it was all my fault – when she learned the horrid news, it was beyond me to imagine.

'Come back to the hotel, Gussie,' I said. 'There's a sportsman there who mixes things he calls "lightning whizzers". Something tells me I need one now. And excuse me for one minute, Gussie, I want to send a cable.'

It was clear to me by now that Aunt Agatha had picked the wrong man for this job of disentangling Gussie from the clutches of the American vaudeville profession. What I needed was reinforcements. For a moment I thought of cabling Aunt Agatha to come over, but reason told me that this would be overdoing it. I wanted assistance, but not so badly as that. I hit what seemed to me the happy mean. I cabled to Gussie's mother and made it urgent.

'What were you cabling about?' asked Gussie, later.

'Oh, just to say I had arrived safely, and all that sort of tosh,' I answered.

Gussie opened his vaudeville career on the following Monday at a rummy sort of place uptown where they had moving pictures some of the time and, in between, one or two vaudeville acts. It had taken a lot of careful handling to bring him up to scratch. He seemed to take my sympathy and assistance for granted, and I couldn't let him down. My only hope, which grew as I listened to him rehearsing, was that he would be such a frightful frost at his first appearance that he would never dare to perform again; and, as that would automatically squash the marriage, it seemed best to me to let the thing go on.

He wasn't taking any chances. On the Saturday and Sunday we practically lived in a beastly little music-room at the offices of the publishers whose songs he proposed to use. A little chappie with a hooked nose sucked a cigarette and played the piano all day. Nothing could tire that lad. He seemed to take a personal interest in the thing.

Gussie would clear his throat and begin:

'There's a great big choo-choo waiting at the deepo.'

THE CHAPPIE (playing chords): 'Is that so? What's it waiting for?'

GUSSIE (rather rattled at the interruption): 'Waiting for me.'

THE CHAPPIE (surprised): 'For you?'

GUSSIE (sticking to it): 'Waiting for me—e—ee!'

THE CHAPPIE (sceptically): 'You don't say!'

GUSSIE: 'For I'm off to Tennessee.'

THE CHAPPIE (conceding a point): 'Now, I live at Yonkers.'

He did this all through the song. At first poor old Gussie asked him to stop, but the chappie said, No, it was always done. It helped to get pep into the thing. He appealed to me whether the thing didn't want a bit of pep, and I said it wanted all the pep it could get. And the chappie said to Gussie, 'There you are!' So Gussie had to stand it.

The other song that he intended to sing was one of those moon songs. He told me in a hushed voice that he was using it because it was one of the songs that the girl Ray sang when lifting them out of their seats at Mosenstein's and elsewhere. The fact seemed to give it sacred associations for him.

You will scarcely believe me, but the management expected Gussie to show up and start performing at one o'clock in the afternoon. I told him they couldn't be serious, as they must know that he would be rolling out for a bit of lunch at that hour, but Gussie said this was the usual thing in the four-a-day, and he didn't suppose he would ever get any lunch again until he landed on the big time. I was just condoling with him, when I found that he was taking it for granted that I should be there at one o'clock, too. My idea had been that I should look in at night, when – if he survived – he would be coming up for the fourth time; but I've never deserted a pal in distress, so I said goodbye to the little lunch I'd been planning at a rather decent tavern I'd discovered on Fifth Avenue, and trailed along. They were showing pictures when I reached my seat. It was one of those Western films, where the cowboy jumps on his horse and rides across country at a hundred and fifty miles an hour to escape the sheriff, not knowing, poor chump! that he might just as well stay where he is, the sheriff having a horse of his own which can do three hundred miles an hour without coughing.

I was just going to close my eyes and try to forget till they put Gussie's name up when I discovered that I was sitting next to a deucedly pretty girl.

No, let me be honest. When I went in I had seen that there was a deucedly pretty girl sitting in that particular seat, so I had taken the next one. What happened now was that I began, as it were, to drink her in. I wished they would turn the lights up so that I could see her better. She was rather small, with great big eyes and a ripping smile. It was a shame to let all that run to seed, so to speak, in semi-darkness.

Suddenly the lights did go up, and the orchestra began to play a tune which, though I haven't much of an ear for music, seemed somehow familiar. The next instant out pranced old Gussie from the wings in a purple frock-coat and a brown top-hat, grinned feebly at the audience, tripped over his feet, blushed, and began to sing the Tennessee song.

It was rotten. The poor nut had got stage fright so badly that it practically eliminated his voice. He sounded like some far-off echo of the past 'yodelling' through a woollen blanket.

For the first time since I heard that he was about to go into vaudeville I felt a faint hope creeping over me. I was sorry for the wretched chap, of course, but there was no denying that the thing had its bright side. No management on earth would go on paying thirty-five dollars a week for this sort of performance. This was going to be Gussie's first and only. He would have to leave the profession. The old boy would say, 'Unhand my daughter'. And, with decent luck, I saw myself leading Gussie on to the next English-bound liner and handing him over intact to Aunt Agatha.

He got through the song somehow and limped off amidst roars of silence from the audience. There was a brief respite, then out he came again.

He sang this time as if nobody loved him. As a song, it was not a very pathetic song, being all about coons spooning in June under the moon, and so on and so forth, but Gussie handled it in such a sad, crushed way that there was genuine anguish in every line. By the time he reached the refrain I was nearly in tears. It seemed such a rotten sort of world with all that kind of thing going on in it.

He started the refrain, and then the most frightful thing happened. The girl next to me got up in her seat, chucked her head back, and began to sing too. I say 'too', but it wasn't really too, because her first note stopped Gussie dead, as if he had been pole-axed.

I never felt so bally conspicuous in my life. I huddled down in my seat and wished I could turn my collar up. Everybody seemed to be looking at me.

In the midst of my agony I caught sight of Gussie. A complete change had taken place in the old lad. He was looking most frightfully bucked. I must say the girl was singing most awfully well, and it seemed to act on Gussie like a tonic. When she came to the end of the refrain, he took it up, and they sang together, and the end of it was that he went off the popular hero. The audience yelled for more, and were only quieted when they turned down the lights and put on a film.

When I recovered I tottered round to see Gussie. I found him sitting on a box behind the stage, looking like one who had seen visions.

'Isn't she a wonder, Bertie?' he said, devoutly. 'I hadn't a notion she was going to be there. She's playing at the Auditorium this week, and she can only just have had time to get back to her *matinée*. She risked being late, just to come and see me through. She's my good angel, Bertie. She saved me. If she hadn't helped me out I don't know what would have happened. I was so nervous I didn't know what I was doing. Now that I've got through the first show I shall be all right.'

I was glad I had sent that cable to his mother. I was going to need her. The thing had got beyond me.

During the next week I saw a lot of old Gussie, and was introduced to the girl. I also met her father, a formidable old boy with thick eyebrows and a sort of determined expression. On the following Wednesday Aunt Julia arrived. Mrs Mannering-Phipps, my Aunt Julia, is, I think, the most dignified person I know. She lacks Aunt Agatha's punch, but in a quiet way she has always contrived to make me feel, from boyhood up, that I was a poor worm. Not that she harries me like Aunt Agatha. The difference between the two is, that Aunt Agatha conveys the impression that she considers me personally responsible for all the sin and sorrow in the world, while Aunt Julia's manner seems to suggest that I am more to be pitied then censured.

If it wasn't that the thing was a matter of historical fact, I should be inclined to believe that Aunt Julia had never been on the vaudeville stage. She is like a stage duchess.

She always seems to me to be in a perpetual state of being about to desire the butler to instruct the head footman to serve lunch in the blue-room overlooking the west terrace. She exudes dignity. Yet, twenty-five years ago, so I've been told by old boys who were lads about town in those days, she was knocking them cold at the Tivoli in a double act called 'Fun in a Tea-Shop', in which she wore tights and sang a song with a chorus that began 'Rumpty-tiddley-umpty-ay'.

There are some things a chappie's mind absolutely refuses to picture, and Aunt Julia singing 'Rumpty-tiddley-umpty-ay' is one of them.

She got straight to the point within five minutes of our meeting.

'What is this about Gussie? Why did you cable for me, Bertie?'

'It's rather a long story,' I said, 'and complicated. If you don't mind, I'll let you have it in a series of motion pictures. Suppose we look in at the Auditorium for a few minutes.'

The girl, Ray, had been re-engaged for a second week at the Auditorium, owing to the big success of her first week. Her act consisted of three songs. She did herself well in the matter of costume and scenery. She had a ripping voice. She looked most awfully pretty; and altogether the act was, broadly speaking, a pippin.

Aunt Julia didn't speak till we were in our seats. Then she gave a sort of sigh.

'It's twenty-five years since I was in a music-hall!'

She didn't say any more, but sat there with her eyes glued on the stage.

After about half an hour the johnnies who work the card-index system at the side of the stage put up the name of Ray Denison, and there was a good deal of applause.

'Watch this act, Aunt Julia,' I said.

She didn't seem to hear me.

'Twenty-five years! What did you say, Bertie?'

'Watch this act and tell me what you think of it.'

'Who is it? Ray. Oh!'

'Exhibit A,' I said. 'The girl Gussie's engaged to.'

The girl did her act, and the house rose at her. They didn't want to let her go. She had to come back again and again. When she had finally disappeared I turned to Aunt Julia.

'Well?' I said.

'I like her work. She's an artist.'

'We will now, if you don't mind, step a goodish way uptown.'

And we took the subway to where Gussie, the human film, was earning his thirty-five per. As luck would have it, we hadn't been in the place ten minutes when out he came.

'Exhibit B,' I said. 'Gussie.'

I don't quite know what I had expected her to do, but I certainly didn't expect her to sit there without a word. She did not move a muscle, but just stared at Gussie as he drooled on about the moon. I was sorry for the woman, for it must have been a shock to her to see her only son in a mauve frock-coat and a brown top-hat, but I thought it best to let her get a strangle-hold on the intricacies of the situation as quickly as possible. If I had tried to explain the affair without the aid of illustrations I should have talked all day and left her muddled up as to who was going to marry whom, and why.

I was astonished at the improvement in dear old Gussie. He had got back his voice and was putting the stuff over well. It reminded me of the night at Oxford when, then but a lad of eighteen, he sang 'Let's All Go Down The Strand' after a bump supper, standing the while up to his knees in the college fountain. He was putting just the same zip into things now.

When he had gone off Aunt Julia sat perfectly still for a long time, and then she turned to me. Her eyes shone queerly.

'What does this mean, Bertie?'

She spoke quite quietly, but her voice shook a bit.

'Gussie went into the business,' I said, 'because the girl's father wouldn't let him marry her unless he did. If you feel up to it perhaps you wouldn't mind tottering round to One Hundred and Thirty-third Street and having a chat with him. He's an old boy with eyebrows, and he's Exhibit C on my list. When I've put you in touch with him I rather fancy my share of the business is concluded, and it's up to you.'

The Danbys lived in one of those big apartments uptown which look as if they cost the earth and really cost about half as much as a hall-room down in the forties. We were shown into the sitting-room, and presently old Danby came in.

'Good afternoon, Mr Danby,' I began.

I had got as far as that when there was a kind of gasping cry at my elbow.

'Joe!' cried Aunt Julia, and staggered against the sofa.

For a moment old Danby stared at her, and then his mouth fell open and his eyebrows shot up like rockets.

'Julie!'

And then they had got hold of each other's hands and were shaking them till I wondered their arms didn't come unscrewed.

I'm not equal to this sort of thing at such short notice. The change in Aunt Julia made me feel quite dizzy. She had shed her *grande-dame* manner completely, and was blushing and smiling. I don't like to say such things of any aunt of mine, or I would go further and put it on record that she was giggling. And old Danby, who usually looked like a cross between a Roman emperor and Napoleon Bonaparte in a bad temper, was behaving like a small boy.

'Joe!'

'Julie!'

'Dear old Joe! Fancy meeting you again!'

'Wherever have you come from, Julie?'

Well, I didn't know what it was all about, but I felt a bit out of it. I butted in:

'Aunt Julia wants to have a talk with you, Mr Danby.'

'I knew you in a second, Joe!'

'It's twenty-five years since I saw you, kid, and you don't look a day older.'

'Oh, Joe! I'm an old woman!'

'What are you doing over here? I suppose' – old Danby's cheerfulness waned a trifle – 'I suppose your husband is with you?'

'My husband died a long, long while ago, Joe.'

Old Danby shook his head.

'You never ought to have married out of the profession, Julie. I'm not saying a word against the late – I can't remember his name; never could – but you shouldn't have done it, an artist like you. Shall I ever forget the way you used to knock them with "Rumpty-tiddley-umpty-ay"?'

'Ah! how wonderful you were in that act, Joe.' Aunt Julia sighed. 'Do you remember the back-fall you used to do down the steps? I always have said that you did the best back-fall in the profession.'

'I couldn't do it now!'

'Do you remember how we put it across at the Canterbury, Joe? Think of it! The Canterbury's a moving-picture house now, and the old Mogul runs French revues.'

'I'm glad I'm not there to see them.'

'Joe, tell me, why did you leave England?'

'Well, I . . . I wanted a change. No, I'll tell you the truth, kid. I wanted you, Julie. You went off and married that – whatever that stage-door johnny's name was – and it broke me all up.'

Aunt Julia was staring at him. She is what they call a well-preserved woman. It's easy to see that, twenty-five years ago, she must have been something quite extraordinary to look at. Even now she's almost beautiful. She has very large brown eyes, a mass of soft grey hair, and the complexion of a girl of seventeen.

'Joe, you aren't going to tell me you were fond of me yourself!'

'Of course I was fond of you. Why did I let you have all the fat in "Fun in a Tea-Shop"? Why did I hang about up-stage while you sang "Rumpty-tiddley-umpty-ay"? Do you remember my giving you a bag of buns when we were on the road at Bristol?'

'Yes, but—'

'Do you remember my giving you the ham sandwiches at Portsmouth?'

'Joe!'

'Do you remember my giving you a seed-cake at Birmingham? What did you think all that meant, if not that I loved you? Why, I was working up by degrees to telling you straight out when you suddenly went off and married that cane-sucking dude. That's why I wouldn't let my daughter marry this young chap, Wilson, unless he went into the profession. She's an artist—'

'She certainly is, Joe.'

'You've seen her? Where?'

'At the Auditorium just now. But, Joe, you mustn't stand in the way of her marrying the man she's in love with. He's an artist, too.'

'In the small time.'

'You were in the small time once, Joe. You musn't look down on him because he's a beginner. I know you feel that your daughter is marrying beneath her, but—'

'How on earth do you know anything about young Wilson?'

'He's my son.'

'Your son?'

'Yes, Joe. And I've just been watching him work. Oh, Joe, you can't think how proud I was of him! He's got it in him. It's fate. He's my son and he's in the profession! Joe, don't you know what I've been through for his sake. They made a lady of me. I never worked so hard in my life as I did to become a real lady. They kept telling me I had got to put it across, no matter what it cost, so that he wouldn't be ashamed of me. The study was something terrible. I had to watch myself every minute for years, and I never knew when I might fluff in my lines or fall down on some bit of business. But I did it, because I didn't want him to be ashamed of me, though all this time I was just aching to be back where I belonged.'

Old Danby made a jump at her, and took her by the shoulders.

'Come back where you belong, Julie!' he cried. 'Your husband's dead, your son's a pro. Come back! It's twenty-five years ago, but I haven't changed. I want you still. I've always wanted you. You've got to come back, kid, where you belong.'

Aunt Julia gave a sort of gulp and looked at him.

'Joe!' she said in a kind of whisper.

'You're here, kid,' said Old Danby, huskily. 'You've come back. . . . Twenty-five years! . . . You've come back and you're going to stay!'

She pitched forward into his arms, and he caught her.

'Oh, Joe! Joe! Joe!' she said. 'Hold me. Don't let me go. Take care of me.'

And I edged for the door and slipped from the room. I felt weak. The old bean will stand a certain amount, but this was too much. I groped my way out into the street and waited for a taxi.

Gussie called on me at the hotel that night. He curveted into the room as if he had bought it and the rest of the city.

'Bertie,' he said, 'I feel as if I were dreaming.'

'I wish I could feel like that, old top,' I said, and I took another glance at a cable that had arrived half an hour ago from Aunt Agatha. I had been looking at it at intervals ever since.

'Ray and I got back to her flat this evening. Who do you think was there? The mater! She was sitting hand in hand with old Danby.'

'Yes?'

'He was sitting hand in hand with her.'

'Really?'

'They are going to be married.'

'Exactly.'

'Ray and I are going to be married.'

'I suppose so.'

'Bertie, old man, I feel immense. I look round me, and everything seems to be absolutely corking. The change in the mater is marvellous. She is twenty-five years younger. She and old Danby are talking of reviving "Fun in a Tea-Shop", and going out on the road with it.'

I got up.

'Gussie, old top,' I said, 'leave me for awhile. I would be alone. I think I've got brain fever or something.'

'Sorry, old man; perhaps New York doesn't agree with you. When do you expect to go back to England?'

I looked again at Aunt Agatha's cable.

'With luck,' I said, 'in about ten years.'

When he was gone I took up the cable and read it again.

'What is happening?' it read. 'Shall I come over?'

I sucked a pencil for a while, and then I wrote the reply.

It was not an easy cable to word, but I managed it.

'No,' I wrote, 'stay where you are. Profession overcrowded.'

'JEEVES MAKES AN OMELETTE'

In these disturbed days in which we live, it has probably occurred to all thinking men that something drastic ought to be done about aunts. Speaking for myself, I have long felt that stones should be turned and avenues explored with a view to putting a stopper on the relatives in question. If someone were to come to me and say, 'Wooster, would you be interested in joining a society I am starting whose aim will be the suppression of aunts or at least will see to it that they are kept on a short chain and not permitted to roam hither and thither at will, scattering desolation on all sides?', I would reply, 'Wilbraham,' if his name was Wilbraham, 'I am with you heart and soul. Put me down as a foundation member.' And my mind would flit to the sinister episode of my Aunt Dahlia and the Fothergill Venus, from which I am making only a slow recovery. Whisper the words 'Marsham Manor' in my ear, and I still quiver like a humming-bird.

At the time of its inception, if inception is the word I want, I was, I recall, feeling at the top of my form and without a care in the world. Pleasantly relaxed after thirty-six holes of golf and dinner at the Drones, I was lying on the *chez Wooster* sofa doing the *Telegraph* crossword puzzle, when the telephone rang. I could hear Jeeves out in the hall dealing with it, and presently he trickled in.

'Mrs Travers, sir.'

'Aunt Dahlia? What does she want?'

'She did not confide in me, sir. But she appears anxious to establish communication with you.'

'To talk to me, do you mean?'

'Precisely, sir.'

A bit oddish it seems to me, looking back on it, that as I went to the instrument I should have had no premonition of an impending doom. Not psychic, that's my trouble. Having no inkling of the soup into which I was so shortly to be plunged,

I welcomed the opportunity of exchanging ideas with this sister of my late father who, as is widely known, is my good and deserving aunt, not to be confused with Aunt Agatha, the werewolf. What with one thing and another, it was some little time since we had chewed the fat together.

'What ho, old blood relation,' I said.

'Hullo, Bertie, you revolting young blot,' she responded in her hearty way. 'Are you sober?'

'As a judge.'

'Then listen attentively. I'm speaking from an undersized hamlet in Hampshire called Marsham-in-the-Vale. I'm staying at Marsham Manor with Cornelia Fothergill, the novelist. Ever heard of her?'

'Vaguely, as it were. She is not on my library list.'

'She would be, if you were a woman. She specializes in rich goo for the female trade.'

'Ah, yes, like Mrs Bingo Little. Rosie M. Banks to you.'

'That sort of thing, yes, but even goo-ier. Where Rosie M. Banks merely touches the heart strings, Cornelia Fothergill grabs them in both hands and ties them into knots. I'm trying to talk her into letting me have her new novel as a serial for the *Boudoir*.'

I got the gist. She has since sold it, but at the time of which I speak this aunt was the proprietor or proprietress of a weekly paper for the half-witted woman called *Milady's Boudoir*, to which I once contributed an article – a 'piece' we old hands call it – on What The Well-Dressed Man Is Wearing. Like all weekly papers, it was in the process of turning the corner, as the expression is, and I could well understand that a serial by a specialist in rich goo would give it a much-needed shot in the arm.

'How's it coming?' I asked. 'Any luck?'

'Not so far. She demurs.'

'Dewhat's?'

'Murs, you silly ass.'

'You mean she meets your pleas with what Jeeves would call a *nolle prosequi*?'

'Not quite that. She has not closed the door to a peaceful settlement, but, as I say, she de—'

'Murs?'

'Murs is right. She doesn't say No, but she won't say Yes. The trouble is that Tom is doing his Gaspard-the-Miser stuff again.'

Her allusion was to my uncle, Thomas Portarlington Travers, who foots the bills for what he always calls *Madame's Nightshirt*. He is as rich as creosote, as I believe the phrase is, but like so many of our wealthier citizens he hates to give up. Until you have heard Uncle Tom on the subject of income tax and supertax, you haven't heard anything.

'He won't let me go above five hundred pounds, and she wants eight.'

'Looks like an impasse.'

'It did till this morning.'

'What happened this morning?'

'Oh, just a sort of break in the clouds. She said something which gave me the impression that she was weakening and that one more shove would do the trick. Are you still sober?'

'I am.'

'Then keep so over this next week-end, because you're coming down here.'

'Who, me?'

'You, in person.'

'But, why?'

'To help me sway her. You will exercise all your charm—'

'I haven't much.'

'Well, exercise what you've got. Give her the old oil. Play on her as on a stringed instrument.'

I chewed the lip somewhat. I'm not keen on these blind dates. And if life has taught me one thing, it is that the prudent man keeps away from female novelists. But it might be, of course, that a gay house-party was contemplated. I probed her on this point.

'Will anyone else be there? Is there any bright young society, I mean?'

'I wouldn't call the society young, but it's very bright. There's Cornelia's husband, Everard Fothergill the artist, and his father Edward Fothergill. He's an artist, too, of a sort. You won't have a dull moment. So tell Jeeves to pack your effects, and we shall expect you on Friday. You will continue to haunt the house till Monday.'

'Cooped up with a couple of artists and a writer of rich goo? I don't like it.'

'You don't have to like it,' the aged relative assured me. 'You just do it. Oh, and by the way, when you get here, I've a little something I want you to do for me.'

'What sort of a little something?'

'I'll tell you about it when I see you. Just a simple little thing to help Auntie. You'll enjoy it,' she said, and with a cordial 'Toodle-oo' rang off.

It surprises many people, I believe, that Bertram Wooster, as a general rule a man of iron, is as wax in the hands of his Aunt Dahlia, jumping to obey her lightest behest like a performing seal going after a slice of fish. They do not know that this woman possesses a secret weapon by means of which she can always bend me to her will – viz. the threat that if I give her any of my lip, she will bar me from her dinner table and deprive me of the roasts and boileds of her French chef Anatole, God's gift to the gastric juices. When she says Go, accordingly, I do not demur, I goeth, as the Bible puts it, and so it came about that toward the quiet evenfall of Friday the 22nd inst. I was at the wheel of the old sports model, tooling through Hants with Jeeves at my side and weighed down with a nameless foreboding.

'Jeeves,' I said, 'I am weighed down with a nameless foreboding.'

'Indeed, sir?'

'Yes. What, I ask myself, is cooking?'

'I do not think I quite follow you, sir.'

'Then you jolly well ought to. I reported my conversation with Aunt Dahlia to you verbatim, and you should have every word of it tucked away beneath your bowler hat. To refresh your memory, after a certain amount of kidding back and forth she said "I've a little something I want you to do for me," and when I enquired what, she fobbed me off . . . is it fobbed?'

'Yes, sir.'

'She fobbed me off with a careless "Oh, just a simple little thing to help Auntie." What construction do you place on those words?'

'One gathers that there is something Mrs Travers wishes you to do for her, sir.'

'One does, but the point is – what? You recall what has happened in the past when the gentler sex have asked me to do things for them. Especially Aunt Dahlia. You have not forgotten the affair of Sir Watkyn Bassett and the silver cow-creamer?'

'No, sir.'

'On that occasion, but for you, Bertram Wooster would have done a stretch in the local hoosegow. Who knows that this little something to which she referred will not land me in a similar peril? I wish I could slide out of this binge, Jeeves.'

'I can readily imagine it, sir.'

'But I can't, I'm like those Light Brigade fellows. You remember how matters stood with them?'

'Very vividly, sir. Theirs not to reason why, theirs but to do and die.'

'Exactly. Cannons to right of them, cannons to left of them volleyed and thundered, but they had to keep snapping into it regardless. I know just how they felt,' I said, moodily stepping on the accelerator. The brow was furrowed and the spirits low.

Arrival at Marsham Manor did little to smooth the former and raise the latter. Shown into the hall, I found myself in as cosy an interior as one could wish – large log fire, comfortable chairs and a tea-table that gave out an invigorating aroma of buttered toast and muffins, all very pleasant to encounter after a long drive on a chilly winter afternoon – but a single glance at the personnel was enough to tell me that I had struck one of those joints where every prospect pleases and only man is vile.

Three human souls were present when I made my entry, each plainly as outstanding a piece of cheese as Hampshire could provide. One was a small, thin citizen with a beard of the type that causes so much distress – my host, I presumed – and seated near him was another bloke of much the same construction but an earlier model, whom I took to be the father. He, too, was bearded to the gills. The third was a large spreading woman wearing the horn-rimmed spectacles which are always an occupational risk for penpushers of the other sex. They gave her a rather remarkable resemblance to my Aunt Agatha, and I would be deceiving my public were I to say that the heart did not sink to some extent. To play on such a woman as on a stringed instrument wasn't going to be the simple task Aunt Dahlia appeared to think it.

After a brief pause for station identification, she introduced me to the gang, and I was on the point of doing the civil thing by asking Everard Fothergill if he had been painting anything lately, when he stiffened.

'Hark!' he said. 'Can you hear a mewing cat?'

'Eh?' I said.

'A mewing cat. I feel sure I hear a mewing cat. Listen!'

While we were listening the door opened and Aunt Dahlia

came in. Everard put the 64,000–dollar question squarely up to her.

'Mrs Travers, did you meet a mewing cat outside?'

'No,' said the aged relative. 'No mewing cat. Why, did you order one?'

'I can't bear mewing cats,' said Everard. 'A mewing cat gets on my nerves.'

That was all about mewing cats for the moment. Tea was dished out, and I had a couple of bits of buttered toast, and so the long day wore on till it was time to dress for dinner. The Fothergill contingent pushed off, and I was heading in the same direction, when Aunt Dahlia arrested my progress.

'Just a second, Bertie, before you put on your clean dickey,' she said. 'I would like to show you something.'

'And I,' I riposted, 'would like to know what this job is you say you want me to do for you.'

'I'll be coming to that later. This thing I'm going to show you is tied in with it. But first a word from our sponsor. Did you notice anything about Everard Fothergill just now?'

I reviewed the recent past.

'Would you describe him as perhaps a bit jumpy? He seemed to me to be stressing the mewing cat motif rather more strongly than might have been expected.'

'Exactly. He's a nervous wreck. Cornelia tells me he used to be very fond of cats.'

'He still appears interested in them.'

'It's this blasted picture that has sapped his morale.'

'Which blasted picture would that be?'

'I'll show you. Step this way.'

She led me into the dining-room and switched on the light. 'Look,' she said.

What she was drawing to my attention was a large oil painting. A classical picture, I suppose you would have called it. Stout female in the minimum of clothing in conference with a dove.

'Venus?' I said. It's usually a safe bet.

'Yes. Old Fothergill painted it. He's just the sort of man who would paint a picture of Ladies' Night In A Turkish Bath and call it Venus. He gave it to Everard as a wedding present.'

'Thus saving money on the customary fish-slice. Shrewd, very shrewd. And I gather from what you were saying that the latter does not like it.'

'Of course he doesn't. It's a mess. The old boy's just an

incompetent amateur. But being devoted to his father and not wanting to hurt his feelings Everard can't have it taken down and put in the cellar. He's stuck with it, and has to sit looking at it every time he puts on the nose-bag. With what result?'

'The food turns to ashes in his mouth?'

'Exactly. It's driving him potty. Everard's a real artist. His stuff's good. Some of it's in the Tate. Look at this,' she said, indicating another canvas. 'That's one of his things.'

I gave it a quick once-over. It, too, was a classical picture, and seemed to my untutored mind very like the other one, but presuming that some sort of art criticism was expected of me I said:

'I like the patina.'

That, too, is generally a safe bet, but it appeared that I had said the wrong thing, for the relative snorted audibly.

'No, you don't, you miserable blighter. You don't even know what a patina is.'

She had me there, of course. I didn't.

'You and your ruddy patinas! Well, anyway, you see why Everard has got the jitters. If a man can paint as well as he can, it naturally cuts him to the quick to have to glue his eyes on a daub like the Venus every time he sits down to break bread. Suppose you were a great musician. Would you like to have to listen to a cheap, vulgar tune – the same tune – day after day? Or suppose that every time you went to lunch at the Drones you had to sit opposite someone who looked like the Hunchback of Notre Dame? Would you enjoy that? Of course you wouldn't. You'd be as sick as mud.'

I saw her point. Many a time at the Drones I have had to sit opposite Oofy Prosser, and it had always taken the edge off a usually keen appetite.

'So now do you grasp the position of affairs, dumbbell?'

'Oh, I grasp it all right, and the heart bleeds, of course. But I don't see there's anything to be done about it.'

'I do. Ask me what.'

'What?'

'You're going to pinch that Venus.'

I looked at her with a wild surmise, silent upon a peak in Darien. Not my own. One of Jeeves's things.

'Pinch it?'

'This very night.'

'When you say "pinch it", do you mean "*pinch it*"?'

'That's right. That's the little something I was speaking of, the simple little thing you're going to do to help Auntie. Good heavens,' she said, her manner betraying impatience, 'I can't see why you're looking like a stuck pig about it. It's right up your street. You're always pinching policemen's helmets, aren't you?'

I had to correct this.

'Not always. Only as an occasional treat, as it might be on a Boat Race night. And, anyway, pinching pictures is a very different thing from lifting the headgear of the Force. Much more complex.'

'There's nothing complex about it. It's as easy as falling off a log. You just cut it out of the frame with a good sharp knife.'

'I haven't got a good sharp knife.'

'You will have. You know, Bertie,' she said, all enthusiasm, 'it's extraordinary how things fit in. These last weeks there's been a gang of picture-thieves operating in this neighbourhood. They got away with a Romney at a house near here and a Gainsborough from another house. It was that that gave me the idea. When his Venus disappears, there won't be a chance of old Fothergill suspecting anything and having his feelings hurt. These marauders are connoisseurs, he'll say to himself, only the best is good enough for them. Cornelia agreed with me.'

'You told her?'

'Well, naturally. I was naming the Price of the Papers. I said that if she gave me her solemn word that she would let the *Boudoir* have this slush she's writing, shaving her price to suit my purse, you would liquidate the Edward Fothergill Venus.'

'You did, did you? And what did she say?'

'She thanked me brokenly, saying it was the only way of keeping Everard from going off his rocker, and I told her I would have you here, ready to the last button, this week-end.'

'God bless your old pea-pickin' heart!'

'So go to it, boy, and heaven speed your efforts. All you have to do is open one of the windows, to make it look like an outside job, collect the picture, take it back to your room and burn it. I'll see that you have a good fire.'

'Oh, thanks.'

'And now you had better be dressing. You haven't much time, and it makes Everard nervous if people are late for dinner.'

It was with bowed head and the feeling that the curse had come upon me that I proceeded to my room. Jeeves was there, studding the shirt, and I lost no time in giving him the low-down. My attitude towards Jeeves on these occasions is always that of a lost sheep getting together with its shepherd.

'Jeeves,' I said, 'you remember me telling you in the car that I was weighed down with a nameless foreboding?'

'Yes, sir.'

'Well, I had every right to be. Let me tell you in a few simple words what Aunt Dahlia has just been springing on me.'

I told him in a few simple words, and his left eyebrow rose perhaps an eighth of an inch, showing how deeply he was stirred.

'Very disturbing, sir.'

'Most. And the ghastly thing is that I suppose I shall have to do it.'

'I fear so, sir. Taking into consideration the probability that, should you decline to cooperate, Mrs Travers will place sanctions on you in the matter of Anatole's cooking, you would appear to have no option but to fall in with her wishes. Are you in pain, sir?' he asked, observing me writhe.

'No, just chafing. This has shocked me, Jeeves. I wouldn't have thought such an idea would ever have occurred to her. One could understand Professor Moriarty, and possibly Doctor Fu Manchu, thinking along these lines, but not a wife and mother highly respected in Market Snodsbury, Worcestershire.'

'The female of the species is more deadly than the male, sir. May I ask if you have formulated a plan of action?'

'She sketched one out. I open a window, to make it look like an outside job—'

'Pardon me for interrupting, sir, but there I think Mrs Travers is in error. A broken window would lend greater verisimilitude.'

'Wouldn't it rouse the house?'

'No, sir, it can be done quite noiselessly by smearing treacle on a sheet of brown paper, attaching the paper to the pane and striking it a sharp blow with the fist. This is the recognized method in vogue in the burgling industry.'

'But where's the brown paper? Where the treacle?'

'I can procure them, sir, and I shall be happy to perform the operation for you, if you wish.'

'You will? That's very white of you, Jeeves.'

'Not at all, sir. It is my aim to give satisfaction. Excuse me, I think I hear someone knocking.'

He went to the door, opened it, said, 'Certainly, madam, I will give it to Mr Wooster immediately,' and came back with a sort of young sabre.

'Your knife, sir.'

'Thank you, Jeeves, curse it,' I said, regarding the object with a shudder, and slipped sombrely into the mesh-knit underwear.

After deliberation, we had pencilled in the kick-off for one in the morning, when the household might be expected to be getting its eight hours, and at one on the dot Jeeves shimmered in.

'Everything is in readiness, sir.'

'The treacle?'

'Yes, sir.'

'The brown p.?'

'Yes, sir.'

'Then just bust the window, would you mind.'

'I have already done so, sir.'

'You have? Well, you were right about it being noiseless. I didn't hear a sound. Then Ho for the dining-room, I suppose. No sense in dillying or, for the matter of that, dallying.'

'No, sir. If it were done when 'tis done, then 'twere well it were done quickly,' he said, and I remember thinking how neatly he puts these things.

It would be idle to pretend that, as I made my way down the stairs, I was my usual debonair self. The feet were cold, and if there had been any sudden noises, I would have started at them. My meditations on Aunt Dahlia, who had let me in for this horror in the night, were rather markedly lacking in a nephew's love. Indeed, it is not too much to say that every step I took deepened my conviction that what the aged relative needed was a swift kick in the pants.

However, in one respect you had to hand it to her. She had said the removal of the picture from the parent frame would be as easy as falling off a log – a thing I have never done myself, but one which, I should imagine, is reasonably simple of accomplishment – and so it proved. She had in no way over-estimated the goodness and sharpness of the knife with which she had provided me. Four quick cuts, and the canvas came out like a winkle at the end of a pin. I rolled it up and streaked back to my room with it.

Jeeves in my absence had been stoking the fire, and it was now in a cheerful blaze. I was about to feed Edward Fothergill's regrettable product to the flames and push it home with the poker, but he stayed my hand.

'It would be injudicious to burn so large an object in one piece, sir. There is the risk of setting the chimney on fire.'

'Ah, yes, I see what you mean. Snip it up, you think?'

'I fear it is unavoidable, sir. Might I suggest that it would relieve the monotony of the task if I were to provide whisky and a syphon?'

'You know where they keep it?'

'Yes, sir.'

'Then lead it to me.'

'Very good, sir.'

'And meanwhile I'll be getting on with the job.'

I did so, and was making good progress, when the door opened without my hearing it and Aunt Dahlia beetled in. She spoke before I was aware of her presence in my midst, causing me to shoot up to the ceiling with a stifled cry.

'Everything pretty smooth, Bertie?'

'I wish you'd toot your horn,' I said, coming back to earth and speaking with not a little bitterness. 'You shook me to the core. Yes, matters have gone according to plan. But Jeeves insists on burning the *corpus delicti* bit by bit.'

'Well, of course. You don't want to set the chimney on fire.'

'That was what he said.'

'And he was right, as always. I've brought my scissors. Where is Jeeves, by the way? Why not at your side, giving selfless service?'

'Because he's giving selfless service elsewhere. He went off to get whisky.'

'What a man! There is none like him, none. Bless my soul,' said the relative some moments later, as we sat before the fire and snipped, 'how this brings back memories of the dear old school and our girlish cocoa parties. Happy days, happy days! Ah, Jeeves, come right in and put the supplies well within my reach. We're getting on, you see. What is that you have hanging on your arm?'

'The garden shears, madam. I am anxious to lend all the assistance that is within my power.'

'Then start lending. Edward Fothergill's masterpiece awaits you.'

With the three of us sparing no effort, we soon completed the work in hand. I had scarcely got through my first whisky and s. and was beginning on another, when all that was left of the Venus, not counting the ashes, was the little bit at the south-east end which Jeeves was holding. He was regarding it with what seemed to me a rather thoughtful eye.

'Excuse me, madam,' he said. 'Did I understand you to say that Mr Fothergill senior's name was Edward?'

'That's right. Think of him as Eddie, if you wish. Why?'

'It is merely that the picture we have with us appears to be signed "Everard Fothergill", madam. I thought I should mention it.'

To say that aunt and nephew did not take this big would be paltering with the truth. We skipped like the high hills.

'Give me that fragment, Jeeves. It looks like Edward to me,' I pronounced, having scrutinized it.

'You're crazy,' said Aunt Dahlia, feverishly wrenching it from my grasp. 'It's Everard. Isn't it, Jeeves?'

'That was certainly the impression I formed, madam.'

'Bertie,' said Aunt Dahlia, speaking in a voice of the kind which I believe is usually called strangled and directing at me the sort of look which in the days when she used to hunt with the Quorn and occasionally the Pytchley she would have given a hound engaged in chasing a rabbit, 'Bertie, you curse of the civilized world, if you've burned the wrong picture . . .'

'Of course I haven't,' I replied stoutly. 'You're both cockeyed. But if it will ease your mind, I'll pop down to the dining-room and take a dekko. Amuse yourselves somehow till my return.'

I had spoken, as I say, stoutly, and hearing me you would no doubt have said to yourself 'All is well with Bertram. He is unperturbed.' But I wasn't. I feared the worst, and already I was wincing at the thought of the impassioned speech, touching on my mental and moral defects, which Aunt Dahlia would be delivering when we forgathered once more. Far less provocation in the past had frequently led her to model her attitude towards me on that of a sergeant dissatisfied with the porting and shouldering arms of a recruit who had not quite got the hang of the thing.

I was consequently in no vein for the receipt of another shock, but I got this when I reached journey's end, for as I entered the dining-room somebody inside it came bounding out and rammed me between wind and water. We staggered into the hall, locked in a close embrace, and as I had switched on the lights there in order to avoid bumping into pieces of furniture

I was enabled to see my dance partner steadily and see him whole, as Jeeves says. It was Fothergill senior in bedroom slippers and a dressing-gown. In his right hand he had a knife, and at his feet there was a bundle of some sort which he had dropped at the moment of impact, and when I picked it up in my courteous way and it came unrolled, what I saw brought a startled 'Golly!' to my lips. It deadheated with a yip of anguish from his. He had paled beneath his whiskers.

'Mr Wooster!' he . . . quavered is, I think, the word. 'Thank God you are not Everard!'

Well, I was pretty pleased about that, too, of course. The last thing I would have wanted to be was a small, thin artist with a beard.

'No doubt,' he proceeded, still quavering, 'you are surprised to find me removing my Venus by stealth in this way, but I can explain everything.'

'Well, that's fine, isn't it?'

'You are not an artist—'

'No, more a literary man. I once wrote an article on What The Well-Dressed Man Is Wearing for *Milady's Boudoir*.'

'Nevertheless, I think I can make you understand what this picture means to me. It was my child. I watched it grow. I loved it. It was part of my life.'

Here he paused, seeming touched in the wind, and I threw in a 'Very creditable' to keep the conversation going.

'And then Everard married, and in a mad moment I gave it to him as a wedding present. How bitterly I regretted it! But the thing was done. It was irrevocable. I saw how he valued the picture. His eyes at meal times were always riveted on it. I could not bring myself to ask him for it back. And yet I was lost without it.'

'Bit of a mix-up,' I agreed. 'Difficult to find a formula.'

'For a while it seemed impossible. And then there was this outbreak of picture robberies in the neighbourhood. You heard about those?'

'Yes, Aunt Dahlia mentioned them.'

'Several valuable paintings have been stolen from houses near here, and it suddenly occurred to me that if I were to . . . er . . . remove my Venus, Everard would assume that it was the work of the same gang and never suspect. I wrestled with the temptation . . . I beg your pardon?'

'I only said "At-a-boy!"'

'Oh? Well, as I say, I did my utmost to resist the temptation, but tonight I yielded. Mr Wooster, you have a kind face.'

For an instant I thought he had said 'kind of face' and drew myself up, a little piqued. Then I got him.

'Nice of you to say so.'

'Yes, I am sure you are kind and would not betray me. You will not tell Everard?'

'Of course not, if you don't want me to. Sealed lips, you suggest?'

'Precisely.'

'Right ho.'

'Thank you, thank you. I am infinitely grateful. Well, it is a little late and one might as well be turning in, I suppose, so I will say good-night,' he said, and having done so, buzzed up the stairs like a homing rabbit. And scarcely had he buzzed, when I found Aunt Dahlia and Jeeves at my side.

'Oh, there you are,' I said.

'Yes, here we are,' replied the relative with a touch of asperity. 'What's kept you all this time?'

'I would have made it snappier, but I was somewhat impeded in my movements by pards.'

'By what?'

'Bearded pards. Shakespeare. Right, Jeeves?'

'Perfectly correct, sir. Shakespeare speaks of the soldier as bearded like the pard.'

'And,' said Aunt Dahlia, 'full of strange oaths. Some of which you will shortly hear, if you don't tell us what you're babbling about.'

'Oh, didn't I mention that? I've been chatting with Edward Fothergill.'

'Bertie, you're blotto.'

'Not blotto, old flesh and blood, but much shaken. Aunt Dahlia, I have an amazing story to relate.'

I related my amazing story.

'And so,' I concluded, 'we learn once again the lesson never, however dark the outlook, to despair. The storm clouds lowered, the skies were black, but now what do we see? The sun shining and the blue bird back once more at the old stand. La Fothergill wanted the Venus expunged, and it has been expunged. *Voilà!*' I said, becoming a bit Parisian.

'And when she finds that owing to your fatheadedness Everard's very valuable picture has also been expunged?'

I h'med. I saw what she had in mind.

'Yes, there's that,' I agreed.

'She'll be madder than a wet hen. There isn't a chance now that she'll let me have that serial.'

'I'm afraid not. I had overlooked that. I withdraw what I said about the sun and the blue bird.'

She inflated her lungs, and it could have been perceived by the dullest eye that she was about to begin.

'Bertie—'

Jeeves coughed that soft cough of his, the one that sounds like a sheep clearing its throat on a distant mountain side.

'I wonder if I might make a suggestion, madam?'

'Yes, Jeeves? Remind me,' said the relative, giving me a burning glance, 'to go on with what I was saying later. You have the floor, Jeeves.'

'Thank you, madam. It was merely that it occurs to me as a passing thought that there *is* a solution of the difficulty that confronts us. If Mr Wooster were to be found here lying stunned, the window broken and both pictures removed, Mrs Fothergill could, I think, readily be persuaded that he found miscreants making a burglarious entry and while endeavouring to protect her property was assaulted and overcome by them. She would, one feels, be grateful.'

Aunt Dahlia came up like a rocket from the depths of gloom in which she had been wallowing. Her face, always red owing to hunting in all weathers in her youth, took on a deeper vermilion.

'Jeeves, you've hit it! I see what you mean. She would be so all over him for his plucky conduct that she couldn't decently fail to come through about the serial.'

'Precisely, madam.'

'Thank you, Jeeves.'

'Not at all, madam.'

'When, many years hence, you hand in your dinner pail, you must have your brain pickled and presented to the nation. It's a colossal scheme, don't you think, Bertie?'

I had been listening to the above exchange of remarks without a trace of Aunt Dahlia's enthusiasm, for I had spotted the flaw in the thing right away – to wit, the fact that I was not lying stunned. I now mentioned this.

'Oh, that?' said Aunt Dahlia. 'We can arrange that. I could give you a tap on the head with . . . with what, Jeeves?'

'The gong stick suggests itself, madam.'

'That's right, with the gong stick. And there we'll be.'

'Well, good-night, all,' I said. 'I'm turning in.'

She stared at me like an aunt unable to believe her ears.

'You mean you won't play ball?'

'I do.'

'Think well, Bertram Wooster. Reflect what the harvest will be. Not a smell of Anatole's cooking will you get for months and months and months. He will dish up his Sylphides à la crème d'Écrevisses and his Timbales de Ris de Veau Toulousaines and what not, but you will not be there to dig in and get yours. This is official.'

I drew myself to my full height.

'There is no terror, Aunt Dahlia, in your threats, for . . . how does it go, Jeeves?'

'For you are armed so strong in honesty, sir, that they pass by you like the idle wind, which you respect not.'

'Exactly. I have been giving considerable thought to this matter of Anatole's cooking, and I have reached the conclusion that the thing is one that cuts both ways. Heaven, of course, to chew his smoked offerings, but what of the waistline? The last time I enjoyed your hospitality for the summer months, I put on a full inch round the middle. I am better without Anatole's cooking. I don't want to look like Uncle George.'

I was alluding to the present Lord Yaxley, a prominent London clubman who gets more prominent yearly, especially seen sideways.

'So,' I continued, 'agony though it may be, I am prepared to kiss those Timbales of which you speak goodbye, and I, therefore, meet your suggestion of giving me taps on the head with the gong stick with a resolute *nolle prosequi*.'

'That is your last word, is it?'

'It is,' I said, and it was, for as I turned on my heel something struck me a violent blow on the back hair, and I fell like some monarch of the forest beneath the axe of the woodman.

What's that word I'm trying to think of? Begins with a 'c'. Chaotic, that's the one. For some time after that conditions were chaotic. The next thing I remember with any clarity is finding myself in bed with a sort of booming noise going on close by. This, the mists having lifted, I was able to diagnose as Aunt Dahlia talking. Hers is a carrying voice. She used, as I have mentioned, to go in a lot for hunting, and though I have never hunted myself, I understand that the whole essence of the thing is to be able to make yourself heard across three ploughed fields and a spinney.

'Bertie,' she was saying, 'I wish you would listen and not let your attention wander. I've got news that will send you dancing about the house.'

'It will be some little time,' I responded coldly, 'before I go dancing about any ruddy houses. My head—'

'Yes, of course. A little the worse for wear, no doubt. But don't let's go off into side issues, I want to tell you the final score. The dirty work is attributed on all sides to the gang, probably international, which has been lifting pictures in these parts of late. Cornelia Fothergill is lost in admiration of your intrepid behaviour, as Jeeves foresaw she would be, and she's giving me the serial on easy terms. You were right about the blue bird. It's singing.'

'So is my head.'

'I'll bet it is, and as you would say, the heart bleeds. But we all have to make sacrifices at these times. You can't make an omelette without breaking eggs.'

'Your own?'

'No, Jeeves's. He said it in a hushed voice as he stood viewing the remains.'

'He did, did he? Well, I trust in future . . . Oh, Jeeves,' I said, as he entered carrying what looked like a cooling drink.

'Sir?'

'This matter of eggs and omelettes. From now on, if you could see your way to cutting out the former and laying off the latter, I should be greatly obliged.'

'Very good, sir,' said the honest fellow. 'I will bear it in mind.'

'JEEVES AND THE GREASY BIRD'

The shades of night were falling fairly fast as I latchkeyed self and suitcase into the Wooster G.H.Q. Jeeves was in the sitting-room messing about with holly, for we would soon be having Christmas at our throats and he is always a stickler for doing the right thing. I gave him a cheery greeting.

'Well, Jeeves, here I am, back again.'

'Good evening, sir. Did you have a pleasant visit?'

'Not too bad. But I'm glad to be home. What was it the fellow said about home?'

'If your allusion is to the American poet John Howard Payne, sir, he compared it to its advantage with pleasures and palaces. He called it sweet and said there was no place like it.'

'And he wasn't so far out. Shrewd chap, John Howard Payne.'

'I believe he gave uniform satisfaction, sir.'

I had just returned from a week-end at the Chuffnell Regis clinic of Sir Roderick Glossop, the eminent loony doctor or nerve specialist as he prefers to call himself – not, I may add, as a patient but as a guest. My Aunt Dahlia's cousin Percy had recently put in there for repairs, and she had asked me to pop down and see how he was making out. He had got the idea, I don't know why, that he was being followed about by little men with black beards, a state of affairs which he naturally wished to have adjusted with all possible speed.

'You know, Jeeves,' I said some moments later, as I sat quaffing the whisky-and-s with which he had supplied me, 'life's odd, you can't say it isn't. You never know where you are with it.'

'There was some particular aspect of it that you had in mind, sir?'

'I was thinking of me and Sir R. Glossop. Who would ever have thought the day would come when he and I would be hobnobbing like a couple of sailors on shore leave? There was a time, you probably remember, when he filled me with a nameless fear and I leaped like a startled grasshopper at the sound of his name. You have not forgotten?'

'No, sir, I recall that you viewed Sir Roderick with concern.'

'And he me with ditto.'

'Yes, sir, a stiffness certainly existed. There was no fusion between your souls.'

'Yet now our relations are as cordial as they can stick. The barriers that separated us have come down with a bump. I beam at him. He beams at me. He calls me Bertie. I call him Roddy. To put the thing in a nutshell, the dove of peace is in a rising market and may quite possibly go to par. Of course, like Shadrach, Meshach and Abednego, if I've got the names right, we passed through the furnace together, and that always forms a bond.'

I was alluding to the time when – from motives I need not go into beyond saying that they were fundamentally sound – we had both blacked our faces, he with burned cork, I with boot polish, and had spent a night of terror wandering through Chuffnell Regis with no place to lay our heads, as the expression is. You don't remain on distant terms with somebody you've shared an experience like that with.

'But I'll tell you something about Roddy Glossop, Jeeves,' I said, having swallowed a rather grave swallow of the strengthening fluid. 'He has something on his mind. Physically I found him in excellent shape – few fiddles could have been fitter – but he was gloomy ... *distrait* ... brooding. Conversing with him, one felt that his thoughts were far away and that those thoughts were stinkers. I could hardly get a word out of him. It made me feel like that fellow in the Bible who tried to charm the deaf adder and didn't get to first base. There was a blighter named Blair Eggleston there, and it may have been this that depressed him, for this Eggleston ... Ever hear of him? He writes books.'

'Yes, sir. Mr Eggleston is one of our angry young novelists. The critics describe his work as frank, forthright and fearless.'

'Oh, do they? Well, whatever his literary merits he struck me as a fairly noxious specimen. What's he angry about?'

'Life, sir.'

'He disapproves of it?'

'So one would gather from his output, sir.'

'Well, I disapproved of him, which makes us all square. But I don't think it was having him around that caused the Glossop gloom. I am convinced that the thing goes deeper than that. I believe it's something to do with his love life.'

I must mention that while at Chuffnell Regis Pop Glossop, who was a widower with one daughter, had become betrothed to Myrtle, Lady Chuffnell, the aunt of my old crony Marmaduke ('Chuffy') Chuffnell, and that I should have found him still single more than a year later seemed strange to me. One would certainly have expected him by this time to have raised the price of a marriage licence and had the Bishop and assistant clergy getting their noses down to it. A redblooded loony doctor under the influence of the divine passion ought surely to have put the thing through months ago.

'Do you think they've had a row, Jeeves?'

'Sir?'

'Sir Roderick and Lady Chuffnell.'

'Oh no, sir. I am sure there is no diminution of affection on either side.'

'Then why the snag?'

'Her ladyship refuses to take part in the wedding ceremony while Sir Roderick's daughter remains unmarried, sir. She has stated in set terms that nothing will induce her to share a home with Miss Glossop. This would naturally render Sir Roderick moody and despondent.'

A bright light flashed upon me. I saw all. As usual, Jeeves had got to the very heart of the matter.

A thing that always bothers me when compiling these memoirs of mine is the problem of what steps to take when I bring on the stage a dramatis persona, as I believe the expression is, who has already appeared in some earlier instalment. Will the customers, I ask myself, remember him or her, or will they have completely forgotten her or him, in which case they will naturally want a few footnotes to put them abreast. This difficulty arises in regard to Honoria Glossop, who got into the act in what I suppose would be about Chapter Two of the Wooster Story. Some will recall her, but there may be those who will protest that they have never heard of the beazel in their lives, so perhaps better be on the safe side and risk the displeasure of the blokes with good memories.

Here, then, is what I recorded with ref to this H. Glossop at the time when owing to circumstances over which I had no control we had become engaged.

'Honoria Glossop,' I wrote, 'was one of those large, strenuous, dynamic girls with the physique of a middleweight catch-as-catch-can wrestler and a laugh resembling the sound made by the Scotch Express going under a bridge. The effect she had on me was to make me slide into a cellar and lie low there till they blew the All Clear.'

One could readily, therefore, understand the reluctance of Myrtle, Lady Chuffnell to team up with Sir Roderick while the above was still a member of the home circle. The stand she had taken reflected great credit on her sturdy commonsense, I considered.

A thought struck me, the thought I so often have when Jeeves starts dishing the dirt.

'How do you know all this, Jeeves? Did he confer with you?' I said, for I knew how wide his consulting practice was. 'Put it up to Jeeves' is so much the slogan in my circle of acquaintance that it might be that even Sir Roderick Glossop, finding himself on a sticky wicket, had decided to place his affairs in his hands. Jeeves is like Sherlock Holmes. The highest in the land come to him with their problems. For all I know, they may give him jewelled snuff boxes.

It appeared that I had guessed wrong.

'No, sir, I have not been honoured with Sir Roderick's confidence.'

'Then how did you find out about his spot of trouble? By extra-whatever-it's-called?'

'Extra-sensory perception? No, sir. I happened to be glancing yesterday at the G section of the club book.'

I got the gist. Jeeves belongs to a butlers' and valets' club in Curzon Street called the Junior Ganymede, and they have a book there in which members are required to enter information about their employers. I remember how stunned I was when he told me one day that there are eleven pages about me in it.

'The data concerning Sir Roderick and the unfortunate situation in which he finds himself were supplied by Mr Dobson.'

'Who?'

'Sir Roderick's butler, sir.'

'Of course, yes,' I said, recalling the dignified figure into whose palm I had pressed a couple of quid on leaving that morning. 'But surely Sir Roderick didn't confide in him?'

'No, sir, but Dobson's hearing is very acute and it enabled him to learn the substance of conversations between Sir Roderick and her ladyship.'

'He listened at the keyhole?'

'So one would be disposed to imagine, sir.'

I mused awhile. So that was how the cookie crumbled. A pang of p. for the toad beneath the harrow whose affairs we were discussing passed through me. It would have been plain to a far duller auditor than Bertram Wooster that poor old Roddy was in a spot. I knew how deep was his affection and esteem for Chuffy's Aunt Myrtle. Even when he was liberally coated with burned cork that night at Chuffnell Regis I had been able to detect the love light in his eyes as he spoke of her. And when I reflected how improbable it was that anyone would ever be ass enough to marry his daughter Honoria, thus making his path straight and ironing out the bugs in the scenario, my heart bled for him.

I mentioned this to Jeeves.

'Jeeves,' I said, 'my heart bleeds for Sir R. Glossop.'

'Yes, sir.'

'Does your heart bleed for him?'

'Profusely, sir.'

'And nothing to be done about it. We are helpless to assist.'

'One fears so, sir.'

'Life can be very sad, Jeeves.'

'Extremely, sir.'

'I'm not surprised that Blair Eggleston has taken a dislike to it.'

'No, sir.'

'Perhaps you had better bring me another whisky-and-s, to cheer me up. And after that I'll pop off to the Drones for a bite to eat.'

He gave me an apologetic look. He does this by allowing one eyebrow to flicker for a moment.

'I am sorry to say I have been remiss, sir. I inadvertently forgot to mention that Mrs Travers is expecting you to entertain her to dinner here tonight.'

'But isn't she at Brinkley?'

'No, sir, she has temporarily left Brinkley Court and taken up residence at her town house in order to complete her Christmas shopping.'

'And she wants me to give her dinner?'

'That was the substance of her words to me on the telephone this morning, sir.'

My gloom lightened perceptibly. This Mrs Travers is my good and deserving Aunt Dahlia, with whom it is always a privilege and pleasure to chew the fat. I would be seeing her, of course, when I went to Brinkley for Christmas, but getting this preview was an added attraction. If anyone could take my mind off the sad case of Roddy Glossop, it was she. I looked forward to the reunion with bright anticipation. I little knew that she had a bombshell up her sleeve and would be touching it off under my trouser seat while the night was yet young.

On these occasions when she comes to town and I give her dinner at the flat there is always a good deal of gossip from Brinkley Court and neighbourhood to be got through before other subjects are broached, and she tends not to allow a nephew to get a word in edgeways. It wasn't till Jeeves had brought the coffee that any mention of Sir Roderick Glossop was made. Having lit a cigarette and sipped her first sip, she asked me how he was, and I gave her the same reply I had given Jeeves.

'In robust health,' I said, 'but gloomy. Sombre. Moody. Despondent.'

'Just because you were there, or was there some other reason?'

'He didn't tell me,' I said guardedly. I always have to be very careful not to reveal my sources when Jeeves gives me information he has gleaned from the club book. The rules about preserving secrecy concerning its contents are frightfully strict at the Junior Ganymede. I don't know what happens to you if you're caught giving away inside stuff, but I should imagine that you get hauled up in a hollow square of valets and butlers and have your buttons snipped off before being formally bunged out of the institution. And it's a very comforting thought that such precautions are taken, for I should hate to think that there was any chance of those eleven pages about me receiving wide publicity. It's bad enough to know that a book like that – pure dynamite, as you might say – is in existence. 'He didn't let me in on what was eating him. He just sat there being gloomy and despondent.'

The old relative laughed one of those booming laughs of hers which in the days when she hunted with the Quorn and Pytchley probably lifted many a sportsman from the saddle. Her vocal delivery when amused always resembles one of those explosions in a London street you read about in the papers.

'Well, Percy had been with him for several weeks. And then you on top of Percy. Enough to blot the sunshine from any man's life. How is Percy, by the way?'

'Quite himself again. A thing I wouldn't care to be, but no doubt it pleases him.'

'Little men no longer following him around?'

'If they are, they've shaved. He hasn't seen a black beard for quite a while, he tells me.'

'That's good. Percy'll be all right if he rids himself of the idea that alcohol is a food. Well, we'll soon buck Glossop up when he comes to Brinkley for Christmas.'

'Will he be there?'

'He certainly will, and joy will be unconfined. We're going to have a real old-fashioned Christmas with all the trimmings.'

'Holly? Mistletoe?'

'Yards of both. And a children's party complete with Santa Claus.'

'With the vicar in the stellar role?'

'No, he's down with flu.'

'The curate?'

'Sprained his ankle.'

'Then who are you going to get?'

'Oh, I'll find someone. Was anyone else at Glossop's?'

'Only a fellow of the name of Eggleston.'

'Blair Eggleston, the writer?'

'Yes, Jeeves tells me he writes books.'

'And articles. He's doing a series for me on the Modern Girl.'

For some years, helped out by doles from old Tom Travers, her husband, Aunt Dahlia had been running a weekly paper for women called *Milady's Boudoir*, to which I once contributed a 'piece', as we journalists call it, on What The Well-Dressed Man Is Wearing. The little sheet has since been sold, but at that time it was still limping along and losing its bit of money each week, a source of considerable spiritual agony to Uncle Tom, who had to foot the bills. He has the stuff in sackfuls, but he hates to part.

'I'm sorry for that boy,' said Aunt Dahlia.

'For Blair Eggleston? Why?'

'He's in love with Honoria Glossop.'

'What!' I cried. She amazed me. I wouldn't have thought it could be done.

'And is too timid to tell her so. It's often that way with these frank, fearless young novelists. They're devils on paper, but put them up against a girl who doesn't come out of their fountain pen and their feet get as cold as a dachshund's nose. You'd think, when you read his novels, that Blair Eggleston was a menace to the sex and ought to be kept on a chain in the interests of pure womanhood, but is he? No, sir. He's just a rabbit. I don't know if he has ever actually found himself in an incense-scented boudoir alone with a girl with sensual lips and dark smouldering eyes, but if he did, I'll bet he would take a chair as far away from her as possible and ask her if she had read any good books lately. Why are you looking like a half-witted fish?'

'I was thinking of something.'

'What?'

'Oh, just something,' I said warily. Her character sketch of Blair Eggleston had given me one of those ideas I do so often get quick as a flash, but I didn't want to spill it till I'd had time to think it over and ponder on it. It never does to expose these brainwaves to the public eye before you've examined them from every angle. 'How do you know all this?' I said.

'He told me in a burst of confidence the other day when we were discussing his Modern Girl Series. I suppose I must have one of those sympathetic personalities which invite confidences. You will recall that you have always told me about your various love affairs.'

'That's different.'

'In what way?'

'Use the loaf, old flesh and blood. You're my aunt. A nephew naturally bares his soul to a loved aunt.'

'I see what you mean. Yes, that makes sense. You do love me dearly, don't you?'

'Like billy-o. Always have.'

'Well, I'm certainly glad to hear you say that—'

'Well deserved tribute.'

'—because there's something I want you to do for me.'

'Consider it done.'

'I want you to play Santa Claus at my children's Christmas party.'

Should I have seen it coming? Possibly. But I hadn't, and I tottered where I sat. I was trembling like an aspen. I don't know if you've ever seen an aspen – I haven't myself as far as I can remember – but I knew they were noted for trembling like the dickens. I uttered a sharp cry, and she said if I was going to sing, would I kindly do it elsewhere, as her ear drum was sensitive.

'Don't say such things even in fun,' I begged her.

'I'm not joking.'

I gazed at her incredulously.

'You seriously expect me to put on white whiskers and a padded stomach and go about saying "Ho, ho, ho" to a bunch of kids as tough as those residing near your rural seat?'

'They aren't tough.'

'Pardon me. I've seen them in action. You will recollect that I was present at the recent school treat.'

'You can't go by that. Naturally they wouldn't have the Christmas spirit at a school treat in the middle of summer. You'll find them as mild as newborn lambs on Christmas Eve.'

I laughed a sharp, barking laugh.

'*I* shan't.'

'Are you trying to tell me you won't do it?'

'I am.'

She snorted emotionally and expressed the opinion that I was a worm.

'But a prudent, levelheaded worm,' I assured her. 'A worm who knows enough not to stick its neck out.'

'You really won't do it?'

'Not for all the rice in China.'

'Not to oblige a loved aunt?'

'Not to oblige a posse of loved aunts.'

'Now listen, young Bertie, you abysmal young blot . . .'

As I closed the front door behind her some twenty minutes later, I had rather the feeling you get when parting company with a tigress of the jungle or one of those fiends with hatchets who are always going about slaying six. Normally the old relative is as genial a soul as ever downed a veal cutlet, but she's apt to get hot under the collar when thwarted, and in the course of the recent meal, as we have seen, I had been compelled to thwart her like a ton of bricks. It was with quite a few beads of persp. bedewing the brow that I went back to the dining room, where Jeeves was cleaning up the debris.

'Jeeves,' I said, brushing away the b. of p. with my cambric handkerchief, 'you were off stage towards the end of dinner, but did you happen to drink in any of the conversation that was taking place?'

'Oh yes, sir.'

'Your hearing, like Dobson's, is acute?'

'Extremely, sir. And Mrs Travers has a robust voice. I received the impression that she was incensed.'

'She was as sore as a gumboil. And why? Because I stoutly refused to portray Santa Claus at the Christmas orgy she is giving down at Brinkley for the children of the local yokels.'

'So I gathered from her *obiter dicta*, sir.'

'I suppose most of the things she called me were picked up on the hunting field in her hunting days.'

'No doubt, sir.'

'Members of the Quorn and Pytchley are not guarded in their speech.'

'Very seldom, sir, I understand.'

'Well, her efforts were . . . what's that word I've heard you use?'

'Bootless, sir?'

'Or fruitless?'

'Whichever you prefer, sir.'

'I was not to be moved. I remained firm. I am not a disobliging man, Jeeves. If somebody wanted me to play Hamlet, I would do my best to give satisfaction. But at dressing up in white whiskers and a synthetic stomach I draw the line and draw it sharply. She huffed and puffed, as you heard, but she might have known that argument would be bootless. As the wise old saying has it, you can take a horse to the water, but you can't make it play Santa Claus.'

'Very true, sir.'

'You think I was justified in being adamant?'

'Fully justified, sir.'

'Thank you, Jeeves.'

I must say I thought it pretty decent of him to give the young master the weight of his support like this, for though I haven't mentioned it before it was only a day or two since I had been compelled to thwart him as inflexibly as I had thwarted the recent aunt. He had been trying to get me to go to Florida after Christmas, handing out a lot of talk about how pleasant it would be for my many American friends, most of whom make a bee line for Hobe Sound in the winter months, to have me with them again, but I recognized this, though specious, as merely the old oil. I knew what was the thought behind his words. He likes the fishing in Florida and yearns some day to catch a tarpon.

Well, I sympathized with his sporting aspirations and would have pushed them along if I could have managed it, but I particularly wanted to be in London for the Drones Club Darts Tournament, which takes place in February and which I confidently expected to win this year, so I said Florida was out and he said 'Very good, sir', and that was that. The point I'm making is that there was no dudgeon or umbrage or anything of that sort on his part, as there would have been if he had been a lesser man, which of course he isn't.

'And yet, Jeeves,' I said, continuing to touch on the affair of the stricken aunt, 'though my firmness and resolution enabled me to emerge victorious from the battle of wills, I can't help feeling a pang.'

'Sir?'

'Of remorse. It's always apt to gnaw you when you've crushed someone beneath the iron heel. You can't help thinking that you ought to do something to bind up the wounds and bring the sunshine back into the poor slob's life. I don't like the thought of Aunt Dahlia biting her pillow tonight and trying to choke back the rising sobs because I couldn't see my way to fulfilling her hopes and dreams. I think I should extend something in the way of an olive branch or *amende honorable*.'

'It would be a graceful act, sir.'

'So I'll blow a few bob on flowers for her. Would you mind nipping out tomorrow morning and purchasing say two dozen long-stemmed roses?'

'Certainly, sir.'

'I think they'll make her face light up, don't you?'

'Unquestionably, sir. I will attend to the matter immediately after breakfast.'

'Thank you, Jeeves.'

I was smiling one of my subtle smiles as he left the room, for in the recent exchanges I had not been altogether frank, and it tickled me to think that he thought that I was merely trying to apply a soothing poultice to my conscience.

Mark you, what I had said about wanting to do the square thing by the aged relative and heal the breach and all that sort of thing was perfectly true, but there was a lot more than that behind the gesture. It was imperative that I get her off the boil, because her cooperation was essential to the success of a scheme or plan or plot which had been fizzing in the Wooster brain ever since the moment after dinner when she had asked me why I was looking like a halfwitted fish. It was a plan designed to bring about the happy ending for Sir R. Glossop, and now that

I had had time to give it the once over it seemed to me that it couldn't miss.

Jeeves brought the blooms while I was in my bath, and having dried the frame and donned the upholstery and breakfasted and smoked a cigarette to put heart into me I started out with them.

I wasn't expecting a warm welcome from the old flesh and blood, which was lucky, because I didn't get one. She was at her haughtiest, and the look she gave me was the sort of look which in her Quorn and Pytchley days she would have given some fellow-sportsman whom she had observed riding over hounds.

'Oh, it's you,' she said.

Well, it was, of course, no argument about that, so I endorsed her view with a civil good morning and a smile – rather a weak smile, probably, for her aspect was formidable. She was plainly sizzling.

'I hope you thoroughly understand,' she said, 'that after your craven exhibition last night I'm not speaking to you.'

'Oh, aren't you?'

'Certainly not. I'm treating you with silent contempt. What's that you've got there?'

'Some long-stemmed roses. For you.'

She sneered visibly.

'You and your long-stemmed roses! It would take more than long-stemmed roses to change my view that you're a despicable cowardy custard and a disgrace to a proud family. Your ancestors fought in the Crusades and were often mentioned in despatches, and you cringe like a salted snail at the thought of appearing as Santa Claus before an audience of charming children who wouldn't hurt a fly. It's enough to make an aunt turn her face to the wall and give up the struggle. But perhaps,' she said, her manner softening for a moment, 'you've come to tell me you've changed your mind?'

'I fear not, aged relative.'

'Then buzz off, and on your way home try if possible to get run over by a motor bus. And may I be there to hear you go pop.'

I saw that I had better come to the *res* without delay.

'Aunt Dahlia,' I said, 'it is within your power to bring happiness and joy into a human life.'

'If it's yours, I don't want to.'

'Not mine. Roddy Glossop's. Sit in with me in a plan or

scheme which I have in mind, and he'll go pirouetting about his clinic like a lamb in Springtime.'

She drew a sharp breath and eyed me keenly.

'What's the time?' she asked.

I consulted the wrist-w.

'A quarter to eleven. Why?'

'I was only thinking that it's very early for anyone, even you, to get pie-eyed.'

'I'm not pie-eyed.'

'Well, you're talking as if you were. Have you got a piece of chalk?'

I tut-tutted impatiently.

'Of course I haven't. Do you think I go about with pieces of chalk on my person? What do you want it for?'

'I would like to draw a line on the carpet and see if you can walk along it, because it's being borne in upon me more emphatically every moment that you're stewed to the gills. Say "Truly rural".'

I did so.

'And "She stood at the door of Burgess's fish sauce shop, welcoming him in".'

Again I passed the test.

'Well,' she said grudgingly, 'you seem as sober as you ever are. What do you mean about bringing happiness and joy into old Glossop's life?'

'The matter is susceptible of a ready explanation. I must begin by saying that Jeeves told me a story yesterday that shocked me to the core. No,' I said in answer to her query, 'it was not the one about the young man of Calcutta. It had to do with Roddy's love life. It's a long story, but I'll condense it into a short-short, and I would like to stress before embarking on my narrative that you can rely on it being accurate, for when Jeeves tells you anything, it's like getting it straight from the mouth of the stable cat. Furthermore, it's substantiated by Mr Dobson, Roddy's butler. You know Myrtle, Lady Chuffnell?'

'I've met her.'

'She and Roddy are betrothed.'

'So I've heard.'

'They love each other fondly.'

'So what's wrong with that?'

'I'll tell you what's wrong. She stoutly declines to go centre-aisleing with him until his daughter Honoria gets married.'

I had expected this to make her sit up, and it did. For the first time her demeanour conveyed the impression that she wasn't labelling my utterances as just delirious babble from the sick bed. She has always been fond of R. Glossop and it came as a shock to her to learn that he was so firmly established in the soup. I wouldn't say she turned pale, for after years of following the hounds in all weathers she can't, but she snorted and I could see that she was deeply moved.

'For heaven's sake! Is this true?'

'Jeeves has all the facts.'

'Does Jeeves know everything?'

'I believe so. Well, you can understand Ma Chuffnell's attitude. If you were a bride, would you want to have Honoria a permanent resident of your little nest?'

'I wouldn't.'

'Exactly. So obviously steps must be taken by Roddy's friends and well-wishers to get her married. And that brings me to the nub. I have a scheme.'

'I'll bet it's rotten.'

'On the contrary, it's a ball of fire. It flashed on me last night, when you were telling me that Blair Eggleston loves Honoria. That is where hope lies.'

'You mean you're thinking that he will marry her and take her off the strength?'

'Precisely.'

'Not a chance. I told you he was too much of a rabbit to suggest a merger. He'll never have the nerve to propose.'

'Unless helped by a push from behind.'

'And who's going to give him that?'

'I am. With your cooperation.'

She gave me another of those long keen looks, and I could see that she was again asking herself if her favourite nephew wasn't steeped to the tonsils in the juice of the grape. Fearing more tests and further references to pieces of chalk, I hastened to explain.

'Here's the idea. I start giving Honoria the rush of a lifetime. I lush her up at lunch and dinner. I take her to theatres and night clubs. I haunt her like a family spectre and cling to her closer than a porous plaster.'

I thought I heard her mutter 'Poor girl', but I ignored the slur and continued.

'You meanwhile . . . Will you be seeing something of Eggleston?'

'I see him daily. He brings me his latest views on the Modern Girl.'

'Then the thing's in the bag. You say he has already confided in you about his warmer-and-deeper-than-ordinary-friendship feelings concerning Honoria, so it won't be difficult for you to bring the subject up in the course of conversation. You warn him in a motherly way that he's a sap if he goes on not telling his love and letting concealment like a worm in the bud feed on his damask cheek – one of Jeeves's gags. I thought he put it rather well – and stress the fact that he had better heat up his feet and grab the girl while the grabbing's good, because you happen to know that your nephew Bertram is making a heavy play in her direction and may sew up the deal at any moment. Use sufficient eloquence, and I can't see how he can fail to respond. He'll be pouring out his love before you know where you are.'

'And suppose she doesn't feel like getting engaged to him?'

'Absurd. Why, she was once engaged to *me*.'

She was silent for a space, plunged in thought, as the expression is.

'I'm not sure,' she said at length, 'that you haven't got something.'

'It's a snip.'

'Yes, I think you're right. Jeeves has a great brain.'

'What's Jeeves got to do with it?'

'Wasn't it his idea?'

I drew myself up rather haughtily – not an easy thing to do when you're sitting in an armchair. I resent this universal tendency to take it for granted that whenever I suggest some particularly ripe scheme, it must be Jeeves's.

'The sequence was entirely mine.'

'Well, it's not at all a bad one. I've often said that you sometimes have lucid intervals.'

'And you'll sit in and do your bit?'

'It will be a pleasure.'

'Fine. Can I use your phone? I want to ask Honoria Glossop to lunch.'

I should imagine that it has often been said of Bertram Wooster that when he sets his hand to the plough he does not readily sheathe the sword. I had told Aunt Dahlia that I was going to give Honoria the rush of a lifetime, and the rush of a lifetime was precisely what I gave her. I lunched, dined and on two occasions nightclubbed her. It ran into money, but you can put up with a few punches in the pocketbook when you're working in a good cause. Even when wincing at the figures at the foot of the bill I was able to console myself with the thought of what all this was in aid of. Nor did I grudge the hours spent in the society of a girl whom in normal circs I would willingly have run a mile in tight shoes to avoid. Pop Glossop's happiness was at stake, and when a pal's happiness is at stake, the undersigned does not count the cost.

Nor were my efforts bootless. Aunt Dahlia was always ringing me up to tell me that Blair Eggleston's temperature was rising steadily day by day and it seemed to her only a question of time before the desired object would be achieved. And came a day when I was able to go to her with the gratifying news that the d.o. had indeed been a.

I found her engrossed in an Erle Stanley Gardner, but she lowered the volume courteously as I entered.

'Well, ugly,' she said, 'what brings you here? Why aren't you off somewhere with Honoria Glossop, doing your South American Joe act? What's the idea of playing hooky like this?'

I smiled one of my quiet smiles.

'Aged relative,' I said, 'I have come to inform you that I think we have reached the end of the long long trail,' and without further preamble I gave her the low-down. 'Have you been out today?'

'I went for a stroll, yes.'

'The weather probably struck you as extraordinarily mild for the latter part of December. More like spring than winter.'

'You haven't come here to talk about the weather?'

'You will find it is germane to the issue. Because the afternoon was so balmy—'

'Like others I could name.'

'I beg your pardon?'

'I didn't speak. Go on.'

'Well, as it was such a nice day I thought I would take a walk in the Park. I did so, and blowed if the first thing I saw wasn't Honoria. She was sitting on a chair by the Serpentine. I was about to duck, but it was too late. She had seen me, so I had to heave alongside and chat. And suddenly who should come along but Blair Eggleston.'

I had enchained her interest. She uttered a yip.

'He saw you?'

'With the naked eye.'

'Then that was your moment. If you'd had an ounce of sense, you'd have kissed her.'

I smiled another of my quiet ones.

'I did.'

'You *did*?'

'Yes, sir, I folded her in a close embrace and let her have it.'

'And what did Eggleston say?'

'I didn't wait to hear. I pushed off.'

'But you're sure he saw you?'

'He couldn't have missed. He was only a yard or two away, and the visibility was good.'

It isn't often that I get unstinted praise from my late father's sister, she as a rule being my best friend and severest critic, but on this occasion she gave me a rave notice. It was a pleasure to listen to her.

'That should have done it,' she said after handing me some stately compliments on my ingenuity and resource. 'I saw Eggleston yesterday, and when I mentioned what fun you and Honoria were having going about together, he looked like a blond Othello. His hands were clenched, his eyes burning, and if he wasn't grinding his teeth, I don't know a ground tooth when I hear one. That kiss was just what he needed to push him over the edge. He probably proposed to her the moment you were out of the way.'

'That's how I had it figured out.'

'Oh, hell,' said the old ancestor, for at this moment the telephone rang, interrupting us just when we wanted to go on discussing the thing undisturbed. She reached for it, and a long one-sided conversation ensued. I say one-sided because her contribution to it consisted merely of Ohs and Whats. Eventually whoever was at the other end appeared to have said his or her say, for she replaced the receiver and turned a grave face in my direction.

'That was Honoria,' she said.

'Oh, really?'

'And what she had to tell me was fraught with interest.'

'Did matters work out according to plan?'

'Not altogether.'

'How do you mean, not altogether?'

'Well, to begin with, it seems that Blair Eggleston, no doubt inflamed by what I told you I had said to him yesterday, proposed to her last night.'

'He did?'

'And was accepted.'

'That's good.'

'Not so good.'

'Why not?'

'Because when he saw you kiss her, he blew his top and broke the engagement.'

'Oh, my God!'

'Nor is that all. The worst is yet to come. She now says she's going to marry you. She said she quite realized your many defects but is sure she can correct them and mould you, and even though you aren't the mate of her dreams, she feels that your patient love should be rewarded. Obviously what happened was that you made yourself too fascinating. There was always that risk, I suppose.'

Long before she had concluded these remarks I had gone into my aspen act again. I goggled at her, stunned.

'But this is frightful!'

'I told you it wasn't so good.'

'You aren't pulling my leg?'

'No, it's official.'

'Then what shall I do for the best?'

She shrugged a moody shoulder.

'Don't ask me,' she said. 'Consult Jeeves. He may be able to suggest something.'

Well, it was all very well to say consult Jeeves, but it wasn't as simple as she seemed to think. The way I looked at it was that to place him in possession of the facts in what you might call pitiless detail would come under the head of bandying a woman's name, which, as everybody knows, is the sort of thing that gets you kicked out of clubs and cut by the County. On the other hand, to be in a jam like this and not seek his counsel would be a loony proceeding. It was only after profound thought that I saw how the thing could be worked. I gave him a hail, and he presented himself with a courteous 'Sir?'

'Oh, Jeeves,' I said, 'I hope I'm not interrupting you when you were curled up with your Spinoza's Ethics or whatever it is, but I wonder if you could spare me a moment of your valuable time?'

'Certainly, sir.'

'A problem has arisen in the life of a friend of mine who shall be nameless, and I want your advice. I must begin by saying that it's one of those delicate problems where not only my friend must be nameless but all the other members of the personnel. In other words, I can't mention names. You see what I mean?'

'I understand you perfectly, sir. You would prefer to term the protagonists A and B.'

'Or North and South?'

'A and B is more customary, sir.'

'Just as you say. Well, A is male, B female. You follow me so far?'

'You have been lucidity itself, sir.'

'And owing to . . . what's that something of circumstances you hear people talking about? Cats enter into it, if I remember rightly.'

'Would concatenation be the word for which you are groping?'

'That's it. Owing to a concatenation of circumstances B has got it into her nut that A's in love with her. But he isn't. Still following?'

'Yes, sir.'

I had to pause here for a moment to marshal my thoughts. Having done so, I proceeded.

'Now until quite recently B was engaged to—'

'Shall we call him C, sir?'

'Caesar's as good a name as any, I suppose. Well, as I was saying, until quite recently B was engaged to Caesar and A hadn't a worry in the world. But now there has been a rift within the lute, the fixture has been scratched, and B is talking freely of teaming up with A, and what I want you to bend your brain to is the problem of how A can oil out of it. Don't get the idea that it's simple, because A is what is known as a *preux chevalier*, and this hampers him. I mean when B comes to him and says "A, I will be yours", he can't just reply "You will, will you? That's what *you* think". He has his code, and the code rules that he must kid her along and accept the situation. And frankly, Jeeves, he would rather be dead in a ditch. So there you are. The facts are before you. Anything stirring?'

'Yes, sir.'

I was astounded. Experience has taught me that he generally knows all the answers, but this was certainly quick service.

'Say on, Jeeves. I'm all agog.'

'Obviously, sir, B's matrimonial plans would be rendered null and void if A were to inform her that his affections were engaged elsewhere.'

'But they aren't.'

'It would be necessary merely to convey the impression that such was the case.'

I began to see what he was driving at.

'You mean if I – or, rather, A – were to produce some female and have her assert that she was betrothed to me – or I should say him – the peril would be averted?'

'Precisely, sir.'

I mused.

'It's a thought,' I agreed, 'but there's the dickens of a snag – viz. how to get hold of the party of the second part. You can't rush about London asking girls to pretend they're engaged to you. At least, I suppose you can, but it would be quite a nervous strain.'

'That, sir, *is* the difficulty.'

'You haven't an alternative plan to suggest?'

'I fear not, sir.'

I confess I was baffled, but it's pretty generally recognized at the Drones and elsewhere that while you can sometimes baffle Bertram Wooster for the nonce, he rarely stays baffled long. I happened to run into Catsmeat Potter-Pirbright at the Drones that night, and I suddenly saw how the snag to which I had alluded could be got around.

Catsmeat is on the stage and now in considerable demand for what are called juvenile roles, but in his early days he had been obliged, like all young hams, to go from agent to agent seeking employment – or trying to get a shop, as I believe the technical term is, and he was telling me anecdotes about them after dinner. And it struck me like a blow in the midriff that if you wanted a girl to exhibit as your fiancée, a theatrical agent was the very man to help you out. Such a bloke would be in an admirable position to supply some resting artiste who would be glad to sit in on an innocent deception in return for a moderate fee.

Catsmeat had told me where these fauna were to be found. The Charing Cross Road is apparently where most of them hang out, and on the following morning I might have been observed entering the premises of Jas Waterbury on the top floor of a building about half-way up that thoroughfare.

The reason my choice had fallen on Jas was not that I had heard glowing reports of him from every side, it was simply because all the other places I had tried had been full of guys and dolls standing bumper to bumper and it hadn't seemed worth while waiting. Entering *chez* Waterbury I found his outer office completely empty. It was as if he had parted company with the human herd.

It was possible, of course, that he had stepped across the road for a quick one, but it was also possible that he was lurking behind the door labelled 'Private', so I rapped on it. I hadn't expected anything to start into life, but I was wrong. A head popped out.

I've seen heads that were more of a feast for the eye. It was what I would describe as a greasy head. Its summit was moist with hair oil and the face, too, suggested that its proprietor after the morning shave had thought fit to rub his cheeks with butter. But I'm a broad-minded man and I had no objection to him being greasy, if he liked being greasy. Possibly, I felt, if I had had the privilege of meeting Kenneth Molyneux, Malcolm McCullen, Edmund Ogilvy and Horace Furnival, the other theatrical agents I had visited, I would have found them greasy, too. It may be that all theatrical agents are. I made a mental note to ask Catsmeat Potter-Pirbright about this.

'Oh, hullo, cocky,' said this oleaginous character, speaking thickly, for he was making an early lunch on what looked like a ham sandwich. 'Something I can do for you?'

'Jas Waterbury?'

'That's me. You want a shop?'

'I want a girl.'

'Don't we all? What's your line? Are you running a touring company?'

'No, it's more like amateur theatricals.'

'Oh, those? Well, let's have the inside story.'

I had told myself that it would be embarrassing confiding one's intimate private affairs to a theatrical agent, and it was embarrassing, but I stiffened the upper lip and had at it, and as my narrative proceeded it was borne in upon me that I had sized up Jas Waterbury all wrong. Misled by his appearance, I had assumed him to be one of those greasy birds who would be slow on the uptake and unable to get hep to the finer points.

He proved to be both quick and intelligent. He punctuated my remarks with understanding nods, and when I had finished said I had come to the right man, for he had a niece called Trixie who would fill the bill to my complete satisfaction. The whole project, he said, was right up Trixie's street. If I placed myself in her hands, he added, the act must infallibly be a smash hit.

It sounded good, but I pursed my lips a bit dubiously. I was asking myself if an uncle's love might not have made him give the above Trixie too enthusiastic a build-up.

'You're sure,' I said, 'that this niece of yours would be equal to this rather testing job? It calls for considerable histrionic skill. Can she make her role convincing?'

'She'll smother you with burning kisses, if that's what you're worrying about.'

'What I had in mind was more the dialogue. We don't want her blowing up in her lines. Don't you think we ought to get a seasoned professional?'

'That's just what Trixie is. Been playing Fairy Queens in panto for years. Never got a shop in London owing to jealousy in high places, but ask them in Leeds and Wigan what they think of her. Ask them in Hull. Ask them in Huddersfield.'

I said I would, always provided I happened to come across them, and he carried on in a sort of ecstasy.

' "This buxom belle" – *Leeds Evening Chronicle*. "A talented bit of all right" – *Hull Daily News*. "Beauty and dignity combined" – *Wigan Intelligencer*. Don't you fret yourself, cocky, Trix'll give you your money's worth. And talking of that, how much does the part pay?'

'I was thinking of a fiver.'

'Make it ten.'

'Right ho.'

'Or, rather, fifteen. That way you'll get every ounce of zest and cooperation.'

I was in no mood to haggle. Aunt Dahlia had rung up while I was breakfasting to tell me that Honoria Glossop had told her that she would be looking in on me at four o'clock, and it was imperative that the reception committee be on hand to greet her. I dished out the fifteen quid and asked how soon he could get hold of his niece, as time was of the essence. He said her services would be at my disposal well ahead of zero hour, and I said Fine.

'Give me a ring when it's all set,' I said. 'I'll be lunching at the Drones Club.'

This seemed to interest him quite a bit.

'Drones Club, eh? You a member there? I've got some good friends at the Drones Club. You know a Mr Widgeon?'

'Freddie Widgeon? Yes, very well.'

'And Mr Prosser?'

'Yes, I know Oofy Prosser.'

'Give them my best, if you see them. Nice lads, both. And now you can trot along and feed your face without a care in the world. I'll have contacted Trixie before you're half-way through your fish and chips.'

And I was called to the phone while having the after-luncheon coffee in the smoking-room. It was, as I had anticipated, Jas Waterbury.

'That you, cocky?'

I said it was, and he said everything was under control. Trixie had been contacted and would be up and doing with a heart for any fate in good time for the rise of the curtain. What, he asked, was the address they were to come to, and I told him and he said they would be there at a quarter to four without fail. So that was all fixed, and I was full of kindly feelings towards Jas Waterbury as I made my way back to the smoking-room. He was a man whom I would have hesitated to invite to come with me on a long walking tour and I still felt that he would have been well advised to go easier on the grease as regarded both his hair and his person, but there was no getting away from it that if circumstances rendered it necessary for you to plot plots, he was the ideal fellow to plot them with.

During my absence from the smoking-room Catsmeat Potter-Pirbright had taken the chair next to mine, and I lost no time in sounding him out on the subject of Jas Waterbury.

'You remember you were telling me about theatrical agents, Catsmeat. Did you ever happen to come across one called Waterbury?'

He pondered awhile.

'The name seems vaguely familiar. What does he look like?'

'Nothing on earth.'

'That doesn't place him. All theatrical agents look like nothing on earth. But it's odd that I seem to know the name. Waterbury? Waterbury? Ha! Is he a greasy bird?'

'Very greasy.'

'And is his first name Jas?'

'That's right.'

'Then I know the chap you mean. I never met him myself – I doubt if he was going at the time when I was hoofing it from agent to agent – but I've heard of him from Freddie Widgeon and Oofy Prosser.'

'Yes, he said they were friends of his.'

'He'd revise that view if he could listen to them talking about him. Oofy in particular. Jas Waterbury once chiselled him out of two thousand pounds.'

I was amazed.

'He chiselled *Oofy* out of two thousand pounds?' I gasped, wondering if I could believe my e. Oofy is the Drones Club millionaire, but it is well known that it's practically impossible to extract as much as five bob from him without using chloroform and a forceps. Dozens have tried it and failed.

'That's what Freddie Widgeon told me. Freddie says that once Jas Waterbury enters your life, you can kiss at least a portion of your holdings goodbye. Has he taken anything off you?'

'Fifteen quid.'

'You're lucky it wasn't fifteen hundred.'

If you're saying to yourself that these words of Catsmeat's must have left me uneasy and apprehensive, you are correct to the last drop. A quarter to four found me pacing the Wooster carpet with furrowed brow. If it had been merely a matter of this grease-coated theatrical agent tapping Freddie Widgeon for a couple of bob, it would have been different. A child can tap Freddie. But when it came to him parting Oofy Prosser, a man in whose wallet moths nest and raise large families, from a colossal sum like two thousand pounds, the brain reeled and one sought in vain for an explanation. Yet so it was. Catsmeat said it was impossible to get the full story, because every time Jas's name was mentioned Oofy just turned purple and spluttered, but the stark fact remained that Jas's bank balance was that amount up and Oofy's that amount down, and it made me feel like a fellow in a novel of suspense who suddenly realizes that he's up against an Octopus of Crime and hasn't the foggiest how he's going to avoid the menacing tentacles.

But it wasn't long before Reason returned to its throne and I saw that I'd been alarming myself unnecessarily. Nothing like that was going to happen to me. It might be that Jas Waterbury would have a shot at luring me into some business venture with the ultimate aim of leaving me holding the baby, but if he did he would find himself stymied by a firm *nolle prosequi*, so, to cut a long story s, by the time the front door bell rang Bertram was himself again.

I answered the bell, for it was Jeeves's afternoon off. Once a week he downs tools and goes off to play Bridge at the Junior Ganymede. I opened the door and Jas and his niece came in, and I stood gaping dumbly. For an instant, you might say I was spellbound.

Not having attended the performance of a pantomime since fairly early childhood, I had forgotten how substantial Fairy Queens were, and the sight of Trixie Waterbury was like a blow from a blunt instrument. A glance was enough to tell me why the dramatic critic of the *Leeds Evening Chronicle* had called her buxom. She stood about five feet nine in her short French vamps and bulged in every direction. Also the flashing eyes and the gleaming teeth. It was some moments before I was able to say Good Afternoon.

'Afternoon,' said Jas Waterbury. He looked about him approvingly. 'Nice little place you've got here. Costs a packet to keep up, I'll bet. This is Mr Wooster, Trixie. You call him Bertie.'

The Fairy Queen said wouldn't 'sweetie-pie' be better, and Jas Waterbury told her with a good deal of enthusiasm that she was quite right.

'Much more box office,' he agreed. 'Didn't I say she would be right for the part, cocky? You can rely on her to give a smooth West End performance. When do you expect your lady friend?'

'Any moment now.'

'Then we'd better be dressing the stage. Discovered, you sitting in that chair there with Trixie on your lap.'

'What!'

He seemed to sense the consternation in my voice, for he frowned a little under the grease.

'We're all working for the good of the show,' he reminded me austerely. 'You want the scene to carry conviction, and there's nothing like a sight gag.'

I could see there was much in what he said. This was not a time for half measures. I sat down. I don't say I sat blithely, but I sat, and Wigan's favourite Fairy Queen descended on my lap with a bump that made the stout chair tremble like an aspen. And scarcely had she started to nestle when the door bell rang.

'Curtain going up,' said Jas Waterbury. 'Let's have that passionate embrace, Trixie, and make it good.'

She made it good, and I felt like a Swiss mountaineer engulfed by an avalanche smelling of patchouli. Jas Waterbury flung wide the gates, and who should come in but Blair Eggleston, the last caller I was expecting.

He stood goggling. I sat goggling. Jas Waterbury goggled, too. One could understand how he was feeling. Anticipating the entrance of the female star and observing coming on left centre a character who wasn't a member of the cast at all, he was pardonably disconcerted. No impresario likes that sort of thing.

I was the first to speak. After all, I was the host and it was for me to get the conversation going.

'Oh, hullo, Eggleston,' I said. 'Come along in. I don't think you've met Mr Waterbury, have you. Mr Eggleston, Mr Jas Waterbury. And his niece Miss Trixie Waterbury, my fiancée.'

'Your *what*?'

'Fiancée. Betrothed. Affianced.'

'Good Lord!'

Jas Waterbury appeared to be feeling that as the act had been shot to pieces like this, there was no sense in hanging around.

'Well, Trix,' he said, 'your Bertie'll be wanting to talk to his gentleman friend, so give him a kiss and we'll be getting along. Pleased to have met you, Mr What-is-it,' and with a greasy smile he led the Fairy Queen from the room.

Blair Eggleston seemed still at a loss. He looked at the door through which they had passed as if asking himself if he had really seen what he thought he had seen, then turned to me with the air of one who intends to demand an explanation.

'What's all this, Wooster?'

'What's all what, Eggleston? Be more explicit.'

'Who on earth is that female?'

'Weren't you listening? My fiancée.'

'You're really engaged to her?'

'That's right.'

'Who is she?'

'She plays Fairy Queens in pantomime. Not in London owing to jealousy in high places, but they think a lot of her in Leeds, Wigan, Hull and Huddersfield. The critic of the *Hull Daily News* describes her as a talented bit of all right.'

He was silent for a space, appearing to be turning this over in his mind. Then he spoke in the frank, forthright and fearless way these modern novelists have.

'She looks like a hippopotamus.'

I conceded this.

'There is a resemblance, perhaps. I suppose Fairy Queens have to be stoutish if they are to keep faith with their public in towns like Leeds and Huddersfield. Those audiences up North want lots for their money.'

'And she exudes a horrible scent which I am unable at the moment to identify.'

'Patchouli. Yes, I noticed that.'

He mused again.

'I can't get over you being engaged to her.'

'Well, I am.'

'It's official?'

'Absolutely.'

'Well, this will be great news for Honoria.'

I didn't get his drift.

'For Honoria?'

'Yes. It will relieve her mind. She was very worried about you, poor child. That's why I'm here. I came to break it to you that she can never be yours. She's going to marry me.'

I stared at him. My first impression was that even though the hour was only about four-thirty he was under the influence of alcoholic stimulants.

'But I learned from a usually reliable source that that was all off.'

'It was, but now it's on again. We have had a complete reconciliation.'

'Well, fancy that!'

'And she shrank from coming and telling you herself. She said she couldn't bear to see the awful dumb agony in your eyes. When I tell her you're engaged, she'll go singing about the West End of London, not only because of the relief of knowing that she hasn't wrecked your life but because she'll be feeling what a merciful escape she's had. Just imagine being married to you! It doesn't bear thinking of. Well, I'll be going along and telling her the good news,' he said, and took his departure.

A moment later the bell rang. I opened the door and found him on the mat.

'What,' he asked, 'was that name again?'

'Name?'

'Your fiancée's.'

'Trixie Waterbury.'

'Good God!' he said, and pushed off. And I returned to the reverie he had interrupted.

There was a time when if somebody had come to me and said 'Mr Wooster, I have been commissioned by a prominent firm of publishers to write your biography and I need some intimate stuff which only you can supply. Looking back, what would you consider the high spot in your career?', I would have had no difficulty in slipping him the info. It occurred, I would have replied, in my fourteenth year when I was a resident pupil at Malvern House, Bramley-on-Sea, the private school conducted by that prince of stinkers, Aubrey Upjohn, M.A. He had told me to present myself in his study on the following morning, which always meant six of the juiciest with a cane that bit like a serpent and stung like an adder, and blowed if when morning came I wasn't all over pink spots. I had contracted measles and the painful interview was of course postponed *sine die*, as the expression is.

That had always been my supreme moment. Only now was I experiencing to an even greater extent the feeling of quiet happiness which comes to you when you've outsmarted the powers of darkness. I felt as if a great weight had been lifted off me. Well, it had of course in one sense, for the Fairy Queen must have clocked in at fully a hundred and sixty pounds ring-side, but what I mean is that a colossal burden had been removed from the Wooster soul. It was as though the storm clouds had called it a day and the sun come smiling through.

The only thing that kept the moment from being absolutely perfect was that Jeeves was not there to share my hour of triumph. I toyed with the idea of ringing him up at the Junior Ganymede, but I didn't want to interrupt him when he was probably in the act of doubling six no trumps.

The thought of Aunt Dahlia presented itself. She of all people should be the one to hear the good news, for she was very fond of Roddy Glossop and had shown herself deeply concerned when informed of his in-the-soup-ness. Furthermore, she could scarcely not be relieved to learn that a loved nephew had escaped the fate that is worse than death – viz. marrying Honoria. It was true that my firm refusal to play Santa Claus at her children's party must still be rankling, if that's the word, but at our last meeting I had found her far less incandescent than she had been, so there was reason to suppose that if I looked in on her now I should get a cordial reception. Well, not absolutely cordial, perhaps, but something near enough to it. So I left a note for Jeeves saying where I'd gone and hared off to her address in a swift taxi.

It was as I had anticipated. I don't say her face lit up when she saw me, but she didn't throw her Perry Mason at me and she called me no new names, and after I had told my story she was all joviality and enthusiasm. We were saying what a wonderful Christmas present the latest development would be for Pop Glossop and speculating as to what it would feel like being married to his daughter Honoria and, for the matter of that, being married to Blair Eggleston, and we had just agreed that both Honoria and Blair had it coming to them, when the telephone rang. The instrument was on a table near her chair, and she reached for it.

'Hullo?' she boomed. 'Who?' Or, rather, WHO, for when at the telephone her vocal delivery is always of much the same calibre as it used to be on the hunting field. She handed me the receiver. 'One of your foul friends wants you. Says his name's Waterbury.'

Jas Waterbury, placed in communication with self, seemed perplexed. In rather an awed voice he asked:

'Where are you, cocky? At the Zoo?'

'I don't follow you, Jas Waterbury.'

'A lion just roared at me.'

'Oh, that was my aunt.'

'Sooner yours than mine. I thought the top of my head had come off.'

'She has a robust voice.'

'I'll say she has. Well, cully, I'm sorry I had to disturb her at feeding time, but I thought you'd like to know that Trix and I have been talking it over and we both think a simple wedding at the registrar's would be best. No need for a lot of fuss and expense. And she says she'd like Brighton for the honeymoon. She's always been fond of Brighton.'

I was at something of a loss to know what on earth he was talking about, but reading between the lines I gathered that the Fairy Queen was thinking of getting married. I asked if this was so, and he chuckled greasily.

'Always kidding, Bertie. You will have your joke. If you don't know she's going to get married, who does?'

'I haven't a notion. Who to?'

'Why, you, of course. Didn't you introduce her to your gentleman friend as your fiancée?'

I lost no time in putting him straight.

'But that was just a ruse. Surely you explained it to her?'

'Explained what?'

'That I just wanted her to pretend that we were engaged.'

'What an extraordinary idea. What would I have done that for?'

'Fifteen quid.'

'I don't remember any fifteen quid. As I recall it, you came to me and told me you'd seen Trixie as the Fairy Queen in Cinderella at the Wigan Hippodrome and fallen in love with her at first sight, as so many young fellows have done. You had found out somehow that she was my niece and you asked me to bring her to your address. And the moment we came in I could see the love light in your eyes, and the love light was in her eyes, too, and it wasn't five minutes after that that you'd got her on your lap and there you were, as snug as two bugs in a rug. Just a case of love at first sight, and I don't mind telling you it touched me. I like to see the young folks getting together in Springtime. Not that it's Springtime now, but the principle's the same.'

At this point Aunt Dahlia, who had been simmering gently, intervened to call me a derogatory name and ask what the hell was going on. I waved her down with an imperious hand. I needed every ounce of concentration to cope with this misunderstanding which seemed to have arisen.

'You're talking through your hat, Jas Waterbury.'

'Who, me?'

'Yes, you. You've got your facts all wrong.'

'You think so, do you?'

'I do, and I will trouble you to break it to Miss Waterbury that those wedding bells will not ring out.'

'That's what I was telling you. Trixie wants it to be at the registrar's.'

'Well, that registrar won't ring out, either.'

He said I amazed him.

'You don't want to marry Trixie?'

'I wouldn't marry her with a ten-foot pole.'

An astonished 'Lord love a duck' came over the wire.

'If that isn't the most remarkable coincidence,' he said. 'Those were the very words Mr Prosser used when refusing to marry another niece of mine after announcing his betrothal before witnesses, same as you did. Shows what a small world it is. I asked him if he hadn't ever heard of breach of promise cases, and he shook visibly and swallowed once or twice. Then he looked me in the eye and said "How much?" I didn't get his meaning at first, and then it suddenly flashed on me. "Oh, you mean you want to break the engagement," I said, "and feel it's your duty as a gentleman to see that the poor girl gets her bit of heart balm," I said. "Well, it'll have to be something substantial," I said, "because there's her despair and desolation to be taken into account." So we talked it over and eventually settled on two thousand quid, and that's what I'd advise in your case. I think I can talk Trixie into accepting that. Nothing, mind you, can ever make life anything but a dreary desert for her after losing you, but two thousand quid would help.'

'BERTIE!' said Aunt Dahlia.

'Ah,' said Jas Waterbury, 'there's that lion again. Well, I'll leave you to think it over. I'll come and see you tomorrow and get your decision, and if you feel that you don't like writing that cheque, I'll ask a friend of mine to try what he can do to persuade you. He's an all-in wrestler of the name of Porky Jupp. I used to manage him at one time. He's retired now because he broke a fellow's spine and for some reason that gave him a distaste for the game. But he's still in wonderful condition. You ought to see him crack Brazil nuts with his fingers. He thinks the world of me and there's nothing he wouldn't do for me. Suppose, for instance, somebody had done me down in a business transaction, Porky would spring to the task of plucking him limb from limb like some innocent little child doing She-loves-me she-loves-me-not with a daisy. Good-night, goodnight,' said Jas Waterbury, and rang off.

I would have preferred, of course, after this exceedingly unpleasant conversation to have gone off into a quiet corner somewhere and sat there with my head between my hands, reviewing the situation from every angle, but Aunt Dahlia was now making her desire for explanatory notes so manifest that I had to give her my attention. In a broken voice I supplied her with the facts and was surprised and touched to find her sympathetic and understanding. It's often this way with the female sex. They put you through it in no uncertain manner if you won't see eye to eye with them in the matter – to take an instance at random – of disguising yourself in white whiskers and stomach padding, but if they see you are really up against it, their hearts melt, rancour is forgotten and they do all they can to give you a shot in the arm. It was so with the aged relative. Having expressed the opinion that I was the king of the fatheads and ought never to be allowed out without a nurse, she continued in gentler strain.

'But after all you are my brother's son whom I frequently dandled on my knee as a baby, and a subhuman baby you were if ever I saw one, though I suppose you were to be pitied rather than censured if you looked like a cross between a poached egg and a ventriloquist's dummy, so I can't let you sink in the soup without a trace. I must rally round and lend a hand.'

'Well, thanks, old flesh and blood. Awfully decent of you to want to assist. But what can you do?'

'Nothing by myself, perhaps, but I can confer with Jeeves and between us we ought to think of something. Ring him up and tell him to come here at once.'

'He won't be home yet. He's playing Bridge at his club.'

'Give him a buzz, anyway.'

I did so, and was surprised when I heard a measured voice say 'Mr Wooster's residence'.

'Why, hullo, Jeeves,' I said. 'I didn't expect you to be home so early.'

'I left in advance of my usual hour, sir. I did not find my Bridge game enjoyable.'

'Bad cards?'

'No, sir, the hands dealt to me were uniformly satisfactory, but I was twice taken out of business doubles, and I had not the heart to continue.'

'Too bad. So you're at a loose end at the moment?'

'Yes, sir.'

'Then will you hasten to Aunt Dahlia's place? You are sorely needed.'

'Very good, sir.'

'Is he coming?' said Aunt Dahlia.

'Like the wind. Just looking for his bowler hat.'

'Then you pop off.'

'You don't want me for the conference?'

'No.'

'Three heads are better than two,' I argued.

'Not if one of them is solid ivory from the neck up,' said the aged relative, reverting to something more like her customary form.

I slept fitfully that night, my slumbers much disturbed by dreams of being chased across country by a pack of Fairy Queens with Jas Waterbury galloping after them shouting Yoicks and Tally-ho. It was past eleven when I presented myself at the breakfast table.

'I take it, Jeeves,' I said as I started to pick at a moody fried egg, 'that Aunt Dahlia has told you all?'

'Yes, sir, Mrs Travers was most informative.'

Well, that was a relief in a way, because all that secrecy and A-and-B stuff is always a strain.

'Disaster looms, wouldn't you say?'

'Certainly your predicament is one of some gravity, sir.'

'I can't face a breach of promise action with a crowded court giving me the horse's laugh and the jury mulcting . . . Is it mulcting?'

'Yes, sir, you are quite correct.'

'And the jury mulcting me in heavy damages. I wouldn't be able to show my face in the Drones again.'

'The publicity would certainly not be agreeable, sir.'

'On the other hand, I thoroughly dislike the idea of paying Jas Waterbury two thousand pounds.'

'I can appreciate your dilemma, sir.'

'But perhaps you have already thought of some terrific scheme for foiling Jas and bringing his greasy hairs in sorrow to the grave. What do you plan to do when he calls?'

'I shall attempt to reason with him, sir.'

The heart turned to lead in the bosom. I suppose I've become so used to having Jeeves wave his magic wand and knock the stuffing out of the stickiest crises that I expect him to produce something brilliant from the hat every time, and though never at my brightest at breakfast I could see that what he was proposing to do was far from being what Jas Waterbury would have called box office. Reason with him, forsooth! To reason successfully with that king of the twisters one would need brass knucks and a stocking full of sand. There was reproach in my voice as I asked him if that was the best he could do.

'You do not think highly of the idea, sir?'

'Well, I don't want to hurt your feelings—'

'Not at all, sir.'

'—but I wouldn't call it one of your top thoughts.'

'I am sorry, sir. Nevertheless—'

I leaped from the table, the fried egg frozen on my lips. The front door bell had given tongue. I don't know if my eyes actually rolled as I gazed at Jeeves, but I should think it extremely likely, for the sound had got in amongst me like the touching off of an ounce or so of trinitrotoluol.

'There he is!'

'Presumably, sir.'

'I can't face him as early in the morning as this.'

'One appreciates your emotion, sir. It might be advisable if you were to conceal yourself while I conduct the negotiations. Behind the piano suggests itself as a suitable locale.'

'How right you are, Jeeves!'

To say that I found it comfortable behind the piano would be to give my public a totally erroneous impression, but I secured privacy, and privacy was just what I was after. The facilities, too, for keeping in touch with what was going on in the great world outside were excellent. I heard the door opening and then Jas Waterbury's voice.

'Morning, cocky.'

'Good morning, sir.'

'Wooster in?'

'No, sir, he has just stepped out.'

'That's odd. He was expecting me.'

'You are Mr Waterbury?'

'That's me. Where's he gone?'

'I think it was Mr Wooster's intention to visit his pawnbroker, sir.'

'What!'

'He mentioned something to me about doing so. He said he hoped to raise, as he expressed it, a few pounds on his watch.'

'You're kidding! What's he want to pop his watch for?'

'His means are extremely straitened.'

There was what I've heard called a pregnant silence. I took it that Jas Waterbury was taking time off to allow this to sink in. I wished I could have joined in the conversation, for I would have liked to say 'Jeeves, you are on the right lines' and offer him an apology for ever having doubted him. I might have known that when he said he was going to reason with Jas he had the ace up his sleeve which makes all the difference.

It was some little time before Jas Waterbury spoke, and when he did his voice had a sort of tremolo in it, as if he'd begun to realize that life wasn't the thing of roses and sunshine he'd been thinking it. I knew how he must be feeling. There is no anguish like that of the man who, supposing that he has found the pot of gold behind the rainbow, suddenly learns from an authoritative source that he hasn't, if you know what I mean. To him until now Bertram Wooster had been a careless scatterer of fifteen quids, a thing you can't do if you haven't a solid bank balance behind you, and to have him presented to him as a popper of watches must have made the iron enter into his soul, if he had onc. He spoke as if stunned.

'But what about this place of his?'

'Sir?'

'You don't get a Park Lane flat for nothing.'

'No, indeed, sir.'

'Let alone a vally.'

'Sir?'

'You're a vally, aren't you?'

'No, sir. I was at one time a gentleman's personal gentleman, but at the moment I am not employed in that capacity. I represent Messrs Alsopp and Wilson, wine merchants, goods supplied to the value of three hundred and four pounds, fifteen shillings and eightpence, a bill which Mr Wooster finds it far beyond his fiscal means to settle. I am what is technically known as the man in possession.'

A hoarse 'Gorblimey' burst from Jas's lips. I thought it rather creditable of him that he did not say anything stronger.

'You mean you're a broker's man?'

'Precisely, sir. I am sorry to say I have come down in the world and my present situation was the only one I could secure. But while not what I have been accustomed to, it has its compensations. Mr Wooster is a very agreeable young gentleman and takes my intrusion in an amiable spirit. We have long and interesting conversations, and in the course of these he has confided his financial position to me. It appears that he is entirely dependent on the bounty of his aunt, a Mrs Travers, a lady of uncertain temper who has several times threatened unless he curbs his extravagance to cancel his allowance and send him to Canada to subsist on a small monthly remittance. She is of course under the impression that I am Mr Wooster's personal attendant. Should she learn of my official status, I do not like to envisage the outcome, though if I may venture on a pleasantry, it would be a case of outgo rather than outcome for Mr Wooster.'

There was another pregnant s, occupied, I should imagine, by Jas Waterbury in wiping his brow, which one presumes had by this time become wet with honest sweat.

Finally he once more said 'Gorblimey'.

Whether or not he would have amplified the remark I cannot say, for his words, if he had intended uttering any, were dashed from his lips. There was a sound like a mighty rushing wind and a loud snort informed me that Aunt Dahlia was with us. In letting Jas Waterbury in, Jeeves must have omitted to close the front door.

'Jeeves,' she boomed, 'can you look me in the face?'

'Certainly, madam, if you wish.'

'Well, I'm surprised you can. You must have the gall of an Army mule. I've just found out that you're a broker's man in valet's clothing. Can you deny it?'

'No, madam. I represent Messrs Alsopp and Wilson, wines, spirits and liqueurs supplied to the value of three hundred and four pounds fifteen shillings and eightpence.'

The piano behind which I cowered hummed like a dynamo as the aged relative unshipped a second snort.

'Good God! What does young Bertie do – bathe in the stuff? Three hundred and four pounds fifteen shillings and eightpence! Probably owes as much, too, in a dozen other places. And in the red to that extent he's planning, I hear, to marry the fat woman in a circus.'

'A portrayer of Fairy Queens in pantomime, madam.'

'Just as bad. Blair Eggleston says she looks like a hippopotamus.'

I couldn't see him, of course, but I imagine Jas Waterbury drew himself to his full height at this description of a loved niece, for his voice when he spoke was stiff and offended.

'That's my Trixie you're talking about, and he's going to marry her or else get sued for breach of promise.'

It's just a guess, but I think Aunt Dahlia must have drawn herself to her full height, too.

'Well, she'll have to go to Canada to bring her action,' she thundered, 'because that's where Bertie Wooster'll be off to on the next boat, and when he's there he won't have money to fritter away on breach of promise cases. It'll be as much as he can manage to keep body and soul together on what I'm going to allow him. If he gets a meat meal every third day, he'll be lucky. You tell that Trixie of yours to forget Bertie and go and marry the Demon King.'

Experience has taught me that except in vital matters like playing Santa Claus at children's parties it's impossible to defy Aunt Dahlia, and apparently Jas Waterbury realized this, for a moment later I heard the front door slam. He had gone without a cry.

'So that's that,' said Aunt Dahlia. 'These emotional scenes take it out of one, Jeeves. Can you get me a drop of something sustaining?'

'Certainly, madam.'

'How was I? All right?'

'Superb, madam.'

'I think I was in good voice.'

'Very sonorous, madam.'

'Well, it's nice to think our efforts were crowned with success. This will relieve young Bertie's mind. I use the word mind loosely. When do you expect him back?'

'Mr Wooster is in residence, madam. Shrinking from confronting Mr Waterbury, he prudently concealed himself. You will find him behind the piano.'

I was already emerging, and my first act was to pay them both a marked tribute. Jeeves accepted it gracefully, Aunt Dahlia with another of those snorts. Having snorted, she spoke as follows.

'Easy enough for you to hand out the soft soap, but what I'd like to see is less guff and more action. If you were really grateful, you would play Santa Claus at my Christmas party.'

I could see her point. It was well taken. I clenched the hands. I set the jaw. I made the great decision.

'Very well, aged relative.'

'You will?'

'I will.'

'That's my boy. What's there to be afraid of? The worst those kids will do is rub chocolate eclairs on your whiskers.'

'Chocolate eclairs?' I said in a low voice.

'Or strawberry jam. It's a tribal custom. Pay no attention, by the way, to stories you may have heard of them setting fire to the curate's beard last year. It was purely accidental.'

I had begun to go into my aspen act, when Jeeves spoke.

'Pardon me, madam.'

'Yes, Jeeves?'

'If I might offer the suggestion, I think that perhaps a maturer artist than Mr Wooster would give a more convincing performance.'

'Don't tell me you're thinking of volunteering?'

'No, madam. The artist I had in mind was Sir Roderick Glossop. Sir Roderick has a fine presence and a somewhat deeper voice than Mr Wooster. His Ho-ho-ho would be more dramatically effective, and I am sure that if you approached him, you could persuade him to undertake the role.'

'Considering,' I said, putting in my oar, 'that he is always blacking up his face with burned cork.'

'Precisely, sir. This will make a nice change.'

Aunt Dahlia pondered.

'I believe you're right, Jeeves,' she said at length. 'It's tough on those children, for it means robbing them of the biggest laugh they've ever had, but they can't expect life to be one round of pleasure. Well, I don't think I'll have that drink after all. It's a bit early.'

She buzzed off, and I turned to Jeeves, deeply moved. He had saved me from an ordeal at the thought of which the flesh crept, for I hadn't believed for a moment the aged r's story of the blaze in the curate's beard having been an accident. The younger element had probably sat up nights planning it out.

'Jeeves,' I said, 'you were saying something not long ago about going to Florida after Christmas.'

'It was merely a suggestion, sir.'

'You want to catch a tarpon, do you not?'

'I confess that it is my ambition, sir.'

I sighed. It wasn't so much that it pained me to think of some tarpon, perhaps a wife and mother, being jerked from the society of its loved ones on the end of a hook. What gashed me like a knife was the thought of missing the Drones Club Darts Tournament, for which I would have been a snip this year. But what would you? I fought down my regret.

'Then will you be booking the tickets.'

'Very good, sir.'

I struck a graver note.

'Heaven help the tarpon that tries to pit its feeble cunning against you, Jeeves,' I said. 'Its efforts will be bootless.'